The stakes are high . . .
The cost of failure higher . . .

THE COMMANDO. This was Michael Rumison's final mission before getting out. But the good life back home has just been eliminated . . . by men who can eliminate him.

THE CIA OPERATIVE. He failed in Afghanistan. This time he can't. Even if he has to sacrifice himself—and Michael Rumison—in the name of American interests.

THE GIRL. Desperate to help Michael Rumison, who came to her father's plantation nearly broken, her love is the only power that can withstand the forces ready to destroy them both.

THE COLONEL. His allegiance is to himself, and to whichever side holds the power to decide a nation's destiny.

THE AGENT-FOR-HIRE. He's the best freelancer in American intelligence. And for getting Michael Rumison, he can name his price. But what will it cost him?

B. L. VAN VORS

AVON
PUBLISHERS OF BARD, CAMELOT, DISCUS AND FLARE BOOKS

END OF THE RIVER is an original publication of Avon Books. This work has never before appeared in book form.

AVON BOOKS
A division of
The Hearst Corporation
1790 Broadway
New York, New York 10019

Published by arrangement with the author
Library of Congress Catalog Card Number: 83-91101
ISBN: 0-380-83428-6

First Avon Printing, November, 1983

Printed in the U. S. A.

WFH 10 9 8 7 6 5 4 3 2 1

Book One

MR. BLACK

On a dark night, I went out without being observed, my house being now empty and at rest.

—San Juan de la Cruz

Chapter One

ALTHOUGH the aircraft was registered as a United States Air Force HC-130, it bore little resemblance to the familiar Hercules cargo plane. Its bulging radar dome gave it the appearance of an awkward, ungainly mutant, but it flew faster and at a higher altitude than any of its more conventional-looking cousins. The special black paint and sophisticated electronics would be used later in the designs of the supersecret, radar-invisible "stealth" aircraft but were in no way apparent to any but the most carefully trained observer. Only the sound of its four supercharged turboprop engines couldn't be camouflaged.

The plane was just one of the reasons Rumison's sleep had been troubled for the second night in a row. The constant drone of the turboprops, the stuffy hold, the mystery the odd aircraft represented seemed only symbols of some deeper disturbance, a psychic imbalance that centered on certain images that dominated his dreams: the blank faces of his parents, now dead; the beach house he had inherited after their car went over a cliff in Big Sur; a large black bird that kept appearing; and Rosso, running somewhere, oblivious to Rumison's cries of warning.

There was something terrifying about Rumison's dreams. Some dark presence, felt rather than seen. A sick feeling of inevitability, of helplessness . . .

A rough hand slapped Rumison's leg, jerking him awake. He opened his eyes to see Mr. Black, the civilian who had been placed in charge of the rescue, looking down at him. For a moment, Rumison couldn't meet Black's eyes. They were pale gray and unreadable, and somehow made Rumison feel like an adolescent caught with his hand on his penis . . . guilty and a little afraid.

"You were having another nightmare," Black said tonelessly.

The unfocused dread Rumison had felt in his sleep momentarily affixed itself to Black's granite features. Rumison shivered involuntarily.

He struggled to sit up. The air in the hold was fetid and smelled like oil and sweat. His mouth tasted like carpet dust as he tried to swallow.

"Sims has found the target," said Black, putting one foot up on Rumison's bench seat as he tied a loose bootlace. "We go in forty-five minutes."

Rumison felt a sudden emptiness in his solar plexus. It must have shown on his face, because Black smiled.

"Don't look so upset," said the older man without much humor. "This is what we came for. Wake up the others and get your gear on."

Rumison nodded mutely and Black returned to the rear of the hold where he began methodically undoing the lashings on their equipment bags. Rumison let out a deep breath and swung his legs off the seat.

Across the hold, Barney was already awake. A nervous smile tugged at his mouth as he caught Rumison's eye. Barney's eyes were blue, sad and strangely innocent. Forcing a casualness he didn't feel, Rumison smiled back.

"I guess they really found it," he said.

Barney nodded. The smile left his mouth, replaced by a slight quiver of determination as he took a deep breath and also sat up.

Barney was dressed in worn Levi's and a blue T-shirt with GREENPEACE stenciled in yellow letters across a green globe of the earth. The letters and globe on his chest straightened as he stretched. He reached under his seat and began lacing on his hiking boots.

Rumison felt a moment's irritation as he watched Barney, as though somehow Barney's premonition two nights before were responsible for Rumison's own unease.

Two nights? How quickly things changed. That night when it had all begun seemed remote now, unreal. Barney's girl friend, Georgiana, had cooked up a spaghetti dinner at Rumison's beach house, and the sunset from the back deck was more colorful than it had been all winter. Catalina Island was visible, for a change, through the smog. Rumison and his other roommate, Rosso, both had dates . . . already Rumison had trouble remembering their names. Met on the beach that day. There had been music and jug wine and the obligatory flirtations no one took seriously.

And then, right in the middle of a sentence, Barney had stopped short and his face had gone white.

"Barney . . . is something wrong?" Georgiana had asked worriedly. Before Barney could answer, the telephone rang. A look of anguish passed over Barney's soft features.

"Rosso, don't answer that."

Rosso, who was closest to the phone, looked up, his eyebrows raised. Barney seemed confused. The phone rang again and Rosso picked it up.

Oddly, Barney showed no surprise or even anger that it was Colonel Ellis calling to order them out to the base for an unscheduled mission . . . despite the fact that they weren't the alert team that week. The events that followed had only made Barney more withdrawn and thoughtful.

Barney finished tying his boots, and Rumison realized with a start that he had been daydreaming. Quickly he reached forward and tapped the black-stockinged feet of Sergeant Sleeper, who was curled up on the bench in front of Rumison's. Sleeper mumbled something and his eyes fluttered open.

Sleeper was an aging lifer with only a few months to go until his thirty-year retirement. He was a difficult man to like and had few, if any, close friends. He was harsh and abrasive with persons of less authority than he and fawning with the officers. He ran his life as though it had been ordered out of an Air Force tech manual.

For a brief moment, as Sleeper stared up at Rumison, his eyes unfocused, his features still slack from sleep, Rumison thought how defenseless the old master sergeant seemed, almost like a small boy. Then, as though remembering who he was, Sleeper hardened his thin, angular features into the lines of the true believer and sat up.

"You'd better have a reason for wakin' me, Rumison," he said, his thin Alabama drawl harsher than usual, as though to compensate for the earlier moments of vulnerability.

"They've found the crash site, Sarge," said Rumison. "Black says we go in forty-five minutes."

"Then what are we waitin' for? Let's move it." Sleeper reached under the seat for his boots, and his watery brown eyes caught sight of Rosso, still asleep on a cargo mat up near the cabin, where the insulation was better and the engine whine not so loud. Rosso at least had gotten a good night's rest. Rumison could hear the loud snoring even above the engine noise.

Sleeper frowned. "Wake Rosso up, Bailey!"

Barney lowered his eyes, nodded without comment and went to do as he was told. Sleeper was more abrupt with Barney than with any of the other enlisted men in the small rescue unit of which they were part. The others, Rosso and Rumison included, were older, tougher, and less inclined to put up with Sleeper's ignorant leadership, but Barney rarely complained. Sleeper seemed to take Barney's deference as a sign of weakness and despised him all the more. It didn't help that Barney had such fine, almost feminine features, or those nervously introspective blue eyes. Sleeper prided himself on his own manly appearance, his close-cropped graying hair, starched uniforms and stiff bearing.

Rumison tried to savor and draw strength from his last few moments of idleness. Meanwhile, near the cabin's door Barney was shaking Rosso awake. Rosso got up immediately, lacing on his boots with short energetic movements. There was nothing in his manner to indicate that only a moment before he had been lost in a deep, untroubled sleep.

Rumison smiled, feeling an overwhelming affection for the short little man he had known most of his life. In all the years he had known Rosso, he had never seen his friend indecisive about anything, including waking up. Rosso was either asleep or wide awake. For him there was no in between.

Rumison found himself wondering if Rosso even dreamed. He couldn't remember Rosso ever mentioning any dreams. The very abstractedness of the dream state was out of character for Rosso.

But didn't everyone dream? Hadn't Rumison read somewhere that dreaming was a psychological necessity, that people went crazy if they weren't allowed to dream? And if Rosso did dream, as he must, wasn't it also likely he had experienced a nightmare or two?

The chain of thinking led Rumison uncomfortably close to the too-recent memories of his own dream state. He shook himself and shifted his attention to Mr. Black, who had finished unstrapping the equipment bags and was busy fastening cargo chute risers to two large canvas parabundles.

Black was an impressive man, Rumison had to admit. Nearly as tall as Rumison's six-three and weighing at least twenty pounds more, none of it noticeably fat. It was hard to guess his age, though it had to be close to fifty. He may have been as old as Sleeper, who was fifty-three. But unlike Sleeper, who often looked drawn and tired despite his self-conscious manliness, there was nothing at all in Black's manner that gave away his years.

Black's hair, like his eyes, was steel gray, the color of the ocean on an overcast day at noon. His face was Nordically classic, the chiseled features resisting any show of emotion. His skin was sunburned, as though he'd just spent two weeks in the desert. Rumison was thirty-three years old. Around Mr. Black he felt fifteen. It was not a feeling he liked.

Black was looking back at him. Abruptly Rumison became aware he was the only one still seated, still without his boots on. Quickly he reached under his seat and began putting them on. Black fastened a last riser into place, rechecked his work, and then walked forward toward the others.

"We'll be over the target shortly," he said without elaboration. "I'll dump out the bundles on the second or third pass, depending on the wind. We'll go around again to see how they land, then jump on the next go-round."

"That doesn't give us much time," said Rosso irritably. He had disliked Black from the start.

"No, it doesn't," agreed Black.

"Where exactly are we?" Rumison asked.

"Just where we expected to be, Rumison. East coast of Nicaragua. Over the Mosquito Rain Forest, about forty-five miles from the coast. As Rosso pointed out, there isn't much time, so don't waste it."

Black turned away, moving toward the jump door. He put on the cargomaster's helmet, plugged the interphone line in, and flipped a switch. Rumison could see his lips moving but couldn't hear what he was saying to the pilot or navigator.

"Move it, Rumison!" grunted Sleeper. "You're still asleep. We've got a rescue going."

"Rescue, my ass," muttered Rosso.

Sleeper pretended not to hear. He had learned from long experience not to get into arguments with Rosso. Besides, thought Rumison as he followed the others back toward the equipment bags, even Sleeper wasn't stupid enough to believe the line they'd been fed at the mission briefing by Colonel Ellis, the small rescue units commander. "Just a simple rescue mission, men. One of our planes has gone down somewhere in Central America, and we're going to find it."

We?

Rosso handed Rumison his nylon jump suit. "How you feeling, Mike?" he asked, concern showing on his square features.

Rumison shrugged. What could he say? He didn't know himself. There was nothing to relate his feelings to, no way of explaining that strange sense of . . . inevitability. He put on the suit and swore as the zipper caught on his denim shirt, tearing it. Their civilian clothes were one of several contradictions to the colonel's assertion that this was a "simple rescue mission." "No regulation dress," Ellis had insisted. It was Rosso who pointed out later, as they made ready to leave, that even the equipment they'd been given was of civilian manufacture, including the parachutes and medical kits.

A partial explanation was apparent, though Black had simply refused to discuss it. The leftist government in Nicaragua had, for some time, been at odds with the new administration in Washington. Even if the mission were, in truth, a simple rescue, it could prove an embarrassment for Washington if members of its armed forces were found poking around in Nicaraguan territory. No matter that these "armed forces" were in fact just a small team of—

disregarding Black—Air Rescue types. No more, really, than older brothers to a Boy Scout troop.

But there were too many questions left unanswered by the glib briefing the colonel had given them. Why, for example, send a team all the way from an out-of-the-way base in California when they could deploy one nearby, just a few short hours away at Howard Air Force Base in Panama? Why the concern with secrecy, why the bizarre black aircraft with its bulging radar dome, why the phlegmatic navigator, Sims, whose duties also included those of copilot and electronics expert? Strangest of all, why had Mr. Black, a civilian, been placed in absolute command of what should have been strictly an Air Rescue operation?

Who was Mr. Black?

Rumison struggled into a parachute harness and adjusted the straps. He attached the reserve chute to the D rings on his chest and then below that the medical kit and survival bag. He strapped a long-bladed survival knife to the inside of his left calf and a small battery-powered strobe light to the inside of the opposite leg. He put on his helmet, adjusted the chin strap, tightened the Plexiglas tree shield down over his eyes and looked around for a place to sit.

The airplane banked into a turn, lining up for the first pass over the target. Sleeper tapped his chest chute, the sign for equipment inspection. Turning clumsily in the jump suit, Rumison found Rosso and they looked over each other's preparations. Rosso found a poorly buckled harness strap and reset it. Rumison was surprised. His mind had been wandering again. Rosso smiled at the mistake, and Rumison nodded his thanks.

Black had dressed quickly, returning to the jump door without bothering to ask anyone to check his suit. The red light over the door winked on and Black pulled the two parabundles closer to the door.

It was sweltering in the heavy suits. Rumison found a seat and collapsed back into it. Sweat trickled off his forehead into his eyes and he had to raise the tree shield to wipe them. Looking up, he was surprised to see the front cabin door open. Major Hawkes, the pilot, entered the hold, striding purposefully toward them, his face set in a determined scowl. He was a small man, no taller than five-five, with a boyishness that belied his forty-three years. His sudden appearance seemed to displease Mr. Black, who frowned as Hawkes approached.

"Better stay up front, Major," said Black quietly. Despite the noise of the engine, his voice was easily heard. "We're getting ready to jump."

Hawkes's jaw jutted out, daring Black to challenge him. "Sims can handle the plane," he said, his voice high and not a little angry. "I don't know what in hell I was even brought along for."

He turned toward the others—Sleeper, Barney, Rosso and Rumison, who were seated on the bench seat facing the jump door. "I wanted to say something before you go," he said, speaking quickly. Rumison suddenly realized the little man was nervous, maybe even frightened.

"I don't have any more idea than you what this whole thing is about, but I do know you aren't volunteers, any more than I was. . . ."

He was referring to the arm-twisting that the colonel had applied—no early outs unless they agreed to the mission.

"I want you to know," Hawkes continued, "that if for some reason you don't make it out like they said you were going to, I'll raise a smell about this thing that'll make the evening news."

Hawkes stopped, suddenly unsure of himself. He looked embarrassed.

"Aw, hell, Larry," said Rosso. "We'll be all right."

Barney's eyes were lowered. He was keeping his thoughts to himself. Sleeper looked perplexed.

"Just so you know," Hawkes finished lamely, "someone's on your side." Giving Black a defiant glare, Hawkes turned and strode back toward the cabin. Black had ignored the whole exchange, talking to Sims on the interphone. The incident left Rumison feeling distinctly worse than before.

"Shit," said Rosso after the cabin door had closed.

Black spoke a few more words into the interphone and then jerked up on the door latch. The door lifted easily on metal runners, and all thoughts were blocked out by the rush of wind and the shrieking whine of the turboprops. The green light came on. Black switched on the strobe lights attached to the parabundles and quickly kicked them out the door.

Rumison glanced at his watch, an expensive Rolex diving watch the Air Force had issued rescue specialists. It was four-thirty in the morning, Eastern Standard Time. Outside the rectangle of the jump door it was still pitch black.

The aircraft circled back and Black leaned out to check the positions of the lights on the bundles. The red light came on again and he straightened.

"Stand up! Get ready!"

Adrenaline made Rumison light-headed. Swaying with the weight of the equipment, he shuffled awkwardly toward the black hole in the fuselage. The aircraft lurched into a final turn and Rumison had to steady himself against an aluminum stanchion. Black leaned closer.

"You're first, Rumison. Remember . . . five seconds before your chute opens. We're pretty high. You'll see a clearing. The target is at its downwind side."

Rumison nodded. Black disconnected his own helmet from the interphone line and backed away from the door, allowing Rumison to move closer. Rumison's mouth was dry and he found himself wishing he'd taken time to brush his teeth. For some reason the thought brought back memories of his grandmother and he suddenly felt small and very alone. Hesitantly he leaned forward and took his first look out at the world that lay beyond the jump door.

It was early morning but as yet there was little sign of daylight. At two thousand feet it was hard to tell where the jungle ended and the sky began. The moon had set but the stars were bright overhead.

They came out of the turn and leveled into the wind, flying at 135 miles an hour. The wind past the jump door was hot and humid. Barney reached down and turned on their strobe lights. The flashes lit the hold in eerie bursts of brightness.

Rumison leaned farther out the door, trying to get a view of the clearing Black had said was their target. At first there was nothing but darkness. Nothing but the hot wind and the cry of the turbines and the mechanical flashes of strobe lights. Like gazing at eternity, Rumison thought, lost for a brief moment in the immensity beyond the door.

Below, in the darkness of the jungle, the clearing appeared suddenly, a light amoeba shape, hardly more than a blur against the surrounding trees. Two pinpoints of blinking light at the opposite end of the amoeba showed where the parabundles had fallen. Rumison's breath stopped in his throat.

Until the moment when Rumison had seen the clearing, the noise of the turbines and the wind had been deafening. But now the world grew quiet and still. Rumison's anxiety lifted, and for a brief, inexplicable moment, relief shook him. And beyond the relief a strange sense of . . . expectancy.

"Why?" came a thought, and he could almost hear the answer. "Because it is over."

"What's over?" a small, frightened part of him wanted to cry, but as Barney pressed in from behind, the cry was aborted and Rumison was alone with eternity.

The green light winked on and he jumped.

Chapter Two

HE floated in a pool of soft, warm liquid. Neither time nor memories existed, only darkness.

A moment later Rumison was slammed awake by the concussion of the jet stream, a huge hand slapping him back into awareness, back into the world.

He fought for balance and almost panicked when he couldn't find it and started to spin. Instinctively he drew himself into the classic pike position that had been drummed into them during airborne training—head down, feet together, hands over the reserve. It was only then that Rumison realized he had forgotten to count. He hesitated only a brief moment, then reached for the rip cord. After a frantic search, he finally found its handle, broken loose from its pocket and floating free at the end of the cable. He yanked hard and the parachute folded out of its sleeve with excruciating slowness. It billowed open with a gentle tug and Rumison let out a great sigh of relief. What had panicked him so? He was glad the others couldn't have seen. He looked up and saw their lights above him, following him down toward the clearing.

The jungle stretched in all directions. A faint brushstroke of dawn was just beginning to color the east. Rumison heard the fading turbines of the Hercules as it headed out toward the Caribbean Sea.

The clearing was about half a mile long, dotted with the dark shapes of scrub trees. Beyond the clearing, the jungle looked tangled and forbidding. As he neared the ground, Rumison could see the symmetrical shape of the crashed jet jammed up against the jungle to his right. That close to the ground, the temperature had risen fifteen degrees and the humidity was overpowering. Cloying vegetable smells, the new and decayed scents of a tropical rain forest, greeted him.

Rumison pulled a steering toggle and turned the parachute into the wind as he settled lightly down into soft, knee-high grass. The canopy collapsed and Rumison lay for a moment as he had landed, watching the others as they came down.

Three of the jumpers were landing nearby, but the fourth, higher than the others, was heading toward the trees at the edge of the clearing.

"Turn! Turn!" Rumison yelled, struggling to his feet. But either the jumper didn't hear him or something was wrong with the parachute, because it drove straight into the nearest tree.

Someone landed ten feet away standing up and Rumison could see it was Black. Close by, first Rosso and then Barney landed.

"Don't yell, Rumison," said Black sharply.

"Huh? Look, Sleeper's para—"

Black unbuckled his harness. "I saw. He'll be all right. Get those lights off. Roll your chutes and get everything out of sight by the target."

"Who're you afraid might find us here, Black?" asked Rosso as he climbed out of his own harness. "Russians?"

Rumison smiled. The idea was ridiculous, out there in the middle of a Nicaraguan rain forest, but Black didn't laugh.

"Do as I say," he answered coldly.

Sleeper's strobe light was blinking on and off regularly in the tree. Black quickly rolled his parachute and started toward the wreck. Barney, not looking at Rumison or Rosso, followed.

Rosso shrugged. "Spook shit," he said, loud enough for Black to hear if he wanted to.

The wrecked aircraft was visible now as the sky grew lighter in the east, a small executive jet whose once-graceful fuselage looked surprisingly intact, though one wing was sheared off and its nose was shoved into a tree like a crumpled beer can.

As Rumison approached it, moving awkwardly under

the weight of the equipment bags and the rolled parachute, he became aware of how quiet the early morning was, how still. It seemed strangely forbidding after the long hours of noise on board the Hercules. He saw Rosso thoughtfully regarding the wreck.

"It doesn't have any markings," said Rosso abruptly.

Rosso was right. The plane, painted a two-tone blue, had no identification markings of any sort. Rumison dropped his load and sat down, still staring at the wreck. Nearby, Black was helping Sleeper out of the tree. Barney was busy cutting the parachute away from the branches with his survival knife. Sleeper reached the ground and immediately collapsed. He was breathing with difficulty. Rumison and Rosso immediately ran over to help.

"I'm all right," Sleeper protested, his face flushed. "Leave me alone. I just hit that damn tree a little too hard is all. Fouled my steering line."

"You might have busted a rib, Sarge," said Rosso. "Better let me look."

"I said leave me alone." Sleeper shoved Rosso's hand away and rolled over on his side, lifting himself up so his back was to the tree.

"Anything you say, Sarge."

"Forget it, Rosso," said Black. "He'll be all right. I want you, Rumison, and Bailey to get those parabundles back here."

Rosso frowned. "What about the jet?" he asked. "We'd better check that out first. Doesn't look too badly damaged. Maybe someone's still alive."

Startled, Rumison looked back at the jet. For some reason the thought that there might be survivors had never occurred to him. After all, it had been three days since it had gone in.

Sleeper was trying to get to his feet. Black eased him back down. "Stay there until you get your breath back, Sergeant. You others, do as I told you. Turn out those strobe lights and don't leave anything behind."

Rosso started to argue, but Black cut him short. "Do as I say, Rosso. Now."

The command was given with such a cold, directed force that Rosso's mouth snapped shut in midprotest.

"Come on," said Rumison, "let's get it over with." Rosso

glared at Black for a moment and then turned to follow Rumison. Barney hurried to catch up.

"We're medics," grumbled Rosso. "And that guy thinks he's James Bond."

Their boots sank into the soft grass, and moisture soaked through the eyelets, wetting their socks. Across the clearing in an easterly direction were the lights from the parabundles. Barney kept looking back over his shoulder at the wrecked jet.

"You think someone might be alive, Rosso?" he asked. He seemed thoughtful and distant.

Rosso sniffed. "Shit. Who knows? We could have at least looked first."

"I knew something was bad," said Barney, watching his boots. "I felt it."

"It's not that mysterious, Barn. We just got caught up in some spook operation is all. Black's probably here to get something off that jet."

"You think so?"

"What else? You see that bird? No markings. Hell, Barn, we're in Nicaragua. You know what kind of shit goes down in this part of the world."

Barney looked uncertain. "I wonder what he's worried about? Out here, I mean."

"Other spook assholes," said Rosso.

"Maybe . . . but if so, why us? What are we doing here?"

That question bothered Rumison also. Back at the jet, Black was just climbing through an open hatch. A chill passed down Rumison's spine. Why are we here? he wondered.

Chapter Three

BLACK let the three men get a quarter of the way across the clearing before he turned his attention toward the wrecked jet. The rear hatch was open, possibly sprung during the forced landing. He stepped up through it, almost gagging. The putrid smell of rotten meat was so overpowering he had to jump back to the grass. Sleeper struggled up.

"You all right, Mr. Black?"

Black nodded. He found a medical kit and unzipped a pocket, looking for alcohol. "Bodies don't keep too well in this heat," he said. He poured the alcohol on a handful of gauze pads and climbed back through the hatch.

Sleeper started to follow but Black stopped him. "If you need something to do, set up the radio," said Black, breathing through the gauze. Sleeper watched as Black disappeared into the wreck, then went to do as he was told. He tried a deep breath and swore as the pain returned. I hit hard, he thought absently.

Inside the small jet, Black quickly worked his way toward the cabin. The interior of the jet looked as though a hurricane had been through it. Pillows and splintered plastic from the interior molding lay everywhere. Broken tables lay in a twisted heap with a chrome and walnut veneer portable bar. Broken glass covered the floor, and an expensive Sony tape recorder had smashed completely through the windowed door of a microwave oven.

Blocking the door to the pilot's cabin was a body. Judging by the torn clothes and the shoes on the bloated feet, it had been a woman, undoubtedly the flight attendant. Insects and animals had been at it and there wasn't much left. Gingerly, the gauze pressed close across his nose and mouth, Black shoved what remained out of the way with his boot and opened the cabin door.

Black had trouble controlling his retching as another gust of bad air, more rotten than the first, greeted him. The swollen bodies of the two pilots sat, still strapped in their seats, their heads tilted forward. Black turned to leave when something caught his eye—a small, round mark in the copilot's temple. He frowned and looked closer. Then he turned to the pilot. Picking up a pencil from the litter on the floor, he carefully parted the hair at the base of the pilot's head. Satisfied, he dropped the pencil and stood for a moment as he considered what he had seen.

Chapter Four

"YOU guys know why they named this place the Mosquito Coast, don't you?" asked Rosso as Rumison and Barney cut shroud lines loose from a tree where one of the parabundles had fallen.

"It was named after the Indians," answered Barney, taking the question seriously. Rumison knew better.

Rosso shook his head. "No. Least that's not what that survival instructor said. You remember, Mike—little black tech sergeant—Leroy or something."

"Sure, I remember," said Rumison.

Rosso gathered in the freed parachute and began rolling it into a bundle. "It's the mosquitos. Some get big enough here to rape turkeys. The Indians keep their windows closed at night because the mosquitos carry off babies. Leroy said there are always snakes some mosquito tried to eat dropping out of the sky."

"You didn't believe him?" Rumison asked.

Rosso laughed. A large mosquito landed on his face and he swatted at it. "No," he said. "Not then, at least."

Rumison had to smile. Behind him Barney seemed not to have heard as he cut the last line loose and pulled it to the ground. Barney seemed preoccupied and even more serious than usual. He was frightened, of course. They all were. Frightened of the unknown . . . even Rosso, though he would be the last to admit it. But something else was bothering Barney, and Rumison worried about it.

Barney believed in premonitions, and there was no arguing he had felt something just before Colonel Ellis's phone call that night. What was it that was eating at him so?

They put the bundled chutes with the parabundles and started back across the clearing. The bundles were heavy, surprisingly so, and the three men sweated in the heat. The sun had risen above the tree line, and the air had grown uncomfortably hot. The clearing had come alive with insects of every type, but the mosquitos were the worst. They billowed up in dark clouds from stagnant pools of water near the small stream that ran through the clearing. Rumison swore as the nylon handle on one bundle cut into his hand. What was in the damn things anyway?

"Rosso," asked Barney as they stopped for a breather to give their hands a rest, "what kind of jet is that thing?"

Back across the clearing they could see Mr. Black moving purposefully near the wrecked aircraft.

"Gulfstream II," Rosso answered. "Hot-shit exec type."

"You think it belongs to our government?"

Rosso shrugged, irritated at the questions, the insects, the heat. "I don't think anything. All I know is Elvis Presley used to own one."

When they arrived back at the crash site, Sleeper was seated on a log next to a small but powerful-looking field radio, and Black was nowhere around. Gratefully they dropped the bundles and sat down to rest. Sleeper grimaced as he turned to face them, still favoring his left side.

"Where's Black?" Rosso asked.

Sleeper nodded toward the jet. "Inside. He told us to wait out here."

At that moment, Black emerged from the hatch. He had a handful of cotton gauze pressed over his nose and was carrying a pillowcase full of papers in his other hand. He dropped the gauze and stepped down to the grass.

"Find anyone alive?" Rosso asked dryly.

Rumison could read no expression on Black's face. Black's answer surprised them all.

"One of the passengers is missing."

Rosso blinked. "Missing?"

"There were four people on board," said Black. "Two pilots, a flight attendant, and a passenger. There are only three bodies. The passenger is missing."

"Something must be screwed up," said Rosso. "Somebody counted wrong."

Black was looking thoughtfully toward the jungle. He seemed not to have heard Rosso.

"He was too smart to have tried walking out," Black said quietly, almost to himself. "He'll be nearby. Probably dead by now, but he'll be nearby. That explains the open hatch."

"May—maybe someone got here before us," said Barney, his manner uncertain around the older man.

Black shook his head. "We've had a monitor on this area ever since that bird went down. He's around, all right. Rosso, Rumison, Bailey: Start looking."

"Shit," said Rosso.

"Sleeper, you rest that rib. I'll join you as soon as I finish some things here."

Black dropped the pillowcase on the grass and bent down to unzip one of the parabundles. When no one moved, he looked back up. "Move it!"

They began the search, using a textbook pattern of expanding circles, with the jet as the center. Thick jungle covered over half the search area. The morning wore on. The heat and humidity increased, but worse were the insects. Even the foul-smelling repellent they'd brought didn't help.

Rumison already had drunk one canteen of water and was refilling it in the stream, making sure to add a chlorine tablet, when he heard Rosso's shout. He found Rosso a hundred yards into the trees, kneeling down by the body of a man lying under a large fern. The man was dressed in a torn and muddy brown suit. He was a big man, larger even than Black. It was hard to tell his age. The thick, swarthy features were caked in mud and dried blood. A small revolver lay in his limp right hand. A black vinyl case was handcuffed to his left wrist by a steel chain. Black and Barney arrived moments after Rumison.

"Is he alive?" Rumison asked.

Rosso, who had his fingers to the man's neck as he checked for a pulse, nodded. "He's alive. Barely, though."

Black reached down and picked the revolver from the man's fingers. He opened the cylinder and emptied the shells into the palm of one hand. Rumison could see that all the shells but one had been fired. Absently, Black placed the gun and shells in a pocket and glanced up through a crack in the trees toward the sky. Earlier Rumison had noticed the clouds building—dark cumulus billows blowing in from the east.

"Storm's coming," he mused. "We'd better get him back to the wreck."

No one mentioned the briefcase as Rosso put it atop the man's chest. They tried to be as gentle as they could but the man was heavy and it was difficult moving him through the thick foliage. More than once they almost dropped him. Sleeper arrived offering to help, but Black waved him away. "I don't want you hurting yourself again."

"I'm all right," Sleeper insisted, but Black was adamant.

"I don't care. We can manage without you."

Watching Sleeper, Rumison felt an unfamiliar sense of compassion for him. Without his starched sergeant's uniform, mirror-polished combat boots, and red beret, Sleeper looked no more than a tired, middle-aged salesman. A man close to retirement who had discovered too late that his life had passed him by, a life he had never really come to grips with. Or was Rumison reading too much into the sergeant's strained features? For a fleeting moment, Rumison felt a chilling sense of identification with Sleeper. It frightened him, and Rumison quickly swept it from his mind. I am not Sleeper, he told himself. I'm still young. In two more months I'll be out of the service. I can sell the house, travel, maybe start a business. . . .

But for some reason the feeling of bleakness wouldn't leave him.

They laid the survivor down in the shade of a thick-limbed tree with bright red flowers, an obis tree. The wind had come up and the sky was growing dark with clouds. Barney, supervised by an abrasive Sleeper, who was trying hard to look useful, set up a poncho roof. Rumison and Rosso tended the survivor, cutting off the torn coat and setting up an intravenous unit of dextran and antibiotics. Rosso swore as the black briefcase kept getting in the way.

"Don't you have a key for this thing, Black?" he asked.

Black, who was fiddling with the field radio, didn't bother

to look up. "Do the best you can," he said shortly. Rosso frowned and turned his attention back to the patient.

Most of the blood that covered the man came from two wounds: a scalp laceration across his forehead and a long, messy, but relatively superficial cut across his back, where a flying shard of plastic may have hit him. Rumison finished bandaging the wounds, and Barney tied the last stay on the roof just as the storm hit.

The rain began slowly, hardly more than a drizzle. In five minutes it had become a torrent, and the accompanying winds tore at the flimsy shelter. The storm raged for twenty minutes, then stopped as abruptly as it had begun. The rain had cooled the air, but it wasn't long before the temperature rose again as the sun broke through the rapidly departing clouds.

Already the rain had begun to erase the scar in the earth where the Gulfstream jet had attempted its last landing. The soft dirt and the thick jungle absorbed rain like a sponge. Half an hour after the rain had stopped there were few visible signs that there had ever been a storm.

The survivor was breathing evenly. Rosso adjusted the flow of blood volume expander into his arm.

"Do you think he'll live?" Barney asked.

"If he's alive after three days in this jungle, he'll live to be a hundred," said Rosso. "He's a tough boy."

Black, squatted down by the radio, adjusted the tuner and picked up the microphone as the others watched. Rumison wondered at the odd sense of apprehension he felt.

"Mother One, come in please. Mother One. This is Baby. Come in."

Rosso made a face. "My God, Black. You could have thought of a better call name?"

Black ignored him, repeating the call. Birds whistled in the trees. Water dripped off broad leaves and once again insects were swarming. Finally from the radio came a distant crackle followed by the boyish voice of Larry Hawkes. Rumison breathed out a sigh of relief. Even Rosso relaxed visibly.

"Come in, Baby. This is Mother."

Black adjusted a dial. "Mother, the delivery was a success. Request transportation home. Add one orphan to the manifest. Repeat, send a chopper."

A lengthy silence followed. Barney sat quietly, his face unreadable. Rumison realized he was biting his lip and stopped.

The receiver crackled. A different voice came on, the deep, emotionless voice of Sims, the procine electronics specialist who had been the navigator and copilot. Sims hadn't spoken more than ten words to anyone but Black on the flight down, but his abrasive bass was distinctive. "Baby, Hospital informs us a foster home is necessary. Mother is unable to provide for you."

The words hung in the tropical air like the guilty verdict of a judge. Black's features tightened.

"Repeat, please, Mother."

"Repeat, Mother is unable to care for you. Truant officers converging on your area. Foster home is necessary. Good luck."

"How much time?" Black asked.

"Truant officers are expected your position no later than 1300 hours. Best get a move on."

The reply was flat and final. Black reached down to switch off the radio but there was another crackle followed by the high, agitated voice of Hawkes. "You PJ's down there, remember what I said. I won't . . ." but Black cut him off. He turned to the others.

"You heard. We're walking out."

Rumison sat, stunned. His surroundings suddenly seemed vague, unreal. His mind struggled to focus. The feeling of inevitability he had experienced just before the jump returned. "Walk out?" he asked dumbly. Surely Black could see how impossible that was. Rumison looked around at the others for support.

Black was looking at his watch. "There isn't much time. We have to be gone from here in less than an hour and there's a lot to do."

Barney's head was lowered and it was hard to tell what he was thinking. Sleeper struggled not to show any emotion but his face had gone white. Rosso smiled thinly. "Why?" he asked simply.

They were accepting it, Rumison thought wildly. Black just shook his head. "I can't tell you that," he said. "Believe me when I say it's not my choice."

"Someone you don't want to find us here is on the way,"

said Rosso. It was a statement of facts. Black didn't answer.

"How far?" asked Rosso.

Black shrugged. He seemed to be judging their acceptance of what he had just told them. His eyes stayed longest on Rumison, who looked away. Abruptly Black reached down into a parabundle and withdrew two collapsible shovels and threw them at Rosso's and Rumison's feet. "There's a town," he said. "A small port named Bluefields. It can't be more than two or three days. Right now I want you and Rumison to dig a hole in the jungle big enough to bury everything we leave behind."

"What about him?" Rosso asked evenly, nodding his head toward the man they'd found in the jungle.

"I'll see to him. Bailey, you give me a hand. Sleeper, stay where you are."

Black turned away and began pulling the thin antenna wires for the radio off the tree limb where Sleeper had placed them. Rosso looked at Rumison and gave a slight shrug of his shoulders. He picked up a shovel and stood up, waiting for Rumison to follow.

"No use bitching," he said quietly to Rumison.

Digging was difficult in the jungle. The loamy topsoil went down for only a few feet before turning to rock-hard laterite. Rosso worked with mute diligence, keeping his thoughts to himse-f. Rumison's hands blistered and sweat poured off his forehead. In the end they had to settle for a hole wider than it was deep. Barney brought over everything Black told him to—parachutes, jump suits, helmets, all the medical kits except for one, the radio and the parabundle bags—and they added it to the pile in the hole.

Black had gone back into the jet, returning a few minutes later with another pillowcase full of papers, which he dumped in a pile. Rumison didn't envy Black the job even as he sweated with the shovel. The smell of rotten meat had grown worse with the heat, pervading the area with a terrible, invisible reminder of what lay on board the ruined Gulfstream II.

Rosso spearated the three medical kits from the rest of the gear Barney had brought over and then took out their dextran bottles and antibiotic kits before shoving the kits back in the hole. "It's going be hell carrying that guy," he mused grimly. "He'll need this."

They finished with the hole and returned to the parabundles to pack for the march. "They figured we'd be walking," said Rosso, indicating all the survival gear that Barney and Black had laid out on a poncho; trail rations in aluminum packets, aluminum-framed Kelty packs, flashlights, hammocks, extra socks. Rosso picked up a neatly balanced and finely honed Swiss-made machete and swung it in the air like a sword.

Sleeper already had his pack filled. "Knock it off, Rosso," he said, but his voice lacked the abrasive certainty it normally had.

Rumison watched Black, some feet away, as Black reached down into the grass near the ruined wing of the jet and picked up something that looked like a glob of pinkish jelly. He sniffed it, then walked over to the pile of papers and magnetic tape he had collected from the interior of the Gulfstream, and threw it down. After carefully wiping his hand, he took a lighter from the pocket on his knaki jacket and touched it to the jelly. Immediately the jelly burst into a bright, blue-white and smokeless flame.

Rumison almost fell on his face as he scrambled to get away from the fire. "Are you crazy?" he cried. "There's jet fuel all over this place!"

Watching unconcernedly, Black shifted the burning pile with a boot. "That was jet fuel," he said calmly. "Or what's left of it. There's nothing to worry about. It won't explode."

Rumison stopped, breathing heavily. For the first time since they had met him, Black smiled. The smile softened his chiseled features, the square jaw and the cold, pale eyes. But the smile was fleeting, and Rumison was left wondering if he had imagined it.

"Someone mullified the Priss," explained Black. "That's a jet-fuel additive that kills bacteria. If they aren't killed they turn the fuel to jelly, like this. The chemicals that neutralize Priss can be added to a fuel supply in gauged amounts, so a person could know within a reasonable time just when the engine would flame out."

"Sabotage," said Rumison without thinking, immediately feeling foolish. Of course sabotage. What else had Black been talking about?

"Gulfstreams have a triple redundancy factor built into their major systems," said Black. "Hard birds to bring down, outside of a missile."

Black kicked the fire again with his boot. He looked at his watch, then upward at the sky. Instinctively Rumison's eyes followed, half expecting to see a squadron of approaching helicopters. But there were only a few scattered puffs of cloud and the blue sky.

A loan moan escaped from the crash survivor, who lay almost forgotten nearby. Barney had already cut down the poncho shelter, and the man lay out in the open, the IV unit still dripping fluid into his arm. Black's attention seemed suddenly absorbed by the fire burning at his feet as the others hurried toward their patient.

The man had opened his eyes, but as Rumison leaned closer they still showed no sign of awareness. The man's broad forehead was damp with perspiration and red with fever around the bandage. Rosso wetted a gauze sponge and wiped the man's face.

"Norris . . . Have . . . have . . . have . . . get to Norris . . ."

The words were mumbled and incoherent. Rosso added water to the sponge, and droplets got into the man's eyes. The man blinked and suddenly his eyes focused. He tried to raise his left arm. The chain attached to his wrist moved and the man's dark eyes shifted to see what was hindering the arm. Then he looked back at Rumison.

"We crashed."

"Easy," said Rumison. "You survived. Must've crawled out."

The man's eyelids closed in a nod. Now that he was conscious, Rumison found himself uneasy around him. The black eyes had looked cold and mechanical. The swarthy features suddenly looked cruel.

The eyes opened again. "Who . . . you?" he asked.

Nearby Rumison could see Black, who had taken a holstered pistol from one of the piles of gear and was buckling it onto his belt. He removed the pistol from its holster and slipped the clip from its butt into the palm of his hand, checking to see if it was full. Then very deliberately he replaced it and holstered the gun.

"We're PJ's, son," said Sleeper, his Alabama drawl thick with a syrupy man-to-man sympathy Rumison detested. "Pararescuemen from Air Rescue. Jumped down to he'p y'all."

The man smiled. "PJ's, huh?" The question was dry and mocking. No, Rumison thought. I really don't like this guy. Apparently Rosso shared his feelings, because he had stepped back and was regarding the man thoughtfully.

Black joined the group and stood staring down at their patient. "Hello, Tom," he said quietly.

The man looked up and his face clouded suddenly. "Bastanchur . . . ahchhh!" A cough interrupted his exclamation.

"That's an awkward case you've got on your arm, Tom," said Black tonelessly. "It's been in the way since we found you."

The man Black called Tom stopped coughing. His eyes shifted warily as he looked at the men surrounding him. Black leaned closer.

"Come on, Tom. Where are the keys?"

"Ease up on him, Black," said Rosso. "The guy's in bad enough shape."

Black ignored the interruption. "The keys," he repeated. "Where are they, Tom?"

"I said the guy is hurting, Black," said Rosso angrily. The man's eyes fastened on Rosso, perhaps sensing an ally. His face twitched.

"Honest . . . I don't know. Only Norris . . ."

But before he could finish, Black took out his pistol, and with a smooth, deliberate motion, put it to the man's head and pulled the trigger. Rumison saw the millisecond of terror in the man's eyes before the explosion. The gunshot echoed in the clearing, sending nearby birds into a frenzy of flight and cries. Rumison stared in shock as the rear of the man's head exploded outward in a fountain of blood, hair and bone. Black holstered the pistol and reached to pick up one of the Swiss machetes that lay nearby.

"Goddamn it!" Rosso cried and, with a speed that surprised them all, threw himself on Black, knocking the larger man back into the grass. Black rolled and Rosso's second flurry of blows lost their mark. In a moment Black was on his feet again, the pistol back in his hand.

"You sonovabitch," growled Rosso.

Black wiped the blood from his lip. "For a short guy you pack quite a punch, Rosso."

"You sick . . . sonovabitch bastard. If you didn't have that gun . . ."

"You'd what? Kill me? And then waht?" Black abruptly holstered the pistol and turned to the others. "I want you all to think about this," he said, "because it is critical if we're to survive . . . remember just where you are."

He bent down to retrieve the machete Rosso had knocked from his hand. He stepped forward and with one effortless swing cut the left hand off the man he had just killed. He picked up the case, shook the severed hand from the handcuffs and motioned toward the body.

"Get those tubes out of his arm and rip those bandages off. Put what's left of his coat back on and drag him back on the jet."

Black kicked the separated hand with a boot. "Take this with you."

Rumison looked around at the others. Sleeper stood dumbly, his face gone slack. He was breathing with quick, shallow breaths and looked ill. Barney hadn't moved and was regarding Black with thoughtful blue eyes. Rosso stood tensely, angry but indecisive.

"Move it!" cried Black, and Rumison found himself helping Barney drag the dead body of the man who had two minutes before been their patient back on board the jet. It was not a pleasant job. Rosso watched, rage and frustration evident in every line of his square face.

"Are you just going to put up with this?" he cried.

Rumison felt guilty, but there was nothing he could do. The world had changed since the gunshot. Fear dominated his thoughts, fear of Black, fear of the jungle, fear of something nameless.

"He's got the gun," Rumison said, trying to sound calm and rational. He didn't think he succeeded.

"The guy would have died anyway," said Barney, seeming oddly unmoved. Of all of them, Rumison thought Barney would have been the most upset.

"Barn—" Rosso began.

"We couldn't have carried him," said Barney. "Not through this jungle. Look how hard it was just getting him to here."

Rumison was glad Barney sounded so reasonable. It made him feel better thinking there might be reasons other than fear for obeying Black.

"I want us gone from here in ten minutes!" cried Black as he strapped the black case onto his pack. "Get a move on it."

Rosso's jaw set. "All right," he said shortly. He bent down and picked up the severed hand, dropping it on the body Barney and Rumison were hoisting into the jet. "Don't forget this," he said.

They didn't leave the clearing in the ten minutes Black had wanted. By the time they had buried the equipment they were leaving behind, arranged their packs for travel, and cleaned up the area as best they could, twice that time had passed.

"They'll know we were here," Black mused quietly as they stood with their packs, looking back at the wreck. "And they'll know we're on foot."

The others were silent and Black shouldered his pack. "We'll travel up that stream for a ways and then turn north. There's a river about twenty miles from here. We'll take it to the coast. Bluefields is north of its mouth."

Black stood for another brief moment as they looked back at the clearing and the ruined jet and the open sky. "Let's go," he said.

Chapter Five

THE sweltering sun somehow found Rumison through an opening in the mat of interlocking ferns, branches, vines and mosses that formed the jungle's canopy, rousing him from a fitful sleep. He awoke instinctively batting at the flies and mosquitos swarming around his swollen head. He swore at himself for not slinging his hammock as Black and Rosso had done. Its mosquito netting would have helped. At the time he had been too tired to care.

He looked at his watch. It was three in the afternoon and outrageously humid. Sweat had soaked his jeans and denim shirt, plastering them against his skin. Still, it wasn't nearly as bad as it had been an hour earlier, when even Black had voted to rest.

The density of the jungle that surrounded them had apparently caught Black by surprise. The map he carried indicated rain forest, but Rumison knew that true rain forests had less undergrowth than what they were traveling through, the result of a higher canopy that blocked more sunlight and retarded growth. The unexpected difficulty of movement had upset Black's schedule and he had driven them mercilessly to make up for it.

Rumison gazed around the small clearing they had hacked out for a rest site. The overriding sensation of fear he had experienced since leaving the plane wreck was quickly being replaced by fatigue, and tempered by the pain in his blistered palms and his aching shoulders. But the fear remained, like a tapeworm lodged somewhere in the emptiness of his stomach, and physical pain was almost a relief from it.

He felt an unfamiliar lump on his ankle and pulled up his sock to find two large, blood-swollen ticks attached to his leg. His hands were wrapped in bandages he'd put on earlier, after his blisters had ripped open from swinging the machete; they trembled slightly as he lit a match. The ticks shriveled in the flame and dropped onto the rotten leaves that covered the ground. Rumison heard a noise and looked up to see Rosso watching him.

"Nice," Rosso commented.

Rumison shrugged. Ticks were the least of it.

"How're you doing?" Rosso asked, concern showing.

"What do you think?"

Rosso smiled thinly. "Well, it's not you I'm worried about." He nodded toward Sergeant Sleeper, who sat some feet away, his back to a tree. Sleeper's eyes were open, but the sergeant seemed oblivious to his surroundings.

"He hasn't moved since we stopped. He didn't even try to sleep."

"You think something's really wrong with him?" Rumison asked, forgetting for a moment his own pain.

Rosso pursed his lips thoughtfully. "His breathing isn't right. Hasn't been since he hit that tree. Busted rib, maybe. But maybe something else."

"Something else?"

Rosso just shook his head. After a moment he said, "He's not going to make it."

The comment was so blunt it took some seconds for Rumison to react. "Aw, hell, Rosso . . ." he began, but as he looked closer at the master sergeant he knew Rosso was right. Sleeper's face was flushed and pale and covered with perspiration. His aquiline nose had the feverish look of an alcoholic's, and his breathing was too shallow and too fast.

"I'll be surprised if Sleeper makes it to lunch tomorrow," said Rosso.

"Punctured lung?"

Rosso lowered his head. "Doesn't matter much, does it? It'll be hard to carry him, even if Black lets us."

"I didn't think of that," Rumison admitted.

"Think of it," said Rosso.

Black was lying in his hammock twenty feet away. The way he was watching them made Rumison wonder if he had overheard.

Black swung out of the hammock and began putting it away. "We've rested enough," he said. "Let's get a move on while there's still light."

They started off again. Black led, doing most of the machete work. He was followed by Barney, Rosso and Rumison, with Sleeper trailing.

Rumison had little sympathy to spare for the master sergeant. It was hard enough just putting one foot in front of the other, swinging a machete that felt as though it were made of lead, carrying a pack that weighed seventy pounds and felt like two hundred. Once, as Rumison looked back to make sure Sleeper was still behind them, Rumison saw a red butterfly. For a brief moment, as his eyes followed its fluttering path, Rumison's mind rose above physical pain and exhaustion. He didn't notice Sergeant Sleeper stumbling blindly along after them or worry about the mosquitos. Instead he saw orchids, oleanders, the countless exotic flowers that broke up the omnipresent shades of green with their bright colors and gave off aromatic scents. A bird flew out of a tree, a bright green parrot. It was followed by a brace of multicolored toucans. High above in the canopy monkeys played, living out their mad lives in the trees.

The butterfly landed and Rumison looked closer. It seemed so delicate and graceful it defied description. But the transcendence was short-lived. Black called after him, and the butterfly flew off. Its disappearance only made the reality of pain, heat, and gnawing fear more terrible.

They struggled on for another two hours. Every now and then Black would motion for a rest, allowing Sleeper to catch up. As the day wore on, Black didn't seem so upset at the delays. He looked on the verge of collapse himself.

Night fell. They made camp in a small, clear area under a huge, moss-covered tree. Rosso had to help Sleeper, who was either too tired or too uncaring to put his hammock into place. They cooked freeze-dried hamburger on Primus stoves and sipped water from their canteens. Sleeper pecked listlessly at his food.

"Better eat it, Sarge," said Rosso. "Remember, 'Eat whatever and wherever you can.' "

Sleeper glared momentarily at Rosso, not liking to be reminded of the Air Force's "first law of survival." "I'm not hungry," Sleeper said, shoving the plate away.

Rosso frowned, and Rumison knew what he was thinking. But Rumison was still unable to feel much sympathy for Sleeper.

In the three years and some-odd months Rumison and Rosso had been stationed with the 68th Aerospace Rescue and Recovery Squadron they had gone on fewer than eight active missions, not one calling for special training. But during the early years of their enlistment they all had been given that training. Sergeant Sleeper had gone through that training, had even trained others. Survival school, scuba school, parachute school, medical school, the countless schools and courses and exercises the Military Air Command offered pararescuemen—all designed to enable them to live up to the Air Rescue motto etched on the medallions of their maroon berets—"That Others May Live"—and to ensure that they could carry out their stated mission, which was to be able, by any means, at any time, under any circumstances to go anywhere to rescue whom they must.

It seemed to Rumison that Sleeper, as a career man, a master sergeant, a lifetime member of Air Rescue, should have been a symbol of that ideal. Instead . . . ?

But life is full of rhetoric and reality, thought Rumison. Sleeper was fine marching around the base with his manualized mind and his starched uniforms and list of regulations. Out where it counted he melted like a Hershey bar in a frying pan.

Maybe I'm being too hard on him, Rumison thought. The Air Force could publish a hundred manuals on survival and the semimystical but absolutely necessary "will to live," but what was this thing, really?

How could Rumison or anyone judge what kinds of pain Sleeper was battling? In acceptable doses pain could be beneficial. Like Alice's mushroom it could make a person grow . . . or shrink, depending on how it was taken. Taken properly, almost any sort of pain could be endured. History and survival literature were full of the heroic deeds of men like Mountain Man Hugh Glass, who had been mauled by a bear yet had managed to crawl two hundred miles across the freezing Rockies to reach safety.

But taken wrongly, pain meant death. Was it a personal decision? Rumison wondered. Suicide? Death chosen over the continuance of the pain? The thought was disturbing. How much pain could Rumison take before calling it quits?

Rumison felt that it would just be a matter of time before the blisters on his hands would heal and then callus over. A few more days and his body would adjust to the heat, the pack, the insects. He had been through enough in his life to realize this.

But what if things got worse? That's what frightened him. How important was mere survival? How much pain would he endure before *he* decided maybe life wasn't so important after all?

Abruptly Rumison recalled the odd emotions he had experienced just before the jump: exhilaration, freshness, rebirth, the strange sense of relief. Perhaps something had been missing from his life to have felt such relief that it might be over.

Why had he felt that way, that any change could only be for the better?

The cold thought occurred to him that maybe life wasn't important enough to accept the pain it offered. Perhaps somewhere in the deep recesses of Sleeper's atrophied consciousness this had been his decision.

No one said much after they had eaten. Night settled. In the dark the jungle seemed forbidding.

"It seems so long ago," mused Barney somewhat wistfully after they'd cleaned the pots and plates with grass and put away the cooking kits. "Only three nights . . ."

A small battery-powered lantern was their only light this first night and it gave Barney a somewhat ghostly appearance. "Oh, well," he said, "it was only a dream, anyway."

"What was a dream, Barn?" Rumison asked uneasily, wondering if Barney were feeling something of what was troubling him. Barney just shrugged, as though the answer should be obvious to everyone.

"You had a feeling when the telephone rang," said Rumison, trying to draw Barney out. "Intuition?"

Barney shrugged again. "Maybe," he said without elaboration. His moodiness was beginning to irritate Rumison.

"Did you know it'd be Gerber Baby?" he asked.

Barney shook his head. "No. It was just a feeling."

"Who's Gerber Baby?" Black asked.

"Colonel Ellis," Rumison explained.

Black smiled. "Fits," he said.

After a while Barney shifted worriedly. "You know, I should've called George. You know how she is."

"She'll call the unit," said Rumison. "They'll explain."

"Really?" grunted Rosso. "And just what will they explain? They wouldn't even explain to us."

Rumison bit his lip, realizing Rosso was right. "They'll tell her something," he said lamely. "She'll be all right."

"Who is George?" Black asked. Was it Rumison's imagination, or had the question been asked too casually? Black had never expressed an interest in their personal lives before.

"Barney's girl friend," said Rumison. "She lives with us down at my house. Takes care of things when we're on alert."

Black nodded, apparently satisfied, but Rumison was unable to dismiss from his mind the vague sense of unease Black's question had aroused in him.

Sleeper's condition was unchanged the next morning, even after the night's rest. Ignoring his bitter protests, the others divided up the contents of the master sergeant's pack and put them in with their own.

The hours and the inches dragged on. Even without appreciable weight in his pack, Sleeper had trouble continuing. After five hours and less than three miles of forward progress through the tangled undergrowth the sergeant stumbled and fell facedown in the loam. He didn't get back up. Rumison was the first to notice his absence and go back for him. Sleeper was still conscious but his eyes were glassy and uncaring. The will seemed to have drained from the sharp features. Large red ants crawled across his slack mouth as Rumison rolled him over on his back.

Black eyed Sleeper wearily. "He can't go any farther today," Black said. "Might as well camp here."

The decision surprised Rumison. Just two hours earlier, Black, looking up at the sky through one of the infrequent breaks in the canopy, had paused, listening as though he had heard a sound inconsistent with the normal mutterings of the rain forest. Rumison had strained to hear but was unable to rid his ears of a persistent high-pitched ringing, the result, probably, of the metal sound the machetes made every now and then glancing off a branch. Black had ordered them on as he continued his own unrelenting attack on the dense foliage. And now it wasn't much past eleven in the morning, with miles to go, and Black had agreed simply to stop—no suggestion of building a litter, or of leaving Sleeper behind.

Black must be feeling it also, Rumison decided. The pain, the exhaustion. He hid it better than the others, but he was no longer a young man, and with the black case strapped to his pack he was carrying more weight than the others.

They cleared another camp area and slung their hammocks. Water in their canteens was low. The day before they had kept them filled from pools of rainwater that formed on the broad leaves of some of the trees, but the pools had now disappeared. With Rumison's help, Rosso began milking sections of water vine. Rosso chopped the vine into foot-long sections while Rumison drained the filmy water into a pan.

"Hell of a way to get a drink of water," Rosso commented. Rumison agreed.

They had filled two canteens and were starting on a third when Rumison noticed Black looking past him. Black's gaze had such an unexpected intensity that Rumison instinctively swung around to see what had caught Black's attention. At first Rumison couldn't see anything unusual. Rosso bent over a vine, getting ready to cut it into sections.

"Rumison, the vine," Black murmured.

Then Rumison saw it. He screamed and threw himself forward just as a green-colored snake he had mistaken for a vine struck at Rosso's head. Rosso was knocked to the ground and the snake, missing its target, fell from the tree. Rumison swept up Rosso's machete and hacked at it wildly.

Rosso picked himself up off the ground. Rumison was trembling. The snake was dead, cut into sections.

"Damn," said Rosso wonderingly.

Black had joined them. "Fer-de-lance," he said. "Nasty thing. Used by assassins in some areas. Hides in trees and goes for the jugular. One of the few snakes known to actually stalk a human."

Anger quickly replaced Rumison's fear. "I don't need a goddamn biology lecture!" he cried. "You saw it! Why in hell didn't you do something sooner? It almost got Bob!"

"You were closer, Rumison. You handled it well enough." There was a grudging note of approval in Black's tone that had the affect of dulling Rumison's anger. Rumison suddenly found himself at a loss. Nearby Barney stood watching and Sleeper was lying unaware in a hammock. Rumison willed himself to relax but was only partially successful.

"Are we moving again?" Sleeper asked from his hammock. The sergeant's voice was brittle yet disturbingly plaintive.

"No," Black said. "We'll be sticking around here for a bit longer, Sergeant."

Sleeper sighed and slumped back into the hammock netting.

Later that afternoon, while Black was squatted down next to his pack, looking over a map, Rumison approached him and said, "We should build a stretcher for Sleeper. He's not going to make it by himself."

Rumison spoke warily, not knowing what to expect, but Black just nodded. "The undergrowth is thinning," he said. "It should be easier from here to the river."

Barney had been listening and he came over to join them. "You think someone is chasing us, don't you, Mr. Black?" he asked.

Black hesitated before answering. "It's possible," he said finally. After a moment he added, "Survival is doing what has to be done, Bailey, whatever the circumstances, going on what you've got . . ." Black looked at them and his eyes were hard. "Which usually isn't a hell of a lot."

"The whole world isn't a jungle, Mr. Black," said Barney, thoughtful.

"Isn't it?"

Barney squatted down at Black's feet. It was a strangely open gesture and like Barney's moodiness the night before it irritated Rumison. Why, he couldn't have said.

"Do you look at the world that way, Mr. Black?" Barney asked.

Black looked up from the map. The question seemed to

have surprised him. "Sometimes," he said. "It changes. Circumstances change . . . for better or worse. You allow for the worst. Not expect it, only consider it, allow for it."

Barney lowered his innocent-looking blue eyes, digesting this. "It . . . it . . . can't be just all survival," he said, sounding unsure. "I mean . . . there must be something . . . some meaning . . ."

Black regarded Barney's intense, boyish face, and Rumison thought he saw something he had never before noticed in Black—some deep well of internal pain, anguished memories behind the iron door of his seamed, rocklike features that Barney's groping questions had tapped into. But then the door closed and Black was once more as he had been, cold and impenetrable.

"You do what you do," he said shortly, ending the conversation as he folded up the map. "What you make of that . . . that's up to you."

The day passed slowly. For the most part they lay in the hammocks and waited for evening. Rosso and Rumison took turns tending Sleeper, whose physical condition deteriorated even as they rested. Sleeper's breathing was ragged and his glazed eyes were sunk in their sockets, as though trying to escape from the external world. There was little they could do but replace the wet dressings on his forehead.

It rained intermittently during the day but the rain had little effect on the heat and only made the humidity worse. The storms rarely penetrated the canopy. The main announcement of their arrival was a flood of water down the tree trunks that supported the jungle's roof, or sometimes the muffled rumble of thunder.

Rumison started. A sudden noise had broken into his daydreams. A large animal? Worriedly he looked around. The sound repeated itself, this time seeming more distant.

Far off in the trees a young monkey was scratching at a branch. Relieved, Rumison settled back. Acoustics were different in the jungle, he had learned. At times he was unable to hear a sound only yards away, the footfall of Barney's boots or Black's machete as it bit into a vine. The rippling green wall that surrounded them seemed almost to swallow sound. At other times, as had just happened,

Rumison could hear the distant scratching of a monkey as if it were only a few feet away.

Under the canopy it was always twilight during the day. Transmitted through the dense foliage the light had an aquarium-like, greenish glow to it. The trees and vegetation flowed in slow, rippling waves, responding to some inner stimulus that was not the wind. There was little wind under the trees, only the hothouse microenvironment created by the canopy and its huge supporting trees.

Rumison heard another sound and looked up to see Barney standing next to his hammock.

"Sorry, Mike," Barney apologized. "I didn't mean to startle you."

Was his fear that obvious? He managed a smile and waited for his racing heart to slow. "Something on your mind, Barn?" he asked.

Barney looked hesitant and unsure of himself. He shifted nervously. "I . . . I don't know . . ." he began. "I . . . I just need to talk . . ."

"Sure, Barn. Does it have anything to do with your telephone-call feeling?"

"Maybe. I don't know. It's . . . something . . ."

Barney paused, looking out into the jungle. His blue eyes wrestled with some internal demon and seemed out of place in his fair-skinned face, even though the face was covered with four days' growth of a light blond beard and covered with sap stain and sweat. Rumison, feeling a need to say something, sat up.

"Hell, Barn, we just had the bad luck to get caught in some spook operation. Once we get out we'll be bragging about it, telling everyone . . ."

Barney shook his head. "That's not what I mean."

"Huh?"

"I said that's not what I'm trying to say."

The fine facial muscles in Barney's face strained as he tried to bring his demon to the surface, to put deep, rootless feelings into words.

"It's something else," he said. "A dream . . ."

Rumison felt a sudden chill go down his spine and found himself not wanting to hear any more. But that was crazy. "A dream?" he asked.

"You know . . . a dream, and you know it's turning,

changing into something else, a nightmare. You know it and there's nothing you can do. . . ."

"Come on, Barn," said Rumison quickly. Barney's thoughts were reaching too close. "Sure it's tough, but we'll make it. A few more days. Cake, really. In a few days you'll be telling George all about it. . . ." But Barney was shaking his head again.

"You don't understand, Mike! It's not just this damn mission!"

Rumison was stunned. "What?" he asked.

"It's everything, Mike. It's all changing. Don't you understand? That feeling about the call . . . it was change. The world, the dream. Don't you see? Even if we get out, what are we going home to? What meaning is there? Don't you feel the purposelessness of it? The days just flowing on, one after another. . . ."

Barney was clutching at Rumison's hammock and there were tears of anguish in his eyes.

"Mike . . . that feeling . . . you see, I felt the joy leave, the meaning gone. Like God had lost interest and it was all running down . . ."

Rumison was lost. Barney had carried this thing way beyond him. "Barn, wait," he said. "Wait until we get out. It's just this damn jungle. Things'll look different. . . ."

Barney's eyes were closed and he was breathing heavily. He seemed disappointed. "No," he said, "I don't think so. It really did change that night, Mike. There are no dreams left. The heroes are gone. You see that? I know you see something of it. What I'm saying . . . what I'm feeling. It's truth. And it doesn't matter if we do make it out."

Barney turned away and left Rumison alone.

Chapter Six

RUMISON looked down at Sergeant Sleeper as the sergeant lay half-conscious on his hammock. Sleeper still looked ill but his breathing was less ragged and, for a change, the rest seemed to have done some good. Rumison lowered the mosquito netting and squatted down below the hammock.

Barney's outburst had disturbed him immensely. In some frightening way it had been a deeper, clearer vision of what he himself had been feeling at different times, afraid and unwilling to examine further. Even now he found himself rationalizing, trying to tell himself it was nothing more than the situation they were in and the subtle twistings of Barney's moodiness and imagination.

Rumison saw Rosso approaching and smiled. Rosso wasn't one to allow himself to be intimidated by off-the-wall mysticisms. Rumison was glad for the company.

"I heard what Barney said," Rosso said, guessing his friend's preoccupation. "I wouldn't let it bother you. He's just scared. We'll make it, despite Black."

"Black?" Rumison asked, looking at Black's hammock thirty feet away, where Black lay resting.

Rosso positioned himself so his back was toward Black's hammock and squatted down next to Rumison. "I've been thinking about things," he said quietly. "About Black."

"Yeah?"

Rosso nodded. "The Sixty-eighth was asked to furnish four pararescuemen for the mission. But not just any four. They specifically asked for Sleeper, you, me, and Barney.

We weren't even on alert. Creighton and Chambers were the alert team. They'd have loved hero shit like this."

"I thought about that," Rumison admitted.

"Figure this, then, Mike. They ordered us to go even though I'm sure there were others who'd give their right arms to do this . . . most who live at the base and who could've gotten there a lot sooner. And why Sleeper? Christ! He's the last man who should've been picked. Everyone knows he is just hanging on till retirement."

"Maybe they thought because he was a master sergeant—" began Rumison, feeling uneasy, but Rosso interrupted with an impatient wave of his hand.

"No, Mike. They wanted us. They wanted us four specifically."

"Yeah. Well, sure, but—"

"No, you don't understand what I'm trying to say. Us. Us specifically. Why? Don't you see? Why us? Why us four? Why did they go out of the way to get us four?"

Rumison was shaking his head. He still couldn't see Rosso's point. Rosso pulled himself closer.

"Mike, have you ever heard Sleeper talk about his family?"

"Me? No. I didn't think he had one."

"He doesn't. He doesn't have any close relatives. None of us do."

Rumison's mind felt sluggish. Something was holding him back from following Rosso's logic.

"Another thing," said Rosso. "Sleeper's retirement comes up this summer. Barney's, yours and my enlistments also are up. We are all due for discharge within three months!"

"Relatives," said Rumison. "My brother Dennis—"

Rosso snorted. "You haven't seen your brother in fifteen years. He didn't even show up when your parents died. You don't even know if he's still alive, and what's important, he couldn't know if you're alive."

Rumison was quiet. After a moment he said, "So you think we might not make it out . . ." But as soon as the words were out another, more horrifying thought occurred. "You think they don't want us to make it out!"

"Quiet, Mike," whispered Rosso. "Easy. Listen to me. I know it sounds crazy, but those James Bond types in the

CIA are crazy. You know that. Look at this. Why is Black the only one with a gun? We could have brought our Colts along . . . they weren't government issue, but we were expressly told to leave them. I mean, whoever outfitted this thing knew what we'd be getting into, knew we'd probably need weapons other than knives. . . ."

Rumison was shaking his head. It was too insane. This wasn't what Barney had been talking about. This was something entirely different. Maybe Rosso's dislike of Black was turning to paranoia. "Think what you're saying, Rosso," he said, trying to remain calm. "I mean, look how many people know where we are. You're trying to say they're going to kill us!"

"It must be that case," said Rosso. "It must be so damned important to someone I don't even want to think about it. . . . But listen, who else besides Larry Hawkes knows where we are?"

There had been dozens of people, Rumison thought wildly. Sims, who had come with Black, and the bus driver who'd taken them out to the flight line, the marines who checked them through the cordon surrounding the plane . . .

Rosso was grimly shaking his head. "The only people back there who know anything are Gerber Baby, Sims, and Major Hawkes. All those others know is that a funny airplane with little red numbers on its wings landed at El Toro and picked up five unidentified people . . . not in uniform. Black was the only one who showed ID. And remember the briefing . . . no mechanics, no radiomen, no cargomaster. . . ."

"But there is Ellis," objected Rumison. "There's Sims and there's Larry. Larry said he'd raise hell if . . ."

Rosso was smiling without humor. "Be serious, Mike. Ellis would sell his daughter to a pimp for a promotion away from El Toro. And Sims? My God."

"But Larry?"

The thin smile stayed on Rosso's lips, and Rumison realized with a shock what Rosso was trying to say. Larry Hawkes didn't have a family either.

"What are the chances," Rosso was saying, "that it's coincidence? I mean, how many people do you know who don't have a family? I'd bet my bottom dollar there's not another unit in the country that has five people without families in it."

Rumison was silent, remembering how others at the unit back home had started calling him, Rosso, and Barney "The Three Orphans" after Barney had moved off base to Rumison's house. Rumison also was remembering a green snake and the look on Black's face. But for some reason Rumison found it hard to accept Rosso's conclusions. It wasn't so much the insanity of it. You expected things like that out of Washington. But Black?

Why, after all Rumison had seen, did he still have trouble accepting that of Black?

Later that evening, after they'd eaten, Black called them together around a small campfire Barney had built. The fire wasn't a necessity. The night air was overly warm as it was, and they had cooked the meal on the pack stoves. But the fire was comforting, raising primordial feelings of security in the unknown. The jungle kept the light and smoke hidden, and Black hadn't objected to it.

Black removed a map from his shirt pocket and marked off their course with a finger. Sleeper was the only one not present, still in his hammock. His dry, rasping breaths had become a fixture of the night.

"We've come maybe ten miles," said Black. "It's another ten to the river . . ."

His finger moved from a small point in the jungle circled in black ink to a river several inches away. In the glare of Black's electric lantern Rumison could just make out its name: El Río de los Brujos . . . the River of the Sorcerers.

"We'll travel down the river to the coast. Bluefields is here, on this lagoon." Black's finger traced a line down the river to the coast and then up the coast to what looked like a fairly large bay. The name "Bluefields" was marked with another circle of ink.

"It used to be a crumbling little Victorian port," Black continued. "It was a British protectorate for two hundred years, and the inhabitants are mostly Indians, blacks, Chinese, and British colonials, none of whom are particularly fond of their new government. Cubans are coming in now, and there's a Mig base being built nearby that we're not supposed to know about, but there's a good chance we can find someone with a boat to sail us out."

"So it's the Sandinistas who are after us," said Rosso.

Black looked up. "Maybe," he said. "Or maybe Cubans or maybe Russians or maybe the FBI, the Mafia, or the Panamanian Salvation Army. Does it make a difference to you, Rosso?"

Rosso stood. "It might," he said. "It damn well might. And knowing what's in that case you've got might make a difference too."

Rosso's growing anger was making Rumison uneasy. Black was watching Rosso carefully.

"I don't know who might be after us," Black said. "And they never told me what was in that case."

Rosso looked dumbfounded. "You're joking."

"No," said Black softly, "I'm not joking."

Rosso went silent at that. Black had killed a man and he didn't even know what for. It was almost too much for Rosso to absorb. Slowly Black folded up the map and put it in his pocket. The lantern light reflected in his gray eyes as he stared at those around him.

"Listen to me, all of you," he said, his voice low, cold, and penetrating, "because I am going to tell you this only once. That case and whatever is in it is no more important to me than most else in this world that people have chosen to call important. My concern . . . my only concern is to get that case to a man in Miami."

"Whoever you have to kill," said Rosso.

For a tense moment Rumison thought Black might actually lose his temper. Black's eyes narrowed and the muscles tightened in his face. But then a sudden cold smile broke through his anger. In a way the smile was worse. For Rumison it spoke of loneliness and pain, the pain of a man without illusions. Or hope.

"Rosso, the world is full of people's fears and miseries and meaningless little doings," said Black. "And for all I know, death may be a great favor to them, and this goes for that man I killed."

The night was silent. The fire burned nearby. Despite the heat Rumison felt a sudden chill. The cold bleakness of Black's words, the personal vision they exposed horrified Rumison. Even Rosso seemed numbed.

Black stood and turned out the lantern. Shadows from the firelight danced off the trees.

"We have a day tomorrow," said Black. "Better get some sleep."

"Mr. Black?"

Black turned to see Barney staring up at him from the fire. "Yes, Bailey?"

"Are you full of fear and misery and meaningless doings also?"

The question was asked in innocence, with no trace of mockery. Black seemed to know this as he paused to consider. "Not fear," he said slowly. "I think that was burned out of me a long time ago. . . ."

He stopped, and for the second time Rumison felt an empathy with the older man so agonizing that he tensed to avoid succumbing to it.

"As for meaningless doings," Black said finally, "at least I'm aware there's little real importance to what I do. But believe me," he continued, adding stress to his last words, "what I do may not have any ultimate meaning to it, but the very fact that I have chosen to do it is enough for me to risk my life for. And to kill for."

Black left them by the fire, digesting his words. Rumison was slowly accepting the fact that there was more to their situation than could be accounted for by the simple mechanical plotting of governmental agencies and the simple physical demands necessary to survive in a Central American jungle.

Something else was going on, and it terrified him. At that moment even Rosso seemed to understand as he stared after Black.

"Damn," said Rosso quietly.

Chapter Seven

It was Rumison who found Sleeper dead the next morning. Hearing no sounds of any sort from Sleeper's hammock, he had pulled back the mosquito netting to find the master sergeant's eyes open, staring up at nothing. In death the body looked curiously waxlike, the skin almost translucent. The expression on the face was one of fatigue. Why were the eyes open? Rumison wondered. What had Sleeper been looking at in those last few moments?

Rumison felt no sadness, not even pity. The death was too pointless. Like Sleeper's life, Rumison thought. And then came the troubling thought, perhaps like all our lives.

Quickly he dropped the netting. He didn't want to see Sleeper's face again. Rosso came up behind him.

"He's dead," said Rumison. Rosso shrugged without comment.

Somewhat later, as they made ready to leave, Barney asked, "Shouldn't we bury him?"

Black vetoed the suggestion. "The animals will get him, whatever we do. We've wasted enough time already."

"I want to say some words," said Rumison, surprising himself. He felt no real grief for the master sergeant and could sense that the feeling was general. But for some reason that made it all the more important.

He hesitated, realizing he didn't know what to say. The others waited.

"Go ahead," said Black.

Rumison took a breath. "Sergeant Kenneth Sleeper was a man . . . like us all. He had his weaknesses . . . like us all. If there is a God to whom his life had meaning, then let that God take care of him. And if not, let him rest in peace."

Rumison could feel the eyes of the others looking at him. He suddenly felt awful and didn't want them to know, so he turned and started off. The others soon followed, leaving the sergeant lying in his hammock, his shroud a thin nylon netting through which Sleeper gazed out at his personal eternity.

They made better time now that Sleeper was gone. The jungle had thinned, becoming more like the textbook descriptions of a true rain forest as the trees grew taller, pushing the canopy higher overhead. For Rumison the present ease of their travel made Sleeper's death even more pointless, if that were possible.

Black, making up for the hours lost, allowed them few breaks. At times in the open spaces between the huge trees he drove them almost at a jog. His concern with speed brought up the question of why he had allowed them to break for Sleeper in the first place. Had it been simple humanity?

His mind lost in thought, Rumison stumbled over a root and fell. He put his right hand on a log for support, but the wood gave way and his hand broke through to the rotten core.

His hand was covered immediately by countless sluglike insects. He cried out in fear and disgust, yanking his hand away as he batted the insects off. Even when they were gone his skin felt as though a thousand tiny feet were crawling over it.

Rosso had come running. "You all right, Mike?"

Rumison pointed at the log, still rubbing his hand against his jeans.

"Let me see your hand," said Rosso.

Rumison showed it to him. It was filthy and, like his face, covered with scratches and mosquito bites, but there was no unusual pain.

"Just big wood mites," said Rosso, dropping the hand. "You're lucky. It could have been muscle worms."

Rumison shivered, instinctively rubbing his hand again. The jungle was full of poisonous insects, but muscle worms were one horror the survival instructors at the jungle school in Panama had been especially fond of describing. The worm burrowed into muscle, living off the tissue until it laid its eggs. When the eggs hatched, the resulting brood of baby worms had to be removed surgically.

They walked twelve miles that day, stopping only for food and water and compass readings. They made camp just before sunset, still without having caught sight of the river, which, according to Black's map, should have been close. As soon as they had slung their hammocks Rosso had taken a nylon hammock sack and started off back the way they had come. Rumison was exhausted but it made him nervous to see his friend wandering off alone.

"I saw some wild tomatoes a ways back," said Rosso. "I won't be long."

"Sit down and stop worrying, Rumison," said Black, bending over a cookstove. "Rosso can take care of himself."

Rosso disappeared. Rumison sat down on a log near the clear area where Barney was building a fire. Black lit the stove and put some water in a pan.

"You sound as though you almost like Rosso, Mr. Black," said Barney, breaking branches for kindling.

Black grunted. "He's honest. That's hard to find."

The comment, given as it had been, seemed a judgment on the rest of them, and it irritated Rumison. "You seem pretty sure he won't get hurt out there," he said.

"I know how it works," said Black.

The answer was not what Rumison had expected. "Works?" he asked. "How what works?"

"Death."

Barney had stopped working and was watching Black with a certain quiet attention. Black, adjusting the flame on his stove, didn't seem to notice.

"Who's talking about death?" Rumison asked.

Satisfied with the flame, Black placed the pan of water on the stove and took out a package of dried apples from his pack. "Aren't we all talking about death?" he asked evenly.

Rumison's irritation grew. "And you think you know how death works?"

Black ignored the irony in Rumison's tone, more intent

on stirring his apples. "Death comes according to how you live," he said simply. "Rosso is a bull. He'll die running after something . . . knowing what that something is. Sleeper had no will of his own, so he died at the whim of chance."

Rumison felt his jaw growing tight, and he turned away. His irritation was growing into anger.

"I've known Rosso only about eight months," said Barney thoughtfully, speaking to Black. "He never seems to worry about . . . things. Not like me. He's like that hero in the *Iliad* . . . Achilles. You know . . . passionate, never doubting. Me? I'm more like Hamlet . . . indecisive, always doubting."

Black looked up from the apples. "Achilles was killed," he said.

"But maybe death as a hero is better than life as a . . ."

"Coward?" Black offered.

Barney lowered his eyes and didn't answer. After a bit, Black said, "But Hamlet *wasn't* a coward. And sometimes doubt and indecision are beneficial . . . though if you carry it too far your brains can slip out your ears. It's easier for the Achilles' of the world. They just leave the mental gymnastics to others. I suppose that's fine if they've been pointed in the right direction. But it doesn't always happen that way for the bulls of this world."

"Is there a right direction?" Barney asked.

"Let's not discuss metaphysics," said Black dryly.

"But how do you decide what to do, Mr. Black? You seem so sure. . . ."

Sure. Yes, that's what bothered Rumison. Black was so goddamn sure of himself. Yet despite his feelings toward Black, Rumison wanted to hear Black's answer.

"It isn't the decisions that matter so much," said Black after turning down the flame on his stove and placing a lid over the pan. "Ultimately we can't know if our decisions are right or wrong. It's the act . . . deciding, then carrying out the decision. Do you live with the courage . . . carrying out your decisions even knowing you may be wrong . . . or . . ." He shrugged as though the alternative wasn't even worth mentioning.

Rosso returned twenty minutes later, walking into camp

just before sunset. His tote sack was filled with wild tomatoes and a large green parrot that he proudly held up for the others to see.

"Hell, that won't feed us all," said Rumison, who was glad to see Rosso back.

"I caught it, I'll eat it," said Rosso. "You can have your freeze-dried rat meat."

Later, after Rosso had boiled, plucked, then roasted the parrot over Barney's fire, he relented and offered pieces to the others, even Black. The stringy meat tasted like chicken gone bad, and Rumison didn't tell his friend he had liked his trail rations better.

"I caught a parrot in survival school," Rosso mused. "We had this little Indian instructor who taught cooking. I once saw him cut down a hunk of bamboo. He tossed it on the fire and ten minutes later shook out ten little fried baby bats. He gave them to us. He thought he was doing us a favor. We had to eat them. Held them by the wings and crunched down. They were crunchy . . . like charred peanut brittle."

"We had to eat dragonflies," said Barney. "Didn't even get to cook them. The first time I bit down, green stuff squirted all down my shirt."

"What'd it taste like, Barn?" asked Rosso.

"I don't know. I was too busy getting sick."

Rumison had to laugh. Darkness had fallen and the laughter helped mitigate the forbidding presence of night.

Night in the jungle was a time of screams, a time for hunting when the larger jungle predators stalked unwary prey. It was a time when the jungle, for everything but man and monkeys, came alive. An eerie chorus of cries signaled final sunset. Even the firelight ghosts, at least to Rumison's imagination, seemed to gain substance.

Rumison found himself remembering the campfire stories told by the wide-eyed native instructors in Panama. They told them to scare the white students, but always ended by scaring themselves too. They called the night the *nagual* or otherness. It was a time for spirits, and men were rarely safe unless the proper rites were observed.

A low, muted rumble of thunder echoed down through

the canopy. Somewhere overhead another storm was gathering. The others seemed content to sit and gaze at the fire, but Rumison found himself watching the shadows, drawn to their movement, their apparent life. He was grateful as he slid onto his hammock, and sleep overtook his fantasies, but even in his dreams the shadows stalked.

Chapter Eight

THEY finally reached the river on the afternoon of the following day. It lay seven miles farther from where they had parachuted than Black's map showed.

The river was wide, at points nearly a hundred yards across, and the water was slow moving and muddy. Rosso, Rumison, and Barney immediately took their clothes off and waded in, indifferent to the thought of leeches, snakes, and the other creatures possibly lurking below the brown surface of the water. They scrubbed off dirt, scabs, and plant sap with abrasive soap, and afterward Rosso passed around a tube of antiseptic. They rubbed it on countless scratches, then lay on their backs in the sunlight for a short time, enjoying the rest.

Black had followed only after moving all their clothes and packs back under a thick copse of bamboo, out of sight from the river.

The sunlight felt good after so many days under the canopy, and for a time at least the mosquitos left them alone. Lying next to Rumison, Barney shifted onto his side and absently began piling sand into a small mound with his left hand. "Feeling better, Barn?" Rumison asked.

"It reminds me of my father," answered Barney, unexpectedly because he rarely talked about his parents. Rumison knew only that they had died sometime past and that Barney had been raised by an elderly aunt.

"He used to take me to this place in Louisiana. We'd fish and talk and sometimes I'd go swimming and lie on the bank like this."

"I didn't know you were from Louisiana."

"I'm not really. My father was Army. We traveled a lot. He was a colonel," Barney added. "I didn't get to see him that much. When he died, Mom went into a blue funk and we moved to Detroit. Later, when she died, I moved in with Aunt Jane in Evanston."

"How did your parents die?" Rumison asked.

Barney had pushed sand into the shape of a pyramid and was smoothing the sides with a twig. "Mom had a bad liver. Aunt Jane said she killed herself, but I don't think so. She just had a bad liver and drank too much and took too many medications."

"And your dad?"

Barney shrugged. "They said it was a plane crash."

"You sound doubtful."

"It was a long time ago. I was pretty young."

"But you think they lied?"

Barney leveled the pyramid with a hand. "My father was a Ranger," he said. "Airborne. He told us he was going to Asia . . . This was just before Viet Nam . . . early sixties. We never saw the body. They said it was burned too bad. I think he probably died in Viet Nam. I couldn't see him dying in some stupid accident."

Barney plunged the twig he'd been holding into the sand, snapping it in two. "It's sorta like Black said, you know . . . about death . . . how it comes. . . ."

He looked suddenly apologetic and looked away. "Later, when Mom died, Aunt Jane took me in. I went to a private school outside Chicago. She wanted me to be a writer. Something refined. She was pretty wealthy . . . into the arts. She disowned me when I enlisted. Said I'd end up like my father. Wrote me out of her will."

"Why did you enlist?" asked Rumison.

At first Rumison didn't think Barney was going to answer. Then Barney sat up and began brushing off sand.

"My father was Army because he loved it," he said. "He was a warrior. I never thought I could match up to him. I thought Rescue might be a good compromise . . . you know, being a hero without having to blow some poor rice farmer away. I blew it both ways."

Barney was quiet, looking out over the river.

"You don't have to be a hero to prove you're a man, Barn," said Rumison.

Barney turned. "Don't you?" he asked.

The mosquitos found them and they dressed quickly. They ate dried fruit and almond-flavored protein bars that tasted like pressed sawdust. The blue sky overhead was the first real sky they had seen in some days.

"We'll have to be careful from here on out," said Black after they'd eaten. "If someone is following us they'll guess we're heading for this river."

"Who could follow us through that mess?" snorted Rosso. "That stuff grew back faster than we could cut it."

"Don't kid yourself," said Black. "There are people around who could track a butterfly through this jungle a month after it passed. And we're hardly butterflies."

Rosso didn't answer, but Rumison could feel what he was thinking: The talk of trackers and unseen followers was Black's way of keeping the real danger hidden . . . Black himself.

They built a raft out of saplings cut into logs with their machetes and bound with shroud line Black had salvaged from the parachutes. It took most of the afternoon to finish. When it was done they dragged it down to the narrow sandy bank of the river for launching.

"When do we go?" Rosso asked.

Black didn't answer. He was looking up at the sky.

"Black, I asked . . ."

Black waved him quiet. "Listen!"

There was nothing at first. And then Rumison heard it, a soft plop somewhere in the distance. Black was standing absolutely still. Suddenly he was in motion.

"Get everything out of sight!" he yelled. "Cover the raft!"

Madly Black began throwing branches over the raft. Rumison was a little slow in following and was almost knocked off his feet.

"Hurry!" cried Black.

Rumison found himself hiding in a tangle of creepers before he was even sure what had panicked Black. He watched as Black threw one last branch over the raft and then leaped under cover with the others.

The jungle's strange acoustics had fooled Rumison again. Just as Black landed next to him he heard a thunderous noise and looked upriver to see an ancient Sikorsky

H-3 American-made helicopter flying low down the river directly toward them. It was painted an olive-drab green, but any markings it may have had were covered over with splotches of gray primer. As it drew nearer, Rumison could see the faces of the pilots as they scanned the jungle. The rear hatch was open and two men in soldiers' uniforms peered out. One was using binoculars.

As it passed over them Rumison slid farther back into the foliage. For one excruciating moment he imagined the aircraft had stopped, but the staccato chug of its rotors soon lessened. Rumison glanced out of his hiding place just in time to see the helicopter disappear around a bend in the river.

Black was the first to emerge. The others were silent. "We'll have to wait until dark," said Black. "Too dangerous now."

Rosso pursed his lips thoughtfully. Rumison wondered if his friend might be reconsidering certain things.

At dusk they slung their hammocks under the canopy and ate. Black wouldn't allow them a fire but he let them sleep until after midnight. When he woke them it was pitch black under the trees where their hammocks were, but closer to the river the stars shone overhead and reflected off the water. They tied the packs to the center of the raft and pushed off, using long bamboo poles. The mosquitos, for a time, were gone. The waning moonlight and the bright starlight gave the water a mirrorlike iridescence.

"Keep your mouths shut and your ears open," Black cautioned before leaving. "Sound carries over water."

The raft was small, too small to lie on. They crouched with their backs to the packs and fended off snags and sandbars with the poles. The bright eyes of dark animal shapes drinking at the river's edge stared out at them as they floated silently past. The cries of the forest seemed louder on the river, more menacing.

They continued on for several hours with no mishap, the slow rhythms of the river lulling Rumison into a sense of complacency. The moon sank below the horizon, and clouds began building in the east. A storm was coming. Flashes of lightning darted down at the jungle, and it wasn't long before the smooth surface of the river was pit-ted with raindrops. Thunder rolled over the forest and a hot, jungle-scented wind drove rain into their faces.

"Maybe we should get over to the bank!" Rumison cried.

"It'll be light soon," said Black.

The river curved southward. Forty minutes passed and a hazy glow through the clouds in the east announced the rising sun. The river narrowed and they entered a section of faster water, broken here and there by rounded rocks that they kept away from by careful use of the poles. The wind eased and the black clouds overhead began breaking up.

"We'd better bring it over to the bank," said Black. "It's getting too light."

Barney turned to say something, but before he could speak the raft dipped into a trough formed around a large snag of tree root and he lost his balance, falling headlong into the root. Before either Rosso or Rumison could react, Black had plunged in after him. In the gloom of the departing storm it was hard to see what was happening.

"We've got to get to the bank!" Rumison cried. Rosso nodded grimly and started poling. The current was strong in the narrows, but ahead a sandbar had created a small inlet, clogged with dead branches. They fought the raft to the sandbar and Rosso jumped off, grabbing the raft.

"Get the packs off!"

Rumison cut through the cord holding down the packs and began tossing them to the bank. Rosso lost his footing and Rumison leaped free just as the raft broke loose and started downstream again. Rosso helped Rumison carry the packs to safer ground and then picked up his machete and ran off upriver, scrambling wildly over roots and fallen trees. "We've got to help Barney!" Rosso yelled back.

"You'll kill yourself, Rosso!" Rumison cried back. "Take it easy! Black's with him!"

"That's what I'm afraid of!"

"Oh, shit," mumbled Rumison tiredly, taking up his own machete as he followed after Rosso.

The way wasn't easy. The jungle was thick near the river, and Rumison had difficulty keeping up with Rosso over the roots and through the thick mud. At places they were forced into the water, struggling against the current. The rain ceased and the sky grew light.

They found Black lying against a tree next to the river. Barney lay next to him. He looked up as they approached. He winced and lifted a hand to an ugly gash on his forehead.

"I think I hit that tree when I fell in," he said.

"Don't you remember?" Rumison asked.

"I think I was knocked out for a minute. The next thing I remember was Black pulling me up here."

"Did you save the packs?" Black asked.

Rumison nodded, feeling relieved and a little foolish. He had begun to think Rosso's worries might be real.

"You all right, Barn?" Rosso asked, not giving up his thoughts as he studied the laceration on Barney's forehead. "Dizzy? Nauseous?"

"Hurts a bit," Barney admitted.

"He'll need stitches," said Black.

"We'll go get the packs," said Rosso shortly.

"That would seem to be in order," said Black dryly.

"I had a dream when I was out," Barney said. "Funny . . . how long it seemed, in just that short time. It was an island somewhere . . . a magical place, like Oz or Middle Earth. . . ."

With the sun, the heat was returning. Steam rose off the trees, and the mosquitos swarmed in dark clouds following the rain.

"Welcome back to reality," said Rosso.

Chapter Nine

THEY came across the abandoned dock the morning of the day following Barney's injury. By Black's calculation they were less than ten miles from the coast. They had traveled by foot again after Black had ruled out as too dangerous the idea of building another raft, sticking as close as they could to the river. The dock stuck out fifty feet into the river from a narrow mud beach. Several wooden sheds roofed in tin stood at the base and there was a large wooden crane at its end. Even from a distance the dock had an unmistakable air of neglect and disuse about it.

Black left his pack with the others, who waited in cover of the jungle that bordered the beach, and went off alone to inspect the dock. The air had grown increasingly humid as they neared the coast, but Rumison no longer noticed the heat, accepting it along with everything else. It may have been mere wish-fulfillment, but he imagined he could smell salt in the light breeze that blew in from the east. The scent, imaginary or not, reminded him of California and his house there. Oddly, the thought brought no fond memories.

Why? he wondered. Why don't I care more?

Since the car accident that killed his parents, Rosso was the only person he had felt particularly close to. He and Rosso had been best friends most of their lives, ever since Rumison's father had tired of tending a failing printing shop in Arizona and moved the family to California to realize his dreams of being a charter boat operator. Rumison had been five at the time. He hadn't wanted to leave Arizona. He had loved the desert, the hot, dry air. It had taken him a long time to accept the change . . . even with the sound of the ocean coming through his new bedroom window.

After the accident, Rumison inherited the house and three aging fishing boats, which he immediately sold to his father's previous skippers. He had yet to appreciate the wealth the house represented. With the incredible rise in the value of beachfront land over the past few years, the house and the land had been appraised close to half a million dollars. Friends urged him to sell and invest the money, but he had wanted to wait until his present enlistment was up—just three months away if Colonel Ellis came through with the early outs he had promised. Land, at least beachfront land, was as good an investment as any, he figured.

Was that why the memories brought no affection? The house was pleasant enough with a good view, but after all, it was just another house. A commodity, like so many other things in California, to be used or mortgaged or sold. A soulless thing, really—as his life had been?

The thought disturbed him. It had come unbidden. More of Barney's influence, he decided irritably. Nearby, Barney was sitting next to his pack, quiet, meditating. Rumison had known him nearly a year and had lived with him for eight months but still he was something of an enigma. He had always seemed out of place in the overtly macho world of Air Rescue. Barney's aunt had been right. He should have been a poet or a writer of some kind. His clothes were dirty and torn now. The GREENPEACE lettering on his shirt was barely readable, and his refined features were scratched, bitten, and bruised. The bandage on his forehead, where Rosso had placed six stitches, was yellow with sweat.

Barney and Rosso were like opposite reflections in a mirror, Rumison thought. Rosso was solid and practical. Put him in a locked room with a book or an idea and he'd go crazy in twenty minutes. Barney was slender and introspective, as comfortable with ideas and emotions as Rosso was with physical stress. And what is my character? Rumison wondered. What traits do I have that others can see but are hidden from myself?

Black returned a few minutes later and Rumison put his

thoughts aside, no closer to answering any of the questions that had generated those thoughts than before.

"The dock is abandoned," said Black, hoisting his pack onto a shoulder. "There are some rusty rail tracks that lead into the jungle. Probably an old plantation nearby. I'm hoping there'll be a back road."

"We're going to follow the tracks?" asked Rosso. He had been sitting on a log, sharpening his machete on a whetstone.

"I thought we might," said Black.

Rosso shrugged. "Seems awfully dangerous," he said.

"From here on it's all dangerous," said Black. "Let's go," and he started off without waiting for the others to follow.

The dock itself was weathered and desolate, littered with debris blown in from the jungle. A broken, faded sign nailed to a shed at the base of the dock read: "SANTA CONCEPCIÓN, R. Harrison, Manager." And below that, "United Foods."

The shed was locked with a small, rusty padlock and had what looked like numerous bullet holes in its wooden front. "Hunters," Rumison decided. Black had noticed the holes also. He kicked open the door, but the shed was empty and the noise startled only the sea gulls that had settled on the tin roof. The narrow-gauge tracks led into the jungle, where after a hundred yards or so, they took an abrupt turn, beyond which Rumison could see nothing. They stayed on a footpath that ran next to the railbed. Three miles farther on, the tracks curved again. In front of them stood a low group of buildings.

A tall, rusty chain-link fence divided the sparse surrounding jungle from the compound where the buildings stood. A gate crossed the tracks. The gate was open, entangled in vines that threatened to engulf the whole fence. There were several large barnlike structures and a number of small buildings, all in advanced stages of disrepair, but the most interesting building was a large, single-story house with a sweeping, red-tile roof. The house was built some feet off the ground on a wooden foundation and had a long, screened veranda that covered the front. It was the only building not roofed in tin, and it looked in surprisingly good condition.

Somewhere in the compound Rumison could hear the softly delicate sound of wind chimes blowing in an imperceptible breeze. Staring at the house, he began to get an uneasy feeling.

"It's lived in," said Rosso abruptly.

Black was regarding the house. Despite the overriding sense of disuse and neglect that surrounded the house, it was obvious that Rosso was right.

"Well," said Black after a moment, "let's see who lives there."

Rosso and Rumison hesitated as Black, followed closely by Barney, started out into the open beyond the fence. "Come on," said Black irritably, "it's just a house. We don't have to worry about the locals."

Rumison wasn't so sure. Nor was he sure whether or not the locals needed to worry about them, or more specifically Mr. Black. He knew these were Rosso's thoughts as well.

"Ah, hell," said Rosso finally, "maybe whoever's here really can help," but he smiled as though he really didn't believe that.

It was early yet, before noon, and the plantation compound was still and silent except for the soft, delicate echo of the wind chimes. Despite the slight breeze it was hot, especially in direct sunlight. Heat waves rose with the dust in the yard as Black led them to the house.

"Lumber," said Black, nodding toward a large iron incinerator that stood next to a sagging barn. The barn probably housed the mill. Nearby on a short spur line stood four flatcars, their wheels overgrown with weeds. The main tracks disappeared into a large shed.

"What do you think happened?" asked Barney. "Why is it abandoned?"

"Vampire bats, Barn," said Rosso dryly. "I heard they drove the Mayans out."

"Maybe we'll find out," said Black, stepping up the wooden stairs to the screen door of the house. But before he could knock, a voice came from behind them.

"Hello. Can I help you gentlemen?"

Standing near the corner of the veranda, one arm holding a reed basket full of freshly picked squash, was a man. He was slightly overweight, of medium height, and dark in coloring, almost black. His hair was well groomed and his face fine featured and intelligent looking, with large, sad compassionate dark eyes. Rumison felt an air of quiet melancholy about the man, evident in the wry grin with which he greeted them and the dark sad eyes. He was dressed in a long-sleeved white shirt, sleeves rolled up to his elbows, and he had on boots and khaki riding breeches. He looked to be in his mid-thirties and he regarded them with no external sign of judgment or fear.

"Please," he said quickly when no one spoke, "I didn't mean to startle you." He stepped forward, holding out the basket as an explorer might show the natives, to show that he was unarmed.

"As you can see, I've been picking squash in the garden. I am Miguel Cordobes . . . uh—caretaker, really, of this place. Please be welcome."

Rumison could feel Rosso tensing as they waited for Black's reaction. Rumison felt a wave of relief as Black stepped down from the screen door and took Cordobes' offered hand.

"I'm Michael Black," said Black politely. "These are my friends, Barney Bailey, Michael Rumison, and Robert Rosso. Excuse us if you did catch us a little by surprise. We came across the dock this morning. We didn't expect . . ."

"Of course, I understand completely," said Cordobes, taking each person's hand in turn. Rumison found Cordobes' grip warm and firm. "The jungle can be a very dangerous place."

"We are trying to get to the coast," Black said. "We were hoping there might be a road."

Cordobes looked surprised. "You are traveling from the west, then? A difficult journey. Yes . . . yes, there is a road. Overgrown now but better than nothing. But we can speak of that later. For now let us go inside, where it is cooler. You can freshen up and I hope will allow me to offer you some lunch. If you don't mind my saying so," he added delicately, "you do look rather traveled out."

Black glanced at the others. His eyes were unreadable. He turned back to Cordobes. "Thank you. We'd like that," he said.

Cordobes smiled. It was a warm smile, like his handshake, and he seemed sincerely pleased. "Excellent. Excellent. I have never met North American hikers . . . at least not who've come in from the west . . . in this area."

He raised a hand and looked up at the roof. *"Bastante, Jorge,"* he yelled, *"estos son amigos!"*

Startled, Black looked up. Rumison stood with the others to see an ancient but surprisingly capable-looking Indian emerge from behind the stone chimney on top of the roof. The old man was dressed in what looked like a faded green Army uniform and he was carrying a Springfield rifle that looked nearly as old as himself. He waved back at Cordobes and then disappeared on the far side of the roof.

"Damn," said Rosso, "he looked serious! Was he up there the whole time?"

Cordobes laughed. "Probably. Jorge is very wily for such an old man. Fighting is all he knows. When he was young he even fought alongside Sandino himself. But please, come inside and we shall see to lunch."

Rumison couldn't help noticing the look on Black's face as Cordobes led them into the large house. Rumison had never before seen that look on Black's face. A look of interest, and respect.

Chapter Ten

THEY left their packs and machetes on the wooden floor of the veranda. A young girl met Cordobes at the door and he spoke some words to her in Spanish and handed her the basket. The girl seemed shyly nervous in the presence of the North Americans, but her large brown eyes were open and loving whenever they rested on Cordobes, which, Rumison noticed, they did frequently. She had a round, childlike, but beautiful Mayan face, and her small body was clothed in a clean white cotton dress.

"This is Taxia," said Cordobes, introducing the girl, who stood holding the basket, her eyes lowered. "My cook and housekeeper, my friend and my lover." Cordobes smiled, unable to hide the affection in his tone. Cordobes nodded at the girl and she left. In motion, Rumison could see the line of her long legs and the upthrust of her just budding breasts under the demure dress.

"Your lover?" Rosso asked. "She's only a kid!"

Cordobes laughed again. "For the Miskito Indians, thirteen is a woman," he said with no trace of embarrassment. "Her father gave her to me with his blessings. . . . But come, I will show you to the bathroom, where you may want to clean up first."

They followed Cordobes through a front living room furnished sparsely in handmade mahogany and rattan furniture down a long hall to a large, modern bathroom.

"Taxia, despite her lack of years, is a woman," he continued, speaking as they walked. "She knows what it is necessary for a woman to know . . . which is how to love. This is all I find of much importance in these sorrowful days of the world . . . this knowledge. So often when people forget it they form arbitrary standards for judging relationships . . . like age. I can think of few things less relevant than age in personal relationships."

"Some people might disagree with you about what's important in life," said Rosso. Only Rumison was aware of the irony in his voice and the meaningful look Rosso had given Black.

"Of course," Cordobes agreed. "But think how beautiful it is if you make love the thing of importance. How dreary is the world when it is absent."

Despite the open smile, it was Cordobes' sad eyes that dominated his handsome face. Unlike Black, whose inner feelings were lost behind the granite mask of his gray eyes and hard features, Cordobes wore his feelings close to the surface. Looking into Cordobes' face, Rumison was assailed by a strange sense of poignancy, the kind one might expect to feel upon seeing a little boy lost at a train station.

Cordobes opened the door at the end of the hall. Beyond was the gleaming modern bathroom, tiled in hand-painted tiles, its faucets shiny with chrome. "It is solar heated," explained Cordobes, pointing toward the large shower stall. "But if you all choose to shower, it is best to make them short."

He left them with towels and bars of Zest soap, apologizing that there were no fresh clothes for them to wear.

"You've done too much already," murmured Black. When Cordobes had left them, Black raised a warning hand.

"Don't volunteer anything," he said quietly. "We're travelers doing a cross-country trek to Bluefields. An adventure. Nothing more."

Black scratched at his short gray hair with a seamed hand. "He likes to talk," he said. "Let him."

The clean water of the shower refreshed Rumison, along with the surprising geniality of their host. They found Cordobes in the living room, seated in a large rattan Solomon's chair and smoking a potent-smelling cigar. He stood when they entered, offering them seats on a couch and handing around a box of the cigars, which they all refused.

"A pity," he sighed. "They are Havanas. There are no other cigars like them. One leaf . . . rolled by hand. The

Cuban women do it, rolling the leaves along their thighs. It is hot in Cuba. They sweat a great deal. That is where the unique flavor of the Cuban cigar comes from—the sweat of a woman's thigh."

They laughed politely. After a moment, Black stood, looking as though he had forgotten something. "Excuse me a minute, Miguel," he said. "There is something in my pack I must see to."

Cordobes nodded graciously. Somewhat uneasily, Rumison watched as the older man left the room. It was a large room, beamed with mahogany gulams and lined with large-paned windows that looked out over a well-kept garden behind the house. A large field choked with low scrub weeds lay on the far side of the garden, and the jungle was beyond that.

There was not much furniture in the room: the sofa, several chairs webbed in leather and rattan, a polished hardwood table, the chair Cordobes sat in, a brass lamp or two and little else. Slow-moving fans hung from the ceiling, their wide blades barely disturbing the hot noon air though it was cooler in the house than outside.

Black returned moments later and took his seat.

"Taxia will have lunch ready shortly," said Cordobes, avoiding comment on Black's absence. "I hope it will be to your liking."

"As long as it's not freeze-dried," said Rosso.

"You said her father gave her to you, Miguel," said Black. "Did you mean that literally?"

Cordobes nodded. "Her father likes me. He is a chief of the tribe that used to work here. The Miskito Indians have a custom of assuming the name of people they like. He gave Taxia to me and began calling himself, along with his other names, Miguel Cordobes. He felt we were the same . . . his daughters were mine. . . ."

Cordobes paused. "Forgive me," he said apologetically. "I run on. Sometimes, with only Jorge and Taxia to speak with . . ."

"It's very interesting," said Black.

"There is no one else?" Barney asked.

"It is not so bad as it sounds," said Cordobes, his sad eyes looking out toward the garden and jungle. "It was my choice. I am comfortable with myself where another may not be. And I have my work. . . ."

Taxia appeared at the doorway, shyly trying to catch Cordobes' eyes. Cordobes stood. "Lunch is waiting," he said.

He led them to a room adjacent to the living room, where Taxia stood waiting by a large table. When they had taken their seats she placed glasses around the table and filled them with amber-colored beer from a pitcher. Rumison could see the beads of condensation forming on the glasses and wondered how the beer had been kept cold. Then for the first time he noticed the muffled chug of a gas motor somewhere off behind the house. By the way it had suddenly cut on, it was probably hooked to an electrical generator.

"Watney's Red," said Cordobes after a long, satisfied draught. "The English drink it warm . . . but in this climate . . . hah! Nothing like cold beer."

Taxia brought out plates and served lunch. Fried rice and tomatoes, squash, and cold meat that tasted like turkey. And the beer, cold and delicious, tasting better than anything Rumison could remember.

The girl waited on them quietly, never once speaking, carrying out their dishes when they were finished, filling their glasses when they were empty. Cordobes, as Black had said, wanted to talk, and he kept up a lively monologue, mostly about mundane things . . . the weather, the food, the plantation. Whether not to appear rude or for some other reason, he kept away from politics or pointed questions concerning his guests. Black sketched out a story about traveling to Bluefields, and if it didn't satisfy Cordobes, their host didn't show it.

"I hope you can stay the night," Cordobes said after they had finished eating, as they sat back and sipped their beers. "I'll have Jorge cook roast pork for dinner."

"Your man . . . you said he fought with Sandino?" commented Black, avoiding a direct answer.

"Yes. He has fought with all the revolutionaries, or so it seems. He is very good, very deadly, even for one so old."

Cordobes paused, frowning thoughtfully. "He traveled with Sandino when he was a young man, returning to the jungle after the Great Betrayal. Recently he was with

Jaime Guerra in the foothills of Cheochitzlan, but Guerra was killed in an ambush by La Guardia during the revolution. Causes mean little to Jorge. Perhaps he has seen too many come and go. He stays with men he respects. Individuals count with him. Little else. He has no family.

"Somehow he found himself here, with me," Cordobes added quietly. "God knows why."

"He doesn't work for you?" Black asked.

Cordobes laughed. "Work? For money? No, I'm afraid Jorge would not work for anyone simply for money. More as though he adopted me. He was with a group of *los muchachos,* revolutionaries who came down from the highlands. . . ."

Cordobes hesitated. "He calls me *Capitán,"* he said, as if trying to unravel the mystery for himself. "But I am not really a captain. He understands the jungle and he understands men in battle, but when the revolution was finally won and the Sandinistas triumphed, his world was doomed, for whom would he fight? Perhaps he would have fought them with as little concern as he fought Somoza.

"He is something of a legend, *El Viejo.* He frightens the young ones. I think that is why they left him with me. But again, I have been doing all the talking. Tell me: How did you end up here, at Santa Concepción?"

Black explained about the raft and about Barney falling off. He kept it as simple and as truthful as he could. Cordobes nodded sympathetically as he looked at the bandage on Barney's forehead.

"You are all right, Barney?" he asked.

Barney nodded. "Bob stitched me up pretty good."

Cordobes raised an eyebrow. "You are a doctor then," he said, looking at Rosso.

Rosso shifted uneasily. "I'm . . . I was a medic. . . ."

"In the military some years ago," said Black. "We brought quite a good kit along."

"A wise precaution in the jungle," Cordobes agreed.

"What about you, Miguel?" Black asked, shifting the conversation to safer waters. "You're obviously educated. Intelligent. What are you doing here, at an abandoned lumber plantation?"

"Educated?" asked Cordobes rhetorically. He lowered his eyes to his glass. "Yes," he continued softly, "perhaps." He looked back toward Black. "But there is education and there is education. Jorge, for example, has been educated in one school, I in another. . . ." He sighed and sipped again at his beer, his sad eyes staring off at something in the distance.

"Yes," he repeated after a moment, "I was educated. I even attended school for a short time in the United States . . . in Texas. . . ."

He set his glass on the table and pushed it slowly away, settling back in his chair. "I was born on this plantation thirty-six years ago," he said. "It is my home."

"But what happened?" Barney asked. "Where did everyone go?"

Cordobes smiled wanly. "It is a long story, I warn you."

"We would like to hear it," said Black. The others nodded assent.

Cordobes hesitated for a moment, smiled again and then began. "My father was foreman here," he said. "My mother was a black field hand who died not long after I was born. My father and the manager, Señor Harrison, were great friends. They wished that I should be . . . educated. With Señor Harrison's help I was enrolled in a private school in Texas. I did not like Texas. It was during the mid-sixties. I ran away.

"I was found and deported, but not until after I had spent some time in the San Francisco area . . . Berkeley. I had run out of money and stolen a woman's purse and I had become radicalized, but my father and Señor Harrison forgave me and I finished college in Mexico. I then enrolled in the University of Chile. This was 1969."

Cordobes had stopped and was looking at Rumison, as if expecting some comment. "Bob and I were in college then," said Rumison, because he could think of nothing else to say.

Cordobes nodded, an enigmatic smile playing on his lips. "I felt as much," he said. "There is a mark, an energy that brands our generation . . . not all, but many."

"A mark?" Rumison asked.

Cordobes' sad eyes were thoughtful. "We have much in common, those of us born in that time in the forties."

"The baby boomers?" Black asked.

Cordobes shook his head. "No. I do not speak of the baby

boomers. I speak specifically of those born between 1942 and 1949. You see, Mr. Black, astrologically speaking, the people born between those years were . . . are the karmic leaders of the world. All the souls of those arrogant people returning to face . . . ?"

Cordobes shrugged and looked at his guests. Rumison suddenly felt embarrassed for Cordobes and he could feel Rosso echoing his thoughts.

"It is an unusual generation by any standards," continued Cordobes, perhaps guessing their feelings. "Proud, willful, spoiled, intelligent beyond the norm. The sixties were a troubled time for such as we . . . with our foolish, romantic notions. We had little choice but to feel the world's pain."

Cordobes turned to Black. "Perhaps you don't understand, Mr. Black. You are older, from a different world, a different order."

Black's face was expressionless. "I'm not sure I follow," he murmured.

"My generation is different, Mr. Black," said Cordobes tensely, as though he expected Black to argue. We were born on the cusp between two visions of reality, and only we as a group can see both sides. Only we are aware that something can be done; for you see, Mr. Black, our generation has a purpose!"

Black sipped quietly at his beer. "Others have thought such things," he said quietly. "From other generations."

Rumison thought this was a particularly tactful way to put it, but Cordobes only shook his head and smiled.

"Perhaps," he said, "but never in such numbers." He paused, his eyes no longer sad but twinkling with humor. "Do I seem overly mystical? Overly optimistic to you?" he asked. "Believing that something can be done in this world?"

"Adolescent visions and hard reality don't often mix well," said Black. Then he added, "But then, you are no longer an adolescent, Miguel, so perhaps you see something the others of us have missed."

Abruptly, Rumison no longer felt embarrassment for Cordobes. Instead he felt a sudden sense of guilt, or loss. Maybe Cordobes was mad, but what had Rumison ever done with his life that was so sane? Had he ever tried to change the world? When he and Rosso had gotten their draft notices, had they protested? They hadn't even had the courage to take the two-year infantry enlistment and get it over with. Instead they'd joined the morally safer Air Rescue, staying in it for ten years, long after it had lost any meaning it might have had for them.

"It was a strange time," Cordobes was saying. "A time when the world almost looked at itself . . . but missed by so very little."

He paused, then shook his head ruefully. "And then, maybe it was not by so little. My perspective has changed. But in any case, the world has fallen asleep again. We can all agree to that. Afraid, of course, to face the probability of its own death. To many it would even seem that nothing was accomplished, that the world continues on in growing confusion."

Dolefully Cordobes stared at a new cigar he had taken from his pocket. "But it was not all wasted," he said, lighting it, sucking in the smoke. Exhaling, he pointed the cigar at Rumison.

"For we have learned truths behind the confusion."

Across the table from Rumison, Barney had been listening to their host with a curious intensity. When no one spoke for several seconds, he asked, "Truths, Mr. Cordobes?"

Cordobes pursed his lips, settling back again in his chair. "Yes," he said. "Some."

Barney stared at him, waiting for him to continue. Instead Black said, "I learned long ago not to get involved in abstract causes, Miguel."

Cordobes smiled. "Aye. No wasted thoughts for the hungry of the world, eh, Mr. Black?"

He leaned forward and the smile had gone. "But I ask you all this: If you were to find a starving child by the side of the road, would you not stop to feed it?"

Black nodded. "I might feed it."

"Of course!" cried Cordobes, as though he had scored a point. "To do so would be appropriate. We are in agreement. Life is too precious to worry about the millions of starving infants in the world, the ones we do not see, do not come in contact with. Life is too short to throw away chasing abstract causes, no matter how well-intentioned. Such causes inevitably go astray, as though mandated by natural law. Perhaps this is because the people who embrace such things have not taken the time to learn their own true intentions in the matter."

"Aren't you contradicting yourself, Mr. Cordobes?" Barney asked.

Cordobes shook his head. "No. We—by we, I mean those of us who understand destiny—are becoming involved again. But this time not because of foolish romantic idealism, or misplaced hippie sentimentality, but because it is our nature. It is why we exist at this particular time in the world's history, because our involvement is absolutely necessary if man is to continue on this planet. There is very little time left. All who have eyes agree, and the collective subconscious cannot be that wrong. We see that starving child by the road, Mr. Black, and that child is ourselves, our world."

Cordobes glared at Black for a full five seconds, but then it was his time to look embarrassed. He dropped his eyes, and the tension drained from his dark features. "Excuse me, please."

"You've a right to your vision," said Black.

"Perhaps I've become a prisoner of that vision," said Cordobes softly. "Out here . . . alone . . ."

"Why are you here, Miguel?"

Cordobes looked up. The sadness had returned to his eyes. "Because of my work," he said. "I am a writer, you see, and what I have told you I will also someday tell the world."

"Miguel," said Black carefully, "earlier you mentioned that there might be a road to Bluefields?"

"You wish to leave so soon?" cried Cordobes, looking sincerely upset at the thought.

"We are behind schedule as it is," said Black.

Cordobes sighed despondently. "Yes. Of course. I understand. There is a road . . . overgrown now. It has not been used regularly since the revolution." He brightened immediately, as though an idea had just occurred to him.

"I will offer you a bargain. It is afternoon and time for me to take my ride to exercise the horses."

"You have horses?" Black asked.

"Yes, several. If you left today, you might miss the road.

You could not reach the coast before dark in any case. But if you agree to stay for dinner and leave in the morning, you can ride with me and I will show you exactly where the road is."

Rosso was fidgeting in his seat. "Look, Mr. Black," he said, "we'd better keep going. . . ." He wanted to say more, but he glanced at Cordobes and closed his mouth.

Black looked at Rumison. "Rumison?" he asked.

Rumison shrugged. He understood Rosso's feelings, his friend's urgency, the need to continue, to get out of Nicaragua as soon as possible, but Cordobes did have a point. They'd have to spend another night in the jungle if they did leave, and Rumison already was hesitant to leave the small comfort Cordobes had provided them.

"Bailey?" Black asked.

"I'd like to stay," said Barney, looking at Cordobes.

Black nodded. "All right. We'll stay the night."

Chapter Eleven

"WE had to slaughter most of the livestock when Señor Harrison left. We gave the meat to the field hands, but I could not bear to kill the horses," said Miguel Cordobes as he showed Black, Rumison and Rosso the barn and small corral some distance from the house where five aging but anxious horses were kept. Barney, complaining of a headache, had remained at the house. Rumison almost envied him. What slight breeze there had been had disappeared, and the sunlight was murderously hot in the open, away from the house and trees. Rumison felt exposed, not just to the sun. Already he was having misgivings about the decision to remain the night. Rosso's urgency to be gone was contagious.

Cordobes and the old man, Jorge, saddled four of the five horses. The old man was another factor in Rumison's growing unease. The brown, weathered face was devoid of humor. The narrow brown eyes regarded the North Americans with a silent mistrust that made Rumison wonder if the old man might not know more than he was saying. Viewed closer he looked even older than Rumison had guessed—certainly past seventy, but the muscles in his lean body were steady and he moved with a quiet, fluid grace. His faded uniform was clean and he wore a deadly-looking throwing knife in a sheath on his belt. The old man reminded Rumison of a force as potentially deadly and implacable as the jungle, and he could understand why Jorge might have made the young and idealistic revolutionaries of the Sandinista movement nervous.

Black seemed unworried, showing a familiarity with

horses as he held the reins of an elderly mare Cordobes was saddling. The horse started as Cordobes placed the saddle on its back and Black rubbed its ears. Cordobes kicked a knee into the horse's stomach and as the horse wheezed out, Cordobes pulled the cinch tight.

"This is Minnow," said Cordobes fondly as he stroked the horse's mane. "Old and gentle but full of tricks."

They mounted, Rosso somewhat awkwardly on Minnow, and Cordobes led off. The area of the plantation that had been under cultivation was large, but the fields were choked now with an ugly, twisted vegetation that looked far more impenetrable than the jungle they had come through. Cordobes explained that the plantation once had employed over a hundred field hands just to clear land.

"It will be extremely costly to clear the land again," Cordobes lamented. "Too costly, perhaps."

"I thought this was a lumber plantation," said Black, who sat easily astride a big gelding.

Cordobes nodded. "Lumber had been the main crop, Mr. Black. Hardwoods. But the trees were becoming more and more difficult to locate in recent years, so the land was cleared and other things were planted: coffee, rubber, more recently citronella grass and peanuts."

"Citronella grass?" Rumison asked.

"Lemon grass," said Black.

"It has many uses," said Cordobes. "But mainly it is a base for perfume."

Cordobes seemed to enjoy the ride, explaining aspects of the plantation's operation as though nothing were amiss with it. If he noticed Rosso's growing impatience or suspected Black's questions of having any other motive, he didn't show it. Rumison suspected their ride to the Bluefields road was made longer by the route Cordobes took, to allow them a better look at the plantation.

"People mistakenly think the jungle is very fertile," said Cordobes as they approached a low row of abandoned houses. "This is not true. The jungle grows on its dead. Often, if you clear the jungle, all you have left is laterite, a hard clay of limestone. To farm it properly takes a great deal of understanding. I've heard that in the Amazon, Japanese immigrants are successfully planting pepper trees. Here we were using the patchwork method, cutting and burning a section of jungle before planting, to give the soil nutriment, moving on when the crop came in. But Señor Harrison was experimenting with other systems. . . . The workers' quarters," he said as they stopped for a minute in front of the forlorn cluster of wooden buildings.

"Hardly seems enough housing for all the hands you said the plantation used," Black commented.

"There are outbuildings you haven't seen," answered Cordobes, "but most of the workers were part-time and many came from Taxia's village, which is a few miles north of here."

It occurred to Rumison that Cordobes had yet to answer the question: What had happened at Santa Concepción? Where were the field hands? Why had Señor Harrison left? Why was Cordobes alone? Rumison wanted to ask, but he hesitated, glancing at Black and wondering why Black or Rosso hadn't brought up the questions again. Perhaps they were all waiting for Cordobes to finish the story he had begun at lunch in his own good time.

They rode on. The heat was intense and Rumison had developed a painful blister on his seat. He was thankful when Cordobes finally pulled them up to a rutted, vine-choked track that led eastward into the jungle.

"The road to Bluefields," said Cordobes.

"Is it passable?" Black asked.

"It goes for several miles, where it touches the river below the dock," said Cordobes. "Then it turns inland. From there on I cannot say. I haven't traveled it in some months but it will be no worse than the jungle. I still say the river is the quickest and easiest way to the coast. You should not let one misfortune stop you. Another raft should be easy to make."

"We'll stick with the road," said Black, staring down the overgrown road. "Where does it lead in the other direction?" he asked.

"Another plantation," answered Cordobes without elaboration. "South of here."

Black raised an eyebrow but Cordobes already had turned his horse away. "We should get back," he said. "The horses grow thirsty."

The old man was waiting for them when they returned

to the stables. Cordobes dismounted and gave Jorge the reins. Rumison and Rosso also dismounted but Black was gazing off across an overgrown field, at a tattered windsock hanging limply on a wooden pole.

"Did this used to be an airfield?" he asked.

"Yes," said Cordobes as he lifted his saddle off his horse. "It was used for the tree spotter. As the hardwoods grew scarcer it was necessary to use an airplane."

"Does that mean you had an airplane here?"

Cordobes hesitated, looking up at Black still on his horse. There was a speculative look in Cordobes' eyes. "No," he answered. "We contracted with a private pilot out of Bluefields. A few of the plantations do have their own, though."

Black swung down, pretending casualness as he undid his saddle cinch. "Oh?" he asked.

"I'm thinking in particular of Encantada," said Cordobes.

"A plantation?"

"Yes. The one the Bluefields road goes to if you were to head south instead of east."

"It's nearby, then?"

"Relatively. Perhaps twenty-five miles, but the road is worse, if it exists at all. There hasn't been traffic between Encantada and Santa Concepción for twelve years."

Black pulled the saddle off his horse and placed it on the fence rail next to the others. One by one, the horses were led by Jorge to a trough in the shade of a large jungle oak tree.

"You seem hesitant to talk about it," said Black.

Cordobes shrugged. "Only because I do not know much," he said. "Encantada is owned by a big Irishman, Sean O'Brien. He came here with his wife after World War II. Encantada is now one of the largest privately owned lumber plantations in Nicaragua. He and Señor Harrison used to be friends."

"What happened?"

A frown creased Cordobes' dark features as he started slowly off toward the house. "There were stories," he said. "But I never really knew, myself."

"You make it sound very mysterious."

"Perhaps. But there is a reason for that. It is something

of a mystery. Twelve years ago something happened there. O'Brien's wife left him. Most of the local landowners refused to visit him. I don't know why. Señor Harrison never discussed it, and of course when this happened, I was . . . involved . . . in other things. I did visit Encantada several times when I was a young boy. O'Brien seemed decent enough—big, gruff, very Irish. . . ."

Cordobes paused, a smile transforming his face. "He had the prettiest little daughter," he murmured, suddenly remembering. "Whitney. I wonder . . ."

Cordobes laughed and shook his head. "Ah," he said wistfully, "I'm still a romantic after so many years. I can't overcome the curse of our generation."

"Were you in love with her?" Rosso asked.

"She was was only ten when I saw her last," smiled Cordobes. "But yes, I believe I was. There was magic in her. Strange," he said, suddenly thoughtful, "that I should think of her after so long."

Barney was on the veranda when they returned to the house, as pensive as ever, sitting on a rattan lounge chair, Cordobes invited Black to play chess and Black agreed. Taxia arrived with another pitcher of Watney's Red beer, and Rosso and Rumison remained on the porch with Barney.

"They're a lot alike," said Barney after Black and Cordobes had retreated inside to play their chess game.

"Are you kidding, Barn?" said Rosso, wiping sweat and dust from his broad forehead as he finished half a glass of beer at one swallow. "They're both nuts, if that's what you mean. What in hell that Cordobes stays here for . . ." He stopped as he drained the glass and then refilled it from the pitcher.

"Damn," he said, "we should've kept going. This place gives me the creeps."

"I don't know," said Barney. "It seems all right."

"How do you mean they're alike?" Rumison asked Barney, afraid Rosso had hurt Barney's feelings.

Barney shrugged vaguely. "Oh, I don't know," he said. "Both pretty self-contained, I guess, or something."

Rosso snorted and finished another half glass of beer.

The sun had settled below the jungle when Cordobes finally came out on the porch and announced dinner. He had split games with Black, two apiece.

"Mr. Black is very clever," he said.

When the others joined him at the table he was already seated. He was smoking another cigar, but the heavy, sweet smoke smelled different from the Havanas he had been smoking. The smell seemed familiar to Rumison. "Marijuana?" he asked, surprised.

"Ganja," said Cordobes. "Our local equivalent. There was a time when United Foods considered growing it as the major crop here, but Señor Harrison objected and they decided it was too dangerous for such a respected corporation. Besides, they needed Santa Concepción as a tax write-off."

Cordobes lifted up a small wood box of the cigars. "Would you care for one?" he asked.

Rosso shook his head irritably. Rumison also declined as did Barney, but only after Barney had glanced toward Black, seeing what the older man would do.

"Thank you," said Black, "but not tonight."

Cordobes lowered the box, unconcerned. "The field hands smoked it," he said. "Enjoyed their work as a result. Someone once called it the twentieth-century avatar, but I wouldn't go so far."

The allusion escaped Rumison. "Avatar?" he asked.

"A god returned to material form to help those not yet enlightened. Traditional avatars have been human, but in our materialistic age, how appropriate if one were to return as a plant or a cigar."

"Crazy," muttered Rosso.

Cordobes nodded amiably. "Absolutely," he said.

The table had been set with clean white linen by the young Indian girl. The knives and forks were tin and battered, out of place on the linen. They ate roast pork and rice and squash off porcelain plates. The beer and the food relaxed Rumison, as did Cordobes' ganja cigar smoke, which hung heavily in the air. The hard knot of urgency that had tightened Rumison's solar plexus loosened. A stillness settled over the room. The light from the candles on the table was friendly and intimate, as outside the night grew darker.

It was not until Taxia cleared away their plates that Black finally asked, "What are you doing here, Miguel?"

For a long moment Cordobes sat as though he hadn't heard. Then, tamping out what remained of his cigar in an ashtray, he turned to Taxia, who had been clearing away his dish, and spoke a few words in a language Rumison didn't understand. The girl touched Cordobes lovingly on the sleeve of his shirt, nodded shyly at the others and left. Outside, the little generator motor switched on again and the few lights in the house, which had been growing dim, brightened.

"It is painful for me," Cordobes began. "And yet I look forward to telling the story. Perhaps it is why I wished you to stay, for you see, I have told no one else, and something like this can fester if it is not released. Even my work, until it is published, does not fulfill the need I have to explain."

Black, Rumison, Barney, and even Rosso were quiet as they waited for Cordobes to continue. Carefully, Cordobes adjusted himself in his chair.

"Where does it begin?" he asked. "Where does anything begin? I told you I went to college in Chile? Yes. Well, I will begin there. You may know that in Chile, liberal students were treated somewhat differently than they were in your country. You of course think of Kent State and Berkeley and Jackson State, but you would agree violence was more the exception than the rule."

"Physical violence," said Barney quietly.

Cordobes nodded. "A good point. Oppression comes in many forms, and I wonder what sort leaves the worst scars. . . ."

Cordobes' voice had trailed off in introspection, but then he took another drink of beer and continued.

"But my point is that in Chile the oppression was more often than not accompanied by extreme physical violence. I remember one protest in particular. I forget exactly what started it. Isn't that terrible? Something or other."

Cordobes smiled sadly and shook his head. "At any rate, the protest became a boycott that soon threatened collection of the garbage in Santiago. The government brought in tanks and machine guns—tanks and machine guns and troops, against all-but-unarmed students. It was not really a battle. All the students had were rocks, a few Molotov cocktails.

"Perhaps I was mistaken. I was not exactly objective in my appraisal of the situation, but the soldiers seemed to . . . delight . . . in prolonging what should have been a short-lived affair. They ransacked the university, the library, the classes, the art center. They dragged all who resisted out into the mall to be shot."

"I may remember the incident," said Black. "August sixty-eight? Twenty students killed, a few soldiers?"

"That was the official news release," said Cordobes. "Actually, over three hundred students were killed, twice that many wounded. And only three soldiers died."

Cordobes stopped, regarding Black curiously. "But how is it you remember this, Mr. Black? It was such a minor accident in the world then."

"I was in Chile at the time," said Black.

"Oh? Traveling again?"

"No," answered Black. "Business."

Cordobes nodded thoughtfully, then continued. "Of course, after it was over, I could not return to my studies," he said. "Instead I joined the staff of an underground newspaper, *La Luz*, The Light. Do you perhaps remember this also, Mr. Black?"

Black nodded. "I do. Radical Marxist, wasn't it?"

Cordobes smiled. "Yes. I wrote articles for it. Emotional things, I'm embarrassed to say now. Most denouncing capitalism and the United States, which in my anger and extreme naïveté I saw as the cause of fascism.

"But I never realized the widespread attention my articles were getting until one day I was given a letter from my father. It was a difficult and painful thing for me to read. He wanted to know how he had failed and why I had turned against him and Señor Harrison so."

Cordobes sighed, looking down at the half-empty glass of beer still in his hand. "I had never before been forced to relate my abstract and rather simplistic theories to reality, to real life, to real people. My enemies were all stereotypes . . . not that in real life many don't fit those molds," he added.

"For many who hate their parents it would not have been so hard, but you see, I loved both my father and Señor

Harrison a great deal." Cordobes stopped, closing his eyes to hide the tears in them. They remained closed for several seconds.

"When I read that letter I realized in a flash who I was really dealing with; with individuals . . . with people like my father and like Señor Harrison. If I were to remain true to the demands of my theories, I would have to denounce all those individuals as the enemy. This I could not do. With this realization my political fervor, the great abstract hate I felt . . . died."

Rumison lowered his own eyes. It was difficult for him to listen. Cordobes was baring his soul to four strangers he'd taken in, none of whom deserved that trust. Cordobes' pain was too sharp and Rumison, feeling like a thief and a coward, did not want to hear more.

"I left Chile and tried to return here," Cordobes said, his voice steady and quiet again. "I wanted to settle down and write nonpolitical novels. But unfortunately my fame as a revolutionary had preceded me. The last thing in the world Somoza wanted was another radical journalist around." This last was said with a rueful half smile that was belied by the sadness in Cordobes' eyes.

He shrugged. "So I was an exile," he said. He finished what was left of the beer in his glass and put the glass aside.

"I traveled, worked here and there doing what work I could. I lived in Algiers, then Paris, where I wrote and sold a few stories to magazines.

"And then, to my great joy, I received a letter from Señor Harrison. He had made a deal with Somoza. If I promised to behave, I could return. Eagerly I accepted. . . . You see, I had a girl. . . ." Cordobes' face clouded for a brief moment before he continued.

"This was in 1978. I returned. I began to write seriously. A book. A great book, I believe. I was to be married. . . ."

Cordobes stood up, somewhat unsteadily. "Shall we go in the other room?" he said abruptly. "More comfortable for conversation." He picked up the pitcher of beer, his empty glass, and the box of ganja cigars, and without waiting for an answer left in the direction of the living room. Barney quickly followed. Black, regarding both Rosso and

Rumison with his unreadable gray eyes, finished off the last of his beer and stood.

"Shall we go?" he said.

Rosso glanced at Rumison and, shrugging his eyebrows, also followed. Suddenly Rumison was alone. Everything was quiet. The generator had stopped for the moment and the only sounds came from the crickets outside the dining room windows. Crazily, for a brief second, Rumison felt certain that the rhythmic chirpings of the crickets were trying to tell him something, something important. If only he could listen, listen in the right places. A chill crept down his back. He shook it off and went to join the others.

"Perhaps you are all aware that the revolution affected this part of Nicaragua much less than it did the West Coast," Cordobes began again as he eased himself back into the rattan Solomon's chair and lifted his dusty boots onto the coffee table. He waited a minute for the others to take their seats before continuing.

"We all thought we were safe here from politics," he said quietly, staring out the large bay window into the night. "I at least should have known better, for not long after I had returned, a group of guerrillas arrived from the West and demanded that Señor Harrison get out. An agent of the capitalists, they called him. An enemy. We did not take them seriously at first. The accusations were so . . . ludicrous. I even tried to reason with them, hoping my previous reputation might be of value, but it was like talking to mud."

Cordobes' eyes narrowed and his voice had hardened noticeably. "Our workers were angry. Who were these *muchachos* anyway, to tell the *patrón* what to do? What right did they have to mess in our affairs? Nothing but bandits, sharp-tongued *pecadores* from the West who knew nothing of the local situation.

"But Señor Harrison, realizing that a confrontation could end only in violence, made ready to leave. 'Just for a short while,' he told us. But that morning at the dock, as Señor Harrison made ready to board the boat, a crowd of his people gathered, armed with cane knives, sticks, rocks. . . ."

Cordobes' right hand had tensed, as though he himself were holding a rock, but suddenly he lowered his head.

When finally he looked back up, the tension had left him and only the sadness remained.

"You can guess what happened," he said. "To this day I do not know who started it. Many were killed. A girl . . . my girl . . . was among the dead. My father also . . . trying to stop the fight . . ."

The bitterness was gone from Cordobes' soft voice. He sat in the Solomon's chair, a wistful smile on his face, seemingly more bemused than angry at the world's absurdity. He poured himself another glass of beer and drank before continuing.

"The bodies were thrown into the river. To me, after my experience in Chile, it was more than coincidence. God had designed a morality play for me to witness, for this time the men with the machine guns were not fascists or capitalists, puppets of imperialism, but the 'liberating' forces of a Marxist revolution.

"I was in pain, great pain, but I was no longer angry . . . not like Chile. I had realized that justice, beauty, honor, these things have little to do with any political movement. Political movements are abstract things, things of the intellect, which is a cold, heartless organ."

"It was a hard lesson," said Black.

Cordobes' dark eyes met Black's gray ones. Cordobes smiled and nodded. "I always was stubborn," he said.

"Were they all killed?" asked Barney. Of all of them, he had been the most intensely interested in Cordobes' story.

Cordobes shook his head. "No. Many lived, but Señor Harrison was gone and the plantation was closed. The workers returned where they had come from. The leader in charge of the Sandinistas felt bad about what had happened. I think it affected him as much as it did me. He asked me to stay on as caretaker until a new management could be found. I agreed. What else was there for me?

"Perhaps as a joke, I was given the commission of captain in the revolutionary army. Jorge, who had not participated in the fight at the docks, stayed here. As I said, I think they were frightened of him."

"And new management has never come?" asked Rumison. "How long will you stay?"

Cordobes released a deep sigh. "Who can say?" he said. "My first book is almost complete. I believe it to be a work of major importance . . . but then what new author doesn't believe what he has to say will shake the world?" He chuckled. "I will at least stay here until I've finished a rough draft of its sequel. Six months longer, maybe."

"Will you try to get the first one published?" Barney asked.

"Of course," said Cordobes, as though shocked at the question. "It is something I have to do. Because of my vision," he added almost apologetically.

He straightened in the chair and for a moment looked at them as Rumison imagined Moses might have looked at the Israelites before leading them away from Egypt: stern, uncompromising, implacable. "There is not much time," he said. "Perhaps seven more years. Fifteen if we are very, very lucky."

"You mentioned that belief before," said Black.

Cordobes snorted. "Belief? It is not belief. What I talk about is simple observation. If people weren't so afraid of opening their eyes, they could see it. . . ."

He stopped abruptly. "I grow angry," he said. "Excuse me. It is only frustration." He took another drink of beer and then waved toward the window and the dark night beyond with the hand that held the beer glass.

"We must learn—that is not our enemy," he said, almost shouting. "The universe is not our enemy!"

Silence followed this statement. Cordobes was smiling, regarding them with amusement. "Don't you understand the importance of that simple concept?" he asked. No one answered.

"Don't you realize the difficulty of achieving that state," Cordobes pressed, "where you no longer fear the world, the fate that world has in store for you? Don't you understand that it is our alienation from that fate, from the universe itself, that is behind all our misdirection? In our fear, we believe that to be secure we must conquer, control. This we can never do, never, though in our attempt we destroy everything we wish to own. Don't you see? It is like a man who wishes love so much he believes he must possess his beloved. But it is this very desire to possess that drives her farther away!"

Cordobes stopped. The others remained silent. It was Rosso who finally spoke. "There's nothing anyone can do about it," he said defensively, as though Cordobes had accused him directly. "So why worry?"

"Nothing?" asked Cordobes. He smiled sadly, took another drink of beer and again looked out the window.

"There is eternity out there," he said softly, "for those who care. For my generation the homework is done, the real trial begins. Yet we can act only one step at a time. Reality exists now, at this moment. It is part of my vision to know that we must, at each moment from here on, behave as we know it is right to behave . . . as we *feel* it is right to behave, whatever direction that behavior, those feelings take us. There is nothing else. We are on a cliff, and every act must be impeccable."

Later that evening the Indian girl, Taxia, led the four North Americans to bedrooms Cordobes had provided for them. As Rumison left the living room, his last view was of Cordobes, his booted feet on the table, smoking another ganja cigar and staring out the window into the night.

That lonely image remained with Rumison until he fell off to sleep.

Chapter Twelve

RUMISON awoke with a start from a dreamless sleep. His heart was racing. It felt like an overwound alarm clock. For some reason he was intensely afraid.

Why?

The silence in the room was almost complete. Even the crickets had stopped their chirpings.

The crickets? Hadn't they been trying to tell him something?

But then he realized something else. In the bed next to him, Rosso also was awake. He glanced at the luminous hands of his watch: Three A.M.

"Rosso!"

"Here. Keep quiet!"

"What's wrong?"

"I thought I heard something."

Rumison strained his ears. Nothing. Or was there? A soft, muffled sound, like a bag of laundry being pulled slowly across a polished floor.

Quietly Rosso got out of bed. Rumison's fear grew. Rosso's quiet footsteps seemed loud in the stillness of the room.

Suddenly a light went on in the hall and before Rumison could think, the louvered door to their room burst open. The bright light momentarily blinded Rumison but he could hear men rushing into the room.

"Alto! Alto!"

The sharp commands were in Spanish. Rosso sprinted for the window but a burst of automatic rifle fire brought him to a halt. To Rumison, frozen in fear, the explosions seemed to arrive several seconds after the bright flashes from the rifle. For one terrifying moment he thought Rosso had been killed, but as he grew accustomed to the light he saw Rosso, standing by the window, his hands raised over his head.

There were five men in the room, all young and grim looking. They were armed with American M-16 rifles and were dressed in new battle fatigues. Two took hold of Rosso's arms and pulled him across the room. Two more grabbed Rumison's legs and yanked him off the bed. He landed painfully on his side. Hey!" he cried, but a booted foot kicked into his back.

"*Silencio!*"

Two men took hold of his arms. They jerked him to his feet and shoved him after Rosso. In the hall more men were waiting. Despite his shock, Rumison found himself seeing things with surprising clarity. There were seven men, dark, Latin-looking, and well armed. One man, the oldest, stood arrogantly aside while Rumison was thrown against the wall, landing heavily next to Rosso, Barney and Black. The man had captain's bars on the shoulders of his battle fatigues.

"You guys all right?" Barney asked, looking concerned but oddly calm. "We heard those shots . . ."

"Shut yore fuckeen mouth!"

The captain stepped forward and slapped Barney with the back of his hand. A heavy signet ring he wore tore a furrow across Barney's cheek. Blood ran down Barney's chin and he wiped it away with his shoulder.

Someone brought rope and tied their hands. The rope was woven hemp and it burned painfully.

"Ease up!" cried Rosso. "That hurts!"

"You learn, you gringo bastards," said the captain, slapping Rosso hard. "You learn to keep yore mouths closed."

He motioned with a hand and Rosso, Barney, Rumison and Black were dragged down the hallway. When Rumison tripped, unable to balance himself because of his bound hands, a rifle butt smashed into the small of his back and he was pulled to his feet and half carried the rest of the way into the living room where he was thrown to his knees.

A small, slender man, probably in his mid-fifties, sat

watching the scene from Cordobes' rattan Solomon's chair. He had thin yellow hair combed neatly across a high, pale forehead in a way that suggested he was trying to cover up spreading baldness. He was dressed in a well-tailored white gabardine suit and wore polished tan Oxford shoes. Perched on a long nose were a pair of thick-lensed, wire-rimmed glasses, which gave his empty, pale eyes a fishlike appearance. He watched without comment as the soldiers brought in their prisoners.

Standing quietly next to the man in the chair was a dark-skinned barefoot Indian dressed in khaki pants and shirt. When the soldiers dumped the contents of Rumison's pack on the floor in front of the man in the chair, the Indian bent down with a hand and sifted through some of the items. He lifted up a roll of toilet paper and then nodded at the man in the chair. The man in the chair waved and the Indian left the room. The man in the chair stood and approached his prisoners. His movements were as delicate and as fragile-seeming as a bird's. He seemed pleased.

"It would have been embarrassing for all concerned," he said in a thin unaccented tenor voice, "if for some reason we had made a mistake."

Before the North Americans could answer, there was a commotion in another part of the house and Cordobes strode angrily into the room, surrounded by more soldiers. "This is wrong!" he cried. "You call yourselves revolutionaries? You're storm troopers, pigs! This is my house!"

"Your house, Cordobes?" asked the man in the white suit calmly. "Since when has the liberated plantation of the people become personal property for one of their soldiers?"

Cordobes saw for the first time who spoke and he stared. "Preitas!"

"Yes, my young colleague. We meet again. I am sorry for the intrusion, but I am sure that when I tell you that these four men are enemies of the revolution, you will allow for the inconvenience."

Cordobes gazed with sympathy at the men. Rumison was so frightened he had trouble keeping his knees from shaking. Rosso glared angrily around, looking for a way out. Barney tried to smile and Black remained enigmatic, watchful.

"They are my guests," said Cordobes. "You have no right to treat them like this."

Preitas smiled. It was the wan smile of an accountant who had just discovered a thirty-dollar tax error on a return he was auditing. "You are living in an illusion, Cordobes. Perhaps you always were."

Preitas turned back to his captives, bound and, with the exception of Rumison, completely naked before him. "So," he said, his pale, fishlike eyes finally meeting theirs, "we finally meet. It has been a hot and miserable chase for my men. I am glad to see it has come to such a satisfactory end."

"We don't know what you're talking about," said Black, but Preitas stopped him with a raised and finely manicured hand.

"Please, spare me the inanities. And spare yourselves the embarrassment of having to utter such absurd lies."

"What is it you want?" Black asked.

Preitas nodded. "That's better."

Preitas walked past them in line, absently curious as he regarded each in turn, stopping in front of Barney. Preitas smiled enigmatically and then turned to them all.

"You have left a trail like a garbage dump," he said abruptly, harshly. "With your parachutes, your equipment so amateurishly hidden. With your toilet crappings, your food packages, your dead. . . ." He paused, smiling thinly.

"How did your friend in the jungle die, anyway? The animals didn't leave much for us to examine."

No one answered. "No matter. In time . . ."

Preitas clasped his hands behind his back and began to rock back and forth. The leather heels on his shoes squeaked irritatingly.

"We also found your raft," he added after a moment. "Tied, of course, with parachute line."

Fine muscles in Cordobes' jaw tightened. It was apparent that he not only knew, but also despised the man he had called Preitas. "What are they accused of?" he asked, barely controlling his anger.

Preitas glanced at him disdainfully. "Does it matter, Cordobes? They are CIA."

"No!" Rosso burst out. "That's not true!"

"Silencio!" ordered the man with the captain's bars, but Rosso kept on. "It's a lie, Cordobes! Barney, Mike and me, we aren't . . . uhhh!" But the outburst was cut off as the captain struck Rosso a hard blow on his neck. Rosso dropped to the floor, holding his throat and gagging. Rumison and Cordobes both cried out, but soldiers grabbed their arms, holding them back.

"This is barbarism!" cried Cordobes.

Preitas looked bored. "Take him to his room," he said. He waved an irritated hand and the soldiers dragged a screaming Cordobes away.

"Your soul is dead, Preitas! You're a butcher! A vampire . . ."

"Poor man," said Preitas once Cordobes' shouts could no longer be heard. "Loneliness and drugs, I suppose." He faced his captives again, focusing on Black.

"We want what you took from the crash," he said, his voice no longer bored but a thin, scalpel-sharp menace. "We want the case you cut from the courier's arm. Tell me: Did you amputate it before or after you shot him?"

Black stood calm and didn't answer. When Preitas had asked about the black case, Rumison's eyes had automatically gone to the contents of Black's pack, which had been spread out on the floor with the other packs. Rumison was suddenly and uncomfortably aware that the case was no longer with the pack.

Preitas smiled. "I did not really expect you to answer without reason," he said, "though it would be to your distinct advantage to do so."

He paused, letting the unspoken meaning sink in. "So," he continued when no one spoke, "I am sorry for you. It will be hard and unpleasant. It will take time, but before we leave this plantation you will have told me everything, even things you thought you would not tell to God himself. If you have heard of me, you know I speak the truth, for I am Colonel Rafael Preitas."

The little man's name meant nothing to Rumison, though he had a feeling the name Preitas was familiar to Black. But the cold pride with which Preitas spoke those words was enough to make Rumison believe he meant what he said. There was something indescribably malevolent about the little man, something loathsome, like the pale bugs that had covered Rumison's hand when it had broken through the rotten log. Such a man, felt Rumison, would be capable of anything.

Preitas was staring at them like a scientist studying slide specimens. His eyes stayed longest on Barney, who refused to meet his gaze. He smiled and reached out a hand as though to touch Barney, but Barney pulled away.

Preitas laughed. "Ruíz," he said, speaking to the man with the captain's bars, "we are all tired."

"*Sí, mi coronel,*" replied Captain Ruíz.

"Post a guard on Cordobes. If he attempts anything, anything at all, kill him."

"*Sí, mi coronel.*"

"What about the old man? The old sergeant?"

Ruíz shrugged. "*Quién sabe?* Maybe he ees dead. He was ver' old."

Preitas looked thoughtful. "Post two guards on Cordobes," he said. "And take these out to the incinerator and post two more guards. I am going to bed. And Ruíz," he added as an afterthought, inclining his head toward Rumison, who was the only one of the four captives who had gone to bed in his underwear, "take that one's pants off. They appeal better to me naked."

Preitas left as rough hands ripped at Rumison's pants. He was taken with the others out to the large incinerator they had seen the day before. Ruíz opened the heavy iron door as the rusty hinges screeched in protest and they were thrown inside. Ruíz looked in at his prisoners, and his face looked like a demon lit in the glare of the flashlight he held.

"We have no drugs or fancy theengs," he growled quietly, "but you weel talk. You may find yore balls burned from yore bodies and yore eyes torn from yore heads, but you weel talk."

And the door slammed home with a solid metallic finality. No one spoke for several minutes. The air in the incinerator was stifling, filled with a fine soot stirred up by their movements. It was pitch black.

Rumison heard a chewing sound and realized that Black had somehow managed to get his hands around to his face and was chewing the hemp bindings loose. Rumison struggled unsuccessfully to do the same, but he soon felt Black's strong fingers working on his knots.

"We're in deep shit," said Rosso.

Rosso sounded so forlorn, and his comment so understated, that Rumison couldn't help but laugh. But the laugh turned to a giggle and threatened to become hysterical and he choked it off.

"What's the plan now, Black?" Rosso asked dryly once his own hands were free. "You got something else up your sleeve?"

Rumison let out another involuntary giggle at the choice of Rosso's metaphor. "Preitas will bargain," said Black.

"For the case?" Barney asked.

"For the case."

"That case must be pretty important," said Barney. Rumison listened for any indication of fear in Barney's voice, but he could find none. Only a calm, dead sort of acceptance.

Black didn't answer immediately. After a moment he said, "I wasn't lying when I told you I don't know what's in that case. But I do know how important some people think it is.

"The President of the United States himself authorized this mission. I was in Afghanistan. My departure could very likely compromise the entire resistance movement there. The President and his best advisers knew that, yet here I am."

The implications of what Black had said were slow to settle in Rumison's mind. When he finally understood Black was serious, the shock momentarily took his mind off his own fear. "My God!"

"Do you have any idea what it might be?" Barney asked.

"Of course!" Black snapped, sounding angry. "Probably pretty accurately. I mean, how many things are there that weigh less than five pounds, are small enough to fit inside that case, that can cause our President to do what he did and that bring out scum like Preitas panting like dogs in heat, at just the hint of what it might contain?"

"What?" asked Barney.

"I'll keep that to myself," said Black shortly, "for obvious reasons."

"But you will bargain with it?" pressed Rosso.

"I'll bargain with my mother's memory," said Black. "Whether I pay off or not is another matter."

"What did you do with it?" asked Rosso. He also had noticed the case was missing.

Black didn't answer. Outside the incinerator Rumison could hear the soft Spanish of their two guards. Could they understand English? he wondered. Did it matter?

"Why us?" he cried suddenly, feeling the dryness in his mouth as he spoke, from the soot that was just now beginning to settle. "Why us, Black? We're not spies, heroes. Why did you choose us?"

"I didn't choose you," said Black, and Rumison could feel his disdain. "The planning was carried out while I was being flown in from Karachi. There wasn't much time. According to your dossiers you all had the necessary training. . . ."

"But why us in particular?" Rosso asked. "Why us instead of the two hundred-odd other PJ's you could have chosen?"

The question was asked with a deceptive calm, but Rumison could sense the tension that lay behind it. Black must have sensed it also, for he didn't answer. Instead he said, "According to your records, you've all been through that mock prison camp up in Washington, right?"

"That's right," said Rosso.

"Then you know what to expect."

"You mean having our balls burned off and our eyes torn out?"

Rumison stifled another hysterical laugh. God, he thought, this is for real! What Rosso just said was for real.

"Preitas used to be head of Somoza's security," said Black. "He defected to Cuba some years back. He has quite a reputation. . . ."

There was a loud clang on the side of the incinerator as one of the guards banged it with his rifle. *"Silencio!"*

"Preitas will come on with that captain, Ruíz, as a whiplash team. Mutt and Jeff. The good guy, Preitas; the bad guy, Ruíz. Our hope is to hold out as long as . . ."

"Silencio! Ahora!"

"As long as possible."

"You're crazy," whispered Rosso fiercely. "Hold out? For what? For that damn case? For you?"

"SILENCIO!"

Their prison became a hell as the sun came up, heating the metal walls of the incinerator. Rumison tried to sleep but found it impossible. His body itched from head to foot and the mosquitos soon found them through the slits in the chimney stack. Remembering a page from a survival manual, Rumison smeared ash over his body, rubbing it in with his sweat as a protection, but it did nothing to stop the mosquitos and only made the itching worse.

With the sun also came light. It beamed in through the chimney slits, forming sharp latticework shadows on the iron walls. Rumison, Rosso, Barney and Black were all seated with their backs to the circular wall. They were all covered in black soot and sweat, looking like blackface comedians in a vaudeville act. Their thirst was painful.

"I guess they're trying to soften us up," Barney said needlessly.

"It's working," answered Rumison.

No one laughed.

The minutes seemed literally like hours. The hours were eternities—time enough, or so it seemed to Rumison, for children to be born, to grow up, to die of old age. What was there but misery? This was the world.

The iron walls soon became too hot to touch, though the thick ash insulated the floor. Rumison tried to force his mind to other things—home, women, the ocean—but this became impossible. There was only one thought in his mind: to get out.

The minutes passed. At one point, he couldn't say when, Rumison's head began to throb. His stomach felt uneasy, nauseous. Dully he reviewed the symptoms of heat exhaustion to himself.

Sleeper died of it, he thought. Not me. This is how Sleeper died. He gave up. Not me. Not me. How bad did Sleeper feel? How bad before . . . ?

A drop of moisture landed on his nose. Imagination? No! There was another one! And another!

Rumison realized that it was raining. Some of the drops were getting through the chimney slits.

"Rain!" he cried, but the others were already on their backs, greedily catching raindrops on their tongues.

The storm, if it could be called that, lasted less than twenty minutes, and when it was over the heat returned with a fury.

Sometime during the day, as his mind slipped in and out of consciousness, Rumison imagined he heard footsteps approaching from the outside. Metal grated against metal as the locking bar was unlatched and the iron door pulled open. Ruíz stood silhouetted in the bright square of sunlight.

"The tall one weeth the brown hair. Come out!"

It took Rumison some seconds to realize Ruíz was talking to him. He didn't know whether to feel elated or terrified.

"Come out! Eef you do not, we weel drag you out."

Rumison looked at the others for support, but no one spoke. Did they envy or pity him? Their faces were expressionless. Rosso did manage a weak but encouraging smile as Rumison crawled toward the door.

"Give in!" said Rosso simply, his voice dry, brittle.

Rumison didn't need the advice. It was what he had intended to do all along. The alternative was unthinkable.

Rough hands grabbed him and pulled him out of the incinerator into the full light of noon. He staggered, and they had to carry him to the house and then to the shower, where they left him.

"Wash yourself!" Ruíz commanded, throwing him a bar of soap.

Rumison swallowed a gallon of water before he found the strength to use the soap. The water eased the painful drumming of his temples, and his stomach settled. When he had washed most of the soot off, Ruíz reached in and shut off the water. He handed Rumison a towel and a clean pair of khaki pants.

Rumison was led into the living room again, where Colonel Preitas was waiting, seated in the rattan chair. Preitas smiled in a grandfatherly way and waved Rumison into a straight-backed chair that faced him.

"You are probably wondering why I chose you first to talk to," Preitas said.

Rumison, unable to talk, nodded. Preitas waved and the

soldiers, all but Ruíz, left the room. Ruíz stood behind Rumison some feet away.

"The older one," said Preitas, "with the scars on his body. Your leader?"

Rumison's thoughts were sluggish. He was afraid his voice couldn't work even if he wished it, so he nodded again.

"He is a hard man, I think," said Preitas. "This is his sort of business. But," he added hopefully, "perhaps not yours. Or the short one, with the square face. He is impulsive. Too impulsive. Nor the other one . . . the slender, blond boy . . ."

Preitas smiled wanly, as though to himself.

"We will speak of him later," he said. "So that leaves you."

Preitas' fishlike eyes regarded Rumison thoughtfully. "An enigma," he said quietly. "A man by looks, but a boy I feel underneath. You are thoughtful, serious. Possibly more intelligent than your friends. Perhaps you will see reason. Will you?"

The question had been asked in such a kind, sincere-sounding manner that Rumison's impulse was to say "yes" immediately. It was what he had intended. But for some reason he couldn't get any sounds to issue from his still-dry mouth.

Taking Rumison's lack of a reply as a negative, Preitas settled back in his chair and pursed his thin lips in a frown. "You are making a mistake," he said. "Why don't you tell me of your mission here?"

But still Rumison couldn't answer. He wanted to. Was he too frightened? Surely Preitas could see that?

But apparently Preitas couldn't. Preitas shook his head sadly. "You are trying to be a hero," he said in a patient, kindly voice. "But unfortunately you are on the wrong side for misguided heroics. I am afraid you have been sent to our country by a corrupt CIA, an organization no intelligent man could possibly give his dying allegiance to."

Preitas paused as his pale eyes sought out Rumison's thoughts. Preitas placed his fingers together, the tips touching in an almost reverential gesture.

"Do you know the history of Nicaragua?" he asked.

Rumison shook his head in a short negative.

"I thought not," said Preitas. "I'll tell you some of it. I won't lie. It is common knowledge.

"Many years ago, in the first part of this century, this country was literally owned by foreign business. The natives, for the most part, were used as little more than slave labor. Rebellion was constant but did not amount to much until a man named Sandino began a guerrilla campaign that nearly succeeded in driving out the foreigners."

Preitas' voice was soft, calm and reassuring. It was the voice of a wise professor speaking to a beloved but errant student.

Perhaps it won't be so bad, Rumison thought.

Preitas continued, "The United States fought hard against Sandino. It sent Marines who destroyed whole villages trying to flush him out. It's a well-known fact that in war colleges the methods learned by the Marines in Nicaragua later were applied to Viet Nam—with, I might add, an equal lack of success. These methods include interdiction of supply lines, assassination of suspected guerrilla infrastructures, indiscriminate bombing, bribery, murder —all the horror that you later saw on television in Viet Nam and that disrupted your country so much. . . ."

Preitas paused again, allowing Rumison time to consider his remarks. Then he continued.

"Finally, appearing to reconsider, the U.S. forces withdrew, after agreeing to certain concessions Sandino had demanded. A new president was elected, a liberal doctor named Sacasa. Sacasa pardoned Sandino and invited him to join in the new coalition government. A banquet was scheduled. People rejoiced."

Preitas leaned forward, lowering his voice dramatically.

"Sandino never arrived at the banquet. A trap was set. He and his lieutenants were arrested, taken out to the airport and executed. It is history's most blatant act of treachery.

"And the man responsible for it was Anastasio Somoza, the forebear of the monster only recently deposed by the Sandinistas. Your Marines had placed the first Somoza in charge of La Guardia, the state police. It is said that those same Marines watched while Sandino was murdered. It is told that even some of the Marines broke down and wept, so great was the tragedy. But they were prevented from doing anything by their officers."

Preitas placed a slender, cold hand on Rumison's, in an apparent gesture of intimacy.

"Don't you see?" he said gently. "The Sandinistas are the spiritual representatives of that great man who was betrayed and murdered that day. You risk your very soul by fighting on the wrong side."

Rumison was still too frightened either to recoil from Preitas' touch or to speak. Preitas, sensing an opening, pressed forward.

"The Somoza regime had strong ties with the United States. After Sacasa was deposed, Somoza appointed himself dictator for life. And the foreign interests returned. But that is all at an end now. Somoza is finished. He went too far. His troops went from village to village, executing all the males between the ages of fifteen and forty, afraid they would join the resistance.

"But now it is over. Justice has triumphed. Your mission, whatever it may be, already is a failure. It is only right you should tell me of that mission."

The cold hand left Rumison's. Preitas waited, but Rumison sat without speaking. His mind seemed incapable of formulating any coherent thoughts. Preitas' story had no meaning to him. He wasn't concerned with sides, with politics, with rights or wrongs or betrayals. He just wanted out, to be gone, to be away from this little man with the soft voice and the fish eyes. But how could he explain that?

No words would come.

Again Preitas misunderstood Rumison's silence. The fatherly patience left him. His lips grew tight.

"You are wrong," he said coldly. "I feel sorry for you. What is your name, so I can remember it when you are too crippled to remember it yourself?"

Panic strangled Rumison's throat. He sat, unable to move as Ruíz stepped forward. Ruíz swung his arm, and something struck Rumison a glancing blow across his mouth. Rumison could taste blood, but for some reason he felt nothing other than the dull impact of Ruíz's hand. Ruíz took Rumison's arms and bound them to the chair with hemp. Rumison was too weak to struggle.

Methodically Ruíz hit him. Still Rumison felt no pain,

only numbness and fear. Blood found its way into his eyes, clouding his vision. A loud ringing sounded in his ears. On the far side of that sound he could hear the soft, insistent voice of Preitas.

"What is your name? You must tell me your name."

Rumison struggled to answer. He wanted to answer. But his mouth simply refused to form around the words.

The beating stopped. Rumison shook blood from his eyes and watched without understanding as Ruíz opened up a small, expensive-looking leather box and withdrew a polished piece of hardwood, one end of which had a long steel needle embedded in it. It looked like a long, thin ice pick with a stubby handle. Ruíz smiled and approached.

Rumison screamed as pain exploded into his consciousness. Ruíz had shoved the needle up into his armpit, into the brachial nerve. And he had twisted and kept twisting.

"Your name," came the quiet voice. "Tell me your name."

"Rumison!" screamed Rumison in agony, the words finally wrenched from his stubborn mouth. "Michael Rumison!"

Ruíz withdrew the needle. But its pain remained. Preitas smiled kindly.

"Very good, Michael. Very good. Now perhaps you are ready to answer my original question. Tell me about your mission here."

Rumison felt he was going to be sick. He was choking on bile welling up from his stomach. The terrible deep pain throbbed in his arm, clouding coherent thoughts. It had all seemed so unreal until the needle.

Overhead the large fans turned slowly. Ruíz waited nearby, the needle, red-tipped now, visible in his hand. He looked eager to begin again.

Prietas held a glass of water to Rumison's lips, and Rumison swallowed gratefully. His heart was beating so rapidly and his breathing came so fast he almost choked trying to swallow.

"Better now?" Preitas asked, withdrawing the glass.

Rumison nodded, anxious to please. It was now his dominant desire.

"Good. Now tell me about your mission."

Rumison wanted to talk. He wanted to tell everything,

to say anything that would keep Ruíz away. But where to start. His mind . . .

"I . . . don't . . . know . . . what . . ." he began.

Why was Preitas looking angry? What had he done wrong? Ruíz moved in from behind.

"No!"

But the needle worked into his arm again.

Rumison screamed. His bowels demanded release, but even this was denied him.

"You are trying to be a hero," Preitas said sternly.

The needle worked farther up into his arm. "My God!" Rumison cried just before he passed out. "You don't know how wrong you are!"

But the cry was only in his mind and Preitas never heard or knew the irony of it.

Afterward, as soldiers dragged him back across the dusty yard toward the incinerator, Rumison was vaguely aware of passing Barney, who was being taken to the house.

"You didn't tell, did you, Mike?" Barney cried.

Rumison didn't answer. He didn't even have the strength to open his eyes.

"I knew you wouldn't tell!" shouted Barney before the guards slapped him quiet. "I knew it!"

Chapter Thirteen

RUMISON finally summoned up the energy to open his eyes. Someone was over him, a dark shape in front of the bright light that came through the chimney slits. He was back in the incinerator. He accepted the knowledge without emotion. He tried to move and realized his head was on someone's lap.

"Easy!" came a cracked voice. But thin and parched as it sounded, it was still recognizable as Rosso's.

"Drink this."

Rosso tilted a small bucket toward Rumison's lips. There was about an inch of water at the bottom. There was none when Rosso lowered the bucket.

Rumison tried to raise himself, but his right arm throbbed painfully near his shoulder, becoming numb below his elbow. He had little muscular control.

"Easy, Mike."

Rumison looked around. Black sat nearby, watching impassively. Barney was gone.

"Wher . . . a . . . Ba . . . r . . . ney?"

"Don't try to talk, Mike."

"Bu . . . t . . ."

"Preitas never wanted you," said Black, his voice dry but clear and even, hinting at underlying strength.

"He wanted Barney from the start. I saw that. They worked on you just to scare him. That's why they messed you up so much. Superficially, I'd guess."

Rumison struggled to roll over on his good side. With Rosso's help he could sit. His whole body hurt. His lips were cut and swollen but he tried to talk.

"Pre . . . ah . . . tas had me wro . . . ong. I ah wan . . . ted to tell ev . . . ah . . . ry . . . thing. . . ."

"And spoil his fun?" said Black. "What did you tell him?"

"My name . . ."

"Only your name?"

Rumison nodded jerkily. "He would . . . n't le . . . ut me talk. . . ."

Rosso was looking at Rumison with an odd, almost embarrassed expression.

"We heard your screams from here," he said. "Was . . . was it . . . bad?"

Rumison couldn't answer. The memory was too fresh. His expression must have been enough, as Rosso didn't ask again.

"Bar . . . ney, he'll ta . . . alk?" Rumison asked.

Rosso looked away.

"Won't he?" Rumison pressed.

"Maybe," said Black.

The temperature inside the incinerator eased as the sun set. Their guards brought another small bucket filled with water, but that was soon gone and no more came. Rumison's mind retreated to some painless gray corner of his being. When the iron door was opened again and Barney's broken body shoved through, Rumison couldn't have said if it was the same day or not.

It was still light enough to see, but the shadows were lengthening and everything was merging once more into darkness.

"No!" cried Rosso. "No, no, no!"

Rosso's cracked groans were barely audible as he leaned over Barney.

"God damn them!"

Miraculously, because as far as Rumison could see no one in Barney's condition should have been alive, Barney's eyes fluttered open. A soft ray of light shone across them. They looked blue and untouched and clear.

"What did you tell them, Bailey?" Black asked.

Rosso shoved Black fiercely away. "Get away from him!" he cried.

Barney's mouth moved. "I . . . didn't . . . tell . . . anything."

The words were soft, pronounced slowly, but they were clear. Barney sounded strangely satisfied.

Black nodded.

"Christ!" croaked Rosso in horror. "Why? You didn't have to go through this." Rosso stared at Black. "He must be kidding," he said. "Out of his mind."

"No," said Barney softly.

"But why? *Why?*"

"I . . . made . . . it . . . important." Barney's last words were formed slowly and lost distinctness even as he spoke them. His eyes closed. Rosso gave out a stifled sob and began pounding on the metal wall.

"Let us out! Let us out!"

Black pulled him away and held him down until he was still. There was no answer from outside.

Darkness came quickly. Rumison's thoughts danced between numb madness and nightmare reality. Barney died without speaking again. The only thing that kept Rumison from giving up completely and following Barney was a mental image burned into his mind of Sergeant Sleeper—Sleeper lying dead in his hammock, staring up at nothing.

It was that image, that picture that came to horrify Rumison more than all the nightmares his present reality could produce.

No reason, he thought. *I won't die for no reason.*

Sometime during the night, when the bright moon overhead could still be seen through the chimney slits, Rumison awoke from his half-trance, half-sleep state and heard unfamiliar sounds coming from outside their prison. He felt a change, without understanding, as Black came alert next to him and Rosso sat bolt upright.

"Are you still alive?"

Was it real or imagined?—Cordobes' voice from outside, calling to them through the door.

"Three of us," Black whispered back.

Silence followed, then the slow, metallic creak of the door as it was carefully and quietly unlatched.

"Hurry," said Cordobes. "I don't know how much time before they change guards."

Rumison tried to crawl, but he had to be helped by Rosso. "You can make it," Rosso urged.

Rumison struggled to help himself through the door. His right arm gave way and he fell forward at Cordobes' feet.

Outside, the stars were bright, the moon directly overhead. In the light, Rumison saw Jorge, the old sergeant, standing at alert next to Cordobes. On the ground lay their guards, dead or unconscious.

"I am sorry about your friend," said Cordobes gently, helping Rumison to his feet. "But I was under guard myself until Jorge came back."

Cordobes handed Rumison a canteen. Rumison almost dropped it before Cordobes realized he didn't have the use of his right arm. Cordobes unscrewed the cap and gave it back to Rumison, who took it in his good hand and drank greedily.

"We must go," urged Cordobes. "Taxia is waiting near the river, where the road comes below the dock. She has horses and clothes."

Black scooped up an automatic rifle that was lying next to an inert guard. "Go ahead," he said. "I'll catch up. There's something I have to do first." And before Cordobes could protest, Black had disappeared in the direction of the house.

"Damn him," Rosso hissed.

"So Preitas was right," Cordobes murmured.

"Only about Black," said Rosso angrily. "Mike, Barney and me had nothing to do with it."

"It doesn't matter," said Cordobes. "I couldn't have acted otherwise. Preitas is an evil man, and I liked your company. My course was clear. But come, we must hurry."

Rumison, too weak to walk 'on his own' had to be helped by Cordobes. Rosso came behind, after following Black's example and picking up the second guard's rifle. Jorge padded along silently to one side.

They had gone only about a hundred yards when the first shots came from the direction of the house. A light came on immediately but was quickly extinguished when a burst of automatic-rifle fire followed. There was shouting and confusion and then more lights came on. They hesitated for a moment by the large shed that the railroad tracks entered. While Cordobes decided what to do, a dark shape appeared, crouching low as it ran toward their position. Jorge raised his old Springfield rifle but Cordobes held out a restraining hand. "Wait," he said softly.

Black stumbled into view, carrying the rifle in one hand and the black case in the other. "They found two guards you killed inside the house," he said, breathing heavily.

"Damn it, Black . . ." Rosso began, but Cordobes silenced him.

"It is too late for recriminations," he said.

"But . . ."

"Please . . . follow me into the shed."

There was a large rusty padlock on the shed door, but Cordobes opened it with a key and hastened them inside. Behind them, silhouetted in the lights from the house, soldiers were fanning out in search of them. It was dark inside, but Cordobes lit a match.

"The engine!" said Black. "Will it work?"

Cordobes nodded. "It will work, if we have time."

The shed contained the engine of a small logging train. The match light died, but Cordobes seemed familiar with the engine as he helped the others into the tiny iron cab. Outside they heard shouts and running feet. Cordobes had bolted the shed door from the inside and so far none of the soldiers had thought to try it.

"How long before it reaches pressure?" whispered Black as Cordobes grimly pumped oil into the engine's hotbox with a lever near the pressure gauge.

"Maybe ten minutes," Cordobes answered.

Black let out an involuntary and exhausted sigh. Rumison, barely able to function himself, thought how tired the older man must be despite his front of iron and steel.

Rosso helped Rumison into the engine cab with Black as Cordobes adjusted more levers. Opening a small door on the hotbox, he struck a match, throwing it inside. The fuel oil exploded with a rush, the flames throwing shadows on the interior of the shed before Cordobes could shut the door. They listened anxiously, but there were no immediate shouts of discovery. The soldiers were still in a state of confusion.

Minutes passed. Rumison counted off the seconds to himself. The sound of the burning oil seemed loud. How could the soldiers miss it?

Apparently they hadn't. The door shook as someone

from outside tried to open it. A cry went up in Spanish. "*Aquí! Están aquí, Coronel!*"

The door trembled as body weight was thrown against it. Black fired his rifle and the shed was lit with flashes smelling of cordite. Someone outside screamed. More shouts followed, then a sharp order. "*Bastante!*"

Then silence. Several more minutes passed. "How much longer?" Black asked.

"Not long," said Cordobes.

Through the walls of the shed came the calm, fatherly voice of Colonel Preitas. Rumison cringed as a sharp stab of pain returned to his arm. "My soldiers are all around you. Sooner or later you will have to come out."

"Listen!" whispered Black. From the front of the shed they could hear the unmistakable sound of lumber being dropped on the tracks in front of the shed door.

"They're trying to block the tracks! We have to go!"

Cordobes threw the large drive lever. The little engine jerked forward with grinding metal and escaping steam. Rumison lay on the floor of the engine by the hotbox, with Cordobes sitting upright on the small metal driver's seat. The others waited, their rifles ready.

Outside, Preitas frantically shouted orders. The engine hit the main shed door and splintered through. Black, Rosso, and the old sergeant began firing as soon as they cleared the rubble. Bullets from return fire whined off the metal sides of the engine. A few pierced the skin of the engine, but it continued forward despite escaping steam, increasing in speed until they were well beyond the shed.

The engine was doing about eight miles an hour as it passed the compound fence. Soldiers ran alongside, firing rifles and cursing in Spanish. Preitas must have sensed failure because Rumison could hear his frantically screamed orders as he urged his men on.

A familiar uniformed face rushed the train. Rosso took careful aim and fired. The figure fell. "Ruíz!" cried Rosso happily. "I got that bastard Ruíz!"

Rumison, lying on the floor, smiled at Rosso with a grim feeling of satisfaction. It was a disturbing feeling, not one Rumison had experienced before . . . hate, revenge, release. Its intensity had surprised him.

The remaining soldiers were dropping back as the engine gained speed. "We made it!" cried Rosso. "Goddamn, we made it!"

"Keep down, Rosso!" shouted Black as Rosso stood to get a better view behind them. "Cordobes, how fast will this thing do?"

But Cordobes didn't answer. Rumison looked up to see the man who had saved them slumped forward across the engine's control levers.

"Capitán!" cried the old sergeant in anguish. He dropped his rifle and lifted Cordobes gently down off the metal seat. Cordobes' dark shirt was damp with blood. There was no life or breath left in the caretaker of Santa Concepción.

It was an agonizing moment for them all. Sharp spasms shook Rumison's chest. Cordobes had been something more than the rest of them. Rumison could see that now. Cordobes had seen something. He had seen hope, purpose, meaning. . . .

"I'm sorry," said Black gently, comforting the old sergeant, who was silently weeping as he held Cordobes' head in his arms.

After a moment the tears stopped and the old man looked up. He took hold of his Springfield and stood. His eyes were dry. He had given what grief he had to give, what was left after so many years of having seen captains die. *"Adiós, señores,"* he said. *"Fueran sus niños que morian de hambre,"* and before Black or Rosso could think to stop him he had turned and jumped from the engine. He rolled once down the railbed, stood unhurt, and was gone in the darkness.

"What did he mean . . . that last about *'hambre'* and *'niños'?"* Rosso asked.

Black's expression was distant and thoughtful in the starlight. "He said we were Cordobes' starving children."

Black was quiet a moment longer. Then he reached down to Cordobes' body and removed a thick manila ten-by-twelve-inch envelope from where Cordobes had kept it under his shirt. Black weighed it in his hand.

"What's that?" Rosso asked.

"I would guess his book," said Black. He put the envelope under his arm and then took hold of Rumison. "Help me get Rumison to his feet. We're going to have to jump. The river's not far."

"Let's just stop it," Rosso argued. "Why risk getting hurt?"

"Help me with Rumison, Rosso."

Rosso shrugged and helped his friend to his feet. The engine chugged around the last bend before the dock. Ahead, visible in the dim light, lay a flat-bottomed riverboat moored under the crane at the end of the dock.

"I figured they came by boat," said Black. He waited a second, judging their speed, and jumped. Rosso, holding Rumison tightly around the waist, followed.

The rough landing with Rosso on top of him knocked the wind from Rumison. He lay still, struggling to regain his breath. He watched as the little engine, doing perhaps fifteen miles an hour, rumbled onto the dock, broke through the crane at the end, and crashed down on the riverboat. The two soldiers who had been left to guard it screamed in fear and scrambled to get out of the way. A muffled explosion was followed by the hiss of cooling iron and escaping steam. Animal shrieks rebounded from the forest, continuing for some time after the explosion.

"How's Rumison?" Black whispered from somewhere nearby.

"All right," answered Rosso. Rumison nodded.

"Come on," said Black. "Preitas won't be far behind."

Between them Black and Rosso helped Rumison along as they followed the riverbank. They had gone possibly half a mile when they reached the Bluefields road. The young Indian girl, Taxia was waiting there with five saddled horses. Her childlike eyes searched the shadowed faces of the three naked men approaching her but showed only the barest hint of emotion, a soft intake of breath, when she couldn't locate Cordobes.

She stood back as Black took the reins to three horses. Burlap bags had been tied to each saddle. Inside were clothes, leather sandals, and some food. Rosso helped Rumison dress and then they mounted. Rumison nearly tumbled off, but Rosso, below, held him until he was stable.

"No!" cried Taxia when Black started his horse back up the road in the direction of the plantation. She motioned frantically the other way. *"Ahí! Ahí!"*

Black shook his head. *"No vaya al costa,"* he said. *"Muy peligroso."*

Taxia watched without comprehension as Rosso, Rumison and Black rode off. She stood alone, holding the reins of the two remaining horses.

Chapter Fourteen

RUMISON knew afterward that if it had not been for Rosso's sheer physical energy and determination, he would never have survived the two days following their escape from the incinerator.

The overgrown Bluefields road Black led them down skirted dangerously close to the compound of Santa Concepción. They could see its lights no more than five hundred yards distant at one point, but finally they had crossed the untilled fields where their greatest danger of discovery lay and entered the even more tangled and ruined southern track Cordobes had told them about earlier.

Somehow Rumison had managed to remain conscious in the open fields near the plantation. Fear played a large part. But once the immediate danger of discovery had passed he slipped into delirium. Rosso, still distrusting Black, washed, tended and fed Rumison for the next twenty-five miles.

For Rumison the delirium was a blessing. No longer could he feel the heat and humidity, the omnipresent insects, the painful, jerking gait of the horse. No longer could he think about Barney or Cordobes or Taxia, who had so carefully masked her emotions from the strange men from the North who had been the chief cause of her lover's death. No longer could Rumison play over in his mind that afternoon he had spent with Preitas and Ruíz and feel the needle as it twisted and hear the sound as it scraped bone.

And there were other things, perhaps even more disturbing, that the delirium kept him from dwelling on, things he was unable to put into words. Things that he intuitively felt underlay it all, the terrible unseen will behind the madness he had been caught up in. Fear had told him that will must be maleficent, evil. But for that time he was spared even from fear.

For the most part Rumison's world was pervaded by a soft, featherlike grayness, only occasionally broken by random, uninvited intrusions of reality: Rosso dripping coconut milk onto his lips, a flash of green jungle, the muddy, rutted track, the dark shadow of Black, who forever seemed to stay just beyond the range of Rumison's vision.

Rosso was his mother and protector, exuding life and affection through his strong, stubby fingers. But the journey was taking its toll on Rosso also. In one of Rumison's infrequent moments of clarity, he heard Rosso talking to him as though Rumison had been conscious all along and were expected to answer.

"Why didn't Barney talk?" he asked. The question seemed important to him. It disturbed him. "Damn it, Mike, it was crazy! He saw what would happen. Who would have thought the little shit had it in him? Just a dumb kid . . . Black probably. Father image or something . . ." Rosso rambled on, repeating the question over and over. During his brief lapse into consciousness, Rumison thought he knew the answer, but he was unable to speak.

There came a time during Rumison's delirium, he couldn't have said what hour or what day, when he heard voices that were neither Black's nor Rosso's. Strong, unfamiliar hands lifted him . . . more voices . . . a feminine one . . . and overriding all of these new sensations a new and remarkable sense of warmth and concern radiating from a single source . . . though he could not recognize the source.

And then the gray returned.

He awoke in a large four-poster bed. The fine white mosquito netting that hung down from the canopy was drawn like a curtain to one side. Rumison's fever was gone, and when he opened his eyes the room came into focus immediately. He looked out at a high, beamed mahogany ceiling, handsome hardwood furniture and a large picture window that faced onto a vast rolling green lawn.

He took a deep breath and exhaled. His head felt light; his body still felt sore in places, but there were no signs of delirium or of the intense pain that had forced him there. A dull ache under his right arm brought back terrible memories, but the numbness in his hand was gone as he clenched and unclenched his fingers.

He had thought he was alone, but as he shifted his head to get a better view of the room he saw that someone was standing in the open doorway.

She is, came his first thought, beautiful! But it was not her physical beauty that held his gaze. He was, after all, used to the golden girls on the beaches of California.

Oddly, despite his certain knowledge that he had never seen her before, he felt that she was familiar—so much so that he could not prevent himself from racking his memory for some hint of a past they might have shared. For several long moments the girl in the doorway gazed back at him, neither smiling nor frowning, seeming to understand—even more than he—the nature of his feelings. Rumison found himself lost in her deep green eyes.

"You're awake," she said, her matter-of-fact words breaking the enchantment. "Are you feeling better?"

Her voice was soft, with a trace of shyness that hadn't been present in her eyes. Her eyes were now lowered, as though she were embarrassed by the earlier moment's intimacy.

Rumison nodded, wondering if he should risk an answer, unsure of his voice.

"Yes," he finally said, "much better."

The sound of his voice surprised him. The words had come as he had wanted . . . which was what had concerned him . . . but his voice sounded deeper than he remembered. More aged.

She stepped farther into the room. Rumison abruptly found himself experiencing such an overwhelming sense of *déjà vu*—an intense feeling that somehow he had lived through that moment before—that he had to shake his head and tell himself such a thing was impossible. She was not someone he was likely to have forgotten.

"I'm Whitney O'Brien," she said. Rumison noticed her accent seemed western American, not unlike his own. "My father owns this plantation. Your friends brought you here two days ago."

She approached the bed and Rumison found himself reassessing her beauty. She was by no stretch of the imagination unattractive. She was wearing faded blue jeans just tight enough to accent long legs, a white cotton shirt over what appeared to be firm but not exceptional breasts, and a small silver cross on a chain around her long neck. Her body was slender, in good shape, though perhaps too angular in places. But Rumison certainly had seen more beautiful women.

Or had he?

"Whitney?" he asked, trying to shake the feeling that he had known her before.

She smiled. The expression was quick, rueful and self-knowing, lacking any attempt at pretense. "I was named after an unconventional aunt," she said.

"Oh."

An awkward silence followed. Rumison finally asked, "Where are my friends?"

"They're here," Whitney answered quickly. "My father agreed to let you take his airplane, but it needs a new prop. They're waiting for one of the men to get back from Bluefields with it. . . ."

A chill crept up Rumison's spine. "Bluefields?" he asked.

Whitney nodded. "My father ordered it several weeks ago but they haven't been flying, so no one bothered to pick it up. The man should be back tonight or tomorrow."

"Do you know why we're here?" Rumison asked.

Whitney smiled sadly. "The revolution has caused a lot of trouble for everyone," she said. "But I think it's for the best. Right now the Sandinistas and their supporters don't like Americans very much. I can understand your problem. They haven't bothered my father, though."

There was something in the way Whitney had added the last statement, an almost undetectable trace of . . . bitterness? that led Rumison to the obvious question: Why hadn't the Sandinistas bothered her father? Instead of asking it, however, Rumison said, "It's good of your father to help us out."

Whitney nodded shortly. "I'll go tell them you're awake," she said, and she turned and left.

Rumison stared after her, and when she was gone he realized how light-headed he felt. He was intensely aware of his surroundings—the soft smoothness of the linen sheets, the smell of fresh orchids, the musky, woodsy odor of milled mahogany. The light coming through the window looked liquid, almost touchable. For a moment it felt good just to be alive.

But as he looked down at his arm and saw the ugly purple bruise discoloring his shoulder, the memories returned. And with them the fear . . .

"Welcome back from never-never land," came a familiar voice, breaking into his thoughts. Rosso, freshly shaved and groomed, dressed in clean khaki, his square, open face set in a self-conscious grin, stood in the doorway. Whitney stood behind him. "How're you feeling, Mike?" Rosso asked.

Rumison let out a deep breath and sat up. Other than a screaming hunger and a slight vertigo, he felt fine . . . better than he had any right to feel. The only real soreness he had was in the area under his arm. He wondered if that would ever go away. "Good," he answered, meaning it.

Rosso nodded. He seemed uncomfortable. Rumison saw that despite Rosso's clean clothes and scrubbed appearance there had been changes in him. Rosso looked thinner than Rumison remembered. His face was scarred with cuts and mottled with insect bites. His brown eyes, usually so straightforward and aggressive, looked almost . . . Rumison couldn't believe it . . . hesitant!

"Thanks for taking care of me," Rumison said.

Rosso shrugged offhandedly. "No big thing. Did Whitney tell you what's happening?"

"Sort of. Everyone's waiting for a propeller so we can fly out."

"Her old man is helping us . . . letting us take the plane. But as you can imagine we're worried Preitas or someone might show up. Those guys we left back at the other place have had plenty of time to get help. It's been four days."

"That long?"

"You were out."

"I guess so."

"Another thing."

"What's that?"

Rosso frowned. "Black thinks Preitas is working with the Cubans. For some reason they're involved with the Sandinistas looking for us. There's something going on—"

Rosso stopped abruptly. A man had appeared at the doorway. He was a large black and he wore a clean white housecoat. Two dark eyes, as black and lusterless as coal, stared out of a massive head that had been completely shaved. His voice was deep and toneless when he spoke. "Miss Whitney, Mista Sean is on de porch, wit de mon Black. He say if de mon Roomesan can do it, to join dem on de porch."

The voice sounded oddly hollow, Rumison thought, as though the man's throat were larger than it looked. Whitney was frowning and Rumison had the distinct impression she feared or disliked the man. Even Rosso looked uncomfortable. The black's attention appeared to be directed solely toward Whitney, but Rumison could have sworn that the man was not only aware of Rumison on the bed, but in a disturbing manner was as intensely aware of him as Whitney had been earlier.

"Tell my father," said Whitney shortly, "that Mr. Rumison is resting and certainly can't—"

"Wait!" said Rumison, sensing some sort of confrontation building, for what reason he couldn't guess, but wanting to avoid it. "I feel all right. I'd like to get out of bed." Whitney turned on him in sudden exasperation. "Really," he added meekly.

The black man nodded slowly. "I'll tell dem to expect Roomesan," he said and backed from the room.

But just before he left, his huge head turned toward the bed until his dark, empty eyes were staring directly into Rumison's. A sudden, inexplicable fear seized Rumison. He shuddered and looked away. When he turned back, the black man was gone.

"Strange guy," he said, trying to cover up his unease.

"You can say that again," said Rosso. Had it been Rumison's imagination, or had Rosso also shuddered?

"He almost talked O'Brien into giving us over to the Sandinistas," Rosso added.

Rumison was startled. "Huh? What for?"

Rosso shrugged. "I guess he doesn't like us."

"Yeah, but why?"

"It might have something to do with his religious beliefs."

"Don't joke with me."

"I'm not. He's obeah . . . or so we've been told, and by the way the people act around him, I guess it's probably true."

"O what?" Rumison asked, confused.

"Sun, our cook, says that obeah is a form of perception," murmured Whitney quietly.

Rumison studied her for a moment, trying to decide if she was serious. He decided she was.

"I still don't understand."

"Voodoo," said Rosso. "Isaiah is the local witch doctor. He hasn't liked us since the moment we showed up. I don't know why. Neither does Black. But he seems harmless enough . . . just spooky."

Rumison was shaking his head. "I don't believe this," he said.

A glimmer of anger appeared in Whitney's green eyes. "You shouldn't judge things you don't understand," she said.

"Wait. I'm sorry. I didn't mean . . . I mean . . . I just . . ." Rumison stopped, unable to finish. What *did* he mean?

"Isaiah is Whitney's father's father-in-law," Rosso explained quickly. "O'Brien married Isaiah's daughter after Whitney's mother left."

Rumison didn't know what to say. He still half thought they were putting him on. Whitney bit her bottom lip. Had Rumison missed something else? He looked to Rosso for help, but Rosso just shrugged helplessly as if to say, It's beyond me.

"You sure you feel good enough to move around?" Rosso asked.

For an answer, Rumison threw off the thin blanket that had been covering him and for the first time realized he was completely naked. Whitney, abruptly laughing at the expression on his face, went over to a dresser, where she took out clean khaki pants and a shirt, underclothes, and a belt, which she brought over and placed on the bed.

"Don't mind me." She smiled impishly. "After all, I helped undress you, and Bob and I fed you and gave you a bath."

"Er . . . yeah. Thanks, I guess. I don't really remember. . . ."

Whitney picked up a pair of leather work boots that had been sitting on the floor. "They belonged to a friend of my father," she said. "He never came back for them."

Whitney, still smiling, pretended to straighten things in the dresser while Rumison pulled his pants on. Rumison tied the boots and stood up, swaying slightly. He took a tentative step and despite his weakness found nothing major wrong. The boots fit well enough and he felt better than he had expected, if still dizzy.

"Well," he said, "show me where to go."

The main house of O'Brien's plantation was larger than the one at Santa Concepción. A rambling, one-story structure with long halls and spacious rooms, O'Brien's plantation had been constructed almost entirely out of stone and mahogany. Indian and Oriental rugs covered the wood floors, and air-conditioning units had been installed in many of the numerous windows, allowing the house to enjoy temperatures in the upper seventies even in the midst of the most extreme heat of summer. Throughout, the house was richly furnished, and many of its furnishings looked as though they had been made by local craftsmen out of native hardwoods. But there was an occasional elegant piece of Continental or English origin, and the sitting room had a large, modern television set.

"Television? Here?" Rumison asked, resting for a moment.

"Betamax," said Whitney, pointing to the wall where Rumison could see a shelf stacked with videotapes.

Black was seated with a man who Rumison knew immediately must be Sean O'Brien, on a wide, screened-in veranda that faced the same rolling lawn seen from Rumison's bedroom window. The lawn ended in a row of palm trees that bordered white sand dunes. The rhythmic sound of slapping surf could be heard in the distance, and sea gulls cried overhead. The air on the veranda was humid and warm; the house, with its air conditioning, had been cooler, but a light sea breeze made the veranda more pleasant, Rumison thought. He hadn't realized they were on the coast.

Black stood politely as Whitney entered, but her father stayed in his chair, hardly bothering to acknowledge his daughter's arrival. Looking at O'Brien, Rumison felt for the third time since he had opened his eyes that someone was taking an unusually intense interest in him.

Paranoia? he wondered, thinking he might be suffering the aftereffects of delirium.

Even seated as he was, slouched in a wooden deck chair, it was apparent Sean O'Brien was a huge man—at least six and a half feet tall, Rumison judged. O'Brien had large hamlike hands, one of which held a frosted glass. But sagging skin and slack muscles indicated that Whitney's father once carried a great deal more weight than he did now. O'Brien looked thin and oddly unhealthy—a man, thought Rumison, in decline. He had a crop of short, strawberry blond hair over a ruddy, freckled face. The freckles might have made the face boyish had it not been for the slack skin and shadows under the eyes. His eyes, green as emeralds, were the only feature Rumison could see in which he even faintly resembled Whitney.

"So you're Rumison," said O'Brien. The man's voice, like his body, seemed to lack something it might once have had, some timbre or resonance. His words carried the remnants of an Irish brogue. He didn't offer Rumison his hand. "At least you're on your feet now. My daughter put enough trouble into getting you there."

"I want to thank you," Rumison said politely.

O'Brien's smile was thin and cold. "If I had my way you'd be tied up and on your way to the authorities . . . whoever they are these days. I've told your friends, I've got no love for the Sandinistas and their revolution—God knows they've screwed up the lumber market—but from a moral standpoint they can't be any worse than that family of thievin' pirates they drove out. I've had enough trouble tryin' to stay out of it. I don't want it spoiled by three gringo fugitives."

Rumison stammered, at a loss for words. O'Brien interrupted him.

"I'm expectin' payment."

Black, who so far as Rumison could remember, didn't look much different from the way he had on that night they had left California, nodded. "I offered O'Brien five thousand dollars," Black said, "for each of us who gets safely out. He asked for ten. We settled on eight . . . payable upon our safe return to the United States."

"And another five thousand for the Piper," grunted O'Brien.

"And five thousand for the plane," Black agreed.

"Not that I trust you any more'n I'd trust an English lawyer," said O'Brien grimly, "but as long as my darlin' daughter has all but threatened to kill herself unless I help—hell's mistake—I may as well try to get something for my troubles."

"You'll be paid," said Black.

O'Brien waved to an Oriental houseboy who was standing nearby. "Chang," he yelled with a slurred belligerency that suddenly made Rumison aware that O'Brien was drunk.

"Bring our . . . uh . . . guests here something to drink. And another of the same for me."

The houseboy bowed and left.

Feeling dizzy, Rumison sat down, though O'Brien hadn't offered him a seat. Whitney remained standing, directly behind Rumison's chair. He could feel her presence like a warm glow at the base of his neck.

"The situation is this," explained Black calmly, his gray eyes as implacable as ever. "O'Brien has a man returning—this evening or tomorrow—with a prop for the plane he has around for spotting trees. The man hasn't been told about us . . . what the prop is for. He thinks it's a routine pickup. I've checked out the plane, ran the engine up. It should get us to Costa Rica—"

"Of course it should," O'Brien growled. "We've been flying it for ten years over these jungles."

Ignoring the interruption, Black continued. "If all goes well we should be in Costa Rica tomorrow. Preitas might show up again, but O'Brien here claims he'll know half an hour before anyone is within fifteen miles of this house—"

"I've put the word out," said O'Brien.

"But just in case," continued Black, "there's a small sailboat moored nearby we might consider—"

"Let's take that damn boat and go," said Rosso as he sat himself in the chair next to Rumison. "Now. This minute."

"Boat or Piper, it'll still cost the same," said O'Brien.

Rosso ignored O'Brien, glaring at Black. "You know what happened when we waited too long before. . . ."

Rosso's barely concealed anger was accusing, but Black just shook his head. "We've been over this, Rosso."

"But Mike's here now. It's different—"

"It's not different. The advantage of the plane is worth the risk."

"Look, Black," said Rosso in an argument that Rumison realized had probably been going on since their arrival at O'Brien's, "it has been four days. That bastard Preitas took less time than that to track us before. He could show up at anytime."

"He ran into trouble," said Black.

"How can you be sure?"

"Because if he hadn't, he would have been here already. If I had been in his shoes, I would have gone back to Bluefields . . . tried to bottle up all possible escape routes. If someone were following us, O'Brien insists he'd know about it."

"That I would," said O'Brien. "There's nothing happens on Encantada I don't know about."

There was a great deal of pride expressed in O'Brien's statement. Rumison found himself remembering the cryptic comments Cordobes had made that day in the fields: O'Brien had come from Ireland and built up the largest privately owned plantation in Nicaragua. He had reason to be proud. But why did that pride seem out of place?

Something had happened, Cordobes had said. Señor Harrison once had been O'Brien's friend, but then something had happened. The local Europeans and Anglos avoided O'Brien now. Why?

Rumison flexed his toes in the boots Whitney had given him. They belonged to a friend of my father, she had said. A friend who had never returned!

Rumison's thoughts were interrupted by the houseboy returning with a tray of drinks. Rumison's was non-alcoholic and tasted like banana and orange juice. As Rumison lowered the glass, he felt queasy. He'd eaten little since the dinner with Cordobes. He looked around and saw the black man, Isaiah, standing near the door to the veranda, watching those at the table. His face was empty and expressionless.

Obeah? Black magic? O'Brien's father-in-law? It all fit . . . except for Whitney. What was she doing here?

"Does me father-in-law bother you, Mr. Rumison?"

Rumison started, realizing he had been lost in thought.

"I asked, does me father-in-law bother you?" repeated O'Brien.

Rumison shifted uncomfortably, not knowing what to say. O'Brien laughed. It was an unpleasant sound.

"He hates you."

The intentional bluntness of O'Brien's statement left Rumison bewildered.

"I . . . uh . . . was told he didn't much . . . ah . . . care for us . . ." he answered awkwardly.

"He hates you, pure and simple," said O'Brien, enjoying Rumison's discomfiture. "It's that hate you feel. He wanted me to ship you back to Bluefields in chains. . . ." O'Brien stopped, frowning thoughtfully as he studied the glass in his large hands. "I've got no good feeling about this thing. Even now I've half a mind to—"

He was interrupted by a cry from Whitney. "Father! You promised!"

O'Brien looked up at his daughter's determined face and sighed. "So I did. So I did."

"He'll keep his word," said Whitney. "He always does."

O'Brien laughed. "A bleedin'-hearted romantic . . . just like her mother."

O'Brien's comment sounded jocular, even contemptuous, but Rumison felt a sadness in it. He was wondering about this when he noticed O'Brien's attention suddenly taken up by something behind him. Rumison turned quickly, half expecting to see Isaiah approaching, but the black man was nowhere around.

A beautiful black girl had come out onto the veranda. Rumison felt the breath leaving his body.

"I hope I'm not interruptin' anythin' important."

O'Brien immediately was on his feet. "Of course not, dear. Just talk. Just small talk."

Rumison thought he had begun to understand.

There was no doubt that this was Isaiah's daughter, O'Brien's wife. She had her father's deep-set black eyes, his proud head . . . but instead of Isaiah's brooding emptiness, her eyes were alive, dancing with a sensual, mocking eroticism.

She was dressed in a flowered sarong that was slit up one side. The slit showed long, well-formed legs. Her skin was as smooth and unblemished as black soap. Her blouse was cut low. Two large, melon-hard breasts rose and fell with her breathing. She moved with a studied sensuality so controlled that it might have been choreographed. Perhaps it had been, Rumison thought. She certainly was aware of the effect it had on the men in the room—all except for Black.

"Good evening, Mrs. O'Brien," said Black, standing politely.

The girl favored Black with a slow, mocking smile, then turned to O'Brien, who couldn't keep the possessiveness out of his eyes. The girl's voice was dusky and, like her movements, studied. She spoke with a featherlike Caribbean lilt.

"Sun is servin' de dinner at fo'. He wondered should we set a place for de sick mon."

An awkward metamorphosis seemed to have come over O'Brien. No longer was he the cynical, slightly drunk Irish lord of the manor. He looked attentive and unsure of himself. "Ah . . . well . . . I guess so, my dear," he fumbled, looking at Rumison.

"How do you feel, Rumison?" Black asked.

Rumison felt the black girl watching him. He felt as awkward as O'Brien.

"So you be de mon Roomesan," she said.

Rumison nodded.

"You'll eat with us?"

Rumison nodded again. "I feel fine," he added quickly to Black.

"I'll tell de cook."

The black girl regarded Rumison a moment longer,

smiled again at her husband and walked from the veranda. She left behind an uncomfortable silence. The effect of her appearance had been so disproportionate to its expressed purpose that Rumison wondered what its real motivation had been.

"Bitch!" said Whitney softly, under her breath. But the word hung by itself in the silence and O'Brien overheard.

"Keep that to yourself."

Whitney's face was expressionless as she replied, "I'll try, Father."

Chapter Fifteen

O'BRIEN's wife was the center of everybody's attention at dinner late that afternoon. Dinner was served by Chang, the houseboy, in the dining room of the large house. Hermilia had changed into a white silk evening dress that exposed large amounts of sleek ebony skin. The dress would have been hard to carry off in most settings and on most women, but on Hermilia O'Brien it looked fitting.

Even Chang seemed unnerved, his hands trembling as he served Hermilia the sugared ham and wild rice. Rumison couldn't keep his eyes off Hermilia and it bothered him. There was no warmth in the young black woman, unless it was the raw warmth of eroticism. But she drew his attention like a magnet.

Rumison wasn't the only one mesmerized by her. Rosso hadn't said a word. O'Brien had become an ingratiating little boy, replying seriously to her bantering comments, relinquishing the floor whenever she interrupted.

Whitney had seated herself next to Rumison. For the most part she tried to ignore the attention her stepmother was getting. Whitney also had changed clothes and was wearing a modest white cotton dress. Rumison noticed she still had on the small silver cross . . . the only jewelry she wore.

"You said that you were in the Air Force, Michael?" she asked, trying to draw his attention.

Rumison started. He had been staring, not for the first time, at Hermilia. He lowered his eyes guiltily. Hermilia's sensuality was a trap, he knew. Like the Sirens of Odysseus, it could lure him to destruction. But for all Hermilia's animal charisma, Rumison still cared more about the quiet blond girl next to him.

"Uh . . . oh. Yes. Rosso and I, at least. And another friend . . ." Rumison stopped, remembering Barney, growing afraid.

Whitney, seeing his expression, placed a hand on his. The gesture was sudden and instinctive and seemed to anger Hermilia, who had been watching.

"All Americans are alike," Hermilia said, jealous of the quick intimacy. "Dey only take, take, take. Money, land, your soul . . . an' when dey maybe give back a small bit, dey 'spect you to lick dem."

She was looking directly at Rumison when she spoke. Rumison felt she wanted him to argue with her . . . another way to reclaim his attention. Her dark eyes, her taunting, controlled anger . . . held out the promise that if he tried hard enough, she might give in.

But Rumison let the challenge pass. For the moment Whitney's touch meant more to him than all of the black girl's sexual promise.

"We're in the Air Force," he said, ignoring Hermilia and continuing his answer to Whitney. "Air Rescue. I never liked the military much, though. Rosso—Bob there—and I got drafted, joined to get out of the infantry."

"But the draft ended a long time back," said Whitney. "If you didn't like it, wouldn't you be out by now?"

For some reason the question seemed to cut to the heart of Rumison's life. Why *had* he stayed in? What *had* he done with all those wasted years?

"I didn't have much money," said Rumison, knowing his answer was lame and feeling ashamed of it. "They offered us a big bonus to re-up. . . ."

"But if you didn't enjoy it?"

"Oh, it wasn't that bad," said Rumison quickly. "Like being a fireman or something. The training was good. We got a lot of time off."

"You were on a rescue mission here?" Whitney asked.

The table was silent. Rumison was uncomfortably aware that everyone was waiting to hear his answer.

"Sort of," he said uneasily. "Rosso, Barney and I weren't told much about it. Mr. Black was in charge."

"I don't buy that 'innocent' bit," O'Brien snorted. "Obvious to me the whole thing stinks. And it's not just the Sandinistas you're runnin' from, I'm thinkin'."

"Look, Mr. O'Brien," said Rosso, "like I've told you: Mike and I just want to get home. We've got no secrets. We haven't hurt anyone. That Preitas is wrong about us. We're just trying to get home after jumping in to help a wrecked airplane."

"An' you, Mr. Black?" Hermilia asked. "Like your friends, are you jus' tryin' to get home?"

Black shrugged and sipped red wine from his glass. "Not as you mean," he said. "No."

"Then what is your excuse, Mr. Black?"

"Excuse?"

"Reason, maybe?"

"A reason for doing what I do?"

"That was the question!" snapped O'Brien, backing up his wife. "What's behind it? You seem the key."

Black shrugged again. "The earth turns, the sun comes up in the east . . . and you ask for a reason?"

"Damn it, Black . . . !"

"Isaiah says he's a goombee," interrupted Hermilia, ignoring her husband as she made slow circles on the rim of her wineglass with the tip of an index finger. "A devil man."

"Maybe I'm just trying to do my job and survive," said Black.

"Dere's more'n one kine o' job, Mista Goombee . . . an more'n one kine o' pay. What do you get paid, Mr. Black? Men's souls?"

Hermilia's smile was mocking. Black returned it with a faint smile of his own.

"I don't know the cash value of a man's soul these days, Mrs. O'Brien," he said. "But I doubt it would cover my expenses. But then you probably know more about that sort of thing than I do."

The slight had been spoken in such a conversational tone that O'Brien, his attention fogged by both alcohol and the presence of his wife, couldn't seem to decide whether to be angry. Hermilia's eyes flared, but before O'Brien could make up his mind, Whitney interrupted. "Can't you tell us *anything,* Mr. Black?" she asked.

With sudden insight, Rumison knew that the strain he had sensed at the table was not something of the moment, something that had come about because of his presence, or Black's, or Rosso's. It was an ongoing battle that Whitney fought daily. It gave him new respect for her. Her warmth and sincerity were threatened, possibly even doomed, by her stepmother's mockery, the brooding antipathy of Hermilia's father, and her own father's apparent indifference.

Why did she stay?

Surprisingly, Black answered her. It came to Rumison that Black had recognized Whitney's plight and sympathized with her. The realization was accompanied by an odd sort of jealousy.

"I don't know the full story myself," said Black. "But Rosso is right. A jet crashed in the jungle. It was supposed to be a rescue mission. What it has become . . . ask the man chasing us—Preitas. A real bastard. I think he works for the Cubans."

"What did you find at the crash?" Whitney asked.

"Six men went down. Five died on impact. There was one survivor. But he died later."

"Oh. That's too bad."

"Perhaps."

Rumison was relieved when the dinner was over and Chang cleared the table. O'Brien had been drinking since early afternoon. It hadn't affected his coordination, but his manner—except where it concerned his wife—had grown steadily more abrasive

"Thank you for an excellent meal," said Black as the last of the plates were removed.

"Sun is still good for something," said O'Brien, "for all his mindless chatter."

"Sun is our cook," explained Whitney.

"An' he's senile as an ol' turkey," laughed Hermilia derisively.

"He is not!" cried Whitney angrily. It was the first time Rumison had seen her lose her temper, or talk directly to her stepmother.

"Whit!" O'Brien warned darkly.

Whitney lowered her head contritely, but Rumison felt that she was angry with herself for letting the black girl get to her. Hermilia's smile was triumphant, as though she had won a round in a battle.

"My daughter has a great fondness for our cook," said O'Brien tightly. "In fact, I'm sure he's the main reason she came back here after being gone so long. . . ."

"That's not true, Father," said Whitney quietly.

"No," he said, "perhaps it wasn't the main reason. But Sun's mind does wander."

Hermilia's low, mocking laughter interrupted any thoughts Rumison may have had. "Poor little Whit. She take de Sun over obeah but still has to believe in obeah's seeing."

Whitney tensed but refused to answer. Before Rumison could ask what Hermilia had meant, O'Brien stood up, signaling that dinner was over.

"I've got things to take care of. I have received word that my man with the prop has reached Karawalla, a fishing camp up the coast a bit. He's got the Whaler, and if I know him he'll leave before first light . . . should be here early. It's an easy ride from there . . . given good weather."

"Good evenin', Mista Goombee," cooed Hermilia.

"Good evening, Mrs. O'Brien," returned Black.

Hermilia flashed the others a smile and left the room with her husband. The tension Rumison had felt all through the dinner left with her.

"One more night," said Rosso dryly.

Whitney helped Chang clear the table, leaving Black, Rumison and Rosso alone together for the first time since their arrival. Black motioned them out to the veranda.

It was still hot outside, despite the nearness of the sea. Several hundred yards away Rumison could see the lights of the workers' quarters and could hear their chatter as they finished their own meals. The sun had almost set in the west and the night seemed peaceful. Only Rumison's growing unease kept him from enjoying it. He hadn't eaten much at dinner because his stomach was still upset.

They were almost out. Only one more night. The thoughts ran through his mind like a chorus.

"I'm sure you two aren't so dense that you don't see something very strange going on around here," said Black once he had assured himself there was no one else within earshot. "Cordobes hinted at it. I don't think it has anything to do with politics, but I still don't like it. Not with that witch doctor haunting the place and urging O'Brien to feed us to the sharks."

"We should have taken the boat," said Rosso. "Hell, we can take it tonight."

"There's no wind," Black pointed out. "And we wouldn't get far rowing those stubby oars."

"We should have left yesterday!"

"You don't hear what I'm saying, Rosso. Either O'Brien is going to help us, or he's not. If he is, the plane is our best bet. If he isn't, we'd be sitting ducks in the boat."

"You think there might be a chance O'Brien will break his word?" Rumison asked worriedly.

"With that wife of his, anything is possible," said Black. "If she takes it in her mind to join forces with her father, O'Brien wouldn't stand a chance. She jerks him around like a yo-yo. So far the only thing keeping us from the wolves is that daughter."

"Whitney?"

Black nodded thoughtfully. "She's been watching over you, Rumison, like a mother bear tending a sick cub. Hard to figure. I guess most good women have a touch of Florence Nightingale in them." But Black didn't sound convinced as his voice trailed off. "You weren't conscious," he said after a moment, "but O'Brien's men found us fifteen miles up the road. O'Brien and the old man weren't anywhere around, but Whitney was out as soon as someone had told her about us. Drove you here in a truck herself. When O'Brien got back to the house he started yelling that we were criminals and devils, but Whitney put up such a fight that he finally gave in to her. She made him promise he'd help. How're you feeling, Rumison? Really."

"Better than I should, I guess. Weak. My arm throbs a bit."

"Sleepy? Tired?"

Rumison shook his head. "Not yet. I don't know what happened to me, but I feel all right."

Black nodded. "I've seen fevers like yours before. Combination of heat exhaustion, pain and mental fatigue. Usually passes in a few days. What I'm asking is, do you feel up to keeping awake for a few more hours?"

"I said I'm all right, Black," said Rosso angrily. "Mike's been out for four days—"

"And you and I have been awake for four days," said Black. He turned to Rumison. "I don't trust anyone around here," he said quietly. "Except maybe the girl. O'Brien's giving in to her was an easy way out for him. Rosso and I had our M-16's, which is more firepower than he was used to. He's not stupid. Whitney's concern gave him an excuse, but I've a feeling he might turn if he thought he could get away without bloodshed."

"We've been keeping watch," said Rosso. "One more night won't hurt me. Not if it means getting out of this goddamn country."

"I wouldn't trust you," said Black. "You're dead on your feet. I've another feeling we're going to need all the rest we can get in the morning."

Rosso did look tired and Rumison realized it. "I can keep awake for a few hours," Rumison said.

"Mike . . . !"

"It's settled," said Black. "It'll only be till midnight, then you can take over, Rosso. You can wake me at three. That should give you five or six hours of good sleep."

Rosso looked up at Rumison, his brown eyes questioning. "I'm not sleepy," said Rumison. "I'll be all right."

Rosso sighed. "I do need some sleep," he said. "I just don't want anything to go wrong."

"Follow me," said Black.

Black led them off the veranda and pointed out toward a small knoll across the grass. There appeared to be some sort of structure on the knoll, but it was difficult to make out in the dark.

"It's a fountain," said Black. "Or at least it used to be. It has a good view of the beach, the house, the workers' compound, the sky. Rosso and I kept watch in our rooms last night, but tonight I think the knoll would be a good place to be."

"If there's trouble?" Rumison asked.

"Wake us. Try to do it silently, but if you can't, just fire off a few rounds and head for the beach. The boat's on the beach about a quarter of a mile south of here. I left some supplies there this morning, just in case."

"I still think we should forget the damn airplane and

take the boat now," argued Rosso tiredly. "We would go a long way before tomorrow."

Black shook his head. "Not far enough. Not without wind. Not without knowing the reefs. We'd have to beach it, come daylight."

"We'd be away from here," said Rosso. He seemed to shudder. "I don't like this place. I've got a bad feeling—"

A soft footfall came from behind them on the veranda. Black raised his hand to his lips. The screen door opened and Whitney looked through. Seeing the three men, she started to withdraw.

"I'm sorry," she said apologetically. "I didn't mean to intrude."

"Pick up a rifle later," said Black quietly to Rumison. "My room is next to yours." Louder, to Whitney, he said, "It's all right. Rosso and I were just going to bed."

"So early?" Whitney asked.

"We've got a big day tomorrow. And Rosso and I haven't gotten much sleep the past few nights."

"Of course. I'm sorry." She looked up at the stars. "I just like to watch the sky sometimes at night," she murmured, as though she felt a need to explain.

"I'm sure Rumison will keep you company," said Black. He took a somewhat startled Rosso by the arm and steered him toward the house.

"Come on, Rosso. We've got to get some sleep."

"What? Oh . . . yeah, sure," stammered Rosso. "Good night, Mike. Whitney."

Rosso and Black disappeared into the house, and Rumison was alone with Whitney O'Brien. A breeze had come up and for a moment Rumison wondered if he should run in and tell Black about it, but the presence of the girl stopped him, and the breeze soon died. Off toward the workers' quarters Rumison could hear guitars and singing. The words were unintelligible, but the rhythm was pure Caribbean. The crescent moon and the stars were bright over the broad lawn, the palms, the sand dunes, and the sea.

"It looks like Mr. Black wanted us to be alone," Whitney ventured.

Rumison nodded. He had been thinking the same thing and wondering why; he had never seen Black do anything without a purpose. Maybe he had thought Rumison could get something out of her. But what? He found himself walking slowly with Whitney out onto the lawn.

"It's so beautiful here . . . sometimes," said Whitney softly.

There was a wistfulness in the comment that Rumison was reluctant to probe, fearing to spoil the peacefulness of the night. Around them the croaks and chirpings of frogs and crickets blended with the music from the workers' quarters.

Peace. And warmth. How different from other nights, other girls he had been with. Walking next to this strange girl whose life held so many mysteries but who also seemed so warm and familiar, for a time he felt his fear stilled.

He thought of Barney. Had he been right, back there in the jungle before Sleeper had died? Had their lives lost something? Had they been as dead, dull, hollow, as lacking in meaning as Barney's words had suggested?

The edges of Rumison's memories, which should have been hard and meaningful, were instead blurred, vague. But blurred by what? What was it that had made that rather pleasant existence in California so . . . so . . . dispensable? What did this moment have that was so different?

"You don't seem to fit in around here," said Rumison, getting as close to an open question as he would allow himself.

"No," said Whitney slowly. "Not anymore. Once, maybe . . . before my mother and I first left . . ."

"When was that?"

"I was twelve," Whitney answered.

"When did you come back?"

"Last year." Whitney seemed unwilling to say more, and Rumison didn't press. After a while she asked, "Where is your home, Michael?"

Home? Rumison wondered. Where was his home? Were vague memories of adolescence and his faint allegiance to an inherited house enough to allow him to call Laguna Beach home?

Home? He felt closer to his birthplace in Arizona. But he hadn't been back there since he was five years old.

"California," he answered finally, not knowing what else to say. "I had a house there . . . Laguna Beach."

Had? Why did he think of it in the past tense?

"Are you married, Michael?"

"No. I lived with Rosso and Barney . . . the guy who was killed."

Was it his imagination, or did Whitney seem relieved? "I'm sorry about your friend. It must be painful."

Rumison shrugged. What was there to say? "I didn't really know him that well," he said. "He had a lot of sides I didn't understand. But I think he was looking . . ." His voice trailed off. He didn't know what he was saying.

She stopped walking and smiled. It was a soft, understanding smile, and it made him feel that words were not necessary.

Sometime later, when the music from the compound had stopped, Rumison said good night to Whitney and sought out Black's bedroom. His Rolex watch, which was miraculously still on his wrist after all that had happened, said it was nine-thirty. Over two hours had passed since Rosso and Black had left him alone with Whitney.

"That you, Rumison?" Black's voice asked when he knocked. Rumison opened the door and entered. Black was propped up on one shoulder in bed and had probably been asleep.

"Uh . . . I'm sorry I took so long," Rumison apologized. "But we got to talking—"

"That's all right," interrupted Black. He nodded toward a rifle that was leaned against the wall near the bed. "There it is. Take it and let me get back to sleep."

Rumison did as he was told, wondering at Black's casualness.

Something didn't seem right.

Chapter Sixteen

THE fountain sat atop the grassy knoll Black had pointed out. As Black had said, it was a good place to keep watch. The fountain was made of rocks and coral and at one time must have been pleasant, but the water had been turned off and the rocks were coated with slippery black algae. There was still water in the fountain's pool but it was covered with a thick layer of stagnant slime. Rumison had at first worried about mosquitos, but there were none about. Possibly O'Brien had sprayed poison or oil on the pool.

Rumison sat at the edge of the pool, his back to the fountain. It gave him a good view of the house, the workers' compound, and the beach. Like Santa Concepción, O'Brien's plantation had a dock that extended some hundred yards out into the sea not far from where Rumison sat.

One by one the lights in the house and in the workers' quarters went out. The comforting choir of crickets and frogs diminished, then ceased entirely. Rumison's right arm began to ache. He let it hang at his side to relieve the pain. Off across the sand he could hear the light surf lapping on the beach.

A screen door slammed. There was still a light burning on the veranda of the house and he could see a figure silhouetted on the steps. Rumison felt a sudden unreasoning chill. He forgot the pain in his arm as he gripped his rifle and hunched lower behind the fountain. The person on the steps was Isaiah. Of this, though he couldn't say why, Rumison was certain.

Does he know I am here? Rumison wondered wildly. Can he see me?

The silhouetted figure stood motionless, appearing to be looking directly out at where Rumison sat, hidden by the fountain. Rumison's fear grew until he had to stifle an impulse to run.

He can't see me, he kept telling himself. Rumison had good eyes and he had barely been able to see the knoll from the house at night, much less anyone hidden there. Isaiah would have to have X-ray vision to see him there. This is stupid! Rumison added to himself.

As though that thought had broken a spell, the figure on the porch stepped down and began walking off in the direction of the workers' yard. Leaving the area illuminated by the light on the porch, whoever it was switched on a flashlight. Rumison breathed a sigh of relief as the light bobbed off down the road.

Rumison sat back up on the fountain. Just jumpy, he thought. It could have been anybody. A servant, going home for the night.

The idea was so reasonable, Rumison let it comfort him. *One more night,* he thought. *Just one more night.* All of a sudden he felt himself growing very sleepy.

"Misser Lumison?"

Rumison almost fell into the pool.

"Wha . . . ?"

"Prease excuse," came a soft, apologetic voice. "I not mean to flighten you."

Trying to slow his racing heart, and straining his eyes, Rumison could just make out the small, slender shape of an old man who had apparently appeared out of nowhere and was standing patiently at the base of the knoll.

"Who are you? What do you want?"

The man took several steps up the knoll until Rumison could see him better—an ancient and exceedingly frail-looking Oriental dressed in a white housecoat and dark pants. He paused; the effort of climbing seemed to have winded him.

"I am Sun. I wish to talk to you, Misser Lumison."

His accent was so heavy, the expression on his face so humble, Rumison almost laughed from relief. The old man fit the stereotyped faithful Chinese servant so closely he seemed a caricature. He even had a thin white goatee that trembled, as though he were on the verge of fleeing. Only his eyes looked real. In the starlight they were bright and alive.

"What are you doing here?" Rumison asked, looking around in the darkness to see if there might be someone else behind the old man.

"No wolly," came the reply. "Only me here."

"Yeah. How did you know I was here? What are you doing here?"

"I sit?"

Somehow the old man had maneuvered himself quite close to Rumison. With a fine-boned hand he was pointing to a space next to Rumison on the ledge of the pool. For a moment Rumison was confused. He was supposed to be on watch. Before he could decide what to do, the old man smiled, as though Rumison had offered him a seat, and sat down.

"Velly good place. Velly good. Can see much from here."

Rumison realized he had been holding the rifle tightly, and he lowered it.

"You're the cook," he said, suddenly remembering the dinner conversation. Suddenly things made sense. O'Brien had said their cook's mind sometimes wandered.

"Oh, yes," said the old man, his head bobbing up and down. "For many years."

"You said you wanted to talk to me?"

The old man ignored Rumison's question. For the first time Sun seemed to notice the rifle. A wide smile covered his face, the smile of a child who had just discovered a new toy. "Oh!" he cried. "Can I see? Prease?"

Rumison pulled the rifle away, suddenly suspicious. "No!" he snapped. "Maybe you'd better go."

The cook's face fell. He looked heartbroken, and large tears appeared in his eyes. "I'm solly," he said apologetically. "I not mean to flighten you. I just want to see."

He looked so forlorn and pathetic, Rumison felt an immediate remorse. Ah, hell, he thought. He's just a harmless old man. Probably a little senile.

Aloud he said, "I'm sorry. I didn't mean to get angry. It's just that this is a dangerous weapon. You might hurt yourself."

"I just want to see," the old man cried.

"It's too dangerous."

"I'm solly. Forgive me. When I was young . . . I remember my own gun."

Rumison weakened. He's so frail, he thought. What harm could he do?

Rumison removed the clip from the rifle and handed it butt first to the old man. "Hell, go ahead and look at it. But just for a minute."

It wasn't until afterward that he realized how foolish the act had been. But at the time it seemed almost natural.

Eagerly the old man took the rifle. He peered at it closely in the dark, holding it clumsily by its plastic stock. His face was so comically inquisitive Rumison had to laugh.

"You kill with this?" the cook asked, his round eyes gazing at Rumison with respect.

The question made Rumison uncomfortable. "Uh . . . no," he answered carefully. "But it can kill someone. You'd better give it back."

The old man nodded, satisfied. But as he lifted the rifle, apparently by accident it slipped out of his fingers and fell with a splash into the stagnant pool. Rumison watched horrified as it sank out of sight.

"Damn!" he cried, frantically reaching after it. But the pool was deeper than he had thought, and all he did was get his shirt wet.

"Now look what you've done!"

"You want the gun?" Sun asked.

"Of course I do, damn it! What do you think?"

"I get then."

Reaching into the fountain, the old man's slender hand disappeared for a moment. When it reappeared it was holding the rifle. He handed it to Rumison.

It wasn't even damp. There was no moisture at all on the rifle. Rumison felt an overwhelming sense of dislocation, as if his mind weren't working properly. A chill ran up his spine.

"I never dlop in," explained the old man happily. "Only make you t'ink so."

Rumison refused to accept the explanation. He had seen

the rifle fall into the water. He had heard the splash as it hit.

Or had he? What other explanation was there?

"How—?" he began, but Sun interrupted.

"No wolly, Misser Lumison. Only small tlick to make you understand t'ings not always what they appear."

"But how—?"

"Save questions for more important t'ings, Misser Lumison. I have come to speak with you 'bout Missy O'Blien."

Rumison was still refusing to accept the impossible. "Missy who?" he asked, examining the rifle closely, as if it might tell him what had happened.

"Missy O'Blien. Velly fine girl."

"Who . . . ?" began Rumison, but then it came to him what Sun was trying to say. "Whitney!"

Sun nodded vigorously and Rumison abruptly forgot about the rifle. "What about her?"

"Have patience, please," said Sun, raising his hand. "Perhaps you should first put burits back in gun."

"Burits?"

Rumison started guiltily. Of course, bullets. The old man was maddening. "What about Whitney?" he asked as he fitted the clip back into the rifle. "Did she send you out here?"

"Many years ago Missy O'Blien small girl," said Sun. "Her mother and Misser O'Blien all happy. Even Hermia . . ."

"Hermia?" Rumison asked.

"Yes. Yes. Hermia. Now Missus O'Blien."

"You mean Hermilia?"

The old man nodded. "Hermia. She good flend to missy. Hermia's mother velly wise person. Velly wise. She told missy many seclets, many t'ings. Then Isaiah come back." Sun paused and frowned. His eyes seemed to lose some of their brightness.

"Go on," urged Rumison.

"He had been gone many years," Sun finally continued. ". . . Then come back. T'ings change. Hermia's mother glow sick and die. Isaiah bad man . . ."

"Just finish!" said Rumison.

Sun nodded, still frowning. "Isaiah teach Hermia many evil t'ings. Teach her how to make crowds and rain—"

"Crowds and rain?"

"Crowds . . . in the sky . . . white . . ."

"Clouds?"

Sun nodded. "Yes. Crowds and rain . . . you know. Sex."

Rumison was growing angry. He was being put on again.

"What do clouds and rain have to do with sex?" he asked, irritated.

"Same t'ing," said Sun quickly. "Same t'ing. Isaiah take his daughter . . . teach her these t'ings. Use her. Hermia enjoy it velly much. Even then, she was beautiful. Her blests lound, like merons. Like so . . ." Sun made circular motions in the air with his hands, then continued. "Hermia learn much. No one knows this. Only I."

Despite himself, Rumison found he was drawn into the old cook's story. "How did you find out all this?"

Sun shrugged but didn't answer. "One day Misser O'Blien come home, find Hermia in his bed," he continued. "Hermia seduce him. Then Hermia use him. Missy know, but say nothing. This go on many months. Then Missus O'Blien find out. Take Missy and leave. Later Missus O'Blien kill self."

"Jeezus!" said Rumison.

"Velly bad," agreed Sun sadly.

"If it's true."

"It is true, Misser Lumison."

For some reason, Rumison didn't doubt the old man. His story explained too many things.

"Why did Whitney come back?" he asked.

"She come back because she roves so much."

Rumison shook his head. He was missing something. "Roves?"

"Missy roves when she was a small girl. Roves her mother, roves her father, she even roved Hermia."

"You mean loves?"

"Yes, yes. Roves. She come back because she cannot forget this rove."

"But she's not stupid," said Rumison. "She must have known how it would be. Her father certainly doesn't care much for her anymore. She must have had some other reason."

Sun shook his head emphatically. "No, Misser Lumison. You wrong. Misser O'Blien rove Missy O'Blien velly much. That's why he dlink so much. But Hermia in control. Missy know this. She understand. . . ." Sun stopped. He regarded Rumison with round, quizzical eyes. "But her father was not the leason she come back," he said abruptly. Rumison waited for him to continue, but Sun remained silent.

For some reason Rumison found himself reluctant to repeat his question. But when silence greeted his silence he finally did so: "Why did she come back?"

Sun shifted himself to a more comfortable position on the rock edge of the pool before he answered. "When Missy small girl," he said, folding his arms and staring out at the bright moon rising over the jungle, "she berieve in many t'ings; in rove and plinces and magic. She wish to melly a handsome plince . . . like the felly stories. So she went to Hermia's mother to make her wish. Hermia's mother told her her plince would come after a rong time. But she must berieve. This is why she come back."

Rumison laughed. The old man's mind had wandered. "So you're trying to tell me that girl in there, Whitney O'Brien, came back to this place—after being gone how many years, ten or more?—because some old woman told her she was going to marry a prince here?"

Sun had missed, or chosen to ignore, the sarcasm in Rumison's tone. "Yes, yes," he said. "Hermia's mother velly good obeah woman. See much. You understand now."

"Look," said Rumison. "Admittedly I don't know her that well, but from what I can see, Whitney doesn't look crazy. She doesn't look like the sort who'd throw her life away on a kid's fantasy. She must know things like that don't happen in reality."

The old man's mouth drew tight. "Perhaps rike guns that fall in water?" he asked coldly.

"I don't see what a cheap trick—"

Abruptly Sun stood up. He bowed and began backing away from Rumison. "I solly," he said. "My mistake. I solly. I t'ink maybe you see."

"I didn't mean to get you angry . . ." Rumison said. Sun raised his head and straightened his shoulders. The gesture made him seem inches taller and a decade younger.

"We have a saying in my homeland," he said softly. "A wise man never settles for the appearance of reality, always seeking to go beyond, while a fool's fear of what lies beyond is what keeps him from being wise. Good evening, Mr. Rumison."

Sun left the knoll and disappeared into the night. It was several full minutes before Rumison realized with a shock what he had just heard. The old cook's parting words had been spoken in a clipped and very precise Oxford English.

Chapter Seventeen

When his watch indicated midnight, Rumison, still disturbed and bemused by Sun's visit, went back into the house to wake Rosso. Rumison stumbled a bit in the darkened hall but finally found Rosso's bedroom.

"Any trouble?" Rosso asked.

"Trouble?" Rumison answered. "No. Not really."

Rosso took the rifle and started to leave. "Wait," said Rumison. "Have you met the O'Briens' cook? An old guy . . . a Chinese named Sun?"

"Seen him around. Little old man, always smiling. Looks senile. Why?"

"No reason. He was out walking around tonight."

"And?"

"Uh . . . nothing. Just curious."

Rumison returned to his room and fell asleep instantly.

It seemed that he had just put his head on the down pillow when he was awakened by someone knocking on his door. He opened his eyes to sunlight dancing in through bamboo blinds. Black entered.

"Get up, Rumison. I've let you sleep longer than I should have. The prop is here. O'Brien is waiting to take us to the field.

There was an uncharacteristic impatience in Black. Rumison dressed quickly and followed the older man outside. O'Brien already was waiting in the driver's seat of a battered, sand-colored Land Rover. Next to him sat a large, muscular black man with pearly white teeth and a narrow, guileless grin on a weathered face. The new propeller for the Piper Cub lay in the rear of the Land Rover along with two medium-size canvas bags.

Rosso, carrying one of the rifles, came running out of the house. He climbed into the back of the jeep with Black and Rumison, and O'Brien started off. Rosso looked strained and anxious, and Rumison wondered at his own lack of emotion. He felt only a vague sense of uneasiness, and regret that he hadn't said goodbye to Whitney. After Sun had left him at the fountain he had spent the remainder of his watch thinking about her, wondering if the old man's story was true. Looking back at the house as they drove off, he half hoped he might catch one last glimpse of her, but he saw no one.

O'Brien, even after the night's rest and dressed in clean khaki, looked haggard and preoccupied. "This here's Pliny," he said, introducing the black with a jerk of his head. "He brought the prop. Also a little news that might interest you."

"Oh?" Black asked.

The black smiled. "Mebbee I could've collected the reward myself," he said.

"Reward?"

"Pliny says the new government has offered a ten-thousand-dollar reward for you three," said O'Brien, his voice even.

"That's a bundle," said Pliny.

"More'n most could resist," said O'Brien. "Most around here would murder their lovin' mother-in-laws for it."

"Mothers even," said Pliny, grinning.

O'Brien drove them through the main compound, where men—mostly blacks, with an occasional Oriental face among them—already were at work milling huge red mahogany logs that had been brought into the yard by tractors. Most of the men were dressed only in khaki work pants, the legs of the pants rolled up below the knee. Sweat dripped from ebony skin as they worked. Red mahogany dust covered the men and the ground and filled the air behind the truck as it drove past.

The plantation had fewer outbuildings than had Santa Concepción, but the ones it did have were newer, roofed with galvanized metal, designed specifically for processing large amounts of lumber.

The narrow but well-graded road took them through a section of uncut jungle before opening up on an empty field Rumison took to be the airstrip. A wooden hangar sat at one end of the field near the road. Next to the hangar an orange wind sock hung forlornly in the still, hot morning air.

O'Brien parked the Land Rover in front of the hangar and with Pliny's help opened the two barnlike doors. Inside, Rumison could see an ancient dull red Piper Cub JR-3. It was a two-seater with cloth-covered fuselage and wings. White lettering on one door read: "O'Brien Lumber Company, Nicaragua."

Working together, the five men trundled the little plane out onto the field.

"Doesn't look like much," said O'Brien gruffly, "but it flies well enough. If you don't mind taking all day to get where you're going."

"Is it fueled?" Rumison asked.

"I checked it all out yesterday," said Black. "All we have to do is get the prop on."

Pliny brought tools from the hangar and began undoing bolts from the old propeller, which Rumison could see had a long crack down one wooden blade. Within fifteen minutes the prop had been replaced. Black threw two canvas bags into the small cockpit and climbed in; Rumison and Rosso waited outside. Black pulled out the throttle, adjusted the magneto and waved out the window to Pliny, who was standing with his hands on the new propeller.

"Contact!"

Pliny yanked down with muscular arms, but nothing happened. Black scowled and they tried it again. Still there were no results. They tried it again and still nothing. Black got out of the plane and lifted the cowling on the engine.

"O'Brien!" he yelled. "Come here!"

Oh, Christ! thought Rumison. Next to him, Rosso's face looked pale.

"What's wrong?" Rosso asked.

"Look," said Black, stepping back from the engine. Inside the cowling both the fuel and oil lines had been smashed flat.

"It must have been done last night," said Black.

"It looks worse than it is," said O'Brien, observing the engine with an almost cursory glance. "Nothing Pliny can't fix in a few minutes."

"Tell him to fix it, then!" said Black, his patience gone.

O'Brien shrugged. "I'll have to go back to the house for some new tubing. We keep spare parts in the storage room off the kitchen.

Black reached back in the cockpit and brought out his rifle. "Rumison and I will go with you," he said to O'Brien. "Rosso will stay here with Pliny."

"As you like," said O'Brien.

"Keep an eye open, Rosso," said Black. "I don't want any more . . . accidents."

Rosso nodded and stepped back with his own rifle. Pliny accepted the situation with a sardonic shrug and sat down to wait in the shade of a wing. Rumison and Black got in the Land Rover, and O'Brien started off.

On the drive back to the house Rumison could feel the tension between Black and O'Brien. O'Brien drove without speaking, staring woodenly ahead. Coming back through the mill area, men stopped in their work and watched them pass, intuitively sensing something wrong. When the Land Rover reached the house, Black got out first.

"Watch the jeep, Rumison," he said, handing Rumison the rifle and taking out his pistol. "Don't let anyone get close."

"I won't."

"Lead the way," Black said curtly to O'Brien.

Rumison waited nervously. The moments passed. He heard someone coming and the back door to the house opened. He felt a wave of relief, along with some other feeling he couldn't analyze, when he saw it was Whitney.

"I thought you had gone," she said quietly, her face unreadable.

Rumison lowered the rifle, embarrassed. Despite everything, he was glad he had gotten a chance to see her before they had left. She was dressed in jeans and a man's shirt and her blond hair was tied back in a ponytail.

"Is something wrong?" she asked.

Rumison shifted his feet. "Somebody banged up the fuel

line on the Piper," he said. "Mr. Black and your father are inside getting some parts."

Whitney looked troubled. "It must have been Isaiah," she said. "He has the keys to everything."

Rumison remembered the night before, his certainty that the man who had appeared on the porch was Isaiah. Perhaps he had been right.

"Why does he hate us so much?" he asked.

Whitney lowered her eyes. "He doesn't hate all of you. It's mostly you. . . ." She stopped. "I mean he's wary of Mr. Black. Mr. Black is . . . a . . . well . . . he's a very strong man, and I'm sure Isaiah is threatened by him."

Completely baffled, Rumison asked, "Why does he hate me?"

Whitney bit her lower lip and didn't answer.

"I had a talk with your cook last night," said Rumison. "He said some things about Isaiah, about Hermilia and your father. . . ."

Whitney's green eyes flashed angrily. "Sun is a very wise man . . . some of the time," she said coldly. "But sometimes he's more like a little boy. You never can tell when he's really serious."

"Was he serious about the reason you and your mother left here?"

Again Whitney bit her lip and didn't answer.

"Why did you come back?" Rumison asked gently.

Whitney looked up and there was anguish in her look. But before she could answer there was a muffled shout from inside the house.

"Stay here!" cried Rumison.

The house seemed empty when Rumison entered. As he ran through the rooms he felt with a despairing certainty that something had gone wrong. Entering the kitchen, he saw a row of eggs laid out on the cutting board next to a mound of chopped onions and grated cheese. Someone had recently been fixing breakfast omelettes. Where was Sun? Where was everybody else?

He saw a partially opened door at the rear of the kitchen and he ran toward it. He heard a noise behind him.

Even as he jerked around, Rumison's last vestige of hope disappeared. Behind him, stepping out of a food storage alcove in the kitchen, stood Sean O'Brien. He held a revolver in his right hand. His florid face was grim and tired-looking.

"I don't want to shoot you, Rumison."

Slowly Rumison laid the rifle on the red tile floor. "Where's Mr. Black?" he asked.

"Keep going through that door. He's in there."

Rumison did as he was told, feeling sick. How could he have been so stupid?

The door led to a large, windowless storage room. Black was standing in one corner, near the door, in front of shelves of canned goods. Hermilia, dressed in tight, form-fitting white pants and a black blouse, stood across from Black, holding another pistol. Isaiah, his huge, malign face set in a remorseless grin, stood next to her.

"We gets him," chortled the black man obscenely, regarding Rumison with dark, hollow eyes. "We gets the pouele fucker good. It's time we sent the mon to Asmodeal. It would be well—"

"No!" O'Brien interrupted sharply, his voice trembling either with anger or fright, Rumison couldn't say which. "There'll be no murder done in my house."

"Isaiah didn't really mean it, Sean," Hermilia soothed, still smiling her strange, mocking smile without taking her eyes off either Black or Rumison.

"After all, the reward is for them alive."

"So that's it," said Black scornfully. "You're selling us out, O'Brien. A bird in the hand, huh? You didn't believe I'd pay."

O'Brien's face contorted. "I'd never sell a man for money, Black. Never."

"For something else then," said Black, nodding at Hermilia.

"And don't you think I'm worth it, Mr. Goombee?" cooed Hermilia.

"I've fucked better," said Black.

"You swine!" growled O'Brien, shoving Rumison aside as he tried to get at Black.

"Stop, Sean! Now!"

O'Brien's hand was white where it gripped the gun.

"He's jus' baitin' you, Sean," said Hermilia. "Don't be more of a fool."

Black was looking steadily at the Irishman's reddening face. "She does have you," he said, "doesn't she?"

"Black, I'm warnin' you . . . !"

"Sean!"

It was a command. O'Brien, every muscle in his body drawn in anger, gave in. His head sagged and the tension left his massive shoulders. Black smiled, but O'Brien refused to meet his eyes.

Isaiah had all but ignored the exchange. The black man's attention was fixed on Rumison. He reminded Rumison of some ancient predatory reptile guarding a chicken egg. Rumison shuddered. Abruptly Isaiah leaned forward and spat. The dark brown spittle landed on Rumison's shirt and dripped downward.

"You ain't no saint, mon. Ain't no saint and ain't no hero. A coward you are, jus' a dumb-ass pouele mo'fucker so scared he want to shit."

Rumison *was* frightened. He was so frightened his legs were shaking. The whole thing was beyond reason.

"Why?" he cried. "What's this all about?"

There was anguish in his question, and O'Brien shook his head sadly. "You really don't know, do you, Rumison."

Hermilia's eyes were full of contempt as she regarded Rumison. "Isaiah's right," she said scornfully. "Jus' look at him. He's weak. Weak and scared. Who'd of thought Whitney . . . ?" She stopped. "Can't blame us, though," she added as an afterthought, almost defensively. "It's Momma's fault."

"Personally I've nothing against you, Rumison," said O'Brien, "but the truth is, given my situation and the political winds in this country, I would have been a fool to have helped you. I couldn't hide something like that. It would have been extremely foolish."

"What does Rumison have to do with it?" Black asked.

O'Brien still wouldn't meet Black's eyes. He looked questioningly toward Hermilia. Hermilia shrugged her indifference.

"What have I got to do with it?" cried Rumison.

"Ten years ago," said O'Brien slowly, as though the words were painful to him, "my daughter made the mistake of listening to an old woman. . . ."

The room began to turn and Rumison felt he was losing

touch with reality. He heard a voice whispering in his ear, the old cook saying, "Appearances, appearances."

"She was a child," O'Brien was saying. "Impressionable. Her mother . . ." He stopped, faltering over the word, and glanced at his wife, whose mocking smile had suddenly left her face.

"Get to de point," she snapped. "Tell him what my Momma said!"

O'Brien looked pained, then turned back toward Rumison. "It was Hermilia's mother, you see," he said. "The old woman. Shortly before she died she told my daughter's fortune. Used the . . . uh . . . tarot. You know? Fortune-telling cards?"

Rumison nodded dumbly.

"Took two hours," continued O'Brien. "I don't know exactly what she said, but Whit took it to heart."

Rumison didn't hear O'Brien finish. For some seconds he was totally numb, unware of his surroundings.

From somewhere came Hermilia's soft, mocking voice.

" 'Three men come ridin', from de north track,
One on de fourth plane, I see him as black . . .
Another is named Red, who too soon will be dead . . .
De last be your prince, held in restraint,
He'll be named with the names of three Holy Saints.' "

Rumison was shaking his head. "It's crazy," he said. "It's all crazy."

"There's more," said Hermilia, the mockery now gone from her voice. "Momma also said, *'Black wins over the dark, whose queen is overthrown. Your prince will return to claim the crown.' "*

Rumison could stand no more. "It's insane! How can anyone believe such crap?"

"Maybe it's not insane," Black suggested evenly. "You have to admit it's a bit much for coincidence. Three men riding down the north road not long after Whitney comes back after being gone ten years. Me and Rosso. Means red or rouge, doesn't it?"

"But I'm not named after three saints," said Rumison, struggling to control himself.

"Isn't your first name Michael?"

"And my second is Paul. But that's it, unless someone has heard of a Saint Rumison somewhere."

A rather enigmatic smile appeared on Black's lips, but he remained quiet.

O'Brien sighed heavily and shifted the revolver uneasily in his hand. "You're hardly my idea of a prince. But that's not important. Whit believes in all this. So does Isaiah. He has great faith in his dead wife's powers. That's why—"

O'Brien didn't finish. He had stopped in midsentence and was staring at the doorway, where his daughter stood mutely.

"Whit—"

Whitney's voice was barely audible. "You promised."

Instinctively, O'Brien reached out, but Whitney shrank away. "Whit . . . please."

"Has she stolen everything from you?" Whitney asked faintly. "Even your word?"

"Whit, it's for our own good. What if they found out I'd helped—"

"Liar!"

The word burst out of his daughter and O'Brien seemed to shrink at her accusation. He looked around, awkward and helpless.

For Rumison, everything that followed happened too fast to remember distinctly. Isaiah screamed something just as Black grabbed Hermilia's arm and twisted the gun from her grip. O'Brien tried to turn but Black struck him in the neck, knocking him back into the shelves, his gun falling at Rumison's feet.

"The gun, Rumison!" cried Black as he dove across the floor trying to get to Hermilia before she recovered hers.

Rumison was slow to react. He bent down for O'Brien's revolver just as Black reached Hermilia. Hermilia struggled, biting Black's arm, but Black pulled away and then hit her with such force that her head snapped back in a loud crack and she was thrown across the room.

"NO!" bellowed O'Brien.

O'Brien lunged, striking Black across the back of the head with a two-pound can of peaches he had scooped up from the floor. Black sank to his knees and O'Brien raised the can to hit him again.

"Please, no!" Whitney screamed.

Rumison couldn't remember pulling the trigger. He was only marginally aware that he had picked up the gun. He fired and the bullet struck O'Brien in the chest, spinning the man sideways.

Strangely, after his initial cry of warning, Isaiah did nothing. He stood like a man in shock, his eyes terror-filled as he looked on. His body had begun jerking spasmodically, like a marionette whose strings had become tangled. His mouth was open but no sound came out, only flecks of spittle.

Black struggled to his feet. "Come on, Rumison!" he cried. "They sent a man to Bluefields to get Preitas. We've got to get out of here!"

Black shoved the jerking Isaiah out of the way and grabbed a length of metal fuel line from a shelf. "Rumison!"

But Rumison seemed not to hear anything. He stood rooted, his total attention on Whitney, who was kneeling down beside her father, dead or unconscious, on the floor.

Black looked at Whitney, then back at Isaiah still standing across the room. He raised Hermilia's pistol and aimed.

Isaiah cried out once, trying to cover his face with his hands. Black shot him in the head. Isaiah jerked one more time and fell in a heap next to his daughter.

Whitney stared up at Rumison. "It . . . it wasn't supposed to be like this," she said, her voice small.

Rumison couldn't answer. Black was tugging at his arm. He turned and ran.

Chapter Eighteen

RUMISON saw Sun hurrying into the house as he followed Black to the Land Rover. "Wait! Mr. Lumison, wait!" cried the cook. But Rumison kept running, afraid to stop, panicked at the thought that Black might leave him behind.

There was no one around when they jumped into the Land Rover. Black drove. The vehicle's knobby off-road tires churned up clouds of red sawdust as they sped through the mill yard. Most of the workers had stopped even pretending to work, looking at one another questioningly when they saw who was in the speeding truck.

"They'll be a problem if we don't get that plane in the air soon," Black murmured.

Rumison didn't answer. He was thinking of Whitney, her face as it had looked up at him at the end. It had been the face of a . . . a betrayed child.

She had no right!

A grown woman, believing in fairy tales. It was madness! Reality was her betrayer, not him, not her "prince." Reality, with its wars and revolutions, its Blacks and Preitases, Hermilias and Isaiahs. It wasn't his fault!

Black, with a surprising sensitivity, guessed his thoughts. "She'll get over it," he said gently. "She's a strong lady, that one."

Even then Rumison wondered at the respect in the older man's tone.

They came out onto the field and saw that Rosso was still alone with Pliny by the plane. Black skidded the truck to a halt and jumped out.

"I already took off the old line," said Rosso. "I think that's all that was wrong."

Pliny was frowning. "Where's Mista O'Brien?"

"Had business," said Black, measuring a section of new tubing against the smashed section Rosso handed him.

Pliny nodded slowly. "Mebbee I bes' go back and see if I can help."

"Suit yourself," said Black. "You'll have to walk, though. We may need the jeep."

Pliny stared at Black for a moment, then turned and walked off. Black began cutting the fuel line with a hacksaw from the hangar tool kit, but he kept an eye on Pliny until he was gone from the field.

"What happened?" Rosso asked.

"O'Brien tried a double cross," said Black. "You'd better take the jeep over and watch the road until I get this line hooked up. We may be getting unwanted company."

Rosso pursed his lips and looked at Rumison.

"I need Rumison with me," said Black.

Rosso shrugged and got into the Land Rover. Off in the north came a sound, the familiar staccato vibrations of a large helicopter approaching. Rumison's heart sank. Black stopped what he was doing and looked up at the sky.

"There it is," he said, pointing to a dark speck on the horizon.

Rosso was thoughtful as he looked out the window of the Land Rover.

"We've got to hurry!" cried Rumison.

"That thing is faster than this Piper," mused Black. "We'd be sitting ducks in the air."

"We've got to do something!"

The helicopter grew larger.

"They might not see us," said Black. "It looks like they're heading toward the house."

"If I could shoot up their engine a little," said Rosso, "they wouldn't be able to follow. "Do it before they know what's happening."

"Rosso, no!" cried Rumison.

"What else can we do?"

"You'd better hurry," said Black.

"Rosso, wait!" cried Rumison as Rosso started up the

Land Rover. Something terrible was about to happen. He could feel it, but what could he do?

"Stay here with me, Rumison!" ordered Black. "I need you here."

"I'll be all right, Mike," said Rosso.

Rumison watched helplessly as Rosso drove off. The helicopter had nearly reached the plantation and was beginning a slow descent. It was an H-3, the same type they had seen on the river, perhaps the same one.

"Give me a hand here," said Black.

It took them only a few minutes to fit the new lines and tighten them into place. Nodding in satisfaction, Black closed the cowling. "Grab the prop, Rumison. Pull down when I yell 'Contact!' "

"What about Rosso?" asked Rumison anxiously.

"I just want to get the engine going," snapped Black impatiently, getting into the cockpit. "Now grab the prop."

Rumison did as he was told. Black adjusted the controls, flipped the magneto switch on, and yelled, "Contact!" Rumison pulled down on the prop, but nothing happened. In the distance, in the direction of the house, he heard the sudden fire of an automatic rifle.

"Listen up, Rumison! I said 'Contact!' "

Rumison brought his mind away from the rifle fire and pulled down again, but still there was no response from the engine.

"Again!" yelled Black.

"It isn't working!"

"I didn't prime it. It'll work. Try again!"

Rumison pulled down four more times, each throw ending in more exhaustion and despair than the one before. The fifth time, his arm aching and his reserves of strength almost gone, the engine caught, fired a few times and then died. The sound of an approaching vehicle drew his attention back to the road, and Black had to yell at him again.

"One more time, Rumison! Now!"

Summoning up his will, Rumison did as he was told. The engine caught, sputtered for a moment, and then, as Black readjusted the throttle, it finally roared to healthy life.

"Get in!"

"Rosso's coming!"

But Rosso for some reason had stopped the Land Rover on the road at the edge of the field and had gotten out.

"Get in, Rumison!" yelled Black.

Rumison hesitated. Across the field Rosso was running toward them. He had left the rifle in the jeep and he was empty-handed.

Black was revving the little engine. A truck had appeared behind the Land Rover and the reason for Rosso's action became evident. Uniformed men scrambled out, some running after Rosso while the others worked to push the Land Rover from where it blocked the road.

Rumison pulled himself into the cockpit with Black. "He'll make it!" he whispered fiercely.

A hundred yards back across the field, a lone soldier dropped to one knee for a better aim and fired. Rosso, who was almost at the plane, staggered.

"No!" cried Rumison.

Blood was streaming from Rosso's shoulder, but he kept running. He reached for the strut just as the Piper started to taxi. Rumison grabbed Rosso's shirt, trying to drag him inside.

"Shit!" said Rosso, struggling to keep up with the plane's increasing speed.

The soldier fired again. Rosso went limp and Rumison could no longer hold him. Rosso's head looked oddly misshapen and there was blood on Rumison's arms.

"Rosso!"

More rifle fire splintered through the Piper's Plexiglas side panel. Rosso's body was torn from Rumison's grip. Black had to grab Rumison's arm to keep him inside the plane.

"He's dead, Rumison. Couldn't you see that? Half his head was gone."

The small airplane bounced crazily down the dirt field. More bullets ripped through the fabric of the fuselage.

They lifted slowly, clearing the treetops at the end of the primitive runway by less than three feet.

Rumison was unaware of the narrowness of their margin of escape. He was cramped into a fetal position, his knees pressed tightly into his chest, his hands clenched into fists, thinking only of Rosso.

Not Rosso! How could it be? His best friend, the only one

he had left. How could Rosso die? Rosso's confident, level-headed approach to life, his steadiness, his dependability were fixed points of reference in Rumison's life.

Rosso had saved his life. Twice! How could Rosso be gone?

They climbed higher and turned away from the field. Black exhaled and relaxed back on the hard bench seat. "We're up," he said simply. "Let's hope Rosso disabled that chopper good enough."

Rumison stiffened. Black put a rough hand on Rumison's shoulder and shook it.

"Snap out of it. We've still got a ways to go."

"To what?" whispered Rumison through clenched teeth. "Where are we going?"

"We're going home," said Black. "Or at least to Costa Rica and then home—that is, if this thing will get us there."

"There's nothing there," said Rumison.

"Nothing?" asked Black. "You have a house there. Friends. A life."

Rumison raised his head and looked at Black. "There is nothing there," he said. *"Nothing!"* Lashing out in despair, Rumison smashed his fist into the bullet-cracked windshield with such force it left a snowflake pattern of fractures in the Plexiglas. Abruptly the tension left him as he accepted what he saw was the ultimate terrifying truth: None of it mattered.

"You're still alive!" Black insisted, almost angrily. "That's enough meaning."

"No!" cried Rumison.

"All there ever is is yourself," Black replied. "The rest is bullshit. It's all there ever was and ever will be. It's all the meaning you need!"

Rumison looked at Black's implacable face. Black was angry, and for the first time Rumison began to understand him. He saw the belief Black had in his own words, and he felt the pain that belief caused Black. Why did Black continue? How could he live with the awful truth that what he did was totally devoid of meaning?

Was this courage? To continue on, despite the void, the empty hopelessness? Was it that quality that Barney had intuitively seen in Black that had made Barney give up his own life for . . . for what? A black briefcase?

Why did it hurt so much? Why was it so painful when you saw through the lies, the illusions, the patent-medicine remedies, when you discovered that incredible aloneness where only the self existed, empty and afraid of the long, inexplicable night?

Chapter Nineteen

WIND whistled through the broken windshield and torn fabric of the airplane. Below, endless, lay the jungle.

Black had turned inland, away from the coast. For tactical reasons he was flying low, low enough for Rumison to smell the familiar hothouse scents of the jungle and see the monkeys as they lived their mad lives in the trees.

Rumison might have hoped that after living through torture, deaths, and delirium, he would have hardened. He had felt better after the fever. His mind had seemed calmer, the world clearer.

But that clarity had been short-lived. He knew now that any hardening he thought had taken place had simply been another illusion, a trick of a vagarious god, to prepare him for the following blows, which would forever shatter his personal view of reality.

Now alone, even though Black was seated next to him in the small cockpit of the Piper Cub, Rumison knew he would never be free of the pain he felt and had felt for many years, though he had hidden from it. The pain had always been there, from the first day he had begun to believe—like most of the other prisoners in the world he knew—that the universe no longer was his friend. The pain remained, hidden in its secret place, forgotten, buried for years in those meaningless doings that stole the dreams of wonder away from life.

Rumison remembered past loves and youthful dreams. Now they all seemed like so many dried leaves. He thought of Cordobes. Cordobes must have known . . . but he'd written a book anyway. Why? Why had he bothered?

For some reason, it seemed to Rumison as though all of his pain and sorrow were somehow symbolized in the last memory he had of Whitney O'Brien.

She still believed. Incredibly, she still held to the misguided notion that the world was not an alien thing, a malign, uncaring, solid-state, random void to be conquered, destroyed . . . but a reasonable, loving place, and that if only she kept her faith and acted appropriately, it would all work out as it was meant to.

On her face and in her horrified green eyes was written, at that final moment, the agonizing knowledge of how wrong she had been.

This was the pain of it all.

Black had remained quiet during their first hour of flight. When the mental projector in Rumison's brain finally switched off, leaving Rumison empty but calm, Black sensed it.

"I'm sorry about Rosso," he said. "Barney was right back in the jungle. I did like him."

Rumison's immediate reaction was cynical, but then he winced. Black wasn't being facetious. He was sorry about Rosso. That's all he was saying.

The controls of the little plane were simple: a joystick, foot rudders, a push-pull-type throttle on the dashboard next to the magneto switch, tachometer and fuel gauge. The fuel gauge consisted of a small orange ball in a glass tube marked Empty at one end and Full at the other. Rumison noted without emotion that the orange ball was very near the Empty mark.

"A bullet must have nicked a line," said Black.

"How far do we have to go?"

Black shrugged. "The Costa Rican border can't be far. Five or ten minutes. But I was hoping to reach San José. There's a lot of jungle between the border and San José. I'm afraid we have another hike ahead . . . that is, if I can find a place to put us down."

Rumison almost laughed. It was getting repetitive. What else could go wrong?

Several more minutes passed and the orange ball settled

to the bottom of the tube. There seemed to be no breaks in the endless green below. Ahead was the dark green-brown line of low mountains Black called the Cordillera de Yolaina. The engine missed and Black pumped the throttle.

"Fasten your seat belt, Rumison. We're going down."

The engine ran for another two minutes before finally quitting entirely. Rumison, nervous but not panicky, thought of the irony of their situation . . . to have parachuted in to rescue air crash survivors, only to end up crashing back into the jungle themselves.

Black was a good pilot. He played with the controls, riding air currents off low ridges as he fought for altitude. Once their wheels touched the treetops, but then the plane caught another updraft and they made it up over another ridge.

"There it is," said Black.

Below, in a wide, shallow valley, Rumison saw what would be their landing strip: a small river, its origins somewhere up in the cordillera, winding its way down through the forest. A tiny, primitive-looking village sat along the northern bank of the river, and a narrow dirt road entered it from the west, also from out of the highlands.

Black banked the plane toward the road, fighting a crosswind rising out of the canyon. Black's movements were sure and calm as he slid the Piper into the wind, wings windward, left stick and right rudder.

The road leveled out before them. Rumison could see Indians with carts and burros watching the plane as it descended. Black dropped the nose and eased back on the stick, flaring to stall their forward speed. The wheels touched hard clay, but the road was heavily rutted. With a lurch the Piper bounced from the road and soared toward the trees. Rumison just had time to cover his head with his arms before they hit. He heard the crashing branches, fabric ripping, the screams of frightened animals, then . . . stillness. They had made it.

"We're down!" he cried in relief. He laughed at the feeling. Was he really glad to be alive, or was it just adrenaline? It didn't seem to matter.

Black was slumped forward, unconscious. "Black?" said Rumison, shaking him lightly. "Black?"

There was no response. Rumison felt Black's carotid pulse. Still strong. There was a bruise on Black's forehead. He had hit himself on the windshield.

Rumison opened a torn door, threw down the two canvas bags Black had brought and then, a bit shakily, climbed down to the ground. He struggled through the broken branches to the other side of the plane and lifted Black down, gently lying him next to the plane's wheel. Rumison looked through the bags, hoping to find some medical supplies, but all he found were several days' supply of food, a change of clothing, some ammunition for the pistol—and the black briefcase.

A sound caught his attention. A small group of Indians, dressed alike in dirty white cotton clothes, were standing just off the road, staring with guarded curiosity at the wrecked plane. Another man, dressed in a brown woolen priest's cassock, moved to the fore of the group.

"My friend needs help," said Rumison. "*Ayuda!* Do you understand?"

After what seemed like an interminable wait, the priest nodded. His face was thin and aged. His long, nervous fingers clutched at a brass crucifix that hung from his neck on a leather cord. "Your friend?" he asked in surprisingly presentable English. "Is he dead?"

"No," answered Rumison. "He hit his head when we crashed. Can we get him somewhere?"

The priest glanced down at Black lying in the tall grass, then quickly looked away as though afraid of what he might see if he looked too closely.

"Is it bad?" he asked apprehensively.

The priest's fear was maddening. "It might be," said Rumison sharply. When the priest still made no move to help, Rumison added, "Look, why don't you get those guys to help me take him someplace?"

The priest wiped his forehead with a cloth he took from one pocket. Rumison wondered how the man could stand the heat in the heavy robe. The priest was a small man, no taller than Rosso had been and much thinner. His features looked European. The numerous lines in his face were all drawn downward, whether by pessimism or simple gravity Rumison didn't know.

"Look," said Rumison, losing patience, "if you can't help . . ."

The priest stepped forward quickly. "Please, *señor.* Do not be angry. I will do what I can, but you see, there are no doctors here, and I am only a poor priest, as you can also see. I was returning to the church with these men when . . ." He waved his arms in the vague direction of the airplane and shrugged helplessly. "Well, *señor,* such things as this do not often occur in Ratanagua."

"Is there somewhere we can take my friend?" asked Rumison.

The priest hesitated. "The church, I suppose. It is poor, but there are some rooms. . . ."

Rumison sighed. "That will be fine. Will those men help carry him?"

The priest nodded. "They are just frightened," he said.

The priest spoke some words in Spanish to the Indians, who stood without moving or giving any sign whatsoever that they had heard. Finally one—the oldest by looks—with flowing white hair and broken teeth, stepped up next to the priest. Soon the man was followed by the others. They took hold of Black's body and lifted him from the ground.

The Indians were all dark-skinned and swarthy, very different from the Mayans and Miskitos to the east. The tallest was not much taller than the priest. Several walked barefoot; others wore leather sandals. Rumison took Black's pistol and stuck it in his own belt. The rifle was still in the plane and Rumison climbed up and retrieved it. He lifted the two canvas bags and started after the Indians. The priest, who had been watching Rumison, peered through the open door of the ruined plane before stumbling along behind.

"It is wise not to leave things of value behind, *señor,*" the priest said after catching up with Rumison. "There are men about who would happily murder you for your shoes. For less than your shoes, in fact. Times are bad. Men grow bad with them. God is not feared so much as he once was."

Rumison shifted one of the bags for a better grip and

nodded politely. "Don't you have any police?" he asked. "Any militia?"

The priest shook his head. "None at all, I'm afraid. We are cut off here completely."

"That's too bad," said Rumison, feeling better.

They followed the road for about half a mile until they reached the small village they had seen from the air. The road was heavily eroded. At places where the jungle grew close it was scarcely more than a path.

The few buildings in the village looked as weathered and corroded as the road. Mud and thatch leaned at dangerous angles, a few of the structures strengthened with jerry-rigged buttresses of logs and bamboo. The place had an air of desolation and rottenness; many of the poorer structures looked abandoned. A handful of half-castes gazed sullenly at the small procession; the few children visible were naked and looked half-starved. They seemed the only humans with any curiosity.

It was an awesomely depressing place. Rumison almost gagged from the pervasive odor of rotten meat, urine and cheap alcohol. Empty bottles littered the mud around the buildings. Rumison saw very few women.

"Qué pasa, Padre?"

The sardonic question had been asked by an enormous fat man who was seated on a wooden bench in front of the only two-story structure in town. The man had a short, scraggly black goatee and wore a dirty, grease-stained Panama hat of indeterminate color. His clothes were as filthy as the hat, a hodgepodge of styles: khaki pants, flowered shirt, a grimy tweed vest that was too small for his huge stomach. He smiled tolerantly when the priest ignored him, and his stained teeth glittered with gold. The priest continued walking, but his pace had quickened.

"That is Juan Tienda," the priest whispered from the side of his mouth as Rumison hurried to keep pace with the little man.

"What's the problem?" Rumison asked.

The priest refused to look in any direction but straight ahead. "He is an evil man, *señor,*" he whispered nervously.

The fat man had lifted himself off his seat with apparent

great effort and followed after them. "Hey, *Yanqui!*" he called. "Wait! I would talk with you!"

"Don't speak with him, *señor,*" the priest whispered urgently. "He is the devil."

Undecided, Rumison hung back. The fat man caught up with him, grabbing his arm in a powerful grip. Rumison winced but the fat man didn't appear to notice until Rumison pulled his arm away. The old priest and the Indians kept walking.

"Wait, *señor,*" wheezed the fat man. "Perhaps I can be of help to you."

He repelled Rumison. His breath was foul, his touch damp and cold. Above his fawning smile, small, piglike eyes glittered. "That old fart of a priest doesn't talk to me," he said and laughed. "He thinks I'm the devil. Isn't that right, son of a mule!" This last was spat at the back of the retreating priest.

"I've got to go," said Rumison, struggling out of the fat man's grip.

"Let the bastard go. I want to talk to you."

Rumison tried to place the man's accent. Not Spanish. Not English. European maybe . . .

"I've got to stay with my friend," said Rumison hastily. "He's been hurt. Maybe later . . ."

"I have a store. Things to sell."

"Maybe later."

The fat man stopped. His expression was veiled as he watched Rumison catch up with the priest.

"As you wish, *señor,*" he called. "You can find me at my store. I also sell information," he added, almost as an afterthought. "To anyone who can pay."

Rumison walked on. The little priest seemed relieved. Rumison didn't blame him. He was relieved himself.

"You were wise not to talk with him, *señor.*"

Rumison looked at the Indians walking stoically and silently along under the burden of Black's unconscious body. He wondered if they too were frightened by Juan Tienda, but their impassive faces gave away nothing.

Soon they reached the church, which was built on a low hill overlooking the river that ran next to the village. The church was old, modeled on Spanish missionary churches of the sixteenth and seventeenth centuries—a frescoed façade between two bell towers and a low wing off to the right as they faced it. It was made of adobe bricks and logs and the thick walls had once, long before, been stuccoed and whitewashed. But the wash had worn off and the gray-brown stucco was chipped and broken. One iron bell hung dolefully in the tower on the right. The tower on the left was empty.

They entered the wing of the building through a low, narrow door that led down to an earthen-floored hallway. The few rooms Rumison saw off the hall were empty of any but the simplest of furnishings. The priest pushed back a dirty brown blanket that served as a door to one of the rooms, and the Indians carried Black inside and laid him down on a corn-husk mattress atop a rough board bed. On one wall above the bed a large, grotesquely realistic carving of the Crucifixion hung, complete with tiny nails pounded through the blood-streaked, finely detailed hands and feet of an effeminate Jesus. A small square of window looked out through the thick adobe walls on the river. The window was covered with a thin piece of dusty cheesecloth that let in a dull, yellowish light.

"It is a poor church, San Término del Río," sighed the priest apologetically as he ineffectually dusted the seat of a wooden chair, the only other piece of furniture in the room, with his handkerchief.

"I am sorry I cannot offer you better. *Gracias, mis niños.*" This last was to the Indians, who, still silent, left the room.

Rumison set the rifle and the bags on the floor and pushed the cheesecloth away from the open window, hoping to let in some fresh air. When he turned back to the bed, Black had opened his eyes.

"Well," Black asked, "where are we?"

"An old church near where we crashed," said Rumison, feeling an inexplicable relief. "This is the *padre.*"

The priest gave a short, nervous bow. "I am Father Pablo del Iglés, *señor.* I am glad to see that you are better."

"How are you?" Rumison asked.

Black touched his bruised forehead and winced. "I've made better landings," he said. "After O'Brien bent that can on my head it must have softened it up. How's the plane?"

"One wing ripped off. Other than that"—Rumison shrugged—"not too bad shape."

"I guess we should thank you for helping, *Padre,*" Black said.

"We do what we can, *señor.*"

"What is this town's name?"

"The town is named Ratanagua, *señor.*"

"Costa Rica or Nicaragua?"

"Nicaragua, *señor.* But the border is not far.

"How far?"

"In kilometers, not far. But the jungle is thick and the Indians are returning to the old ways. . . ."

"How far in kilometers?" Black asked patiently.

The priest considered. "Five, perhaps six, señor."

"That means the San Juan River is nearby?"

"Oh, *sí.* The stream that is just outside meets it not far from here. Ratanagua used to be where passengers from the San Juan riverboats met with the overland caravans going to the West, before the Panama Canal was built. But now . . ." The little priest shrugged dejectedly. "Now there are no more visitors. You are the first in some time."

"The canal was built a long time ago," said Black.

"Sí. Before even I was born."

"Why do you stay, then?"

The question seemed to startle the priest. "But where would I go? I travel across the mountains to Santa Helena once every three months. I hear news there. It is the same the world over. Godless times are upon us. There is nowhere to go, nowhere to hide."

The little priest shifted back and forth on his feet uneasily. *"Señores,* if you will forgive me, I have many things to attend to. . . ."

"Perhaps you could bring me some water before you go," suggested Black.

"I'll do what I can," said the priest.

"Jeezus!" said Black after Pablo del Iglés had left. "Where did you find him?"

"He found us," said Rumison. "He was near where we came down. Had some Indians carry you here."

"Any militia around? Guerrillas? Anyone who might wonder what we're doing here in a bullet-riddled Piper Cub?"

Rumison shook his head. "I didn't see any, and the priest said there weren't any police. It's pretty primitive. A few Indians and dead dogs. No telephone or power lines. No antennas. The priest says they're completely cut off here. There's a fat storekeeper who said he sells information. The priest is scared to death of him . . . called him the devil. I didn't like him myself."

"There's always someone with an angle," Black mused. "But let's hope it will be safe to stay here for a day or two."

"You not up to going on?" Rumison asked.

"Not if it's not necessary," Black answered. "I have concussion fever. I've had it before. Headache, temperature. It will last only a short while . . . a day or two. Best you get some more rest also, at least today and tonight; see what we feel like in the morning. By the way, where did the Piper end up? Can you spot it from the air?"

"It swung into some trees. If someone were looking, they probably could see it."

"Maybe you could do something about that," said Black, "without looking too conspicuous."

"Might be hard."

"Might at that," Black said, picking up a large black flea that had crawled off the bed onto his chest. He squeezed it between his fingers. "I guess it can't be helped right now. My head hurts like hell and I need some rest." Another flea crossed his forearm and he flicked it away. "That is, if my friends here let me rest," he added dryly.

Chapter Twenty

FOR the rest of the morning Rumison remained in the room with Black and kept watch. Rumison hadn't wanted to fall asleep himself but the heat was enervating and he was exhausted. As the afternoon wore on he closed his eyes and lay back against one of the canvas bags. When he opened them again it was evening. He lit a match and touched it to a candle on the windowsill. Black was still asleep. Rumison took a long drink of tepid water from the earthenware jug the priest had brought, then left the room, almost colliding with Father Iglés in the hall.

"Ah, *señor.* You are awake. How is your friend?"

"Still sleeping," said Rumison. "*Padre,* I was wondering if we could get something to eat."

"Certainly, *señor.* I'll get you what I can. But we are a poor church and—"

"We aren't particular, *Padre,*" said Rumison quickly. "We can pay a little."

"I will do what I can," said the priest. "But . . . oh, yes, the reason I came. There is a boy outside who wishes to speak with you."

"A boy? What for?"

"He would not say, *señor.* His name is Ponce. He is the son of a carpenter."

Curious, Rumison followed the priest down the dark hallway to a door so low that he had to stoop to get through it. The door led to the nave of the church. The first thing Rumison noticed, besides the size of the room, was a large gilt statue of the Virgin Mary holding the baby Jesus. It overlooked rows of wooden pews. On both sides of the statue stood rows of candles, some of them burning. Their light and the light of the larger candles around the statue were the room's only illumination. One lone Indian woman, her head covered with a black shawl, knelt below the statue, oblivious to both the priest and Rumison.

The boy was waiting outside the church's large doors; his feet were bare and he wore no shirt. He was dark-complexioned, but he stood with a natural dignity and his face was open and guileless. Rumison was immediately drawn to him.

"Do you speak English?" Rumison asked.

The boy, who looked to be about fourteen, shook his head and then burst into a torrent of Spanish. Rumison looked at the priest.

"He says his father is the best carpenter in the world," said the priest. "He says his father can fix anything and that for a price he will fix your airplane."

The boy looked so serious that Rumison had to laugh. Not understanding, the boy looked up at the priest. *"Qué pasa, Padre?"*

"He wonders why you laugh," said the priest.

The boy looked so earnest Rumison felt immediately contrite. "I'm sorry," he said. "Please tell him that I'm sure his father is a good carpenter as he says, but that I don't think anyone could fix that airplane out there."

The boy grew indignant as the priest translated. He let out another burst of angry Spanish, ending it by placing his hands on his hips and glaring at Rumison.

The priest shrugged. *"Señor,* he insists his father can fix your airplane."

"Look," said Rumison patiently, "it would take a well-equipped air mechanic's shop to fix that thing, *Padre.* A carpenter out here, no matter how good . . ."

Rumison stopped as an idea suddenly occurred to him. "Wait," he said. "Don't tell him that. I could be wrong. Tell him I'll accept his father's offer. Tell him that if his father can fix our airplane we will give him five hundred American dollars. But tell him that when he works on it, to make sure it is out of the sun. Tell him to keep it in the shade of the trees, to protect it from lightning. This is very important."

The priest's eyes had grown large when Rumison mentioned the amount he was willing to pay Ponce's father. He translated the message, and the boy's face beamed. *"Gracias, señor,"* he said, grinning. *"Gracias."* Still grinning, he turned and ran from the church.

Rumison felt ashamed at what he had done. He half expected to see a frown of disapproval from the priest, but Father Iglés was grinning.

"His father is a good carpenter, *señor.* Perhaps you may not have to walk to Santa Helena after all. It is a bad journey, especially if the *señores* are carrying such large amounts of money. . . ."

The priest lowered his eyes, gazing at the ground, waiting for affirmation. "It is a dangerous journey, even if one carries little money," he added.

Another pause. Rumison remained silent and the priest sighed. "I've tried to exercise the ideals of the holy Church among these people," he said sadly, "but I am only a poor and weak man and their perfidy runs deep. They come to worship on Sunday and holy days and to confess when it suits them, but still they continue to live their wicked lives and when it is time to repair the bell or give a coat of gilt to the statue of the Blessed Virgin, they look the other way, spending their money instead—what little they have—on drink from Juan Tienda's store. Why, *señor,* you would not believe it, but in the past eighteen years we have taken in less than the cost of new stucco for the church."

"I understand, *Padre,"* Rumison said sympathetically. "It must be hard. Maybe when Mr. Black and I are ready to go, we could make a small donation."

"Señor, I did not wish to imply that I am only looking for money!"

"No, of course not," Rumison said quickly. "It would be our pleasure. A gift, in appreciation for your generosity. All the help you are giving us."

"Señor . . ."

"For the Church, *Padre."*

The little priest hesitated, raising his eyes to the statue of the Virgin Mary. "Yes, of course. In that case . . . for the church."

"About getting us something to eat, *Padre . . ."*

Was it Rumison's imagination, or was there a new

bounce in the priest's steps? "Yes, yes, *señor.* I believe the cook has some mutton stew for dinner."

The church kitchen was large and gloomy and was lit only by a Coleman lantern hung on a bracket near a large rusty wood-burning stove. An old woman—an Indian crone whose face looked as leathery as the meat she was chopping—scowled at Rumison as he followed the priest into the room. The priest said a few words in a language Rumison had never heard. The crone nodded and pulled more vegetables from a bin and began adding them to a large kettle on the stove without comment.

There was a rough wooden table in one corner, and the priest offered Rumison a seat. A small boy stuck his head in the doorway. The crone scolded him, but the priest silenced the woman with a wave of his hand and called the boy in. The boy, thin and listless-looking, poured some milk into a glass from a pitcher, gave Rumison a sour look and then left. The priest didn't offer any explanation and Rumison didn't press. Instead he asked about the town.

"No," said the priest, answering one of Rumison's questions, "there are no radios here, or telephones. The only electricity is from a small generator in Juan Tienda's store. Our only link with civilization is the road . . . so who would have expected to see an airplane land here?"

"It wasn't by choice," said Rumison. "What can you tell me about Santa Helena?"

"It is a large town," said the priest. "Maybe four thousand people live there. It is a full day's ride by burro from Ratanagua, if the burro is fast and doesn't stop. Generally I take two days to travel there. Santa Helena has bus service, because it is not far from the main highway."

"Is that where the town gets its supplies?" Rumison asked, indicating the well-stocked shelves of the kitchen.

"Yes, *señor.* We buy from Juan Tienda. He has eight burros and makes the journey once a month."

"So you do business with him?"

The priest shifted uncomfortably. "*Sí, señor.* Sadly we must. The whole town depends on him."

"He doesn't look to be in good enough shape to do much traveling."

"Appearances can be deceiving," said the priest. "The

man has the strength of a bull. And he has men who help him."

"The nearest police are in Santa Helena?"

"Yes, *señor.* Some months ago *la guardia* was here . . . chasing guerrillas who were trying to escape into Costa Rica, but they did not stay long."

"Did they get them?"

"Señor?"

"Did they get them? The guerrillas?"

"Those particular ones they did, yes . . . or so I heard. Their bodies were dismembered and thrown into the river. Or—again, so I heard. But other guerrillas and bandits have escaped the wrath of *la guardia.* The jungle is thick and the borders are ignored for miles on either side."

"Do you know the revolution is over, *Padre?"* Rumison asked. "The Sandinistas have won. Somoza is dead."

The priest looked thoughtful. "So," he said, "I had heard such, but one never knows. Or cares, I might add. It is all the same to the Church. Our business lies not with secular matters."

"You speak very good English," Rumison observed.

The priest nodded. "I learned in the seminary. Along with Greek and Latin. The fathers were very strict. But it is all useless knowledge in Ratanagua. You are the first I've spoken English to in many months."

"Tienda speaks it," Rumison pointed out.

The priest grimaced. "I try not to speak to Tienda, and when I do, it is not in English. Where he learned English, I neither know nor care."

The crone stirred the kettle. The smell reminded Rumison how hungry he was; he hadn't eaten anything since dinner the night before at O'Brien's.

"Father Pablo," he said, "if by chance Ponce's father can't fix our airplane, what would be the best way to get to Costa Rica?"

"The best way? The bus from Santa Helena, of course. There is no other way."

"How do the guerrillas go?"

"The guerrillas? Why would you want to enter the jungle, *señor?"*

"Just curious, *Padre."*

"The jungle is hard, *señor.* It has untold dangers. The Indians say the ghosts of their ancestors from the lost city of Tecún roam near the ybris trees, because the red color of the bark reminds them of the warmth of living blood. Myself, I believe the devil uses the jungle instead to persecute lost souls. It is the primitive superstitions of the natives that make it difficult for the Church to do its work."

Rumison regarded the priest, wondering if he were serious.

"But," the priest continued sorrowfully, seeming unaware of the contradictoriness of his sentiments, "a man may be brave in the face of hardships and ghosts, yet still be wary of the devils who have taken the form of men. Like Tienda. There are many unexplained murders nearby. The road is very dangerous. I travel myself only with extreme reluctance. Yet Tienda makes the journey often to Santa Helena and is never attacked. It can only lead one to the conclusion that he himself is behind the murders."

"And yet you still do business with him."

"As I said, *señor,* we have no choice."

Rumison returned to Black's room some time later with two bowls of stew. While they ate he told the older man what he had learned. Black ate slowly and deliberately. Even the slight movement of eating seemed to pain him.

"That was a good idea about the plane," said Black. "In more ways than one. Besides getting it hidden, it'll confuse the locals about our real intentions."

"Just what *are* our real intentions?" Rumison asked.

"The jungle, of course." Black grinned dryly. "Despite lost souls and ghosts and fat storekeepers."

"We're not exactly equipped for that anymore," said Rumison. He avoided mentioning there were only two of them now, and neither was in shape for rough travel.

"It's best to keep away from small towns that have bus lines and newspapers," Black said. "It won't be so bad. The jungle is nowhere near as thick here."

"I hope you're right," said Rumison.

Chapter Twenty-One

THE priest had fried eggs and goat's milk for their breakfast the next morning. The swelling on Black's bruised forehead had gone down during the night and he moved more like his old self. Black and Rumison ate breakfast in the kitchen with the priest. The boy Rumison had seen in the kitchen the day before also ate, holding his plate on his lap as he sat in one corner. The priest looked uneasy when Black asked why the boy didn't join them at the table.

"He is used to the floor," said the priest quickly. "Pablito is an orphan. He lives here in return for a few small chores."

The boy glanced up, regarding the table with dark, leaden eyes, but didn't speak.

"He understands English?" Black asked.

"Yes," said the priest. "What little I taught him."

The boy continued eating.

After they'd eaten, Black went back to his room to lie down, complaining that he still had a headache. Rumison, uncomfortable in the company of the priest, left the church and walked down the worn path toward the village. Before leaving he had stuck a pistol in his belt.

"As a man of God, I should not say this," said the priest, "but you are wise to carry a weapon in Ratanagua."

There seemed, to Rumison, to be more people around in the village than he remembered from the day before. They stood or sat, following his movements with their eyes, but otherwise giving no notice that he existed. The men scratched their bodies and drank urine-yellow alcohol from clear glass bottles. The few visible women were either suckling scrawny babies or pounding flour for corn cakes or tortillas.

" '. . . No joy in Mudville,' " muttered Rumison to himself.

He came to the plaza, where a few sullen stallkeepers halfheartedly tried to sell him their wares: pork, fish, vegetables. Flies swarmed everywhere. The plaza stank of meat, excrement and vegetables rotting in the heat.

The fat storekeeper, Juan Tienda, was seated on the same bench as the day before. Indeed, he looked as if he hadn't moved from it. He smiled amiably as Rumison walked past.

"*Buenos días, señor.* I knew you would be back."

"Oh?" said Rumison, stopping. "How so?"

"I am not stupid, whatever people say," said Tienda. "I have heard Manuel Trabajo is fixing your aircraft. I also know it has no gasoline. Since I sell the only gasoline around, I knew you must come to see me. Simple, no?"

Rumison was thoughtful. "How much is your gasoline?" he asked.

Tienda shrugged his massive shoulders. "There is nowhere else you can go, *señor.* My gasoline is brought in many miles by burro. Sometimes I sell it to the *riodero*s, though mostly I use it to run my electrical generator. It is dear to me. I will sell it, however, for fifty American dollars a gallon. I can sell you ten gallons."

"Expensive," said Rumison.

Tienda nodded. "It is. But then you are lucky I have gasoline at all."

Rumison peered past the storekeeper, trying to see through the dirty window of the store. "What else do you sell?" he asked. "Hammocks? Machetes?"

Tienda raised a thick eyebrow. "Hammocks? Machetes? What would you do with those things?" His pig eyes were thoughtful.

Realizing his mistake, Rumison said quickly, "We need the machetes to clear the road to take off."

"You could hire five of these bastard *indios* for the price of two machetes, *señor,*" said Tienda.

"I didn't know that," said Rumison.

"And the hammocks?"

"The beds at the church are full of bugs."

Tienda laughed. "I've never slept there," he said. "The good father buys my goods through that old hag who cooks for him, but he pisses in his pants if I get too close."

The storekeeper spat on the wooden porch and waved toward the door to his store. "It is all in there, *señor.* Go in and look around."

Rumison hesitated, but when it became obvious Tienda wasn't going to follow him, he entered. Once inside he had to adjust his eyes to the poor light. The glass windows were nearly opaque with dirt. Shelves and tables of assorted goods were heaped about in apparent randomness: blankets, Coleman stoves and lanterns, clothes, picks, shovels, machetes, mosquito netting, canned goods. Most of the dry goods looked used. Rumison remembered the priest's warnings about murders in the area and wondered where the previous owners of the goods were now.

Rumison started. He thought he was alone, but seated in the corner on a wooden stool a young girl watched him. She looked to be about eleven or twelve. She was wearing a short, sacklike dress. In the dim light she looked fairly pretty but when Rumison smiled at her, the indolent expression on her face didn't change.

Rumison noted two machetes, two knitted hemp hammocks and a bolt of mosquito netting. Then he walked outside.

"I saw some things we might want," he said. "I'll be back with my partner if we decide we need them."

"Your partner is well, then?" asked Tienda.

"Pretty much."

Tienda nodded, absently picking at a tear in his flowered shirt.

"And the gasoline, *señor.* You of course will want that?"

"Uh . . . yeah. Of course," stammered Rumison. "As soon as the plane is ready."

"Of course, *señor.*"

Just then a chorus of angry shouts drew Rumison's attention across the street. A small group of Indians standing on the porch of a mud hut were shoving one another. As Rumison looked closer he saw the argument was over a bottle of whiskey one of the Indians had and refused to give up. The Indian with the bottle was grabbed from behind, and the bottle shattered against the adobe. The Indian who had been carrying it screamed in rage and pulled a long knife from his waistband. Before anyone else could react, the Indian drove the knife into the stomach of the man who had knocked his arm. The man screamed and sank to the ground. While the others watched with a wary sort of amusement, the Indian with the knife grabbed the wounded man's long hair, pulled his head back and cut his throat.

"Jeezus Christ!" cried Rumison, horrified.

Tienda was smiling as he watched Rumison's reaction. "This is Ratanagua, *señor,*" he said, chuckling. "Death is very easy to come by here, as you see."

The fat storekeeper's words sounded so much like a threat that Rumison instinctively reached for the gun in his belt. The smile left Tienda's face. "*Señor,* please! I did not mean anything."

Rumison shook his head to clear it. Across the street the Indians had found another bottle and were passing it around. Someone giggled. The corpse of the dead Indian was ignored.

"His wife will bury him," said Tienda, reading Rumison's thoughts.

Rumison left. The laughter of the drunken Indians followed him. He took a deep breath and held it. His hands were shaking badly. It took several minutes before the shaking stopped. He walked up the road, trying to put the scene he had just witnessed from his mind.

Before he realized it, Rumison had come to the place on the road where they had crashed the plane. A small group of ragged-looking children shouted and then stepped shyly back as he approached. Beyond them, all but hidden from view under the trees and looking in better shape than it had any right to be, was the Piper. A man was perched on one wing, busily tightening a large bolt. The boy, Ponce, was squatting down in the tall grass, carving at a piece of hardwood with a knife. He saw Rumison and waved, then shouted at his father, who climbed down from the wing.

Rumison stared at the plane in amazement. Ponce and his father must have been up all night working on it. The entire airframe had been strengthened with new hardwood braces and the damaged wing had been solidly bolted back into place. From an aesthetic standpoint all the plane needed was new cloth over the tears in the fabric. But from a functional standpoint, Rumison knew that the little airplane would never fly again. The wing would have made anyone a beautiful front door, but it wouldn't get off the ground. Ponce's father had used thick, heavy pieces of wood, bolting them together with huge iron bolts and bands of iron. The metal looked as if it had been scavenged from a steamship or a train engine.

"Ees goo', *señor?*" asked Ponce, standing proudly next to his father.

Rumison didn't know whether to laugh or cry. "It is very beautiful, Ponce," he said. "*Muy bonito.* Your father is an excellent carpenter . . . *un hombre magnífico.*"

Ponce beamed in pride while Rumison nodded at the reserved-looking father.

"*Está bueno, señor. Muy bueno. Cuantas más días?*"

The father puzzled over Rumison's accent for several seconds, then smiled. "*Uno más día, señor. Uno más.*"

Rumison nodded, unable to meet the father's eyes. "Very good," he said. "*Gracias.* We will pay you."

Rumison took another path back to the church, avoiding the main street and Tienda's store. He didn't want to know if the dead Indian still lay on the porch of the hut. Black was in the room, studying a map the priest must have given him. Black listened to Rumison's story and nodded. "Sounds like the storekeep is The Man in these parts," he mused. "Which means he won't be happy selling us a few gallons of gas, even at fifty dollars a gallon."

"How do you mean?"

"Just this. If we could afford that, we could afford more. From what you've said I don't think anyone around here would grieve over two dead gringos."

For some reason Black's suggestion did not come as a surprise to Rumison. "So he might try to kill us?" he asked, knowing the answer.

Black nodded. "Probably. The priest hinted at it today and Tienda follows a type. The fat spider at the center of a web. No matter that it's a very small web. Power works like a pyramid, the spider at the top controlling the strings. Ratanagua is a pretty unsophisticated place. The web strands are harder to follow back in civilization, unless you know what to look for."

"What should we do?"

"Wait. Hope Tienda doesn't get wise before we bail out early tomorrow morning. It may have been a mistake asking about machetes and hammocks. The *padre* has some of what we need right here."

"I wasn't really thinking," said Rumison.

"You'll learn."

"Are you going to be all right to leave in the morning?"

Black shrugged. "Right enough." He indicated the map with a finger. "According to this, we don't have far to go."

"I've heard that before," said Rumison.

"Well, we'll see. Why don't you go out and let me get some more rest. Talking gives me a headache."

Rumison nodded and left. He spent the rest of the afternoon wandering around the old church, thinking. His thoughts were as restless as the monkeys scrambling about in the trees of the jungle. Was life just a series of pyramids, one fat spider after another? Was Tienda a spider, or just a fat fly caught in some other spider's web? Everyone had some web they were struggling to escape, or so it seemed. Each waiting in fear for that moment when the web's maker would feel the vibrations coming from their frantic effort to escape.

Rumison saw his own web, the gilded mesh of unimportant California days, the painless, joyless existence. What had changed all that? For it had changed, somewhere back on O'Brien's plantation, somewhere with Whitney's face and Rosso's blood.

Barney had held out because for once in his life he wanted to do something that made a difference. To flick his finger in the face of the spider. Why was that so important to him?

Black had said, "Nothing is important but what we choose to give importance to." But faced with the inevitability of death, the impending arrival of the spider, how could anyone believe anything to be important?

Rumison found himself outside the front of the church, watching as a flock of pigeons passed over the bell towers. In a sudden flash he realized what purpose religion played in the human drama. How easy it was to let someone else worry about questions of value, of importance. How hard it was to face those things yourself.

Rumison's thoughts were broken by the approach of an old Indian. "*Almas, por favor,*" the Indian called. "*Un cordoba, por favor.*"

The beggar's teeth were broken or missing and his breath was rotten. His yellow skin was wrinkled like birchbark and his rheumy eyes were fawning.

"*Señor, por favor. Un cordoba.*"

Rumison saw that the Indian didn't really see him. He saw instead an illusion, a symbol, a young white who represented everything that the beggar thought he wasn't.

"*No tengo dinero,*" said Rumison, shaking the Indian's clutching hand from his arm. "*Nada.*"

Brief hate blazed in the Indian's dark eyes, then fear, then indifference. He shuffled off away from the church.

His soul was stolen from him, Rumison decided. Stolen by things he'd been taught by others to believe were important.

Rumison went back inside. Walking down the hallway to the room, he heard Black's angry voice. He hurried to find Black with the boy Pablito, shaking him violently.

"What were you doing in this room? Why were you looking through my bags?" Black was asking.

The boy looked too frightened to speak. He was wailing loudly and didn't answer, even after Black repeated the question in Spanish. Black threw the boy disgustedly on the bed just as the priest pushed excitedly past Rumison.

"What is going on here? What are you doing to Pablito?"

"I caught the little bastard going through our bags," said Black.

The priest, looking as frightened as the boy, turned to him and asked, "*Es verdad, niño?*"

"*No, no, Padre,*" the boy said, sobbing. "*Quiero a ver el equipaje. Está todo. Está todo.*"

The priest look anxiously toward Black. "He rarely sees men such as you, *señor,*" he said apologetically. "He is young and curious. I am sure he won't do it again."

"I'm sure also," said Black curtly.

Bowing, the priest grabbed the boy by the arm and dragged him wailing from the room.

"You were pretty rough on the kid," said Rumison when they could no longer hear Pablito's cries.

"He saw the case."

"So?"

"Figure it out, Rumison. Those handcuffs would tell quite a story to someone."

"You're worried about the priest?"

"I'm not worried about anyone. I'm stating a fact. I think the kid was lying about why he was in here."

"Huh? What for?"

Black held up his left forearm. Blood was forming on it in the pattern of human teeth. "He tried to run past me when I found him. I grabbed him and he bit me. He didn't start the scared-little-kid routine until after I started asking questions."

"And you think the priest may have put him up to it?"

"Not the priest," said Black. "He's a bit hard to take, but somewhere beneath his self-pity I think he's still a priest."

"Who then?"

Black shrugged. "It doesn't matter," he said. "I just hope it doesn't speed up the inevitable."

Black and Rumison spent the remainder of the afternoon resting and discussing strategy. The route Black had chosen on the map followed a small nearby creek toward the mountains.

"Once over the ridge, we'll drop down to this flat area bordering the San Juan," said Black. "It's a roundabout way, but it keeps us out of the jungle for a ways, and the creek can cover our tracks if anyone might want to follow."

That night they ate roast chicken with the priest in the kitchen. Pablito was nowhere around. They had almost finished when there was a loud pounding at the doors to the church. The priest stopped midsentence. He looked frightened.

"Aren't you going to see who it is?" Black asked.

The priest didn't answer. Black stood. "Then I will, *Padre.*"

"*Señor,* wait!" cried the priest. "These are evil days. Perhaps what is out there is best left alone."

"And maybe it's someone wanting to light a candle," said Black.

"*Señor,* you joke."

"We do only what we have to do, *Padre.*"

Reluctantly the priest followed Black out of the kitchen. The racket had stopped by the time Black opened one door.

"Ponce!" cried Rumison, recognizing immediately the carpenter's son. Ponce stood with blood running down his face from a cut above his eye. The blood mixed with his tears. The boy was sobbing loudly.

"Ponce, what happened? *Qué pasa?*"

The boy looked up at Rumison and blurted out a stream of unintelligible Spanish. Then he began to weep again. Black looked grim and the priest quickly shut and bolted the door.

"What's wrong?" asked Rumison.

"The boy says his father is dead," said Black evenly. "He says Juan Tienda came with two men to the airplane. He says his father tried to keep them away, but they shot him and would have shot the boy, but he ran away. He waited until Tienda had left, then went to find his father, but his father was dead!"

"Oh, God, no!"

Black bent over and asked the boy a question. The boy stopped crying long enough to answer.

"He said it happened over an hour ago," said Black. "He took his father to their house before coming here."

"*Señores,* please," cried the priest, his fingers worrying the brass crucifix hanging from his neck. "I do not want trouble. Not with Tienda. He is an evil man."

"Then you won't mind if we have to kill him, *Padre,*" said Black coldly.

The priest gasped. "Kill him! No! Please, *señor,* you must not. It is against our laws, and who then would make the journey to Santa Helena for supplies?"

"I thought Tienda was a devil," said Rumison.

"*Sí,* the very devil! But to exist here, we must have him. He is necessary!"

"Let's go, Rumison," said Black sharply, "we've got things to do."

"Please! *Señores!*" wailed the priest.

"Wait, Mr. Black," said Rumison. "Do you have any money at all?"

Black shook his head. Rumison had trouble meeting the

questioning eyes of the carpenter's son. He took off his watch and handed it to the boy. "I'm sorry I lied to you and your father," he said. "I'm sorry for what it's done to you and your family. I wish this could be more."

Uncomprehending, but controlling his tears, the boy slowly reached out and took the watch. *"Gra . . gra . . . gracias, señor,"* he said brokenly.

"Señores, please!" cried the priest. "You must not do this thing!"

But neither Black nor Rumison listened to him.

Chapter Twenty-Two

MOONLIGHT reflected off the wispy smoke that rose into the hot night air from the chimneys of mud huts. The village had closed itself up for the night. Candlelight and lamplight filtered through a few narrow windows but the streets and the plaza were deserted. From somewhere came that loneliest of sounds, the distant, mournful barking of a dog.

"Is that Tienda's store?" Black asked quietly, indicating the two-story structure several hundred yards away.

Rumison nodded. He still wasn't sure what Black had in mind, but in his own hatred of Tienda, he didn't care. Every time Rumison thought of Ponce, he winced, and every time he thought of Tienda, his anger deepened.

Black dropped the canvas bag he was carrying near the trunk of a huge Venus oblado tree. The large red blossoms looked purple and malign in the moonlight. He took the clip out of his rifle and checked it and then turned to Rumison.

"I'll go it alone," he offered.

"I'm not sure what you're planning," said Rumison.

Black shrugged. "Tienda has figured things out by now. He's seen the plane, the bullet holes in it. He knows it won't fly. He'll try to get us. So we have to get him first. Besides, he has things we need."

"I'll help," said Rumison, surprised at his own determination and calmness.

"I'd hoped so," said Black. He reached over and grabbed the pistol from Rumison's belt.

"Hey!"

"Quiet. I want you to put this in the small of your back, under your shirt. Tienda probably will be armed. He may be expecting trouble. He probably has others with him. You'll go to the store."

"What about you?"

"I'm going to scout around outside here, then join you once you've talked with Tienda."

"What will I talk about?"

"Anything. Ask him what he wants."

Rumison took the gun back from Black and put it in his belt the way Black had suggested.

"I'll see you there," Black said, and then disappeared down a dark street.

Rumison walked toward the store. The upstairs windows were dark, but an electric light was on downstairs in the rear of the building. Rumison could hear the chugging of a small gas motor, probably the generator, behind the building. For a moment he waited. There was another sound, an odd sound, yet somehow familiar . . .

The motor shut itself off. Rumison suddenly understood what the other sound was. On the second floor of the building, someone was making love. He was disgusted to think it might be Tienda. With whom? The rhythmic squeaking of a bed intensified. Small animal sounds, the deep grunt of a man, the higher-pitched cries—too high for a woman—of a young girl, ecstatic, totally involved. The sounds grew into orgasm, then abruptly stopped.

Rumison knocked loudly on the front door and waited. There was no immediate answer. He tested the door, rattling it. It was locked. He knocked again.

"Qué pasa?" cried Tienda's voice from somewhere upstairs.

"It's me, the American!" called Rumison. "I want to talk with you!"

There was a pause, then, "Just a minute!"

It wasn't long before Rumison heard heavy shuffling footsteps. Another light came on downstairs. A bolt was thrown and the latch on the door turned. Tienda stood facing Rumison.

"Ah," snorted Tienda loudly, "the gringo. I expected you back, but not in the middle of the night. Few people in Ratanagua discuss business at night. It is a time for other things."

Tienda was naked except for a dirty pair of shorts and his sandals. He carried a large pistol, but he lowered it when he saw who was at the door. He laughed and waved Rumison inside.

"Come in. Come in."

Rumison entered. A large bare light bulb hung by a cord from the ceiling. The bright light made the store look even shabbier than Rumison remembered.

Tienda placed his pistol casually on a dirty counter top before shuffling over to an ancient electric refrigerator. Taking out a bottle of Miller's beer, he snapped the cap off with the fingers of one bearlike hand and took a long, noisy swallow. He wiped foam from his goatee with the back of his hand and held out the bottle to Rumison. *"Señor?"*

Rumison shook his head.

Tienda shrugged. "Why are you here?" he asked.

"Why did you kill Ponce's father?" asked Rumison, struggling to control his rising anger and revulsion.

Tienda looked perplexed. "Who?" he asked.

"Ponce's father. The man who was working on our airplane."

"Oh, him." Tienda dismissed the matter with a wave of his hand. "He got in the way. He tried to keep myself and my friends from admiring your aircraft. They had never seen one up close, so I decided to show them. I can't understand what got into the old man. He was always so timid."

Tienda belched loudly and then took another swallow of beer. His huge stomach quivered like a giant pale slug as it hung over his belt. He belched a second time and said, "Come, *señor.* Let us stop playing games. You know I did you no real disservice by killing that peasant. He could not fix your aircraft. He ruined it. My store could as well fly after he'd finished bolting that carved-up tree to it. He made a cabinet out of it. It will never fly again. So obviously Trabajo meant nothing to you."

Rumison couldn't trust himself to speak. Tienda, mistaking his silence, grinned.

"You planned to walk from Ratanagua," he said conspiratorially. "The work on the aircraft was a trick to make people believe otherwise. This is why you wanted my machetes, my hammocks, the mosquito netting."

Tienda looked pleased with himself. "Go on," said Rumison, forcing the words out.

"I thought this strange," said Tienda slyly. "I said to myself, 'Juan, why would two Americans wish to fool simple people like us into believing they are going to fly away, when in fact they must walk, like the rest of us?' "

Rumison didn't answer. Behind Tienda, on the stairs leading to the upper story, Rumison saw the young girl he had noticed in the store earlier. She was naked. In the sharp light he could see the small patch of hair between her slender legs, and her small breasts, which were just beginning to bud.

"I told you to wait!" said Tienda, in English.

The girl brushed a strand of dirty brown hair from her eyes. "I jos' wan' to see," she pouted.

Tienda shrugged. "See, then," he said. He turned back to Rumison.

"My daughter," he explained.

The girl found a stool and sat, her legs spread wide. She watched Rumison steadily, staring with an almost indecent curiosity. Rumison tried hard to ignore her.

Tienda laughed, amused at Rumison's discomfiture. "My daughter likes men," he said.

"Just finish what you were saying!" snapped Rumison.

"Ah, you Americans," chuckled Tienda. "So to the point. But where was I . . . ? Ah, yes, the question: Why would you wish to fool us? I had no answer, so I sent a man to speak to the *padre.* Perhaps the good father would explain. He believes you are rich *yanquis* and he expects a large 'donation' for helping you. But I . . . I think maybe no. You see, I had already been told of the little holes in your plane . . . the bullet holes. . . ."

Finished with his beer, Tienda threw the empty bottle on a trash heap in the corner. He took another bottle from the refrigerator.

"There is a boy who lives with the old priest," he said, popping off the cap of the new bottle. "I asked him to look through those two strange bags carried from the airplane."

"Pablito?"

Tienda grinned. "Ah, yes. Pablito. The priest's bastard. You knew that, didn't you?"

Rumison didn't answer.

"Yes, Pablito is the son of our good celibate priest. He tries to pretend no one knows, but it is a joke. The mother was an Indian. . . ." Tienda paused. "I can see you are not interested in that. But perhaps you would be interested in knowing that Pablito likes my daughter. He likes her a great deal, or at least what she does with him. . . ."

Tienda grinned again, winking at the girl. "Isn't that right, Carla?"

The girl nodded languidly.

"Of course, she likes men better than boys, don't you, my dear?" Tienda continued.

The girl shrugged her thin shoulders, all the while watching Rumison. "I like the men becus' they mooch beeger," she said. "They feel mooch bedder eenside me."

Tienda laughed heartily.

Rumison's anger finally overcame his disgust. "I'm not interested in your daughter's sex life," he snapped. "We were talking about something else."

Tienda wiped his mouth and set the beer down on the counter next to his pistol. "Go to bed, Carla," he said abruptly.

Without arguing, the girl got down from the stool. "Go'nigh, *señor,*" she said.

Tienda waited until she had climbed the stairs. Then, almost disinterestedly, as if his thick fingers merely needed something with which to busy themselves, he picked up the pistol.

"No more games, eh?" he said finally. "I know you and your friend are running from someone, no?"

"What makes you say that?" said Rumison.

Tienda stroked his beard reflectively. "It makes much sense. Two *yanquis* in a country that no longer likes them very much. A small aircraft of Nicaraguan registry, full of bullet holes. Not just any bullet holes, now, but machine-gun bullets. And who has machine guns? The government? No, it is gone, or so I have heard. *Los Muchachos,* I suspect. And what did Pablito see in your bags? A black suitcase . . . with handcuffs. So I ask, What does it all mean?"

Tienda played with the pistol, eyeing it as though looking for dirt, turning the cylinder, placing it again on the counter.

Rumison was wondering what to do when the decision was abruptly taken from him. Outside the store a gun went off. Then another, followed by the loud thunder of a shotgun. The pistol was immediately in Tienda's hand, pointed directly at Rumison's heart.

"Don't move!" he cried, his slovenly body tense, suddenly alert, his thick face angry and red.

"So," he said, more calmly, "your friend was outside all this time."

"I don't know what you're talking about," said Rumison, nervously taking a step backward.

A hamlike fist came out of nowhere, knocking Rumison to the floor. "Don't lie to me!" bellowed Tienda. "The shotgun was Gonzales. None of my other men have guns. Those other shots must have been your friend."

Tienda swung his fist again but this time Rumison managed to deflect it partially with his arm. Even so, the force of the blow jolted him.

Tienda glared at him. Rumison could see the madness in the pig eyes. Rumison tried to stand, but Tienda hit him with the pistol, almost paralyzing Rumison's forearm. Rumison crawled away and Tienda followed.

"Gonzales must have killed your friend," said Tienda, his voice brittle with anger. "Now it is your turn, you faggot bastard!"

Two more shots sounded outside. Tienda paused in astonishment, giving Rumison time to scramble to his feet. Rumison kicked up with everything he had, catching Tienda directly in the crotch. Tienda grunted in agony, trying to raise the pistol. Rumison grabbed the thick arm with both hands and slammed it into the counter. The gun fell and Rumison kicked it away just as Tienda's free hand caught him by the throat.

Tienda was incredibly strong. Rumison couldn't throw him off. The muscles in Rumison's neck were weakening. Desperately Rumison worked one arm free, clutching at the gun hidden under his shirt. He brought the barrel in against Tienda's sweaty stomach and pulled the trigger. Tienda jerked, but the pressure on Rumison's throat didn't ease. The world grew dark. Rumison fired again and again and finally the grip began to lessen. Rumison yanked himself free and stood back, gasping for air as his vision cleared.

Tienda was still alive, dragging his massive, blood-covered body toward the gun that Rumison had kicked by the trash heap. Rumison steadied himself against the counter and raised the pistol. His shot hit Tienda in the neck and the fat man fell dead next to the trash.

The door flew open and Black was revealed crouched, ready to fire. When he saw Rumison, he lowered the rifle.

"You all right?"

Rumison nodded, unable to talk.

"We've got to hurry," said Black. "Tienda had men waiting outside. I got two, but another got away."

Black picked up a backpack from a shelf and began shoving things into it. "Get one for yourself, Rumison. Throw what you need into it."

Rumison nodded and did as he was told. Then he saw Tienda's daughter watching from the stairs.

"Ees dead?" she asked, matter-of-factly.

Rumison nodded.

"Yo' tek me weef yo'?" she asked.

"We can't do that."

"We need money," said Black. "Where did your father keep it?"

Rumison hated himself at that moment. But the girl was quiet. She seemed to be weighing, balancing.

"Eef I get, mebbe yo' tek me weef yo'?"

Black shook his head. "I'm sorry, we can't do that. But we'll leave you with some money. If you don't help us, we'll take it all."

The girl stood a moment, then nodded.

She led them to the second floor, down a short, dark hallway into a bedroom. A huge bamboo bed with a down mattress took up most of the room. The air stank of sex and sweat. The girl removed a bamboo log from the bed's headboard and took out three small leather bags, handing them to Black.

"Yo' leave some," she said.

The bags contained currency, a few precious stones, some gold nuggets and coins. Most of the currency was in

Nicaraguan cordobas, but there was a tight string-bound bundle of U.S. bills. Black took the gold and the U.S. currency and gave the rest back to the girl. She took it without comment and put it back in its hiding place. Turning to leave, Rumison felt a soft hand take hold of his.

"Tek me weef yo'."

The small voice was pleading. There were tears in her eyes. She had been transformed into a small, frightened little girl.

"We can't," said Rumison.

"I hef no one now. I'm afraid."

Gently, Rumison disengaged his hand. "I'm sorry," he said.

Chapter Twenty-Three

THE village was quiet, still. Where there had been lights, it was now dark. Rumison followed Black down a narrow path to the stream, where Black turned toward the mountains. Rumison tripped over branches and roots, slipping on wet rocks, dropping the machete he had taken from Tienda's store, wasting precious time scrambling in the shallow water to find it. More than once he heard the rustle of a startled animal and wondered how long before they met something that wouldn't frighten so easily.

Finally, after an hour of painful and exhausting travel, Black called a halt and they slung the hammocks, also stolen from Tienda's store, between trees near the river.

"How's your head?" Rumison asked. In the dark he couldn't see Black's face, but he had an instinctive feeling that the older man was in some amount of pain.

"It'll be better in the morning," said Black shortly. His voice sounded weary.

"Maybe I can carry something extra tomorrow." Rumison suggested. "That briefcase or something."

"That won't help my head," said Black.

Traveling was easier the next morning. The river was shallow, allowing them to walk on exposed rocks and hard sand, avoiding the jungle along the bank. They followed it for half a day before reaching the base of the cordillera. The banks of the stream grew into canyon walls and they found themselves climbing at steeper and steeper angles. If Black still had headaches from his concussion, he didn't show it, and Rumison was hard put to keep up with him.

By early afternoon they had reached a waterfall. It was over thirty feet high but easy enough to climb on the right side, away from the spray and slippery moss that coated the rocks nearer the water.

They stopped to eat a cold lunch of beans and canned apricots. A fine mist from the fall cooled the air around them. A bright-colored macaw flew past, then a large hawk, its tail feathers twitching in a thermal created by the canyon winds and the mist. They weren't yet high enough to see Ratanagua, but they were well above the jungle. In the distance a thin column of smoke rose into the air.

"When Rosso was killed, I didn't think anything mattered much anymore," mused Rumison philosophically. "But I'm still afraid. I don't want to die. When I survived that crash, I was really happy."

"That's normal," said Black.

"But would it be normal if I really believed it didn't matter?"

Black shrugged, seeming uninterested.

"And that boy, Ponce," said Rumison. "I felt awful . . . I feel awful."

"Don't let it bother you too much," said Black. "Our time is up when it's up. His father's time was up, that's all. Like Barney's and Cordobes' and Rosso's. And nothing you or I do changes that."

"You really believe that?"

"Yes."

"Then why do we fear death so much?"

"Fear has a purpose, I suppose," said Black quietly. "Focuses things, puts them in perspective. But death comes in spite of fear . . . or not, as the case may be. It's irrelevant to dying."

"But if it really doesn't matter, why do I feel these things?" Rumison asked. "Why does it hurt so much when I think of Rosso or that boy? Why am I afraid of dying?"

Black sighed. "It's no mental trip, Rumison. Don't try to make it one. Reasons? Who really knows much of anything? It's just us, trying to survive because that's what our bodies tells us to do and we may as well listen to them as anything."

"That isn't much to base your life on."

"No?"

They finished the meal and started off again, coming almost immediately to another waterfall. This one also was fairly easy to climb, at least at first, with good handholds where the rocks were dry. But as they climbed higher the walls of the canyon narrowed, forcing them closer to the mist; the rocks became slippery with moss. Rumison found himself being afraid, but as Black had said, he noticed his fear helped him to climb better, more attentively.

They continued on, reaching more falls. Most were only ten or fifteen feet, but a few, like the first, were over thirty feet high. The climbing wasn't particularly difficult, none of it harder than a 5.5—or advanced beginner's climb in rock-climbing jargon—but as the day wore on and without ropes or climbing gear, Rumison's fear grew. He worried most that eventually they would reach a falls too high or too difficult to scale; going on would be next to impossible without ropes. It was late afternoon and his arm was aching again.

"I think this is the last one before the top," said Black as they gazed up at the next falls, the largest they had yet come to. It was fully fifty feet high and the water cascading over it doused them with spray.

Rumison was doubtful. "We'd better wait until morning."

Black looked around the area where they were standing. There was a large pool underneath the falls, but other than that only rocks and moss-covered ledges. "No place to camp," he said.

Rumison felt a rising sense of foreboding. "There's a dark area behind the falls," he said. "I bet there's a cave there."

Black shook his head. "If there is, it'll be wetter than sleeping out here."

"I don't know. At least we could look."

"Come on, Rumison," said Black. "We'll have to climb it sooner or later. Let's get going. We don't have much time. Looks like a good route to the right here."

Rumison gave in. He led off, taking each move with deliberate, thought-out care. Thirty feet above the pool he looked up to see that the final approach to the top was blocked by a granite overhang. He climbed another five feet and waited, jamming his leg into a narrow crack for support.

"Doesn't look like much to hang on to," said Black, coming up beneath him and studying the overhang. "But it's hard to tell in this light. How's your position?"

"It's no bomb shelter, but I'm safe enough."

"Could you take my weight if I stood on your shoulders?"

"It's a long way down," said Rumison.

"Only thirty or forty feet. The pool should break a fall. It doesn't look like we have a choice."

Rumison glanced down. He couldn't see below the surface of the pool; it was obscured by foam and dead branches. He felt weak. What if there were rocks? Nervously he rechecked his footing.

Black inched his way up and around Rumison. Rumison felt the weight of Black's boot, then it was gone. He looked up to see Black slowly making his way up the overhang in the direction of a stunted but hardy-looking tree that grew down from the top.

Black had almost made it. He straightened cautiously, balancing himself for the final step. At the exact moment that he reached forward toward the tree, the unexpected happened. A large blackbird, startled by the motion of Black's arm, flew screaming out of the tree and struck Black in the forehead. Black grimaced in pain and wavered.

There was nothing Rumison could do except watch in horror. For a brief moment he thought Black might still make it. Black seemed to hold himself to the smooth stone by sheer force of will. But then the bird attacked again and Black fell. He tried to adjust his body, but the heavy pack hampered his efforts and he landed sideways in the pool and quickly swirled out of sight beneath the falls. The triumphant scream of the bird sounded like steam escaping from a crack in a boiler as it flew up out of the canyon.

Fear and urgency gave Rumison's flagging muscles strength but also made him careless. He misjudged a toehold and fell the last fifteen feet, landing unhurt in the pool. He pushed his pack up on a rock and then swam after Black, who was floating on his back in an eddy between some rocks. The briefcase tied to Black's pack had acted as a float, keeping the pack from pulling him under.

"I think I need some help," said Black weakly. "I got the wind knocked out of me."

"Thank God!" breathed Rumison. "I thought you were dead."

He pulled Black over to a calmer part of the pool and then undid Black's pack, pushing it up with his own. Then he dragged Black onto a ledge by the falls. The ledge led to a cave, the one Rumison had thought was there; it was drier than he'd expected, and he pulled Black inside.

"I guess I should have listened to you in the first place," said Black.

"Are you all right?" Rumison asked. Black's breathing was easy enough but something about the older man bothered him; Black's hands were clenched, as though he were in pain.

"I'll do," said Black. "Stunned, I guess." He glanced around the small cave. It's going to be damp in here unless you get a fire going."

"I saw some dead trees a ways back," said Rumison.

"Worth trying."

Rumison hesitated. "Are you sure you're all right?"

"We'll see," said Black. As Rumison continued to watch him, he added, "You'd better get the packs in here and find some wood before it gets dark."

The light coming through the veil of the waterfall was already growing dimmer. Rumison left the cave, returning a few minutes later with the two packs. Then he went to look for the dead trees and found some fifty yards back down the canyon. He made several trips with armloads of branches and logs he'd broken loose. The matches they'd taken from Tienda's store were in a waterproof container and with a little coaxing he got a fire going. Its smoke curled up into a draft that carried it past the falls out into the canyon.

It was dark now. The sun had set quickly behind the high canyon walls. Rumison took out some cans from a pack and started to fix a meal. The crackle of the dry wood harmonized with the falling water, and the fire's flames left shadows on the stone ceiling of the cave.

Black had changed position only slightly since Rumison

had first pulled him inside the cave. He was lying on his back, staring into the waterfall, which was lit by the firelight. "It's almost pleasant here," he said quietly.

"I'd feel better somewhere else," said Rumison. "I hope you're all right in the morning."

Black didn't answer. After a moment he said, "It's not far to Costa Rica. This'll all be over soon."

"Thank heaven," said Rumison.

Black seemed not to have heard. "Have you wondered yet, Rumison, what it all means?" he asked.

Rumison, who had been opening a can of beans, stopped. There was something about Black's choice of words, or their reflective tone, that made him uneasy.

"I'm not sure," he said.

Black still was gazing at the waterfall. "That girl back there . . . Whitney . . ."

"Yes," said Rumison carefully.

"A strong woman. I knew someone like her once . . . in fact, she reminded me of her a great deal."

"Oh?"

"Same green eyes, same warmth, sincerity. Innocent in an odd way, but not naïve. Tough as nails, really."

Rumison suddenly was uncomfortably aware that Black no longer was staring at the waterfall, but was looking at him, judging him in some inexplicable way. Rumison quickly looked away from those penetrating gray eyes and finished opening the can of beans. "Care what you eat?" he asked shortly.

Black shook his head. He seemed angry. "That black woman was right about you," he said. "You are weak. God alone knows why you're still alive. Baily and Rosso were hard as nails compared to you."

The unexpected outburst both startled and hurt Rumison. What was Black thinking? Rumison had never claimed to be a hero. "Look, Black," he said, anger replacing his hurt, "I don't care what you think. You think I like it Barney and Rosso died, or Cordobes? Maybe they all were better than I but I didn't ask to come on this thing and I didn't ask to be the one left here with you. God damn it, it—"

"Take it easy," said Black, interrupting with a wry smile and a raised hand. "It doesn't really matter."

"Then why in hell . . . ?"

"What matters is that you are the one here, left with me. What matters is that you are the one still living. That's what I was asking. Have you thought about what that means?"

Rumison was confused again. Black seemed to be trying to get at something. What did he want? "What can it mean?" Rumison said, a trace of his earlier bitterness showing through. "It doesn't mean anything. It doesn't matter."

"God damn it! It does matter!" shouted Black, jerking his head up. The movement seemed to cause him pain and he winced.

"You'd better take it easy yourself," said Rumison, worried again. "You might have hurt something."

Black let out a disgusted sigh. He reached over and pulled a pack under his head so he could see Rumison better. That movement also seemed to cause him pain, but he controlled it better.

"You're like them all," said Black, still angry but no longer looking at Rumison. "You think you see things, understand them when all you really know are your own miserable little prejudices. You live your whole life in a state of numbness, like you think it's nothing more than a vaguely pleasant walk in the park, and when you experience something real where you might learn something, you block it from your mind and say it's all meaningless, that nothing matters!"

"Mr. Black . . . ?"

"Listen to me, Rumison!" cried Black, turning his eyes toward Rumison again. "Listen to me, because I'm trying to tell you something!"

Rumison listened. He had no choice. The anger in Black's eyes had given way to an intensity so strong it was frightening. Black hesitated, choosing his words carefully, his hands clenched.

"Sometimes . . . something . . . may happen in a person's life, Rumison. Things that change that life so drastically, the person never again can see the world the same way as they had. Nothing seems important anymore . . . the old values are shattered and nothing has replaced them. That person has seen the lies behind all those many things we've all been so conditioned to believe are important. . . ."

Black stopped. The intensity seemed to drain away from him, leaving only a quiet inner anguish. Rumison had been put into a state of near shock by Black's unexpected passion and didn't know what to say or feel. Black was trying to tell him something, of that he was certain. But what, and why?

"So there's nothing," said Rumison as Black's gaze returned to the waterfall.

"There are our affections," replied Black softly.

"That isn't much."

"They're all we have. And when you understand them, you realize that's quite a lot. The only validity any faith can have is given by our affections. But who understands this? Who trusts his affections anymore? We all look for that wise man on the mountain to tell us where to go, what to do, what to believe. Afraid, the world is afraid. Afraid of being cast out, lonely. Afraid of being wrong, of being weak. Afraid of being the only thing that makes sense . . . ourselves. Our affections are not just egocentric desires, Rumison. They are the only way we know what is really going on. Can't you see that?"

Rumison was hearing and seeing a side of Black he would never have believed existed. He felt off balance, as at the fountain when the old cook had pulled the rifle out of the water, or later, when Rumison had heard that precise, impeccable English . . . only fools trust appearances.

"Someone should get something out of this mess," Black was saying. "It looks as though it has to be you."

Rumison felt a chill go down his back. Was it the dampness in the cave? "I'd better fix dinner," he said quickly, picking up another can.

Black sighed. "I'm not a philosopher," he said, almost apologetically. "Maybe my words aren't right."

Rumison was looking at the can he'd picked up. Peaches. A random question stirred his mind.

"That old man, Isaiah?" he said. "Why did you kill him?"

Black regarded Rumison for a moment and then a sardonic smile broke his lips. "We couldn't very well leave him behind," he said.

"Was that your only reason?" asked Rumison.

"Did I need more?"

Rumison shrugged. He returned his attention to the peaches.

"Are you thinking about that prophecy?" asked Black.

Rumison stabbed his knife into the can and didn't answer.

"Are you so certain it was a lie?"

Rumison looked up, irritated. "Of course," he snapped. "Look what happened!"

The smile remained on Black's lips. "Have you ever been to Persia?" he asked.

Rumison stared at him. "What in hell does that have to do with anything?"

"Have you?"

"No."

"You should read up on Persian history when you get home," said Black. "You see, they have this saint there. Very well known. His name is Rumi."

A loud ringing suddenly filled Rumison's ears. He could see the old Chinese man grinning at him. He remembered Hermilia. . . . "Three saints . . ."

And abruptly it occurred to Rumison just what it was about Black that had been bothering him. Black had not once moved his legs since Rumison had dragged him out of the pool.

"Have you wondered," Black asked again, "what it all meant? Why you are the only one still alive after all that has happened?"

"You're still alive," Rumison objected nervously.

"I'm talking about you."

Rumison shook his head. "There is no reason."

Black's gray eyes seemed to bore holes through Rumison, and Rumison couldn't look away. "Maybe there's no reason now, Rumison," said Black, his eyes glinting with a strange light of inner amusement. "But wash yourself in the dew, boy, there still is time to make one. You owe it to the others."

It was not until sometime later that Rumison really understood what Black had meant.

Chapter Twenty-Four

THE next morning, while Rumison was outside the cave, Black shot and killed himself. Rumison heard the shot as a muffled pop, more a change in air pressure than anything. Slowly, knowing what he would find, he entered the cave.

Black lay as he had been, his eyes closed, blood running from his mouth, and a small penny-size hole under his jaw. Ever the professional, he had held the barrel not into his mouth, but upward, into the soft area between the jaw and neck where the trajectory of the bullet would carry it through the carotid artery and into the pons and midbrain.

Rumison had known without Black having told him that Black had broken his back when he had fallen from the overhang. The knowledge helped to explain Black's odd behavior the night before—the last sentiments of a man who knew he was soon to die.

Rumison's thoughts were shapeless as he gazed at the body, still clutching the pistol in its muscular right hand.

Rumison took what supplies he felt he needed. The rest he left at Black's feet, thinking vaguely of Celtic warrior burials. He pulled the black briefcase out and stared at it. Underneath it, in Black's pack, was a thick envelope he hadn't noticed before. He knew immediately it was the manuscript to Cordobes' book. The paper was wet and heavy, but he put it in his pack with the other supplies. He stared at the black briefcase a moment longer and then placed it at Black's feet with the other things that he was leaving behind.

Rumison went outside and began bringing in rocks from

the ledge around the pool to the cave, stacking them around Black's body. It took him most of the morning to complete the rough cairn. Maybe the animals will get him anyway, he thought, but he hoped not. When he had finished he rested and ate and then made ready to leave.

In the bright midmorning sunlight the waterfall seemed childishly easy to climb. Rumison found a route that hadn't been apparent the evening before and skirted the troublesome overhang. He saw no sign of the blackbird. The day was hot and still.

It took him another day to hike out of the jungle. He crossed the San Juan River, the border to Costa Rica, and caught a ride on the Pan American Highway with a churlish Scotsman who introduced himself as Robert Charon, a tree finder for a Costa Rican lumber company. Rumison considered going directly to the American embassy in San José but decided against it and had Charon leave him on the outskirts of the little port town of Punto Arenas. Three hours later he had signed aboard a small diesel yacht, heading north as a crewman. The yacht was being delivered by the hired crew to its owner in Puerto Vallarta, Mexico. Ten days later, during the night to avoid questions, Rumison swam ashore in Mexico and bought a bus ticket to Mexicali.

The American border guard eyed his gaunt face suspiciously. "Are you an American citizen?"

Rumison, who was now wearing clothes he had bought in Mexicali and carrying nothing but the money he'd taken from Tienda's store and a small wool bag with Cordobes' manuscript inside, nodded.

"Say it," said the guard.

"I'm a U.S. citizen," said Rumison.

"All right. Go on through."

Rumison was back in the United States. It seemed strange to him. New. Fresh. The people looked innocent and unaware, going about their lives as though there weren't the terrible unknown lurking just over their shoulders, waiting to pounce. Waxwork figures, living waxwork lives. And yet there was a compassion Rumison felt now that also was new, and a sweet poignancy that came from the realization of how fragile that world he saw before him really was.

He took a Greyhound bus to Laguna Beach and then walked the extra two miles to his house. It was summer already and the streets were crowded with tourists. The house was locked. He got the spare key from where it always had been kept under a flower pot and entered. On the kitchen table he found a handwritten note from Barney's girl friend, Georgiana:

Dear Guys:

I'm so worried . . . you've been gone two weeks and no one says anything. I've gone home. My father is a jerk but he has connections and has offered to try and find out something. If you get home, please call me immediately.

P.S. URGENT.

The note was signed, "Love, George," and underneath was a Los Angeles area telephone number. Rumison dialed it, surprised to find the telephone still working.

"The Van Mannon residence," answered a male voice with a stiff British accent.

"I'd like to talk to Georgiana, please."

There was a pause. "Who is calling, please?"

Rumison hesitated. "Michael Rumison," he said. "A friend."

He waited. He heard quick footsteps, followed by Georgiana's high, excited voice. "Mike? Oh, Mike, is it really you?"

"It's me, George," said Rumison

He really knew very little about Barney's girl friend and he couldn't judge how she'd react.

"Oh, Mike!" she cried. "I was so worried. I tried everything to find out where you went, but they wouldn't tell me anything. Are you all right? Where's Barney? Oh, why didn't he call me? Damn him! Is Rosso there? Oh, Mike! What happened? Where have you been?"

"Barney and Rosso are dead," he said.

There was silence. "Dead?" came the small voice.

"I'm sorry," he said, feeling her pain as though it were his.

"Oh . . ."

"It's a long story, George."

"I'll be right down. Are you at the house?"

"Yes. I'll wait for you."

Rumison put the receiver back in its cradle and sighed. He hadn't realized it would be so hard. After some minutes had passed he picked it up again and dialed the administration office of the 68th Aerospace Rescue and Recovery Squadron. A voice he didn't recognize answered, identifying himself as Sergeant Kibik.

"I'm trying to find someone I heard was stationed with you," said Rumison. "His name is Michael Rumison, a pararescueman."

"Sergeant Rumison is no longer with his unit," said Kibik. "There was a rearrangement of manning allocations a few months ago and he and several others were given early outs just a couple of weeks ago. Can I ask what this concerns?"

"Uh, yeah. I wanted to ask about his house in Laguna. I heard it might be up for sale."

"As far as I know, that's where he should be," said Kibik. "After the discharge, we lose track."

"I understand he had a friend out there . . . a Major Larry Hawkes? Maybe I could talk to him?"

"Hawkes?" asked Kibik. The voice seemed surprised.

"Yeah. Maybe he could help me find where Rumison is."

There was a dead silence on the other end of the line. Finally Kibik answered. "I'm sorry," he said stiffly, "but Major Hawkes was killed in an automobile accident two weeks ago."

"Killed?"

"An accident. Excuse me, sir, but who did you say was calling?"

Rumison hung up, feeling empty.

Georgiana arrived an hour later. She was driving a new Mercedes sedan, and the makeup she was wearing around her pale blue eyes was streaked. When she saw Rumison, thin, bearded, his face still scabbed from his ordeals, she almost broke into tears again.

"Oh, Mike!" she cried, throwing her arms around him as though he were a small boy.

Rumison was thinking of how much she reminded him of

Barney . . . slender, blond, fey. He was also thinking of how he had never really looked at her before, understood her.

They sat down on the couch and he told her the story. She didn't interrupt, not even when he told her how Barney had died. When he finished she was quiet.

"George," asked Rumison, "you said your father tried to help. What did he do?"

Georgiana shook her head. "I really don't know," she said softly. "He called, talked to some people. He has a friend who is a state senator. Everyone just said the same thing. You all had been discharged. No one knew where you were. Even my dad believed it. . . ."

Georgiana looked like she was going to cry again. Rumison sighed. "Rosso always thought we'd been set up," he said. It didn't seem that important anymore. There were other things. . . . "What should I do?" he asked.

Georgiana looked up at him with something like surprise on her face. "Do?" she asked. "Of course you know what to do."

Rumison was confused. Georgiana was staring at him with a strange look, and tears glistened her eyes. He misunderstood and put his arm around her to try to comfort her. "Come on, George," he said. "It'll work out."

She pulled away, incredulous. "You idiot!" she cried. "You really don't know what to do, do you?"

Rumison stopped, in shock. "What are you talking about?" he finally asked.

The tears had left Georgiana's eyes now, and she seemed angry. "I'm talking about the same thing you said that man Black talked about. . . ."

"Yes, but—"

"Listen to me! The girl, Mike. You have to go back for the girl. Don't you see? It's the only thing that would make sense. You have to go back for the girl!"

Rumison was stunned, as though he had been struck a physical blow. "I killed her father," he said weakly. "I ran out on her."

"Damn it!" cried Georgiana. "You don't know he's dead. And if you go back, you wouldn't have run out on her. Don't you understand? She's the key. You said yourself she's the symbol of the broken dream . . . but the dream doesn't have to be broken. It doesn't have to be meaningless!"

Understanding rushed in on Rumison like an ocean wave, bringing with it a terrible, numbing responsibility, and with that responsibility an overwhelming fear. The terror of a small boy given a dangerous task he knows he might not be up to. I'm not who she thinks I am! cried that small, despairing voice in his heart.

But with the fear and the terror and the knowledge of his own inadequacies there also came a quiet but growing sense of release, similar to what he had experienced before parachuting into the Nicaraguan jungle, a feeling that some great weight had been taken off his soul. He knew now, in truth, that there was indeed only one thing he could do.

His body shuddered with conflicting emotions, but when the spasms had passed, Rumison was calm.

Book Two

McGREGOR

I am forever shutting out the sunrise,
lest the sunrise kill me.

—Walt Whitman

Chapter Twenty-Five

"He's the best man for the job," said the general, his still boyish face earnest with the lines of a man who believes totally in what he is saying. The director didn't answer immediately. He had seen the act too many times before. Instead he looked to the other man in the room, a grim, ascetic-faced man twenty years the general's junior but appearing five years older.

"Nat?"

"You know what I think, director."

The director picked up a thick yellow personnel file from his desk, weighed it in his hand, and then let it drop from a height of four inches back onto the desk. "Do we have a choice?" he asked.

"Even if we did, we couldn't get anyone better," broke in the general, his right hand clenched in a fist as he leaned toward the director. "The man is tailor-made for the assignment. Speaks fluent Spanish, comes from a Caribbean background, knew Bastanchury intimately, in fact was one of his closest friends."

"I didn't know Bastanchury had any friends," said the director, frowning.

The general shrugged. The move hardly broke the crease in his Air Force blues. "He fought with him in Asia. Learned from him. Respected him. Other than Bastanchury, I'd say he was the best unattached in the business."

"When he's of a mind. What about Nat's objections?"

The general paused. Some of the certainty left his blue eyes, a fact the director noted.

"You have to realize, sir," began the general carefully,

"That when dealing with men of this type you are bound to find eccentricities. Why, Bastanchury himself was—"

"We are dealing with more here than 'eccentricities,' " broke in the other man, his voice heavy with sarcasm. He looked at the director and nodded at the personnel folder. "You've read the psychological profile, sir. I need say no more other than the obvious fact that we can't let this project go wrong. We all know the wager. If Castro, or the Communist-bloc countries should ever—"

"That's exactly why I am standing by him," said the general.

The director had already made his decision when he looked up from his mahogany desk at the two aides. Nat Bishop was young and educated with a Ph.D. from Yale in political science. In private Bishop's staff referred to him as "the Housewife," referring to his mindless attention to detail and constant fault-finding proclivities. General Gwilyn S. Norris was Bishop's exact opposite. Positive and eager, he had been one of the Air Force's youngest generals before going to work full time for the intelligence community some twenty years earlier. In public the two men men appeared almost to hate one another, but in private, the director knew, they operated very well as a team.

The director slowly picked up the file and handed it across the desk to Norris, who took it with a wide smile. Bishop's expression didn't change. "It's your ball game, Gwil. You know what happens if this McGregor blows it."

"We'll see that he doesn't, sir."

"Use Nat's people for that. They're good at that sort of thing."

Bishop took the comment without smiling. Now that he thought about it, the director couldn't remember if he'd ever seen Bishop smile.

The two aides left the polished-hardwood-paneled office and the director leaned back in his leather chair and sighed. It would be a rough one, he thought. According to the reports and all logic, a tremendous amount depended on its successful completion, perhaps a major shift in the delicate balance of the world's power structure. Not perhaps—definitely. And much of its success depended on the as-yet-obscure motivations of an Air Force sergeant named Rumison and the ability of a temperamental, extremely eccentric (at best) free-lance intelligence agent named McGregor.

The director sighed because, in spite of his positaon, in spite of the thousands of sources of information he had access to, the microfilm, the telephones, the computers, the men, the libraries, the scientists, the help of the CIA, the FBI, the military intelligence agencies, the cameras, the machines, the energy, he knew how very little he really knew about what was happening in the world. He believed that history is made by men, and when the outcome of a major historical event was to be determined by the acts of one or two of those frail creatures, it was humbling to realize how little one knew about one's fellow man, or the world.

"I'm becoming a mystic," thought the director, and then his thoughts turned to Richard Francis Burton McGregor and he sighed again.

Chapter Twenty-Six

THE late-summer Taos sun was hot even in the afternoon as McGregor ran. He had been running for ten miles and had five to go. It was Sunday. Most days he only ran five miles, but Sundays, a day for rest, he ran fifteen. Today something was troubling him and the running came hard.

He didn't run on a set course. There was a deer trail that started somewhere near his adobe but it had many branches. He judged distance by time, figuring that he could run five miles in just under thirty minutes and fifteen in about an hour and forty minutes. Most days he enjoyed the running, but today, in spite of the crystal fresh air, his breathing was labored and his muscles ached. He didn't think about what might be troubling him. For one thing he had no idea what it was, and for another he knew thinking about it wouldn't help. Whatever it was would surface, sooner or later. Sometimes it irritated him that his mind's ability to grasp information lagged so far behind his body's, but not now. Now he only wanted to finish the run.

He had seen no one since beginning the run. He'd started off on a trail branch that led around the Indian reservation, and you didn't normally meet people other than Indians in that area. The Indians were protective of their land and much of it was sacred. They had been known to get very nasty with trespassers, and it was not uncommon for some unsuspecting hunter or modern flower child to cross into a sacred area, only to be found later beaten and bewildered by the side of the road. McGregor had lived off and on in Taos for seven years, and though the Indians he knew he considered friends, he had never been invited onto the mountain or to Blue Lake.

There were stories of white men who had been taken into the tribe, blood brothers allowed to participate in the rituals, the myths, the lore of the Pueblo Indians of Taos. McGregor had even met one—Frank Cheshire, who had written several books on American Indians. He'd pumped Cheshire for every ounce of information the writer had, but Cheshire had remained as silent as a midnight grave when it came to speaking of the religion of Blue Lake and the ways of the Pueblo Indians.

Once McGregor had climbed up into the mountains during Ka'in'oetek, the Ritual of the Snake Festival, and watched from a ridge overlooking the lake as the Indian participants sat in a circle, eating what he speculated might be peyote, and every now and then, as if at random, rising and chanting or moving in a ritualized dance.

McGregor remembered again the words of one of his Indian friends: "The *cacique*, the holy one, says you could be the greatest, McGregor," Riley Dancing Waters Concha had said, answering McGregor's prodding one night at La Cocina Bar and Restaurant in Taos. Normally Riley kept his mouth shut on such matters, but that night McGregor had been drinking Cuervo Gold Tequila, and for every shooter he drank, Riley had finished two.

"Then why don't they accept me?" asked McGregor.

Riley looked sad and stared down at an empty shooter on the bar. His dark Indian features looked as if they were battling themselves, trying to find a way to tell a friend something that he might not want to hear.

"Leave it alone, McGregor. It's no big deal, being an Indian. Sometimes I think I'd rather have a Cadillac."

McGregor didn't answer. He knew Riley was trying to spare his feelings. He motioned to the bartender and another shooter was placed in front of the Indian. Riley didn't touch it. Instead he said, "The *cacique* said that you are not yourself, McGregor. He said that you could be one of the greatest but that you are not yourself. He asked, 'How can we trust one who is not himself?' I told him you looked like yourself to me, that you know a lot and have been through your own warrior training, but it didn't help. He is an old man. Perhaps he doesn't know. I'm sorry, McGregor."

McGregor's foot slipped on a loose rock and he almost fell. The feelings that had been troubling his body and his thoughts about what Riley had told him were making it difficult to hold a pace on the narrow path. With difficulty, for his mind wanted to wander, he forced his consciousness back to the here and now, concentrating on the path, the rocks, the red-brown dirt, the streams, the fences and animals, the cottonwood and piñon trees, and the mountains which loomed up enticingly on his left like a massive wall. But for all his concentration, a thought stayed in the back of his mind, dancing back and forth like a leaf caught in a canyon thermal. "If I am not myself, then who am I?"

Chapter Twenty-Seven

McGregor ran along the boundary of the reservation for another two miles before circling back down from the foothills toward Arroyo Seco, where he began seeing people again, Anglos mostly, post-flower children, skiers staying through the summer, artists, women living the new liberation, college dropouts, and one or two local ranchers. McGregor knew many of them but was in too much pain to wave back as they smiled greetings. He looked down at his watch, a gold-and-steel Rolex diver's watch. Five minutes to go, he thought. Judged it just about right. His house was a mile away.

The end of the run neared and McGregor's pain turned to agony. He could feel cramps forming in the muscles of his calves and his head was pounding. He saw his house in the distance and glanced down again at his watch. The hour and forty minutes had passed, but McGregor ran on for another full minute before finally coming to an exhausted stop. He stood for several minutes with his head down between his knees, taking in deep fast breaths and fighting off an urge to collapse on the hard clay ground. As he raised his head he saw his house still several hundred yards in front of him. His eyes cleared and he could see a car parked on the dirt road in front of his house. It was a dull green Plymouth four-door. McGregor had seen its like many times before. He knew without thinking that its license plates would be government and he also knew that the car had something to do with the thing that had been bothering him.

"How far did'ye run?"

McGregor turned, his senses not yet clear. A man was standing watching him from his right. Five foot nine or ten, close-cropped hair, straight posture, casual clothes, boyish friendly smile, middle-aged but looking much younger because of the boyishness.

"Fifteen miles," answered McGregor, expecting the man to be surprised, but the man just nodded.

"That's right, it's Sunday," he said.

McGregor made a mental note to rearrange his running schedule, probably on a random basis. He didn't like to be predictable in anything he did.

"What do you people want?" he asked, shaking his head to get the perspiration off his forehead.

The man laughed good-naturedly. "Are we that obvious?" he asked.

"Interagency motor-pool car, short hair. Yeah, you're that obvious. Besides, I had a feeling."

"I've heard about your feelings," said the man.

"Military," continued McGregor, ignoring him. "Not robot enough for the Marines. Not shaggy enough for the Navy. Army or Air Force. I'd say Air Force. Colonel probably. Intelligence. You have a job that needs a free agent. Something sticky."

"General," said the man. "But you're right on the other counts."

"General," repeated McGregor and then his mind cleared. "Norris?" he asked.

"Gwil Norris," said the general, holding out his hand. McGregor looked at it for a full five seconds before deciding to take it. He had nothing against Norris, had in fact heard good things about him. The Air Force's boy wonder, after Lauris Norstad, until he'd gone to work full-time with the Agency.

"It's a little sweaty," apologized McGregor.

"Fifteen miles is a long way to run."

McGregor nodded. "You don't mind if I walk around a bit," he said, beginning a slow loosening walk before Norris had a chance to answer. Norris followed him.

"You up for a job?" he asked.

McGregor's first impulse was to say no, that he had retired and the Agency knew it, but there was something about that feeling. . . .

"What sort of job?"

"Sticky one, all right. Recovery mission, maybe down to Central America."

"Nicaragua or El Salvador?"

The general smiled. "You still keep up on current events," he said.

"Not hard to figure."

McGregor walked for another five minutes without talking, and Norris didn't press him. McGregor didn't want the mission. He didn't want anything to do with the Agency, but there was that feeling, and General Gwilyn Norris didn't do errand-boy chores. Whatever the mission was, it was big and messy.

"Nice house," commented Norris after a while. "You build it yourself?"

McGregor nodded, knowing Norris already knew the answer plus a lot more about him than the fact that he had built his own house out of river rocks, logs, and hand-blocked adobe. He kicked off his blue Adidas running shoes, stepped out of his shorts, and walked under an outdoor shower he had made off to the side of the house out of old barnwood. Norris appeared to watch unconcernedly as McGregor showered.

"I'm retired," said McGregor several minutes later as he turned off the shower. He picked up a towel hung on a nail by the shower and toweled off.

"It would pay well," said Norris unperturbed.

Why am I even considering this? thought McGregor to himself. Out loud he said, "Not well enough. I don't need money."

"We estimate you have less than eighty thousand. Conservatively invested, after taxes that doesn't leave much."

"I don't need much."

McGregor's body was beginning to feel better and the pain in his head was clearing. Vaguely he wondered if Norris had picked that exact time to show up, believing it might catch him off guard.

"Nice house," said Norris again, following as McGregor picked up his clothes and walked around to the front door. McGregor was proud of the house. He'd built it without plans from an idea he'd had in his mind. Nine sided, an enneagon, everything was hand fitted and finished in rough-hewn natural wood. It wasn't a large house but seemed spacious because it had only four rooms: the central room, which included the kitchen, den, living room, and dining area; one bedroom; one bathroom; and an exercise room.

"Mind if I look around?" asked Norris.

McGregor shrugged. "Help yourself. I've got to get some clothes on."

McGregor took his time getting dressed, trying to feel himself out so he could deal with Norris. He put on old Levi's, desert boots, and a faded Hawaiian shirt, and sat on his bed for several minutes staring at the Indian rug on the floor. When he returned to the central room he found Norris looking over his library, one wall of books in the area he called his den.

"Strange assortment," commented Norris.

"Let's get to the point, Norris," said McGregor finally. "Money won't do it and you know that. What's this mission all about?"

Norris smiled his boyish smile. "You could write your own ticket on this one," he said. "Half a million."

McGregor blinked. The most he'd ever been offered before was a tenth of that, but this in itself wouldn't make him change his mind. That feeling . . .

The smile left Norris' face and he was looking straight into McGregor's eyes. Something few men ever did.

"Bastanchury is dead," he said, his voice without inflection

Nothing the general could have said would have affected McGregor more than those three words. McGregor stood dumbly. It was seconds before he could even think, much less talk.

"How?" was all he could ask.

"That's the mission, McGregor. You're to find out how." The general's voice was low and sympathetic, but McGregor wasn't listening. He was thinking of Bastanchury. No one's death should have affected him that much. Why Bastanchury's?

"How do you know he's dead?"

"It's a long, involved story," said the general. "Mind if I sit down? I could use something cold too. It's hot outside. I don't see how you run in this weather."

McGregor nodded, and without thinking went over to

the refrigerator and poured two large glasses of cold apple juice. The general took his gratefully.

"Several months ago," began Norris after taking a long drink of juice, "before summer, a private jet went down in the Mosquito Rain Forest area on the east coast of Nicaragua. A passenger on that jet was carrying something absolutely critical to the welfare of this country—"

"So Castro was right," said McGregor.

"Not exactly," answered Norris. "The item in question was not directly involved in any so-called CIA plans to overthrow that government. So far Castro is just making an ass of himself at the U.N."

"So far?"

"It all ties in. Bastanchury was given the mission to sterilize the aircraft before the Sandinistas could get to it. A sneaky-Pete operation was mounted with Bastanchury and four military types. Air Force . . ." The general looked strangely apologetic as he said this, and McGregor wondered why.

"It was necessarily a quick operation," continued Norris, "or should have been. The jet itself wasn't difficult to locate. We had the electronic signals from the transcorder. Bastanchury apparently accomplished the sterilization while means were being readied to get the team out; either a helicopter from Guantanamo or the Fulton Recovery System. Bastanchury radioed up that they'd located a survivor, but by this time Howard gave us word the Nicaraguan Air Force was in the area. No way to get them out. An alternate pickup point had been scheduled, and the team took off through the jungle. They never reached that pickup point."

"He was good in the jungle," said McGregor absently. He was remembering a day fifteen years earlier when he had first met Michael Bastanchury, a major in the Special Forces and commander of a small group advising a Montagnard hill village in Viet Nam before the real war broke out. McGregor had been a nervous, green lieutenant straight out of Fort Bragg.

"Richard Francis Burton McGregor," Bastanchury had said before anything else. "That name mean anything to you?" Bastanchury was one of the most formidable-looking men McGregor had ever met, thick-boned but muscularly lean, with piercing pale eyes.

McGregor was confused. "Sir?"

"Your name. The Richard Francis Burton part. It mean anything to you?"

"My mother named me," answered McGregor, still not sure what the major wanted. "Burton was an English explorer she admired."

Bastanchury snorted. "English explorer, my ass. I would have liked to have known your mother. She must have been a great lady, admiring a man like Burton. She is dead, isn't she? That's what the report says."

McGregor nodded.

"Well, if you want to live to be one-tenth the man your namesake was, we have a lot of work ahead. How are you at languages?"

Bastanchury had a way of looking at people that made them feel guilty or inadequate somehow, and McGregor didn't like that feeling. He remembered wanting to prove himself. "I know four languages well, sir," he said, trying hard not to let any pride show in his voice. "And they ran me through a short course in Yard before I flew here."

"What languages?"

"English, Spanish, French, and a bit of Chinese."

"I thought you said you knew four languages *well.*"

McGregor's face burned.

"No matter," continued Bastanchury. "You have a long way to go. The original Burton knew thirty-nine languages."

"Thirty-nine . . ." choked McGregor.

"Thirty-nine. I know twelve and I don't even like languages. I'll give you over to one of the Yards to get that language down and then you can start on Vietnamese. That's all, Lieutenant. Report back to your hutch."

Memory after memory crowded through McGregor's mind, and then he realized General Norris had asked him a question.

"You and Bastanchury were in Asia together, weren't you?" said Norris, repeating himself.

McGregor nodded. "You know we were, General. Finish your story."

"Officially, that's all there is."

"And unofficially?"

"Unofficially it's a different story. We've put together a scenario from isolated facts and suppositions that goes like this: On June first of this year, the Sandinistas announced capture of a team of American agents engaged in espionage in Nicaragua. The description they gave matched Bastanchury's team to a T. Pressed for proof, they stalled and finally had to back down. Indications were that they had planned to produce three dead bodies for proof, but without identification they probably realized it was useless. They needed something more."

"Three dead bodies? I thought you said there were five on the team plus a survivor?"

Norris waved his hand. "Let me finish. It was known to us that the Sandinistas did indeed have three bodies whose descriptions match Rosso, Sleeper, and Bailey, members of Bastanchury's team. Bastanchury and an Air Force sergeant named Michael Rumison were never caught by them. The survivor Bastanchury had reported never left the wreck. Probably killed by Bastanchury, at least that's what they've been saying, and we have no reason to doubt it."

"Why would Bastanchury have killed his own man?"

"Bastanchury was a realist."

"Yes, but . . ." began McGregor, but then he remembered again a part of the personality of the man who had taught him what his name meant, and he understood. Norris saw this and continued.

"During this time one of our men in the Bluefields area, not far actually from the alternate pickup point Bastanchury's team missed, reported that a reward had been offered for three American agents whose descriptions again matched Bastanchury, Rumison, and Rosso. We assume from this that by then Sleeper and Bailey were already dead. A woman, wife of one of the local plantation owners, subsequently claimed, and was paid, the reward. Sergeant Rosso apparently bought it on that plantation but Bastanchury and Rumison escaped again, rumor has it in a small Piper used by the plantation for tree spotting and dusting. Bastanchury was never heard from again."

"Then you can't be sure if he's really dead."

"There's one last fact," said Norris. The way he said it made McGregor halt the chain of his thoughts.

"Sergeant Michael Rumison is definitely known to have returned to the U.S. alone before disappearing again."

There was quiet in the house. A bird whistled outside. General Norris finished his apple juice. McGregor waited.

"We're whistling in the breeze, like that bird there," said Norris finally. "Nobody knows what is going on. The Sandinistas don't have them, we know that much. You knew Bastanchury as well as anyone. You know if he was still alive he'd have let us know. Some of my colleagues figure Rumison found out what was in the case and is trying a blackmail, but that doesn't fit, either with my estimation of Rumison's character or certain other facts. Besides, he would have contacted someone by now."

"Case?" asked McGregor casually.

Norris sighed. "That's what it's really all about," he said quietly. "Bastanchury took it off the courier on the jet. Black attaché case. Bondex lock, reinforced stainless steel. Need special tools to get into it. Not even Bastanchury knew what was in it. In fact, I don't know what's in it, but you can believe it's hot. Very hot."

"Yeah, I can believe that, but I can't believe you don't know what it contains. You're practically second to the director, from what I hear. If you don't know . . . ?"

"That's the rub," said the general. "It's ironic, but this isn't even really the Agency's game, yet it could mean its end if what's in that case ever gets out."

"Whose game is it, then, General?"

"I can't tell you that, McGregor. Believe me, I wish I could, but that's where the line on our information to you is drawn. Anything else, but not that."

McGregor sighed, his eyes staring out the front plate-glass window at the mountains. It was getting close to evening and sunset. McGregor had paced the window so it would face the mountains at sunset. He liked sunsets more than sunrises. He like the evening better than the morning. Judging by the cloud formations, it would be a good sunset that evening.

"That's the mission," said the general. "Rumison is the key. Find out what happened to Bastanchury and get that case. Either bring it to us or destroy it."

"I haven't said I'd take the mission, Norris."

"You'll take it."

"You seem to think you know me, General. It could be a mistake on your part."

General Norris looked over at McGregor's face, into his eyes again. He seemed to be looking for something. Suddenly the boyish enthusiasm left, and McGregor saw an aging man in front of him. "I had a hero once, McGregor," said the general quietly, so quietly McGregor could barely hear him. "Among other things, he was an English explorer. I've always been sorry I never had the guts to be like that person."

McGregor felt inexplicably embarrassed. A scene from the Orson Welles movie *Citizen Kane* flashed across his mind, the Rosebud scene at the end. It made him very sad and left him at a disadvantage with the general, whose face was once more masked by the eager, boyish, calculating career military man.

Maybe you do know something about me, General, he thought.

Chapter Twenty-Eight

"THAT'S it, McGregor," said Norris, setting two attaché cases down on the dining table in McGregor's house. "In those two cases is everything we know about Bastanchury's mission, beginning from the time he was called in. They're expecting me in Albuquerque at eight, so I have to hurry."

"You mean that's it?" asked McGregor. "No hype sessions, no funny guns and fake ID?"

"There's ten thousand dollars cash in one case, and forms for fake ID. You know why we hire you, McGregor. Because the Agency doesn't want to get directly involved. This time it's crucial. You're all but on your own." Norris took out a pad and wrote a telephone number on it. McGregor recognized the area code as Virginia.

"If you need something—information, more money, weapons, whatever—call this number. A pickup spot will be arranged for the transfer." Norris paused. "Perhaps I should tell you, in the event you are caught . . ."

"You never heard of me."

"Oh, we've heard of you all right. A free-lance agent employed by Great Britain at the time of your capture. The background is all set."

"Won't that strain relations with England a bit?" asked McGregor sarcastically.

Norris shrugged. "England's fair game now. No power, no prestige. She's sinking. She can't afford to object, and people can't pick on her as much as they used to. That end's taken care of also."

"You guys are real bastards, sometimes."

"I've heard the same about you, McGregor. But enough name-calling. I shouldn't have come here personally anyway. My neck is on the line, but I knew anyone else would have had a hard time convincing you. . . ." Norris held out his hand again. This time McGregor ignored it.

"Well," said the general, lowering it. "Can't say as I blame you." He turned to go.

"One last thing," he said. "About Rumison." McGregor could hear that strange note of apology in the general's voice. "None of those Air Force types knew what the mission was about. All they were told was that it was a rescue mission. They were from Air Rescue. Bailey and Rosso were Rumison's best friends. It's my personal belief that Rumison blames the U.S. for their deaths, which is why he disappeared without reporting in."

"And you aren't to blame?" asked McGregor.

Norris shrugged. "Just thought I'd tell you. You ought to be able to understand something like that." The boyish grin returned to his face. "Whatever, McGregor. Good luck." He turned again and left.

McGregor left the cases on the table and poured himself a glass of white wine before starting dinner. He ate by himself—lamb chops, rice, and salad—and watched the sunset, the red-golden rays highlighting the cumulus clouds and disappearing over the mountains. After dinner he washed the dishes. His housework done, he put a Bob Dylan tape on an elaborate built-in stereo system and sat down to study what Norris had given him. All the time a small voice in the back of his head was telling him that he shouldn't have accepted the mission, while the rest of him knew he had no other choice. The Agency and the case could go to hell, but McGregor had to find out how and why Bastanchury had died—if he was dead. And if not, he had to find Bastanchury.

Photos, personnel files, intelligence briefs, ten thousand dollars cash in hundreds and twenties, blank ID cards for everything from the FBI to a Cuban bureaucrat—that was it. Not much, considering the importance of the mission. Someone must have a lot of faith in him, McGregor thought. Either that or things weren't quite what they seemed. He thought the latter much more likely but it didn't change matters. He opened up the file on Air Force

Pararescue Technical Sergeant Michael Paul Rumison: Born May 3, 1951, Tucson, Arizona. Raised in Laguna Beach after the family moved there in 1956. Graduated high school 1969, B student, lettered in swimming. Graduated from the University of California at Santa Barbara in 1973, C average, lettered four years swimming, three water polo. Joined the Air Force to avoid induction into the infantry.

On the surface, Michael P. Rumison seemed a fairly normal California beach boy, intelligent and athletically able but lacking in motivation. His greatest interests seemed to be surfing, mountain climbing, and skiing, with a few other sports thrown in for good measure. Surprisingly, his IQ rating was near genius and his service-record scores were in the ninety-ninth percentile. His father had owned and run a small charter business that operated out of Newport Beach and then Dana Point marina until he died along with Rumison's mother a year earlier in an automobile accident. Since Rumison's only sibling, a brother, had been missing for several years, he was sole heir to a small beach house and ten thousand dollars in insurance money, which he had used to upgrade the charter business before selling it.

The psychological profile didn't tell him anything he hadn't already deducted from the personal history. It had been quickly done, obviously after the fact. The handwriting analysis was equally blank. Rumison was a strong, capable, intelligent individual who lacked real motivation—the result, the report read, of being raised in a middle-class family in the rather idyllic surrounds of a Southern California beach town where surfing, swimming, and boating were a way of life. The report was in all respects typical of every one-dimensional, shallow case history that filled governmental files.

What McGregor wanted to know, what he would have to find out, was where and what Rumison was now. He held up two photos of Rumison, one a blown-up passport photo and another of him in Air Force blues wearing a red beret. They both showed a rugged-looking man, cleft chin, dark hair which probably grew curlier as it got longer, and bright-blue eyes that seemed innocent and almost childlike in an otherwise mature face.

The files on Rosso, Bailey, and Sleeper were no more enlightening. Master Sergeant Kenneth Allan Sleeper, McGregor dismissed. An Air Force lifer ready for retirement. No family, no close friends, low IQ compared to the others. Why Bastanchury had chosen him for such a strenuous and important mission posed a question, but the answer could wait. Rosso's history was remarkably similar to Rumison's. Both parents dead. They were beach raised, athletic and intelligent. Bailey was ten years younger; an army brat who enlisted voluntarily, highly intelligent but less physically capable than either Rosso or Rumison. No known living relatives . . .

No known living relatives? The information filed itself under unlikely coincidences in McGregor's brain. Norris had said that the four Air Force men hadn't known what they were getting into. He'd been strangely reserved, almost embarrassed by the fact. Maybe he hadn't let on all he knew. The Agency wasn't likely to use assassination in these days of congressional hearings and investigations, but this mission had been no ordinary one. If Rumison suspected as much, it would explain his never reporting in and his later disappearance.

McGregor put the files down and sat back in the soft leather couch. Dylan was singing "Just Like a Woman." He was tired and sore from his run and needed a quiet night's sleep. He sipped some apple juice and returned to his studies.

Chapter Twenty-Nine

LAGUNA BEACH used to be a small art colony located sixty miles south of the great sprawl of Los Angeles, but sometime during the seventies, it had been discovered by the doctors, lawyers, insurance brokers, and professors trying to escape the high-intensity squeeze of Los Angeles county, and now most of the good artists are gone. The ones who remained had to jack up the prices on their art and go commercial in order to afford the cost of living in the suddenly wealthy town.

McGregor had been to Laguna Beach before and it made him sad to see the changes time had brought. The traffic was terrible and crowds of middle-class tourists thronged the streets. On the ocean's horizon he could see a brown trail of smog that blocked the view of Catalina Island. Some things hadn't changed, however, and McGregor thanked God for small favors. The city hadn't let high-rise in yet and the local architecture was still clapboard beach houses, lots of trees, and small, hilly streets that ended at rocky coves and small, sandy beaches.

McGregor pulled his rented Volkswagen into the parking lot of a beachside motel called the Riviera. He'd left Taos early that morning for the Santa Fe airport and rented the car in L.A. It was still before noon and a surprisingly hot day for the area, so, after checking into a room overlooking the beach, McGregor put on a pair of Hawaiian-print swimming trunks, grabbed a towel out of the bathroom, and walked down to the beach.

"Sorry."

McGregor looked at the boy who had spoken. Young,

tan, blond, he had thrown a Frisbee which barely missed McGregor's head. The "Sorry" had been automatic and perfunctory. There were too many tourists on the beach to worry about whom your Frisbee hit. The boy was playing with a young girl wearing a string bikini. Every time she caught the Frisbee her breasts would bounce almost free of the small crochet top, and McGregor watched her with a mixture of pleasure and wonder. Her moves were loose and unconsciously sexy though she couldn't have been over fourteen. The blond boy seemed immune to her charms, intent on making good passes with the plastic Frisbee.

McGregor was exhausted and had planned originally to lie down on the beach in front of the hotel, but it seemed to be a hangout for prepubescent surfers, so he decided to walk until he found a quieter area of sand.

The surf was good-sized, and McGregor thought he might go body-surfing later. Like Rumison, he also had been raised around the water and he even had a small house in Hawaii, on Kauai, that he hoped no one else knew about. He visited it occasionally under a different name. As he walked he watched the beach crowds, mostly younger, all tanned, the girls almost uniformly beautiful. The girl with the Frisbee was the rule rather than the exception. He remembered reading an interview a magazine had done with Timothy Leary, the ex–Harvard professor who had established a worldwide drug ring centered in Laguna Beach. The interview was conducted in Switzerland, where Leary was in hiding. "Do you miss the United States?" the interviewer had asked. Leary had replied that all he missed was Mexican marijuana and Laguna Beach girls. McGregor could see why.

After walking for nearly a mile, McGregor gave up on finding an uncrowded bit of sand. Even though it wasn't a weekend it was a hot summer day and the beach was jammed. He laid his towel down near a volleyball court and sat down. The group around the court were obviously locals, most of them in the high school–college age bracket, but a few older people too. McGregor watched a game of good two-man for a few rounds before his attention started wandering back to the girls. He made eye-contact with one girl he found particularly attractive, and, to his surprise, she didn't look away but smiled. He smiled back and then was amazed at himself for being the first to break eye-contact. He looked at the girl again, a pretty brunette in a maroon string bikini, but she was talking to a boy next to her, seemingly unaware of the previous moment's intimacy with the dark stranger who had just sat down.

McGregor was a handsome man, by any standards. He was one-fourth black, which gave his skin an ebony tinge that women found attractive, especially when contrasted with his green Irish eyes. He'd shaved off his beard the night before, making him look younger than his forty years, but somehow he didn't think age was much of a factor in Laguna Beach. The girl he'd been drawn to couldn't have been much out of high school, but if he had read her eyes right, she liked what she saw. His hair was long and his body was incredibly fit after forty miles a week hard running, an hour a day weight and yoga workout, and a three-times-a-week martial-arts workout. He'd never before had much problem with women, and it seemed easier as he got older, but there was something about the girls here, an ease and boldness, that was putting him into an unfamiliar defensive position. He found himself thinking up reasons why he shouldn't pursue things farther with the girl who had smiled: her age, the job he was in town to do, the surrounding crowd.

Maybe it's jet lag, he thought. He stood up from the towel and dove into the water.

The water was warm. McGregor saw a buoy about five hundred yards offshore and began a slow, easy crawl out toward it. Rumison was raised in this town, he thought. Among girls like that. It must have been a shock for him and the others, finding themselves involved with a man like Bastanchury. McGregor wondered if Rumison might not have gone insane from the experience. He remembered the story of the Buddha, who had been kept in a beautiful palace away from the evils of a corrupt world by his father until one day he chanced to look over the palace walls. From then on the Buddha's philosophy had been: "It is all suffering, all illusion." Maybe Rumison had experienced something like that. McGregor laughed to himself as he wondered what Norris and the others would think about his speculations. Everything to them was cut-and-dried, filed away in neat, tidy packages that could be punched into a computer. When things went wrong for them, they always returned to the computer looking for the answer.

The swim did McGregor good, and he made up his mind on the return to shore to find a young lady for the night, maybe the one in the maroon bikini.

When he returned to the towel he looked for her, but her beach chair was empty and he couldn't see her in the crowd. He lay on his back and thought about Rumison and Bastanchury and pretty beach girls. After a while he decided it was time to get to work. He still had the whole afternoon in which to see the real-estate agent who had sold Rumison's house and perhaps to talk to some of the Air Force sergeant's friends. He looked over one last time to the girl's chair and saw that it was still empty, but as he began walking back toward the hotel he saw her standing by herself at the water's edge, apparently unaware of him as he approached.

"Hello," he said as he reached her. She looked up at him without surprise and smiled.

"Hello," she answered. "I saw you lying there. I was hoping you'd talk to me."

"You were? Well, in that case, what are you doing tonight?" McGregor had decided to be at least as forward as she was.

"Nothing. Let's go out."

"O.K. What's your name?"

"Jamie. What's yours?"

"McGregor," answered McGregor.

"McGregor?" asked the girl, still smiling, her eyes looking directly into his. "Is that all. Just McGregor?"

"Just McGregor. How 'bout dinner?"

"I'm on a diet," said Jamie. "Do you like to dance?"

McGregor shrugged. "Depends on who with. Do you want to go dancing?"

The girl nodded, pleased with herself. "Why don't you pick me up at my house," she said. "About eight. I know a good place in Newport we can go."

McGregor started to have second thoughts about the girl. He didn't particularly want to drive ten miles to Newport to go dancing at some noisy bar, and he didn't particularly feel like talking to some irate father if Jamie turned out to be as young as he thought she was, but then again she was the sexiest young woman he had talked to in several years.

"All right," he said. "Where do you live?"

"Do you have a good memory?"

"Excellent."

"Five-oh-nine Bluebird Canyon. I'll see you at eight." The girl broadened her smile and then turned and ran back off toward her seat at the volleyball court.

Chapter Thirty

"YOU don't look like an Air Force man," said the bird-like little real-estate woman, eyeing first McGregor's forged ID card and then his long hair. McGregor was still trying to decide whether to act like a hard-nosed cop or the boy next door. The woman looked sharp. "Intelligence, ma'am," he said, smiling. He decided that the hard nose wouldn't go over too well with her.

"Intelligence? Don't tell me Michael Rumison is in trouble. I know better. I've known his family for years. Besides, he told me he was out of the Air Force."

"He is, ma'am. We're just tying up some loose ends. Just routine. The Air Force owes him a great deal of per-diem time that he was unaware of, and we can't seem to find him. He has to fill out some forms."

"He always was careless with money," said the woman, handing the green card back to McGregor, who made a show of putting it back into the plastic window in his wallet. She looked somewhat appeased but not enough for her to be careless with information. McGregor decided he liked her, which was unusual. He felt most real-estate people rated just above politicians and union leaders.

"Still and all," continued the woman, "there are some unusual things about it all. I don't know—"

"You said you knew him well," said McGregor quickly. "We're just trying to locate him. Perhaps you could tell me exactly what your involvement with him was after . . . say, June first."

The woman pursed her lips. Her eyes looked into McGregor's for a moment and then shifted away. "There's more to this than per-diem," she said decisively. "But then, I don't suppose you military types are going to tell an old lady what it is." Her eyes shifted back to McGregor's for confirmation. McGregor just stood, letting her come to her own conclusions.

"Ah, well, Major McGregor. I suppose I have to accept you on your word. However, I tell you this: I don't want to do anything that will hurt Michael Rumison. I don't think a real-estate agent's commitment to a client is exactly like a priest's or a lawyer's, but I feel strongly about the Rumisons. Always have."

The woman was sharp, thought McGregor, but not that sharp. Something had happened that was putting her on her guard, and he wanted to know what that was. He searched around for the best way to break through that guard, but the woman surprised him.

"Have a seat, Major. I'll tell you what I can."

McGregor took the offered chair and the woman told her story.

"Like I said, Major, I've known the Rumisons for years. Dan and Sue died just a while back. Automobile accident. Michael inherited it all. There was another brother, but he left home years ago. No one has heard from him since. Last June Michael approached me through this office and said he wanted to sell the house. Quickly. He offered to sell it for a hundred and fifty thousand dollars. The house originally cost only twenty-two thousand back in 1956, but with real-estate values being what they are today, particularly for beachfront property, the market value of the Rumisons' house couldn't have been less than three hundred thousand. Possibly as much as half a million, with the right buyer."

"Did he act troubled?" asked McGregor. "Frantic, anything like that?"

"It wasn't how he acted," answered the woman. She hadn't given her name to McGregor, but the placard on her desk read "Amy Witherwill," and he thought the name fit her. "He acted quite calm and deliberate. I tried to tell him that if he waited he could sell the house for twice what he was asking, but he said he needed the money and didn't want to bother with selling the place." Amy Witherwill paused, frowning. "No," she continued. "It wasn't how he acted. It was how he looked."

"Looked?"

"Maybe it was the beard, but I don't think so. He looked older. A lot older. When I'd seen him last he was a beach boy. Young, tanned, you know the type. This time he was older. You noticed it mostly in his eyes, but he was thinner. Gaunt almost. I asked him about it and all he said was that he'd been down in South America and gotten sick."

The phone on Amy Witherwill's desk rang and she answered it. Outside on the Coast Highway the traffic got worse as the inland tourists began leaving the beaches. McGregor's eyes glanced around the office, noting the faded black-and-white pictures of Laguna Beach down through the years that adorned the walls. They saddened him.

"A friend," apologized the woman, putting down the receiver on the phone.

"So you sold his house for him, Mrs. Witherwill," said McGregor.

"Not sold. Bought. And it's Miss, not Mrs. I couldn't pass up a bargain like that, so I bought it myself. Had to hock my underwear to do it."

McGregor chuckled at the woman's choice of language. "Do you remember the exact date?" he asked.

Miss Witherwill nodded. "June third. I told him I'd buy the house from him the next day. The deal was closed, escrow went through, and the last papers were signed two weeks to the day after that. Fastest I'd ever known it to happen."

"He took the money and left?"

"I haven't seen him since. He said he was leaving Laguna, but he never said where."

"Did he mention his friends, Bob Rosso or Barney Bailey?"

"You know, that was strange," said Miss Witherwill. "They'd all lived together ever since joining the Air Force, and I never saw them. When I asked Michael about them he said they were still in South America. He seemed very calm. Quite aware, but all the same he didn't talk much."

"After you bought the house, did you notice if Michael left any personal items around?"

"That was another strange thing, Major," said Miss Witherwill. "He left nearly everything. All the furniture. Clothes, books, chinaware, television—it was as if the house hadn't been touched. I imagine he took some of his own clothes with him when he left, but the dressers were still full. All of them, Bob's and Barney's also."

"Where did you store them?"

"Why, in the house. I haven't sold it yet. I'm waiting a bit before I put it on the market, for tax purposes. It's all there, just as it was. When I get ready to sell it, then perhaps I'll store it, but no use paying storage too soon if it's not necessary." Miss Witherwill sighed. "I suppose you would like to look through it?"

"If I could."

Miss Witherwill tapped a pencil on her desk blotter, laid it carefully down and then stood up. "I have no more business here today," she said finally. "I'll drive you over there. Not that I don't trust you alone, you understand, but . . ."

"I understand. I certainly appreciate it."

On the way over to the Rumison house McGregor kept asking Amy Witherwill questions that might give him more information about Air Force Sergeant Michael Paul Rumison's whereabouts, but there seemed little more she could offer other than the names of a few of Rumison's local friends. The real-estate woman was as good a driver as she was a businesswoman, maneuvering her silver Cadillac through the traffic and side streets like a New York taxi driver. It wasn't long before she found a just-vacated parking place on the small dead-end street that ran in front of the Rumisons' two-story beach house. McGregor got out and was walking around to help her, but she was out of the car before he got to her.

"It's a good house," she said as if talking to a customer. "Built strong, not like a lot of old beach houses. Doesn't look like much on the outside. Needs paint and a few repairs, but built well." She took out a key chain with numerous keys on it, selected one, and unlocked the front door. Once inside, she hurried around to open the curtains to let some light in.

The house was simply decorated in knotty pine and mahogany, looking like a home that a charter skipper might live in. As Miss Witherwill had said, it appeared as if little had been touched.

"Help yourself, Major," said Miss Witherwill. "I don't think there's much you can learn here, though. I've been through most of it."

McGregor knew that to get the most out of searching the house a team of experts would be necessary. Again he wondered why the Agency had entrusted such a supposedly important mission to one lone man, and again he came to the conclusion that he was being used somehow, that things were not what they seemed. He looked through the bedrooms, searching briefly through the one that must have been Rumison's. He couldn't tell what, if anything, had been taken. The dressers and closets looked full. Even the bathroom had razors and toothbrushes.

"How many people were living here with Baily, Rosso, and Rumison, Miss Witherwill?" asked McGregor.

"Why, just those three, I believe. Why do you ask?"

"It seems strange that what appeared to be Bailey's room was the largest and had a king-sized bed, when this was Rumison's house. I also noticed some feminine things in the bathroom. I thought maybe Bailey had a girl living with him."

"Why, I don't know. You know youngsters these days."

"It should be easy enough to check."

"Is it important?"

It could be very important, thought McGregor, without answering. It could be very, very important. The whole idea had been just a feeling, a hunch on McGregor's part, but over the years he had learned to trust his feelings more than most men trusted their reason.

McGregor looked at the wastepaper baskets, but they were all empty. The writing desk in the den was likewise empty of any recent doings. Rumison had left behind a very clean house. He probably knew someone would be after him, thought McGregor. If he was really running, he was too intelligent to be tripped up on something like leaving an airplane reservation stub in a trashcan.

McGregor paused in order to look at the numerous pictures which were hung on one wall in the den: pictures of Rumison's father on a small fishing boat, his two sons smiling by his side, the mother in a bathing suit, looking very pretty and stylish for 1959. Rumison in a Pararescue Graduation picture with Rosso, a picture of Rumison on the university swim team, another of him on a rock face climbing with ropes, and yet another with a surfboard under one arm, probably taken while he was in high school. Nothing to change the image in the intelligence report Norris had given McGregor, yet . . .

"I've seen enough, Miss Witherwill," said McGregor. "We can leave now."

"It is a mystery, isn't it?" said Amy Witherwill. "It's almost as if they had never really left."

"They've left, all right," said McGregor. He didn't add that at least two of them would never return.

Chapter Thirty-One

McGregor left Amy Witherwill at the Rumisons' house after giving her his room number at the motel and asking her to contact him if she should have any more information. It was only two miles back to his Volkswagen, and he wanted to talk to neighbors who might have known Rumison.

"I know there's something going on," said Miss Witherwill, getting into her Cadillac. "Someday I'll learn about it."

"You will, I'm sure," said McGregor.

The Rumisons' house overlooked a small cove and there were houses all around it, but most were summer rentals, and Miss Witherwill had said that their occupants probably wouldn't know the Rumisons. The house directly across the street was owned by a Hollywood scriptwriter named Barry Epecris. McGregor didn't recognize the name, but if the real-estate lady was right he had seen one or two of the man's movies. Epecris had been friends with the Rumisons. McGregor crossed the street and knocked on the large door.

"Can I help you?" The person who had spoken was a small girl. She looked up shyly at the man in front of her.

"Is your father in?"

The girl left McGregor standing at the door without answering. Seconds later a woman came to the door. She looked to be approaching forty but was still girlishly attractive though dressed in clay-spattered jeans and an oversized man's flannel work shirt. She brushed long brunette hair from her eyes in a coquettish manner and smiled at McGregor.

"Can I help you?"

"My name is McGregor. Major with Air Force Intelligence. I'm trying to locate Michael Rumison. Asking anyone in the area who may have seen him in the last few months."

The woman barely glanced at McGregor's proffered identification. "Barry knew the Rumisons better than I did," she said. "But he won't be back for several weeks. He's filming a script he did over in Hawaii."

McGregor couldn't decide if Mrs. Epecris was just being friendly or if she had other things on her mind, but she did have a very warm smile.

"Won't you come in Mr.—uh—Major . . . McGregor."

"Thank you, Mrs. Epecris."

The house inside was done in deep reds, with heavy, dark Spanish furniture, comfortable-looking but definitely not beach decor. Mrs. Epecris didn't have much of a tan, and McGregor guessed that the Epecris family didn't spend much time on the beach.

"I knew Mike sold the house for a very low figure. Everyone on the cove knew about it. Thought it might drop property values, but I hear that dike Amy Witherwill is asking double what she payed."

"Dike?" asked McGregor. Mrs. Epecris had said the word casually, offhandedly, and it had caught McGregor off guard.

"Dike. Gay—you know."

McGregor smiled ruefully. "Oh, right."

"You know her?"

"Met her today. She showed me the house. I liked her."

Mrs. Taylor shrugged. "Most real-estate people around here are gay. Along with a lot of the other permanent residents. Funny. Barry and I moved down here to get away from the Hollywood weirdness, but . . ." Her eyes dropped to her dirty jeans and she looked up apologetically.

"I was throwing some pots in the back," she explained.

She is attractive, thought McGregor. Out loud he said, "What I'm really interested in is meeting someone who may have seen Mike Rumison just before or just after he sold the house."

"He's gone? I hope he's not in trouble."

"He's gone," said McGregor. "But all we need him for is to sign some paperwork."

"And they send an Air Force major for that?"

I'm going to have to get a better story, thought McGregor. "I wasn't doing anything else," he said.

"I can't believe that," said Mrs. Epecris, and again McGregor thought he caught a double meaning. She looked like an ex-model, sophisticated even in work clothes, with faultless teeth and complexion, all the grace of a person with good training or a lot of money. McGregor was attracted to her and momentarily considered forgetting the beach girl he had a date with, but then he remembered Jamie's dark tanned breasts and slender young body. The little girl was seated on the bottom step of the stairwell watching with large shy eyes. McGregor flinched from an old hurt that was so far removed from his consciousness that he couldn't even remember the origin.

"Barry knew the Rumisons better than I did," said Mrs. Epecris, suddenly very businesslike. Funny how women could sense things. No, it wasn't funny at all, thought McGregor. No funnier than how he sensed certain things.

"Barry was good friends with Mike's father. Used to go fishing with him, and then when he died and the other two boys moved in . . . well, he was friendly, but it wasn't the same thing, I guess."

"Was there anyone else living with them?" asked McGregor.

Mrs. Epecris frowned. "There was a girl for a while, I believe. I don't know her name. . . ."

"Geroge!" cried the girl. "Her name was George."

"Thank you, Amy. That's right, Mr.—uh—there I go again, Major McGregor. George. I remember now. Short for Georgina or Georgiana or something. Pretty girl in an intellectual sort of way. Had more class than most of the beach girls around here. I don't know where she went to."

"Do you remember her last name or anybody that might know her?"

"Amy?"

The girl shook her head. "Lots of people know her," she said. "Go down to the beach. The lifeguard, Chris, knows her. He was friends with them."

"That would be your best bet, Major. Find people their

own age. People say there's no generation gap in Laguna Beach, but I can assure you there is. The young people are so casual about everything, you know."

McGregor stood up from his seat and held out his hand. "Thank you, Mrs. Epecris." He looked over at Amy. "You too, Amy." The girl beamed.

"I'm sorry I couldn't help you more, Major. I hope nothing has happened to Michael. Have you tried contacting the other two boys?"

McGregor nodded. "No luck," he said.

"If there's anything else I can do for you . . ." Again the suggestion of a double meaning. What had she said?—"They're so causal about everything." Suddenly McGregor found Mrs. Epecris' intimations distasteful. But then he thought they might all have been just in his imagination. It disturbed him that he still had any ideals concerning personal relations. He thought he'd lost them long ago.

"Good day, Mrs. Epecris," he said and left the house.

The beach was across the street and down a flight of brick stairs bordered by pepper trees and ferns. McGregor felt awkward walking out on the cove sand in his suit and Oxford shoes. It was late afternoon but there were still people on the beach. Luckily the lifeguard hadn't gotten off work yet, and McGregor headed toward him.

The lifeguard was young and tanned and blond. Every girl's summer dream, thought McGregor. He was seated in a beach chair atop a low iron stand painted red, surrounded by young girls on beach towels and laughing and arguing children. The guard was apparently well liked, and he talked with the crowd while his eyes kept up a constant scan of the cove. McGregor didn't blame him. The surf looked bigger in the cove, and rocks jutted out dangerously from either side of the bathing area.

"Sure, I know Mike," answered the lifeguard after McGregor had introduced himself and asked his question. "Barney and Rosso also. I haven't seen them for ages, but I saw Mike in June."

"Did you talk to him?"

The young man shrugged. "A little. He'd changed. Didn't have much to say."

"Changed?"

"Yeah. Hard to explain. We used to be pretty good

friends. Used to guard together. Last time I saw him I couldn't relate. He looked a lot . . . older. Maybe not older . . . physically. Just older. Like . . ." The lifeguard's eyes turned inward for a moment. Just a moment, and then he shook his head. "He had a beard," he finished lamely.

"When you said older, did you mean more mature?"

"Yeah, I guess so. I guess that's what I meant. Like he knew a lot more or something. He wasn't a kid any longer, that's for sure."

"Did you ask him what he'd been doing?"

"Sure. Said he'd been down in South America."

"Did he say if he'd be going anywhere?"

The lifeguard shook his head. "Not that I remember. I heard he sold the house. I haven't seen him around for a while."

McGregor asked him a few more questions before getting to the one he hoped might help him. Somehow he felt the girl might provide a key.

"George. Sure. Great lady. Barney's old lady. Used to come down to the beach all the time."

"Do you know her last name?"

"Uh huh. Van Mannon. Rich parents up in Beverly Hills. She split home and moved in with Barney. They got along pretty good. Both pretty intellectual."

"You know how I can get in touch with her?"

"Beats me. I haven't seen her since I last saw Mike."

"You did see her then?"

"Yeah, with Mike. They both came down to body-surf. It was June sometime. Say, Mike isn't in any real trouble, is he?"

McGregor shook his head. "Don't know anything. Just trying to find him."

"Good luck."

Chapter Thirty-Two

McGregor spent the rest of the day talking to people who had known ex–beach boy Air Force Sergeant Michael Rumison and found that the answers were all very much the same. Mike had changed. Not upset, in fact quite calm and seemingly at peace, but different. Bearded, older-looking. He'd come back to town, sold his house, and left. No one knew for where. No one had talked with him about anything of consequence. Some admitted feeling awkward when they saw him, though most couldn't explain why.

"Hard to say," said one girl when McGregor pressed. "It was his eyes. They looked too close. Like yours, sort of, but you have control. He just looked, like, he didn't care what he saw or that he was making you nervous. They weren't unkind. They were just . . ." She shrugged without finishing.

The girl had been one of the names the lifeguard had given him to talk to, and there were several more, but it was getting late and he remembered his date with the beach girl, Jamie. It excited him, with a feeling he hadn't felt for many years, in spite of an aversion to discotheques and most dancing. But even as he returned to the motel and got ready for the date the riddle of Michael Rumison sat uncomfortably on his mind, mingling with the question of Bastanchury's death, the reality of which McGregor was beginning to accept.

He showered, shaved, and dressed in desert boots, tan corduroy Levi's, an Indian turquoise belt, and a blue Hawaiian-print shirt, and left without eating. The night was warm, like the day had been, the offshore winds blowing, smelling of trees and grass and auto fumes. The winds blew off the desert, across Southern California, across the hills and freeways. They used to clear the air, and sometimes they still did. That night the winds weren't strong enough—there were too many freeways and too many housing developments and too many people—but the winds had an exhilarating effect all the same. McGregor had read somewhere that the French had done a study on their equivalent wind, *le mistral,* and found that the air became positively charged when they blew, causing definite changes in the personality. They even had an ancient law that said men couldn't be tried for crimes of passion when *le mistral* blew.

Bluebird Canyon turned off the Coast Highway and ran up into the hills. McGregor was mildly surprised to find 509 a large home, tastefully designed in different woods with large areas of glass. A young man, blond and blue-eyed, answered the door. His presence made McGregor conscious of his age, but the young man smiled as if McGregor were nothing unusual and motioned him inside.

"I'm Mark," he said. "Jamie'll be right down. Make yourself comfortable."

McGregor took the offered hand. "McGregor," he said.

"Jamie couldn't remember your name," said Mark. "Glad to meet you."

Mark led McGregor into a spacious living room furnished in old but comfortable-looking furniture before he left with the excuse that he had a date. McGregor busied himself by reading the titles of the books lining one wall. He was impressed. Rows of books on psychology, philosophy, classics, many written in French, and even a few on mysticism that he himself had in his library, some of the ones General Norris had commented on as being an "odd assortment."

"Hello," came a voice from behind him. It was a liquid voice, filled with promise. McGregor turned. Jamie was smiling at him. She was barefoot and dressed in a one-piece knee-length dress that looked like it was made out of silk and clung to her body. As far as McGregor could tell she wore nothing under it.

"It's McGregor," said McGregor, putting down a book he had taken from the shelf.

The girl laughed. "I forget names easily," she said. "How could I forget McGregor, though?"

"Are you ready to go dancing?" asked McGregor.

Jamie shook her head. The move was calculated, and her hair fell across her eyes. She pushed it away with one hand. "No. I don't feel like dancing now. Would you like some dope? I think I'll have some."

McGregor didn't normally smoke marijuana. It made him think too much, and when he thought too much he would get drowsy and fall asleep, but he accepted a joint from the girl and sat down on an overpadded but comfortable couch. Jamie went over to a stereo and put on some mild jazz. Miles Davis, McGregor thought.

"You met Mark?" asked Jamie.

McGregor nodded. "Friend?" he asked.

"Brother. He's in a band. Has to play tonight. He's cute, don't you think? All the little girls think so. He gets tons of phone calls." Jamie hadn't sat down but was rocking rhythmically back and forth to the music while she talked and smoked. McGregor felt an erection growing as he watched her. She saw it and let him know that she saw it and smiled. McGregor took another smoke.

"How old are you?" he asked suddenly. He knew it was rude, but the question just fell out.

"Twenty-four. And you?"

"Thirty-eight."

"You don't look that old," said Jamie unconcernedly. "You look more like . . . thirty."

"Thanks. I figured you for nineteen."

"Are you disappointed?" asked Jamie mischievously.

"Nope. Now I don't have to deal with irate fathers."

"You wouldn't anyway. My father lives up in Santa Barbara. I live with Mark and my mother."

"What about your mother?"

Jamie laughed. "Her lover is twenty-four," she said. "He used to be my boyfriend."

Jamie took McGregor's hand and lifted him up to her. "Would you like to dance here?"

McGregor took her in his arms and together they started

a slow dance. Things moved fast. McGregor began kissing her neck. His hands caressed the silk dress, feeling her softness. Jamie didn't resist, but when his hands moved down she pulled away with a soft laugh. "You do like to dance, don't you?" she smiled, while her eyes held his steady. "You have beautiful eyes," she said. "They were the first thing I noticed about you when I saw you walking down the beach. Your body of course, but mostly those piercing green eyes. I've never seen eyes so . . ." She looked up at him accusingly. "Do you wear contacts?"

"No, they're real."

Jamie smiled and her hand rested lightly on his belt, brushed against his erection and moved back to his waist. McGregor pulled her closer and they began dancing again. This time his hands moved up under her dress, across the sides of her breasts, which hardened as they danced. She blew lightly in his ear and then began to move her tongue across it. His hands moved downward, and this time she didn't pull away. McGregor wouldn't have stopped if she had. They remained standing for several minutes as he felt her juices, neither noticing that the record had finished, and then McGregor drew her down to the rose Chinese carpet. Without taking any clothes off he unzipped his trousers, pulled up her dress, and made love to her on the floor. It was violent and over very quickly, and when he had finished McGregor felt like he ought to apologize.

Jamie laughed quietly, stroking his hair. "That was good," she said. "You're so strong. It was much better than going to Newport."

McGregor agreed. It had been good. And would be again.

"Can you stay tonight?"

"Yes."

The girl stood up and led McGregor to a large bedroom where they undressed before falling into a soft king-size bed. "It's Mom's," said Jamie. "It's much better than mine."

"Won't she mind?"

"No."

During the night McGregor heard a soft knock on the door and a woman's voice.

Jamie stirred drowsily, like a cat. "I'm in here, Mom," she answered.

"I'll sleep in your room. Good night, dear," said her mother.

Chapter Thirty-Three

THE telephone was ringing when McGregor returned the next morning to his hotel room after having breakfast with Jamie and her mother. The brother, Mark, hadn't returned. The mother had been a rather attractive and intelligent woman. It was she who owned most of the books in the house, though McGregor was surprised to learn that Jamie had a degree in French Literature and had studied a year at the Sorbonne. Talking to the mother depressed McGregor. He had had an enjoyable night, but in spite of Jamie's beauty, her seductiveness, and her youth, it had been just another forgettable incident in McGregor's life, and the mother's casualness reminded McGregor of his own inability to care more.

McGregor hurriedly unlocked the door and ran to answer the ringing phone. He recognized the caller immediately.

"Mr. McGregor, this is Amy Witherwill . . . Pelican Realty? I thought I might tell you that I was visited by another man after I left you yesterday who was interested in the Rumison boy and wanted to see the house."

"Oh? Did he give his name?" McGregor sounded calm but his mind was turning.

"Meade. Mr. Meade. Said he was with the Internal Revenue Service. I didn't like his looks so didn't volunteer the information I gave you."

"His looks?"

"He was black . . . not that I have anything against blacks, but he acted strange. Also wouldn't give me any identification. Spoke with a slight accent. Not foreign, really. Just not a Californian. Possibly a Southerner. Anyway, I went back to the house to make sure I remembered to close the curtains, and the house had been broken into."

Broken into, thought McGregor. A black man interested in Rumison? Accent? Wouldn't be who he claimed, of course. The Agency wouldn't send another agent. Or would they? Who else could it be?

"Did you call the police?"

"I thought I'd better talk with you first, Mr. McGregor. Find out what is going on." Miss Witherwill's voice was angry and indignant, but betrayed no apparent fear.

"Could you give me a description of the man?"

"Well, big. About your size but thicker. Wore a nice suit. Expensive but not stylish. Brown. Short hair." There was a pause. "That's about it, I guess."

"How did you know the house had been broken into?"

"How? Why, the back door had been pried open with a crowbar or something, and inside there were drawers opened all over. It was a mess."

Amateur, thought McGregor. Either that or he wanted us to think he was an amateur, or was something else happening? There were always so many variables.

"Should I call the police?"

"I don't think it would help, Miss Witherwill. Only confuse things more."

"This man, he wasn't a friend of yours?"

"No. No friend of mine, or Mr. Rumison's, I feel. There was a question I forgot to ask you, though. What bank was the check drawn through that you paid Rumison with?"

"I'll answer only on one condition, Mr. McGregor."

"What's that?"

"That when this is all over you tell me what happened."

"Done."

"Bank of America. Laguna Branch. Made out for one hundred and fifty thousand dollars even, a cashier's check."

"Thank you very much, Miss Witherwill. For everything. Take it easy, now. I don't think the other man will be back. If you see him again, though, you might call the police and have him arrested."

"Not call you?"

"I won't be around. Goodbye, Miss Witherwill."

McGregor put the phone down and thought. Somebody representing somebody else was close behind him. A black man. Not hard to spot in Laguna Beach. Things were beginning to heat up and McGregor liked the feeling. He operated best under pressure. It intensified his concentration by taking his mind off other things.

He packed quickly, paid his motel bill, and got into the Volkswagen. At the bank he learned that the check had been cashed by a local bank, Laguna Federal Savings. He learned there that Rumison had had an account with that bank but had closed it out in mid-June. All two hundred and four thousand dollars of it. Taken all of it in cash, hundred-dollar bills. McGregor also learned that Rumison had made another large deposit of money, fifty thousand dollars, gotten from the sale of his father's charter business. Another thirty-eight hundred had been deposited from Air Force paychecks made out to Rosso, Bailey, and Rumison, Rosso's and Bailey's having been signed over to Rumison. McGregor laughed at that. He was beginning to like this man. Aloud, he thanked the bank official who had let him look at the Rumison account statements.

"Always pleased to help a Treasury agent," said the man. "I thought something was strange when a man his age comes in and withdraws that much money in cash, but there didn't seem to be any reason not to give it to him at the time. We had it delivered here, new hundred-dollar bills."

The man's attitude was questioning, but McGregor just nodded. "You've been a big help, Mr. Doodle."

"Daedle. With an *ae.*"

"Yes, Mr. Daedle. You've been a big help."

McGregor decided against visiting the charter company. He suspected he wouldn't learn much and he was in a hurry now, thanks to the mysterious black man named Mr. Meade. There were two places he had yet to visit that topped his priority list. He got back in his rented car and headed out the windy and thankfully still-undeveloped Laguna Canyon Road.

El Toro was a Marine air base, but the Air Force had been allowed to use a hangar for an Air Rescue squadron. McGregor showed his Treasury credentials to an uncomprehending corporal at the gate and was allowed to pass after signing a registry and being issued a guest pass.

The 68th Aerospace Rescue and Recovery Squadron's administration was in a new and rather sterile-looking building out near the flight line. It was painted white and trimmed with Air Force blue, which distinguished it from the many buildings painted Marine green. Inside, a dour-faced woman receptionist referred him to the NCOIC of administration, Sergeant Kibik. Kibik was young to be a master sergeant, possibly not over thirty, but he looked aware and efficient. McGregor could feel himself being sized up as he approached Kibik's desk.

"Treasury, huh? What's your interest in Rumison?" The man sounded unwarrantedly suspicious, and McGregor wondered why. No one else was supposed to have known about Bastanchury's mission other than the commanding officer of the 68th and a few key personnel. McGregor didn't think Kibik was one of them, but the word could have gotten out and an administrative type would probably be the first to pick up on it.

"He cashed some checks that weren't his. Air Force paychecks. Forged signatures."

"You don't say? Where'd he get the checks?"

"They were sent to his house. Two airmen lived with him?"

"Rosso and Bailey?"

McGregor nodded.

"Why would he forge their names? I heard they were best friends."

The man's attitude was putting McGregor on the defensive, and he didn't like the feeling. "Don't know," he replied. "That's what I'm here to find out. Something suspicious is going on and Treasury wants to know what."

Kibik looked thoughtfully up from his desk at McGregor. Then, as if he had made a sudden decision, he stood up and motioned McGregor to follow him.

"I don't want the others to know," he explained quietly, leading McGregor into an empty coffee room. He took a cup down from a shelf of cups and poured black coffee into it.

"You care for a cup, McGregor?"

"I don't drink coffee."

Kibik sat down. "I probably shouldn't either," he said. "But you get in the habit around here."

"What don't you want the others to know?" asked McGregor.

Kibik sipped at his coffee. "I'm not sure," he said finally. "Just a series of things that have happened. I'm like you. I don't know what's going on but I am suspicious."

"Oh?"

"I was transferred to this dogshit outfit in June, McGregor. I had a cushy job at Hickum, in Hawaii. A house, kids in school. I didn't want to come. I thought I was in over there, and then I'm yanked ass-end back to smogland, and on a goddamn Marine base to top it off." Kibik looked as disgusted as he sounded.

"And?"

"I asked why, of course," continued Kibik, staring down at his cup. "I just got the brass runaround. Supposedly I was replacing the old admin NCOIC, a guy named McPhee or something, but why me, and why jerk me like that? I was given two weeks and that's all."

"What happened to McPhee?"

"Damned if I know. Nobody's told me. Nobody really seems to know. Nobody but 'the Gerber Baby.' "

"Who?"

"Lookit, McGregor," said Kibik suddenly. "You tell anyone else this outside of a military court and I'll deny it."

"I understand."

"The Gerber Baby is Ellis, the C.O. Everyone calls him that. You'll see why if you meet him."

"What does all this have to do with Rumison?"

"I don't know, exactly. Let me finish and judge for yourself. A week after I got here, my section got orders from up above . . . above Ellis even . . . to cut retroactive discharge papers for five men from the unit. Five men I didn't know. Sleeper, the old NCOIC of the PJ section . . ."

"PJ?"

"Pararescue. The so-called heroes of this outfit. Red Berets. The guys who jump out the ass end of our birds. Bullshit."

"Go on, Sergeant Kibik."

"Yeah, well, anyway, the men they wanted discharged

were Sleeper, Rosso, Bailey, Rumison, and Major Hawkes, a pilot who was killed before I even got here."

"What reason did they give for the orders?"

"Overmanned. Supposedly all those named were due to get out shortly anyway. I didn't buy it."

"No? Why?"

"They don't do things that way. I never even saw those guys. They're supposed to check themselves out. Hand-carry the papers to about ten different spots and get them signed off . . . equipment, medical, insurance, pay. Christ, you don't just fill out a paper and then sit back and assume the guy is out of the Air Force. We could be open for all kinds of lawsuits that way."

"So what did you do?"

"Went to Ellis, naturally, but he told me to forget it. To just do as I was told. These are his exact words, 'Make it look good for the records, is all, just make it look good for the records.' Hawkes was already dead, and no one, and I mean no one, seemed to know where the others were. It suddenly came to me that this was a whitewash. For some reason the Air Force didn't want anything to do with those guys. I asked around the squadron about them. Even went down to the PJ section, but seems like most of the crew that had been around and knew those guys had been suddenly transferred, just like McPhee, and the ones who had been around either didn't know anything or weren't talking. One day those guys were all around and another day they were gone. That simple. No birds had flown out from the squadron either. I checked the logs. They were just gone, and then I got orders to make it appear as if they had all been discharged months before they were due for separation." Kibik paused, finishing off his coffee with a gulp. He stood up and poured himself another cup.

"That isn't all," he continued. "A few days later I got a phone call from a guy who wanted to find Rumison. Said he was interested in buying his house and couldn't seem to find out where he was. Sounded authentic at first, so I gave him the party line . . . Rumison had been discharged along with Bailey and Rosso and Sleeper. Then he asked something that sent me up the wall. He asked to talk to Major Hawkes. Now, how would some strange dude from Laguna

Beach know about Major Hawkes? So I started asking what his name was. All I got was a dead line."

Kibik sat back down at the table and stared for a second at McGregor but then his eyes shifted away.

"And then you come along," he said. "Saying that Rumison is wanted for forging Rosso's and Bailey's paychecks. Boy, you can't tell me something isn't very smelly in Denmark."

"It sounds like it," said McGregor noncommittally. Kibik was a smart man. Smart like Amy Witherwill had been smart.

"There are a lot of smart people in this world, McGregor," Bastanchury had once said. "Lots and lots of them, and most die just like everybody else, living their lives as housewife or store clerk, worried over petty things that never mattered anyhow. Their brains only feed their vanity, and they believe they don't have to do anything because they know better. Lots of smart people in the world, McGregor, but the only ones that count are the ones that *do.*"

McGregor had found out that Bastanchury spoke the truth. Kibik could find out what was happening, if he wanted. But to dig too deep into matters might upset an otherwise secure existence. It would be all right if someone else dug and told, told him in an empty room where no one else could hear. Told him so he could go home and say he knew one more thing that other people didn't, but not bothering to do anything about it because that would upset things.

McGregor stood up. "Thanks for letting me in on your suspicions, Sergeant," he said. "If anything comes up I'll try and let you know."

"I'd appreciate it, McGregor. This thing has been driving me balmy, trying to figure it out."

"Dig a little deeper, Sergeant."

"Can't do. Too many things at stake. Ellis made that perfectly clear."

McGregor nodded. "I understand," he said.

Chapter Thirty-Four

A SENSE of urgency dominated McGregor's mood as he drove the Volkswagen along the Santa Ana Freeway toward Beverly Hills. The speed limit was posted as 55, but the only cars that were keeping to it were the slower trucks and oil-burning cars in the right lane. McGregor couldn't have said why he had the feeling, but he'd learned from experience to put faith in his feelings. The gas pedal was almost to the floor as he maneuvered through a traffic heavy for a summer's late morning, his eyes constantly checking behind him for patrol cars. On either side of the freeway the endless suburbs of Los Angeles slid by in ghastly monotony; miles and miles of shopping centers, tract homes, macadam roads, neon signs, telephone wires and the ever-increasing traffic which was the main cause of the floating brown haze that Los Angeleans call air.

McGregor usually didn't allow himself to daydream for any length of time, but daydreams offered an escape from the tedium of the freeway and the surrounding suburbs. They also took his mind off the question of why he felt he didn't have much time. Was it the mysterious Mr. Meade?

McGregor thought of Michael Bastanchury. He wondered if Bastanchury had ever felt anxiety or a sense of urgency. Bastanchury had been the toughest man McGregor had ever known, both mentally and physically. Bastanchury had been wounded once during a fire fight, trying to pull a Yard chieftain to safety. Bastanchury normally didn't take such risks, only when he felt they were absolutely needed, but he knew the Yards had been getting nervous listening to Cong propaganda about the decadent

Americans, and he felt that some sort of significant gesture was needed. Rescuing the chieftain was just the sort of move that was necessary. It was at this time that Bastanchury had first talked about death.

"Shut up, McGregor," he said harshly when McGregor had commented on the serious nature of his wound, a bullet through his right side. "I'm not going to die. It isn't time for me to die."

McGregor could sense even then that it wasn't bravado that made the major say that. That Bastanchury really believed it. It made him curious, and later, when he visited Bastanchury in the camp's small infirmary, he asked him about his views on death and dying and why he had been so sure he wasn't going to die.

"We're given two things in this life," said Bastanchury. "A certain, determined amount of time to live. And if we are tough enough, the ability to organize that time into any game we want."

"I don't quite understand, Major."

"I don't expect you do, Lieutenant. Not many men do understand it. Your namesake did."

"You mean you believe in fate?"

"We die when we're going to die. Not sooner. Not later. If you know this, you can determine how you want to die. I have some things to do yet. I didn't feel like dying there in the jungle with some slopehead's bullet in my liver. It's that simple."

It wasn't that simple, but McGregor didn't press. Later, over the years, he thought he'd figured out what Bastanchury had been talking about. He'd even molded his own life, his own thoughts and actions, around what he thought he understood, but now that Bastanchury had apparently died, McGregor wasn't sure any longer. He needed to know how the older man had met his death.

McGregor's sense of urgency grew as the Volkswagen neared central Los Angeles. He was hungry but he obeyed his feelings and didn't stop for lunch. He did stop at a gas station off Wilshire Boulevard to check the phone-directory listing for Van Mannon. There was no listing for Georgiana Van Mannon in Beverly Hills, but there were three other names. He called the numbers. Two had never heard of Georgiana and the third wasn't answered. He memorized the address of the third and got back in his car, hoping that the Van Mannon he was after had a listed number and that he wouldn't have to waste time calling the number Norris had given him and getting them to trace the girl. He somehow knew he didn't have that time.

The address McGregor had gotten was in upper Beverly Hills, toward the mountains. It was a very wealthy neighborhood, with most of the houses being in the mansion category, hidden behind high walls and hedges, their driveways guarded by tall wrought-iron gates that were probably electrified. The address belonged to a Raymond McAllister Van Mannon, and his house was unusual in only one way: Its gate was open.

McGregor drove up a long, winding cement driveway and as he looked up at the large Spanish house in front of him he knew that he was too late. The driveway circled around a huge fountain in the front yard of the house, forming a parking area for as many as ten cars. Most of the area was now filled with black-and-white police units, and police were milling around an ambulance with its doors open at the front entrance.

"Can I help you, sir?" a uniformed officer asked McGregor as he pulled to a stop behind a police car.

"What happened?" asked McGregor, fearing he knew the answer.

The officer shrugged. "Triple murder," he said. "Are you a friend of the family?"

McGregor took out his forged Treasury ID and showed it to the officer, who handed it back to him without comment. "I'm investigating a forgery case," explained McGregor. "I'm looking for a Georgiana Van Mannon."

"You'd better talk to Lieutenant Barnes," said the officer. "Georgiana Van Mannon was one of those killed."

McGregor got out of the Volkswagen and followed the officer past the ambulance, past police photographers and attendants and into the main house. The house was huge inside, tiled with porcelain tile, the floors covered in expensive Oriental carpets, the walls hung with paintings by famous artists. Lieutenant Barnes was in the library talking to an older man with graying hair and a woman who was crying.

"Kelso?" asked the lieutenant, looking up at the officer who had led McGregor into the room.

"This man's a Treasury agent, Lieutenant. He's investigating a forgery case. Wanted to talk to one of the deceased."

Barnes looked capable and bored, but his interest pricked when the officer mentioned forgery.

"Treasury, huh? Which of the deceased?"

"Georgiana Van Mannon," answered McGregor.

"Oh, I knew it," cried the woman. "If only George hadn't gotten mixed up with that beach riffraff."

"Knew what, Mrs. Haskill?" asked the lieutenant.

"I knew that's what brought this all about. I knew she'd gotten mixed up in something bad."

The woman started crying again as the man put his arm around her and tried to comfort her. Barnes was looking bored again. McGregor didn't let the look fool him. He might be in for a rough time of it if he didn't play his role just right, but he also knew he might be able to get good information from the lieutenant. Barnes nodded to another uniformed officer who had been taking notes, and the officer ushered the man and the woman from the room.

"If there's any way we can help, officer . . ."

"You will be contacted, Mr. Haskill," answered the lieutenant. "You've been more than a help already."

"They found the bodies," he explained after the Haskills had left the room. "Friends. Mrs. Haskill gets these feelings, she said. Felt something was wrong. Found the door open and then the bodies. Found the butler dead in the hall and the old man in the living room. The girl, the one you're after, was upstairs in a bedroom." He looked at McGregor curiously, and McGregor knew he was noting his long hair, his clothes, his shoes, and his reactions.

"Why are you looking for her, Mr.—ah—?"

"McGregor. I'm not actually after the girl. I'm looking for a friend of hers."

"Name?"

McGregor paused, wondering if he ought to say, but then he figured he'd better.

"Rumison. Michael Paul Rumison. We're investigating him for forgery."

Barnes nodded. "Maybe murder too," he said.

"How so, Lieutenant?"

"No other suspects so far. We found a car registered to Rumison in the garage. Mrs. Haskill says that's who the girl was living with down at some beach town . . ."

"Laguna Beach," said McGregor.

"Anyway no other suspects unless you have a lead."

"You really think that's enough to go after Rumison? The fact that this girl was staying at his house and that his car happens to be in her garage?"

Barnes shrugged. "I hadn't even considered it until you came along talking about forgery. You sound like you're defending him. Boyfriends have been known to kill their girl friends, you know . . . and their girl friends' parents. From what the Haskills said, old man Van Mannon wasn't too hot on his daughter living with Rumison."

"The girl was living with another man at Rumison's house," said McGregor. "Man named Bailey. Friend of Rumison's. Bailey's been missing for three months. I'm tracing Rumison because he cashed a couple of paychecks issued by the Air Force to Bailey and another roommate named Rosso by forging their signatures."

"Maybe he killed them too . . . for the money. The girl knew it and he offed her and her old man and the butler?"

"No reason."

"The money."

"Thirty-two hundred is hardly enough reason to kill your best friends when you've just sold a house and a family business for two hundred thousand cash. Besides, Rosso and Bailey had been missing for some time before Rumison cashed the checks."

"I'm just fishing," said the lieutenant, standing up from his position on the sofa back. "But I can see we have a lot to talk about, McGregor. You'll forgive me if I seem a little less than open, but you Treasury boys . . . By the way," he asked, "you don't mind if I see some ID? You know, with the long hair and all . . ."

McGregor took out his wallet and handed it to the lieutenant, who looked closely at the Treasury card and then began to thumb through the other ID's. McGregor hadn't had time to forge a complete set, and he hoped Barnes didn't have a good enough memory to remember the numbers on his credit cards.

"No driver's license."

"It's in another wallet."

"You should carry it with you. Where you working out of?"

"Washington."

Barnes raised an eyebrow but didn't comment. He handed the wallet back. "Care for some lunch?" he asked. "I'm hungry as hell, and we can talk. There are some strange things about this case and maybe we can help each other."

McGregor breathed an inward sigh of relief and nodded. "I'm hungry too," he said truthfully.

Chapter Thirty-Five

"THE old man and the butler were shot in the forehead by a small-caliber pistol, possibly a .22. Beautiful shots. The old man was killed at a fairly close range, I think. Can't tell about the butler until pathology gets back to us. The girl didn't have a mark on her except a bruise across the back left side of the neck."

Lieutenant Barnes was on his second hamburger in a lunchroom on the Sunset Strip.

"Professional?" asked McGregor, knowing the answer better than Barnes.

"Looks like it. What did this guy Rumison do in the Air Force, anyway?"

"Pararescue and survival expert. Rescued people. Medical technician."

"Think he knows anything about weapons?"

McGregor hesitated. "He has an Expert rating with both rifle and pistol, according to his records," he answered finally.

Barnes wiped catsup off his thin-lipped mouth with a paper napkin and then sat back in his seat. The lunchroom was crowded, but the crowd was fairly quiet and McGregor could hear the traffic on the Strip above the dim murmur in the café.

"Lookit, McGregor," said Barnes. "Something is going on, and I want to know what. This is my district. A murder of a wealthy and respected citizen and his daughter, not to mention their butler, has taken place, and brother, you don't know what pressure is until you have the good people of Beverly Hills on your case. There's more money and power in those few square miles than . . ." The lieutenant paused and looked down at his coffee cup.

"Washington does not send T-agents out on a miserable three-thousand-buck forgery rap. They'd use the locals for that. This killing has all the signs of an assassination." Barnes waited for McGregor to say something.

"Does the coroner go to work right away on this thing?" asked McGregor while Barnes finished his coffee off in one long swallow. Barnes put the cup down impatiently.

"On this they will. I told them to."

"They normally check for drugs?"

Barnes nodded slowly, his interest growing. "Usually," he answered. "If they can't find any visible outward signs of death, and sometimes even then, if the case warrants it. Do you think this has something to do with narcotics?"

"What about uncommon drugs?"

"Uncommon drugs? What do you mean, uncommon drugs? What's uncommon these days?"

McGregor sighed, deciding what to tell the lieutenant. The man was clever and a good cop. Unlike Sergeant Kibik he was paid to dig deep.

"There is something going on, Lieutenant," answered McGregor finally. "How the murders tie in is anybody's guess at this point. I can't tell you much, but the drugs I think the coroner should check the girl's body for belong in the category of certain alkaloids. . . ."

"Psychedelics?"

"Let me finish. Belong in the category of certain alkaloids of the benthium chain or perhaps pentothol or Colium."

"Truth serum?"

McGregor nodded. Barnes looked thoughtful for a moment and then stood up. Five minutes later he was back.

"I called the coroner," he said. "We should have the results by tomorrow. Now can you tell me what's going on?"

"National security, Lieutenant."

"That big, huh?"

McGregor nodded. "Sorry," he said.

"I'm not going to accept just your word, you know, McGregor," said Barnes. "I'll need something in writing."

"Go on with the case, Lieutenant. I'm sorry I can't help you any more."

"Answer me one question, McGregor, and then I'll take you back to your car."

"If I can."

"Who do you think might have killed those people?"

McGregor smiled. "It wasn't Rumison, Lieutenant," he said. "I can guarantee that. You might put out an A.P.B. on a black man named Meade, about my size but heavier, short hair, business suit, talks with a slight accent, possibly Caribbean. It's only a guess and not much to go on, but it's all I have."

"You're right, McGregor. It's not much to go on." Barnes drove McGregor back to the Van Mannon house where McGregor had left the VW. The ambulance and most of the police cars were gone.

"By the way, McGregor," said Barnes as McGregor got into his car. "Where can I locate you when I need you?"

"Office in L.A.," answered McGregor.

"Good. You might as well know I'm running a check on you, and if Washington doesn't come down with something, I'm taking you in as a material witness."

McGregor cursed silently to himself as he drove off. He didn't have much time left to do what he had to do in L.A.

Barnes had given him the address of the Haskills, and he drove to their house wanting answers to questions Barnes couldn't have asked. Their house was close by, within walking distance of the Van Mannons' and another large one. It was reminiscent of the antebellum South, and when a black maid answered the door wearing an ankle-length uniform McGregor shook his head.

"Ah'm sorry, sir, but Missus Haskill is not feelin' too well."

McGregor showed his ID. "It's important," he said.

"Well, in that case . . ."

Mr. and Mrs. Haskill were just finishing lunch on their veranda, which looked out over a huge backyard, part of which was a well-kept putting green. After introductions McGregor sat down. Mrs. Haskill was pale-skinned with lines in her face that indicated she was either a perpetual complainer, or a perpetual sufferer, McGregor didn't quite know which yet. But he despised both and had disliked Mrs. Haskill from the moment he saw her with the lieutenant. Mr. Haskill was gray and unobtrusive. A bank executive or a retired stockbroker.

"Excuse us if we seem a little . . . uh . . ."

"I understand, Mr. Haskill," said McGregor quickly. "I just needed to know the answers to a few questions and then I'll be leaving."

"Anything to help. My wife is rather upset and I'm not too surefooted right now myself."

"Lieutenant Barnes told me pretty much what you said," began McGregor. "The girl, Georgiana, left home last year. The old man—Van Mannon—had her traced to a house in Laguna where she'd been staying, but she refused to come home. Since she was of age, nothing could be done. Am I right so far?"

Mrs. Haskill nodded, and it looked like she was ready to break out crying again. "Ray was so patient with her," she said. "After May died. May was the mother, you know."

McGregor nodded as though he did.

"He offered her everything she wanted. But kids these days . . . I just knew something like this would happen."

"When did she return home?" asked McGregor.

"May," said Mrs. Haskill. "May thirteenth. I remember because it was a Friday and I should never have gone over there. They were in a terrible argument."

"Do you remember what they were arguing about?"

Mrs. Haskill shook her head. "I left as soon as I could," she said.

"Mrs. Haskill, the question I really need you to answer is, when did Georgiana return with the Volkswagen? If you don't know, maybe you can tell me of someone who might."

"I can answer that," said Mr. Haskill. "She came back in May on the bus. Ray told me that. Thought it odd, when he'd given her a Mercedes to use. She left again in early June. Ray called me, said she'd gotten a phone call from those people she'd been living with. I don't know the exact date, but Ray was pretty upset."

"She came back, though."

Haskill nodded. "This time with the car. Told Ray she was keeping it instead of the Mercedes, that it had been given to her." He laughed quietly with no understanding.

"Strange, don't you think, Mr. McGregor? Wanting to keep an old Volkswagen rather than a Mercedes?"

"Real strange," said McGregor, but the irony in his tone was lost on the older man and his wife.

"You remember the exact day when she returned?" he asked.

"I could check. Ray and I had a golfing date that day. He had to cancel, but I'm sure it's still on my calendar."

"It is all so awful," said Mrs. Haskill after her husband had left. "To see poor Robert lying there and then . . ." She began to sob. McGregor didn't bother to try and comfort her. The husband returned a few minutes later.

"Tuesday the fifteenth of June," he said.

"Such a horrible thing," said Mrs. Haskill, still sniffling.

"Thank you both very much," said McGregor, taking his leave. "You've both been a very great help."

Chapter Thirty-Six

IT had been a scream that woke him up, his own, but McGregor didn't know that. All he knew was that he was awake, and with that knowledge came relief. The nightmare had been a bad one, one that he knew well. He thought he had outgrown it, but that had been wishful thinking, and now he was shaking and sweaty because the nightmare had returned.

The small motel room offered no comfort. It was impersonal and cold, cheap prints of sailing ships decorating white stucco walls. A block away, across the Coast Highway, the ocean slapped the empty Malibu sands, but it could not comfort him either.

McGregor checked his watch: 4:30 A.M. Too early to get up, but he didn't feel like going back to sleep. Not with the nightmare still fresh in his consciousness. He lay on his back and thought, reviewing his activities of the last several days, trying almost desperately to destroy the images of the dream.

After leaving the Haskills' McGregor had taken his rented Volkswagen back to the rental agency at International Airport and gotten another one from another agency using different identification. Then he had stopped in at a pay phone in the TWA terminal at the airport and placed a call to Virginia. A man's voice had answered.

"McGregor here. I need some help."

"Who?"

"McGregor, damn it."

"Just a minute, please." Three minutes later another voice answered the line. A voice like a computer.

"Go ahead, McGregor."

"I need some things."

"Go ahead."

"There's been a murder in Beverly Hills. An old man, Van Mannon, his daughter Georgiana, and the butler. I need to get hold of the autopsy report on all three. I also need some interference. I used an ID from the Treasury Department under the name McGregor. A cop in Beverly Hills named Barnes, Lieutenant Barnes, ran a check on me. They'll be after me when a negative comes through. Thirdly, I want to have the passenger lists checked for the date June fifteenth, this year, for a man fitting Michael Rumison's description at all the bus stations, airports, and train stations. Possibly wearing a beard."

"That's impossible, McGregor. It's been too long."

"He would have been traveling light and probably paid with a hundred-dollar bill. He withdrew two hundred thousand dollars cash from Laguna Federal Savings just prior to the fifteenth. You could get the serial numbers from the bank and run a trace."

The voice was silent. "We'll do what we can, McGregor," it said finally, unemotionally.

"One more thing," said McGregor. "A man named Meade. Black, six foot two or three inches, over two hundred pounds, possibly a foreigner. He's been hanging around."

"We'll do what we can, McGregor," said the voice again.

McGregor had hung up after getting the address of a lawyer in Santa Monica who had a telecopier where the autopsy results could be sent. Then he had driven to Malibu and rented the room. The sense of urgency hadn't passed with the Van Mannon murders, and the next three days were hard for McGregor. He had met a woman named Isadora in a nearby bar and spent the night with her, but he couldn't obliterate the emptiness he felt. She left the next morning and then there was nothing but the room and the beach and the ocean lapping against the warm Malibu sand.

On the third day of waiting the autopsy had come through to the lawyer's office, and McGregor had something to do besides run and swim, which he'd been doing a lot of in an effort to rid himself of his growing impatience and his dislike for everything that Los Angeles represented.

Raymond McAllister Van Mannon and his butler had died instantly as the result of .25-caliber slugs in the forehead, fired from not more than ten or less than five feet away. There was no other mark on them, though Van Mannon's blood was heavy with alcohol. The report concluded that Van Mannon was probably a heavy drinker, on the evidence of the general condition of his body. The girl had died of an overdose of trepanin bentholate, injected purposefully and directly into the heart, causing instant cardiac arrest. There were numerous marks on her right arm, the result of Pentothal injections. It was the coroner's conclusion that Miss Van Mannon had been professionally interrogated for at least an hour before the fatal injection was administered. The bruise across the back of the neck probably stunned her but nothing more. Miss Van Mannon was also two months pregnant.

The report hadn't helped McGregor's mood any, and it meant someone was very probably three days ahead of him, if the girl had known where Rumison was heading, and McGregor had a feeling she had. It had been a professional job, unlike the break-in at Rumison's house. How many people were involved? How many interests?

On the fourth night of waiting the nightmare had come. It was a dream with a different feel from other dreams, with a meaning and a dark reality all its own. McGregor had dreamed it before, many times when he was younger and then with steadily decreasing frequency, until he had thought it gone forever. Somehow he connected its return with Bastanchury's disappearance. And now he lay on the hard motel bed and tried to think about anything but the dream.

He thought about the beach girl, Jamie, and Mrs. Epecris, and the lady who called herself Isadora who had been a bit actress and was now living off alimony from her third husband. But his thoughts couldn't stay with any of the attractive women he had spent time with recently, and he was surprised to find them turning to Amy Witherwill. She was a tough old bird and McGregor had liked her, felt a kinship with her. She was also a lesbian and McGregor wondered what that meant about him.

He thought then about the girls from Taos. He knew many, and they would come to make love, to stay for a week or even a month before moving on to Sun Valley or Boulder or Hawaii. None satisfied his craving for something deeper, for something like the lifetime romance of Richard Francis Burton and his wife, Lady Isabel Arundel Burton.

And the dream was tied to these thoughts also, so McGregor didn't follow them too closely.

Sunrise came slowly. McGregor put on running shorts and jogged down to the sand, where he ran barefoot for five miles up to Malibu Point. The surfers were just paddling out into the sun's rays breaking through the brown line of early-morning smog. He swam around the pier and then, because his feet and his leg muscles weren't used to the sand, he walked back to the motel, where he showered and dressed before putting in the call to the number in Virginia.

"We've got it, McGregor," said the voice, emotionless. "Rumison's money turned up in Las Vegas. We ran a flight check and the computer came up with one Michael White leaving Orange County Airport on June fifteenth, arriving via Hughes Air West in Las Vegas at twelve noon. Fits your man's description. People on both sides remembered him. Paid for everything with new hundred-dollar bills. Didn't bother to hide them. Gambled heavily and apparently lost heavily. Stayed at the Dunes Hotel, where most of the bills turned up. Checked out three days later. No record of a flight or a bus out of town."

Gambled? It didn't fit with the picture McGregor had been forming in his mind about Rumison. Didn't fit at all . . . and then Rumison had disappeared again.

"What about Meade?" he asked.

The voice hesitated. "No reference, McGregor."

"What about the police here?"

"Couldn't help, McGregor. Got orders not to interfere."

McGregor took a deep breath. "Sure," he said and hung up.

He thought about what the voice had told him. One thing made him curious, and for some reason it gave him hope that his picture of Rumison was still partly accurate. Rumison had used the name White. Why had he chosen that name? Bastanchury's code name on the mission had been Black, and that was the only name Rumison would have known him by.

McGregor packed, ate a quick breakfast at the motel coffee shop, and then left for the airport and Las Vegas.

Chapter Thirty-Seven

THE dream had always been the same. Stormy skies, a dark man whose face is hidden underneath a flat-brimmed hat pointing, McGregor running as the ground starts to break up, finally making it to a large brick building, like a university or a library, hiding in a room as the walls begin to shake. The pressure builds up and the building collapses. McGregor feels a large sliver of glass enter his right eye, and he passes out. When he comes to, the dream is still going on. The storm is past, a Gypsy woman helps him with the glass, the buildings are all destroyed, the air is clean, and then the dark man appears again, pointing, and McGregor doesn't want to go, to leave the Gypsy. He feels himself being torn in two, one side himself or the person who he thought was himself, the other side a woman, a feminine side. He screams. . . .

In the daylight, in the safety of the 707 jet, McGregor could remember the dream. He remembered the feelings he associated with it. The feelings were central to much of what he did, he knew that now. The dream was connected to Bastanchury because Bastanchury also was connected to much of what McGregor thought. Bastanchury had offered McGregor a system of thought that had replaced the subconscious patterns of the dream, but now Bastanchury was gone and the dream had returned. . . .

The stewardess walked by and smiled. Automatically McGregor smiled back, part of him attracted to the girl, a pretty blonde, and another part repelled by the idea of another surface encounter, another connection that, once the sex was over with, would only remind him of how unconnected he was to anybody.

"You don't look like a gambler," said the girl.

"Never can tell," said McGregor. "Wait till I get a pair of dice in my hands. My palms begin to sweat and my eyes get glassy. You stopping over in Vegas?"

The girl nodded. A man near the rear caught her eye with a raised hand. She grimaced at McGregor. "We'll be there in five minutes," she said. "I'm staying over the night." She looked down the aisle again, sighed and left. McGregor sighed also. It was all too easy.

The jet landed. Outside, in the desert air, it was hot, the temperature over a hundred. The blonde had been by the door as McGregor disembarked and had smiled again.

"Maybe we'll run into each other," said McGregor.

McGregor was traveling under the name of David Francis, thanks to the Agency's refusal to clear up the problem with Lieutenant Barnes and the L.A.P.D. He knew that eventually that loose end would cause him some problems, particularly if Barnes had remembered much from his ID cards, but there was nothing he could do about it for now.

He got into a waiting taxi. "The Dunes," he said. The taxi driver looked unconcernedly into his mirror at McGregor's face.

"You got reservations?" he asked.

"Didn't know you needed them."

The driver shrugged. "Might," he said. "Having a big convention there. Teamsters Union. It might be filled. I got another place just as good and cheaper rooms—"

"Just the Dunes, please. I'll get a room."

"All right, Mac, but you don't know what you're missing. This other place has more to offer. Better women . . ." The driver's voice trailed off, leaving his meaning clear. McGregor laughed humorlessly to himself.

"Just drive."

"Sure, Mac, sure. Just wanted to help."

"Save it for the Red Cross."

"Sure, sure."

The taxi driver hadn't been lying about the convention, but there were still rooms left at the Dunes, and McGregor took a key to a second-floor double and threaded his way through the noisy crowd to the elevator. There were few females in the crowd. Most were large men in cheap suits, and most were drunk or well on the way even though it was still officially morning. McGregor had been through Las Vegas many times. He had never liked the place, with its gaudy life-style, its neon signs and cheap plastic architecture, its strange, harried, pale-looking residents, but in spite of the stewardess's assessment of him, he did like to gamble, and he picked up on the gambler's excitement that permeated the place.

His room was no more and no less than he had expected it to be. McGregor wondered if they purposefully designed the rooms so the occupants wouldn't want to be in them, and would instead be out in the casinos spending their money. He set his bags on the bed, took out two thousand dollars from the roll of money Norris had given him, put the rest back in the suitcase, locked it, and then went downstairs.

McGregor cornered a harried desk clerk who sent him to the floor manager who in turn gave him the name of a pit boss named Sharkey McGuire. McGregor found McGuire taking a fifteen-minute break in the employee's lounge. The room smelled of hair grease and cigarette smoke.

"Sure, I remember him. How could I forget, when all you guys keep reminding me?"

"All us guys?" asked McGregor, sensing something wrong.

"Yeah. Must have been three or four the last week. Two FBI guys and then another T-agent."

"When did the FBI show up?"

"Three days ago," said McGuire, scratching his black thinning hair. "Must have been three days ago. I picked them for Feds right away. College look, cheap suits, you know."

Three days ago! The Agency could have used the FBI to check Rumison out, but the voice in Virginia hadn't reported to McGregor until just that morning. Either the FBI types were phony or the Agency was holding back.

"When'd this other guy show up?"

"Day later. I told him just what I told you, that I'd already said everything I could to the FBI. He wanted it all anyway, so I told him."

"You happen to remember his name?"

McGuire shook his head. "Can't remember," he said, eyeing McGregor suspiciously. "Say, what's the matter? Don't you guys keep in touch?"

"Normally. This is a pretty unusual case. You remember what the agent looked like?"

"Sure. Big, about your size but thicker, colored guy. Expensive suit. Mild-looking, but I wouldn't want to tangle with him. I wouldn't have taken him for a fed."

"Was his name Meade?"

"Could have been. Could have been Sandusky for all I remember. Names don't mean much to me, people changing them too often. Say, this guy White. What'd he do anyway? Must've been something big."

"The others didn't tell you?"

"Not a thing."

"There's a lot involved," answered McGregor noncommittally. "We don't have it sorted out yet. You seen Meade around since then?"

McGuire shook his head. "I'd think you guys would keep in touch," he repeated.

"I've been trying to catch up with him. What'd you tell him?"

"Not much. I remember the guy is all—White—because it was hot then, hotter than now, and not much business, and I always remember high rollers. He came in the middle of June. Checked the records, signed in June fifteenth. Casually dressed, 'bout like you. Had a beard. Looked suspicious until he started throwing out the bucks. Hundred-dollar bills everywhere. Rented a nice room, stayed here three days, gambled twelve hours a day, always at blackjack, and then left. Don't know where he went."

"Make any friends? See any women?"

McGuire shook his head. "He was a real loner, not that people didn't try to get close to him, especially some of the ladies. He wouldn't talk to no one."

"The home office said he lost a lot of money."

The pit boss scratched his hair again. "That's what I told the FBI boys," he said, "but then I started thinking. I mean it seemed like he lost a lot because his hundred-dollar-bills were turning up everywhere and he gambled, like I said, all day long, but after they left I realized I didn't know how much he'd lost, so I started checking into it. He tipped heavy but didn't spend nothing but eats and his room. Played blackjack for high stakes and looked like he was dropping a lot, but Danny, the dealer he played with mostly, said he didn't really lose that much. Other people remember him changing those hundreds a lot, like he was cleaning them."

"Cleaning?"

"Yeah, you know. Exchanging them. So they couldn't be traced. You know, around Vegas no one cares a rat's shit how you made your money, long as you have it, but there's always questions. Where did this man get that much money in cash? Figured he must have had close to a hundred G's, according to the cashier."

"Two hundred," said McGregor absently. His mind was somewhere else. So that's it, he thought. Rumison hadn't gone to Las Vegas to gamble, to lose himself in the fast life or forget his past. He'd come to cover his tracks, to change his easily traceable bank money into lower-denomination unmarked bills. Rumison had a purpose, a direction, a destination.

"He steal the money?" asked the pit boss, breaking into McGregor's sudden flood of understanding.

McGregor shook his head. "It's his," he said. "We're after something else. Did you tell Meade about White not losing as much money as the FBI thought he had?"

"The black? Yeah, I told him."

"Where's this Danny, the dealer?"

McGuire checked his watch. "He's on at two. Don't know where he is now. You want me to get his phone number for you?"

"That's all right. I'll wait. You point him out to me when he comes in. I'd like to do some gambling myself a bit."

"Sure. I'll be around."

Chapter Thirty-Eight

THE casino was crowded and noisy, even at noon. McGregor didn't know how many rooms the Dunes had or how many had been taken by drunken union members with buttons on the lapels of their suits identifying their local number, but he guessed it was a lot. He couldn't find any poker tables that looked interesting, so he stood by a twenty-five-dollar-limit blackjack table for fifteen minutes waiting for the far-left seat to open up. McGregor always sat in that seat, and he only played at a table that used one deck. It gave him time to count the cards and make his decision and made it easier for him to calculate the odds. He took out a stack of twenty-five-dollar chips and laid them in front. The stakes were fairly high for blue-collar workers, and most of the players at the table were quiet and serious about playing.

"Twenty," said the dealer in a bored monotone as he read McGregor's first hand. "Pay twenty-one." McGregor had drawn a six to a fifteen, and he took his winnings. He had been the only one at the table to win.

Play continued, and McGregor won steadily. The man next to him stood up disgustedly and cashed in. His place was taken by a drunken, loud-mouthed Teamster who had shoved his way through the small crowd watching the game to get at the empty seat.

"Five hunner' in chips, dealer," said the man rudely. He was a big man, overweight but still strong-looking. A cocktail waitress came past and he grabbed her arm, almost knocking her off balance.

"Jack Daniels, neat. I've been waiting for a drink."

"Yes, sir," said the waitress. McGregor watched her leave, feeling sorry for her. There was a class of people he would always feel sorry for, and middle-aged waitresses with beehive hairdos belonged to that group.

"Bets out," said the dealer.

McGregor was still winning, approaching the peak of a probable backslide, but he wanted to wait for the losing hand that would signal it. The man next to him lost steadily and became more belligerent with every loss. McGregor knew that normally the dealer would signal the pit boss when a player became too offensive and the offender would be hustled out of the casino by security officers, but this time the management must have had some sort of agreement with the union, because nothing was done.

"Twenty," said the dealer. "Pay twenty-one."

McGregor had drawn a nineteen, and he knew it was time to leave. His watch said two o'clock and he wanted to talk to Danny. As he started to collect his winnings a meaty arm swung across the table, knocking down his row of carefully stacked chips.

"Sorry, there, fella," said the big man, grinning. "I was just reaching over to point at a fella I know over there. Didn't mean to bump your chips over like that."

McGregor was a violent man. He knew this, but very few others did, because there was always a point in his rising anger when he could decide whether to let it build or to quell it. He could only remember three times in his life when the anger had caught him off guard. He could feel his anger rising now. Others must have felt it also, for there was sudden quiet at the table. The teamster was smiling. McGregor continued to pick up his chips. He was subconsciously aware that the dealer was looking around for the pit boss.

The teamster seemed to lose interest, and McGregor bent down to pick up the chips that had fallen on the floor. Suddenly a leg came out and hit him in the side of the head. The teamster laughed.

"Uh—gosh, fella. You seem to be getting it today, don't you. I was just stretching my leg—"

He didn't have time to finish the sentence. McGregor's elbow had jammed up into his side and made him grunt in pain. In quick succession McGregor hit him in the jaw, the neck, and the stomach, and as he fell from the stool McGregor kicked him in the crotch for good measure. The man probably didn't feel it. He was out cold.

"It's all right, Sharkey," said the dealer as the pit boss appeared, followed by two security officers with drawn pistols. "The man had it coming."

Sharkey looked at McGregor appraisingly. "Big guy," he said noncommittally.

"He didn't have much choice," said the dealer, obviously on McGregor's side. "The guy was drunk. Hassling him."

"Take him to the first-aid room," said the pit boss, motioning toward the unconscious teamster. He looked around at the crowd that had formed, noisy again now that the tension was gone. "All right," he said, "all right. Break it up, just a little too much to drink." McGuire looked at McGregor again.

"Danny's here," he said. "You'd better come with me."

"My chips . . ."

"We'll collect them for you."

"Thanks."

"Don't mention it."

The pit boss was trying to get McGregor away from the table, and it was several seconds after his anger had died down before he could think clearly enough to realize why. The big teamster may have been an obnoxious loud-mouth drunk, but he was a teamster and some men in the crowd probably wouldn't like the idea of a long-haired man beating up on one of theirs. McGregor followed Sharkey through the crowd as several elbows jostled him.

"That group could get mean," said Sharkey, once they had left the floor and returned to the employees' lounge.

"I see that," said McGregor. "Next time I'll control my temper."

"I thought you guys always controlled your tempers."

McGregor shrugged. "When we want to," he answered.

Danny was waiting for McGregor in a small office behind the employees' lounge. He was a young man, pale, with colorless blond hair slicked back and held down with hair cream.

"I've got to get back to the floor," said Sharkey after introducing the two men. "Don't take too long with Danny. Sam's filling in for a bit, but he didn't especially like it."

"Just a few questions," said McGregor.

"I can't tell you any more than I told the other guy," said Danny.

"How many guys you talk to about this?" asked McGregor.

"Just one. T-agent, like you."

"You didn't talk to two FBI agents?"

Danny shook his head. "Just the black guy."

"Remember his name?"

Again Danny shook his head.

"What'd you tell him?"

"Not much. The guy—White they said his name was, I never knew it—played blackjack. Bet hundreds. Played a system, sat in the far-left seat. My guess is he played with me the most because my table is the only hundred table that uses one deck."

McGregor nodded and smiled inwardly to himself. He and Rumison must have read the same book.

"He turned a lot of money over," continued Danny. "But I don't think he lost that much, if any. He played a loose system, could have won if he'd kept it tighter."

"Tighter?"

"Yeah, he probably counted tens only. Makes odds about even."

"You guys know about systems?"

Danny smiled. "Of course. Know they work too, if the guy knows what he's doing. We're supposed to shuffle a lot to break it if we catch a guy using them, but with that guy I just played straight. No reason, him playing even like that. Some of the places would bring in a mechanic, but the Dunes is pretty clean that way."

"And you're sure this guy was using a system."

Danny nodded. "Sure. He played every hand the same way. Played quickly, no decisions. Guy can't play that fast less he knows what he's doing, following a system. I know. I must've played five hundred hands with the guy. Made out, too. He tipped real well."

"Which is maybe another reason you didn't shuffle the cards as much?"

Danny shrugged. "Didn't hurt nobody," he said.

"You ever talk with him? He ever say anything?"

Danny shook his head. "Not a thing."

"Nothing? Nothing at all?"

"Well, just before he quit he picked up his chips, gave me two hundred bucks, and said he was leaving."

"Leaving? He say to where?"

"Nope. Just said he was going home."

Going home? The phrase hit something in McGregor's mind. He didn't know what, but he knew it was important.

"You remember exactly the words he used, Danny?" he asked.

Danny looked thoughtful. "Just that he was going home," he said. "He said, 'Thanks for the games,' then he handed me the two hundred. I asked him if he was coming back, and he shook his head and then said, 'No, not for a long while. I've got to be going home.' "

Home? Rumison's home was in Laguna Beach. He'd never known any other. He wouldn't have called his room at the Dunes home. Was he just talking?

"Thanks, Danny," said McGregor out loud. "You've been a big help. By the way, you haven't seen the black guy around, the other T-agent, have you?"

"Sorry, Mr. Francis."

Chapter Thirty-Nine

BASTANCHURY had taught him about the varieties of fear: about the fear that clogs the mind and keeps the motor neurons from firing properly; about the clinging fear, the dread that comes for no apparent reason in the dead of the night or during certain unpleasant moments in the day; about the fear of people that makes a person turn his eyes away when someone looks too long or too close. Bastanchury had known about fear and what it was and he had taught McGregor.

"Fear serves a purpose," he'd said at a small campfire in the hills of Viet Nam while they waited for the Viet Cong to launch another strike before the rains came. "It can focus attention in critical situations when the attention needs to be focused, heighten perceptions, give us adrenaline, quicken reactions. But when it goes to the mind, when we think about it, it defeats its own purpose. The secret is to do. Still the mind, utilize the energy."

"But it's impossible to do that," protested Lieutenant McGregor. "Like now. Waiting, just waiting. What do you focus your mind on? Just waiting like this."

"You must have trust," said Bastanchury. "Trust is your ability to handle the situation, your body's ability to handle the situation. And trust in your fate, the knowledge that you will die when it's time, and not before, in spite of anything you can do. You must accept the situation as it is."

"How can I repeat something I don't know is true, something I don't even understand or believe in?"

"You just do," said Bastanchury. "It's just something

you decide to do, in spite of doubts. That's the enemy, those doubts that keep you from doing what you would."

McGregor had learned. He had learned what Bastanchury meant, and he'd developed the ability to do what he would, in spite of fear, in spite of doubt. He'd learned to face everything, no matter how frightening, as it came, and it had given him a tremendous amount of power. Bastanchury had warned him about that also.

"When you no longer fear, then people no longer have control over you; you have control over them. Use it only to accomplish what you would, otherwise it becomes another trap, another way to keep you from doing what you would."

"But how do you know what to do?"

McGregor remembered Bastanchury's sad smile, seen in the flickering of the firelight. "You decide and then you do," said the major simply.

What McGregor hadn't realized at the time was how much he was beginning to trust Bastanchury. Bastanchury needed no one. He had a certainty that could have made him a master teacher or leader, if he'd wanted that. McGregor didn't have that certainty, but he'd trusted Bastanchury, formed his thoughts around Bastanchury's, and gained his own center from the older man because he saw how things happened to Bastanchury and how Bastanchury dealt with them.

It was dark in the hall by McGregor's room. The overhead light must have blown. The power wasn't off, because farther down the hall, around a corner, another light cast shadows in the darkness. Normally darkness heightened McGregor's senses, but it had been a long day, flying into Las Vegas, the fight, the interviews, the investigations, trying to turn up something the Agency's men might have missed, someone who may have seen Rumison leaving town, or talked to him in a weak moment. But he'd learned nothing more and he was tired.

His key clicked into the lock. Off in the distance he could hear the muted sounds of the casino. The door opened and there was another sound, one not quite right. He turned too late and something hit him across the side of the head, stunning him as he fell into the room.

"That's the bastard," said a voice. It was vaguely familiar, and he sensed figures in the room. Somebody kicked him in the side. Someone else's foot came up and kicked his face and he was afraid. The fear built and with it the energy, but no clarity with which to use the energy. A doubt. Bastanchury was dead. Bastanchury's ideas hadn't helped him after all. It was all a farce; McGregor had lost his trust.

Another foot kicked and another. "They're killing me," screamed McGregor's mind, and the mind panicked. The body fought to blunt the blows, to roll with the punches and parry the kicks, but it also had to fight the mind, and it was a losing battle. McGregor remembered no more.

Chapter Forty

WHEN McGregor regained consciousness it was light outside. His first thought was pain, total and complete, but with broadening consciousness the pain became more localized. His head, his fingers on his right hand, his ribs. He raised his hand to look at the fingers. They were smashed and broken. He rolled and his ribs screamed out in agony. Some were broken, but his legs seemed all right, as did his left arm, and he lifted himself with its help and stood up. He fell again and the pain washed over him.

When he came to again the pain had diminished to a dull throbbing. He checked his watch. Remarkably, it hadn't been broken. Eleven-twenty. This time when he stood up he didn't fall.

He checked his bags, to find them still in place and still locked. It hadn't been a robbery. McGregor knew it wasn't a robbery. Through his pain he'd recognized the voice that had spoken as the man he'd knocked unconscious at the blackjack table. A very mean fellow, he thought ruefully.

He staggered into the bathroom and looked in the mirror, knowing what to expect. It wasn't as bad as he'd thought, but it was bad enough. There wouldn't be any pretty beach girls for some time. His face was cut and bloody and his nose was broken. Both his eyes were black, swollen nearly shut.

He limped out to the phone and dialed the desk clerk. "Could you have someone bring up a roll of gauze and some antiseptic?" he asked.

"Certainly, sir. Is anything wrong?"

"No. I just cut myself. Just have him leave it on the dresser as soon as possible. I'll be taking a bath."

"Right away, sir."

McGregor went back to the bathroom and turned on the water in order to fill the tub. Not being able to use his right hand made things difficult, but he finally got his clothes off and sank down into the warm water, feeling thankful that his groin seemed to be untouched. The water hurt his cuts at first, but then its warmth began to have an easing effect.

He heard a knock on the door but didn't answer. The door opened, there was the sound of movement, and then the door closed again. That would be the bellboy with the antiseptic, he thought. And if it wasn't, McGregor was beyond caring. The beating had done only minor damage to him physically; professionals would have crippled him. But McGregor was much more worried about his mental state. He'd almost let himself be killed by three drunken truckdrivers, simply because he had doubted himself, given into fear. It was not a pleasant knowledge.

Twenty minutes later McGregor dried himself off with one hand, got the antiseptic and gauze bandaging the bell boy had left, and began splinting his hand. Only three fingers were broken, and he straightened them out, then wrapped them tightly, and then wrapped the whole hand. He ignored the pain, taking it as just punishment for his mental laxity the night before. When he had finished with his hand he daubed antiseptic cream on his facial cuts, ignoring his sore ribs. When he had time he would get them X-rayed. After he was finished he called the desk clerk for an outside line to an airline ticket agency and booked a two-o'clock flight to Miami Beach. He also arranged for a cab to be waiting in front of the hotel at one-forty. Then he dialed the desk clerk again and asked to talk to Sharkey McGuire.

"I'm sorry, sir, but we can't take him off the floor. I'll have him return your call during his next break."

"All right. It's important, though."

McGregor dressed and then packed his bags. It was after twelve already. The telephone rang, and it was the raspy voice of McGuire.

"I heard you wanted to talk to me, Mr. Francis."

"Yeah, McGuire. I wondered if you ever found out the name of that guy I hit, down in the casino."

McGuire laughed dryly. "Boy, did I. Name's Kirkpatrick. Head of Local 541. Bad dude, supposed to have heavy mob connections. Lot of his friends were pissed off at you. He's all right, left the first-aid room just a few minutes after we took him in, madder'n hell. If I was you I'd stay away from him for a while. Might even be wise to stay away from the floor."

"Thanks for the warning," said McGregor. "Kirkpatrick, huh? You know his room number?"

"Not offhand. What'd you want with his room number?"

"Just wanted to apologize for my behavior yesterday. Well, thanks, McGuire. I'll see you around."

"Sure, Mr. Francis."

Time was running out for McGregor. He'd felt this ever since leaving Laguna Beach, but now he felt it more than ever. The assignment had become very personal and very important to him, but there was one small matter he had to take care of first. He dialed the desk clerk again.

"This is B-31. Could you have a lunch sent up? Steak and potatoes and a salad, and some cold fruit juice."

"Certainly, sir."

"And page a Mr. Kirkpatrick. Tell him that someone wants to see him in his room at one-thirty, that it is very important."

"I don't know . . ." began the clerk, obviously hesitant. "I mean, you are Mr. Francis, aren't you . . . ?"

"I am. I want to apologize to Mr. Kirkpatrick for yesterday. But don't tell him that, he might not come up to see me otherwise."

"I don't know, I'd better—"

"Look," broke in McGregor, "I'd call him myself, but I don't have time. I'm leaving at two. Now, just be a good guy and page him and tell him someone wants to meet him at his room at one-thirty and that it is important. You don't have to tell him who it is. I'll leave you a good tip on the bill."

"O.K., Mr. Francis. I guess it's all right, you just wanting to apologize and all."

McGregor sighed and hung up. It was shaky but it would have to do. If Kirkpatrick didn't show up it would just be another loose end, like Barnes back in L.A. He lay back on the bed, careful of his ribs and hand, and waited for his lunch.

Chapter Forty-One

McGregor had given the bellboy who brought him his lunch a twenty-dollar tip to make sure his bags were brought down to the taxi at one-forty, and to get him the number of Kirkpatrick's room. It was nearing one-thirty now, and he waited, sitting in a telephone booth in the hall just down from the room number the bellboy had come up with. He wasn't nervous or scared. He didn't try to rationalize what was going to happen. It was just a job, just something he had to do in order to feel better about himself later on.

He knew Kirkpatrick would show up. It was a feeling he had, and he wasn't surprised when he saw the big teamster walking toward his room with one other man. McGregor would have preferred to find Kirkpatrick alone, but the presence of the other man didn't change his mind. The two men opened the door and entered the room. Two seconds later McGregor walked up to the door and knocked. Kirkpatrick opened the door.

"Wha . . . ?"

He didn't finish. McGregor's foot came up in an expertly timed and placed aikido kick to the groin, and Kirkpatrick doubled up in pain. McGregor's left hand shot out and struck him in the neck, knocking him sideways. McGregor stepped over the man into the room just as Kirkpatrick's companion started to come at him. He spun and his foot shot out, catching the other man in the knee joint and snapping his leg. The man fell in a grunt of agony.

"Christ, you've broken my leg!"

Kirkpatrick was trying to get up again. McGregor

kicked him in the head. Then he closed the apartment's door.

Kirkpatrick's companion was almost sobbing. "What're you going to do?" he cried. "What're you going to do?"

McGregor looked at him without compassion. He was smaller than Kirkpatrick by quite a bit. He could have been with Kirkpatrick the night before, but McGregor doubted it. The man didn't look like he had the stomach for such things. His face was pale, shocked, and his eyes were scared.

"Tell Kirkpatrick, when they take him to the hospital, not to take people so lightly," said McGregor quietly. "Tell him that what I am going to do to him could happen again, anytime."

"What . . . what are you going to do . . . ?"

McGregor showed him.

When it was over, McGregor called room service and asked for two stretchers to be sent to the room. Then he walked downstairs. The cab was waiting as it was supposed to be, and his bags were in the back.

"The airport," he said.

The driver looked at McGregor's bruised face and shook his head. "Man," he said, "you look like you just lost a fifteen-round decision to Larry Holmes."

McGregor didn't answer. It hurt too much.

Nat Bishop put the telphone back on the receiver. His expression didn't change, but those who knew him well would have known he was angry. Very angry.

"He's gone to Jamaica," he said to the other man in the room

"Jamaica?"

"He's from Jamaica."

"Why would he go home at a time like this?"

Bishop shook his head, signifying he didn't know.

"How are the two teamsters?" asked the other man.

"One will be all right. Broken patella. The other is still in intensive care. Broken ribs, broken jaw, broken arm, internal injuries."

"And you men see no connection between them and his assignment?"

"None whatsoever," said Bishop, standing up from his desk as he began putting several open files that lay on the desk into a black briefcase. "None whatsoever. I told that ass Norris that McGregor is not psychologically sound. He may have gone off the deep end. Total vindictiveness. He may have blown the assignment completely."

"Does it matter?"

Bishop finished with the files and snapped the briefcase. "Maybe," he answered. "Maybe not. Norris was right in one thing, though. McGregor has a good track record. He's just weird enough to come up with a new line. God knows we haven't got anything else going."

Bishop picked up the telephone again and dialed one digit. "Carter. Pack it up. We're leaving in twenty minutes." He put the telephone down.

The other man in the room smiled. "Jamaica?" he asked.

Bishop nodded.

"There is one thing," said the other man quietly as he removed a cigarette from a gold case in his vest pocket and lit it.

"What's that?"

"Jamaica is in the Caribbean, you know."

"So?"

"It's easier to get to Nicaragua from Jamaica than it is from Las Vegas these days."

Bishop didn't say anything for several minutes. "I hope you're right," he said finally. "But if he is, it brings up another question."

"It brings up many questions."

"Why would Rumison have gone back to Nicaragua?"

The man with the cigarette shrugged. "Why do criminals return to the scene of their crimes? A meaningless question, for me. If this is the case, however, and McGregor is following Rumison back to Nicaragua, then I would be very curious to know how McGregor found out."

"Who knows what goes on in McGregor's mind?"

"But this is all speculation, of course," said the man, smiling again.

Bishop started to pick up the briefcase, and then he

looked up sharply at the other man. He started to speak and then decided against it. Sometimes he wondered if the black man in front of him were any more sane than Mc-Gregor.

Chapter Forty-Two

JAMAICA is a large island, 4,412 square miles of beaches, hills, forests, roads, fine hotels, beautiful rivers, and a seemingly carefree and healthy populace. There is poverty there, but even the wretched shantytown in Kingston has a unique Jamaican flavor that somehow seems to mitigate the pain of being so poor that secondhand shoes are an unaffordable luxury.

McGregor had been born in Jamaica and it should have been home for him, but for some reason only his subconscious knew, the island made him uncomfortable. There was a darkness there or in his heart, and it was for this reason he'd been back only three times since he first left to attend school in the States. He'd never admitted the fact to himself, much less anyone else, but each of his three previous visits had been short and unpleasant. Now as he drove up the long hilly road that led to the island's interior region called Cockpit Country, where his grandmother lived along with Indians and the other *maroons,* descendants of runaway slaves, that same darkness began to return. It took its place beside the fleeting images of his nightmare and settled in with the growing loneliness and the alienation he felt from women. Somehow these things tied together. This he had sensed back in his room in Las Vegas when he had thought Kirkpatrick and his friends were going to kill him, in that timeless moment between shattering fear and unconsciousness. In that same moment, strangely interconnected with his own karmic history, had come the certainty of where Michael Paul Rumison, ex-sergeant in the United States Air Force, had been going.

There had been two clues. The first had been the name he had chosen to travel under—White. Rumison was still connected somehow with the mission, with Bastanchury, whose code name had been Black. The second clue had been Danny's recollection of Rumison's words, "I've got to be going home." McGregor couldn't explain his reasoning in words or rational thought, but he knew Rumison was heading back to Nicaragua. Why, he didn't know, but he hoped that it had to do with Bastanchury. What other reason could there be? he thought. It was known that the others were dead; Rosso, Bailey, Sleeper. McGregor knew what a man like Bastanchury could do to a young man's head. Was Bastanchury in some sort of trouble? If so, why hadn't Rumison reported in? Why was he doing his best to cover his tracks?

These thoughts had followed McGregor since leaving Kingston, but as he drew closer to Cockpit Country they suddenly ceased. It was sunset. The sun was dropping into the ocean, growing incredibly large and incredibly pale, its color reflecting off the scattered clouds, the shadows growing in the forest on either side of the new macadam road just as they grew in McGregor's heart.

McGregor had rented a small open-topped M.G., and the warm wind of the trades wisped through his hair, reminding him of the California Santa Anas and the French *mistral.* The trees of the forest, the casuarinas and coconut palms, the banana trees and the magnificent flowering poincianas, were losing their identity in the darkness, but McGregor had no trouble finding the narrow dirt road that broke off from the main highway and led to the little village of Dominique, where his grandmother lived.

McGregor slammed on the brakes just in time to avoid hitting the rear end of an ancient black Ford pickup truck that appeared to be caught in a pothole in the road. The truck had no rear lights, which was why he hadn't seen it sooner. The dark shape of a man was hunched down by the wheel caught in the hole. The man didn't look up from his work, but in the light of the M.G.'s headlamps McGregor could see that he was old—an old man with flowing long white hair. McGregor had a sudden irrational desire to back up and return to the highway, but he suppressed it with an irritated shake of his head and got out of the car.

"You need some help?" he asked.

The old man looked up, and McGregor saw now that he was black, a mulatto probably. McGregor's nerves were keyed up, as if he were expecting something. There was no sound in the forest but the wind.

"No help needed," said the old man. His voice was strong, with the singsong cadence of most Jamaicans. "I've got a board under her now. She'll make it. Serves me right for not payin' attention. I knowed that hole was there." The old man stood up as if to signify that no help was needed, and he approached McGregor.

"You must be heading to Dominique," he said. McGregor could see his eyes squinting in the bright glare of the headlamps. "No other place this road goes to."

The old man drew closer. McGregor could smell the coconut smell of his dark skin.

"You don't look to be in much shape to help anyone," said the old man, laughing suddenly as he seemed to notice McGregor's face and bandaged hand. "Why you goin' to Dominique?"

"My grandmother lives there."

The old man laughed again. It wasn't a warm laugh. It reminded McGregor of dry sugarcane stalks breaking in a high wind. "You're McGregor," he said.

"Do I know you?"

"You will," said the old man cryptically, laughing again and turning back to his truck. McGregor watched as he got in and started the old flathead engine. The engine ran smoothly, and after a short grinding of gears the old man drove off, the wheel that had been caught coming out of the hole easily. McGregor looked at the hole in the light of the headlamps but couldn't see any board. The thought disturbed him and he climbed back into the M.G.

Chapter Forty-Three

DOMINIQUE wasn't a town. In the nineteenth century, it had been a large sugar plantation owned by a crazed Frenchman who was later murdered in his sleep by his servants. With the freeing of the slaves and the subsequent rise in the cost of labor the plantation had been abandoned by the Frenchman's relatives. Maroons, mulattoes, and renegade whites had taken up residence in the old buildings and started a little village whose economy was based on what was left of the sugar and tobacco fields along with a minor trade in "ganja," the island's name for marijuana.

McGregor's mother had been born in Dominique, in an old house that used to be slaves' quarters. His mother had inherited her pride and beauty from McGregor's grandmother, and an unusual intelligence from his grandfather, a white Catholic missionary who had dropped away from the Church after falling in love with a black woman. The grandfather had died of yellow fever, *la fièvre jaune,* before McGregor was born. McGregor's mother had run away from home when she was just thirteen but had returned shortly after McGregor's Irish father had left Jamaica and his young wife and son. McGregor had been four years old at the time.

He'd never known his grandfather, and what he remembered about his father was not much more than a half-forgotten dream. Years later he had heard a rumor that his father, John McGregor, had died in South America, trying to start a lumber plantation in the Amazon Basin. McGregor's mother, forever a wild and impulsive woman, began running around with different men, and since she was very beautiful she was also very popular. A white official of the British colonial government had taken her as his mistress and McGregor had been sent off to the States to boarding school. McGregor was fourteen when he learned of his mother's death in an automobile accident outside Paris. The Englishman had also been killed, the deaths causing a minor scandal among the more respectable population on the island.

Until he had met Bastanchury, McGregor had resented his mother. He'd resented her self-centeredness, her apparent lack of affection for him, her abandoning him when he was sent off to school, and later the embarrassment she had caused him by her manner of death. Bastanchury had changed all that by making him see her as the woman she must have been, full of life, frustrated by her own upbringing, beautiful, willful, and most of all a romantic, forever hoping for that someday when her knight would ride up and save her from the dragon of her existence.

McGregor didn't resent Isabelle Beleforte McGregor anymore. He would never feel a son's love for her, but he had learned to respect her memory. The knight had never come, but she had lived as if he really had existed somewhere, and as Bastanchury had said, "Perhaps that is all that matters in this life; that we live as if our dreams really existed."

McGregor couldn't see the old man's truck ahead on the road. It had disappeared as if it had never existed. Either the old man had driven at breakneck speed or McGregor had missed seeing a turnoff somewhere back on the road. The thought, like the missing board back at the pothole, disturbed him, but he shoved it from his mind and concentrated on trying to find the old slave quarters where he hoped his grandmother still lived.

He passed the plantation house, lying atop a small hill, shattered and gutted from an old fire, surrounded by trees and covered with lianas and ivy. It had been abandoned for over eighty years, but the area around it had grown and the old barns, the old mill, the old slave quarters, all had been turned into dwelling places for homeless field workers, defrocked priests, and young girls too uneducated to follow the dreams of their childhood.

McGregor stopped the M.G. in front of his childhood home, wondering how he could have thought that he might forget where it was. The low stone building stood as it had always stood in his mind, unchanged, or so it seemed in the dark. Candlelight burned through the lightly curtained front windows, and McGregor knocked on the thick wooden plank door. The door opened with a struggle. McGregor's grandmother stood there in the candlelight.

"Come in," she said calmly. "I've been expecting you."

McGregor's grandmother was tall and regal. Even old age hadn't diminished her bearing or taken away the pride with which she held her head. McGregor could see that she had gotten old. There was a timelessness to her despite the gray hair and wrinkles that had always been different from the short-lived fast-burning passion of her daughter's life. McGregor stepped inside the house with a strange reluctance.

"Expecting me, Grandmother?" he asked.

Mrs. Beleforte nodded. "Louis told me you were coming."

"Louis?" McGregor was puzzled for a moment and then the puzzle seemed to clear up. "Would he be an old man, drives a black Ford pickup?"

"Yes. That is Louis."

"He must be a crazy driver," said McGregor. "I just met him on the road a ways back. He must have just left."

"Oh, no, Richard. Louis told me three days ago you were coming. I have not seen him since then."

"Three days ago? But . . ." Conflicting thoughts ran through McGregor's mind. It was impossible. He himself hadn't even known he would be here three days ago, yet in all his early life, the one thing that stood out most about his grandmother had been her total honesty.

"Louis is a strange man," said Mrs. Beleforte. "Sometimes he sees things. But he could not see, or he would not tell me that he did see, why you have returned?" She put the statement as a question, and it caught McGregor off guard.

"I'm sorry," said Mrs. Beleforte. "I'm being rude. You can talk later. Have you eaten?"

McGregor shook his head.

"Will you be staying?"

"Perhaps a day or two, if it is all right."

"It is all right. You can get your bag and I will serve you dinner."

The old woman turned and left McGregor alone by the door in the small living room. McGregor took a deep breath and exhaled it slowly. It helped to calm him. Too many things, too many images, too many feelings, too many words. A strangeness as if everything were slightly out of focus, yet his perceptions were incredibly clear. Above it all a hurt. His grandmother was his last living relative. He had been gone for many years, and yet she had shown no surprise, no happiness, no love, even when it was obvious he had recently been hurt. Instead she had seemed . . . ? McGregor returned to the car and took out first one bag and then the other with his good hand and carried each one back into the house.

He knew the house well. Little had changed. Bamboo furniture and West Indian tapestries, hand-carved ashtrays, a large deep-red Oriental rug that somehow didn't look at all out of place in the rough house, low ceilings held up by aging beams, and a brass oil lamp hanging in the center.

He carried the bags into the bedroom he had lived in when he was a little boy and put them down near the door, which was open. The lamp in the room was off, and it was too dark to see in clearly. He lit a match, located the oil lamp, and lit it.

"That's my room," said a voice from behind him. The voice startled McGregor and he turned. He had thought his grandmother to be alone. A young black girl stood before him, no older than fifteen. She was dressed in a hand-stitched peasant blouse and a Jamaican sarong that fell almost to her bare feet. She was very beautiful and she looked at McGregor with unwavering brown eyes.

"Who are you?" he asked.

"I'm Isidra. That's my room," said the girl.

"Isidra? That's a pretty name. Are you staying here?"

"She lives here," said Mrs. Beleforte, coming into the living room with a tray on which was McGregor's dinner—fish and rice and a tall glass of mango juice. McGregor knew the meal well. He had eaten it many times as a boy.

"She lives here," repeated his grandmother as she set the tray down on a table. "Her parents are dead."

McGregor didn't answer. He looked into his old room. It had changed. It was lived in by a young woman now, and it reflected the difference.

"Your meal will get cold."

McGregor picked up his bags and moved them back out into the living room. Then he sat down and began eating.

"We go to bed early here, you remember," said Mrs. Beleforte. "It is Isidra's and my bedtime. You may sleep on the couch here. It is big enough for you, and comfortable. We can talk in the morning."

She gave a nod toward the girl, who had been watching McGregor with intent eyes. The girl nodded at Mrs. Beleforte, went into her room, and closed the door. Mrs. Beleforte looked at her grandson for several moments, then walked over to the front door and bolted it. McGregor remembered his grandmother's insistence that the door be locked at night. She wouldn't sleep if the door wasn't locked.

"Good night, Richard," she said.

"Good night, Grandmother. Thank you for the meal."

"Could I have done less?" said the old woman, and she left for her own room on the other side of the kitchen, leaving McGregor alone with his meal and his thoughts.

Chapter Forty-Four

ISIDRA was beautiful. McGregor watched her in the morning, as the sun came up over the jungle and the surrounding hills and the birds sang to the accompaniment of the smell and sound of eggs frying in his grandmother's kitchen. He watched her move with the grace of a young fawn, as she showered in the outdoor shower that stood next to the outhouse, unconscious and uncaring about her nakedness. McGregor remembered his own thoughts when he had been young and growing up around Dominique, and he wondered when he had lost such innocence.

Isidra was shy but not nervously so, quiet but not unresponsive to McGregor's questions. She exuded a feeling of trust which surrounded her, like that of a puppy, a complete receptiveness that McGregor found both admirable and erotic.

"Your breakfast is ready, Richard."

McGregor looked up from his seat on the porch bench, wondering why he suddenly felt ashamed. Long ago he'd come to terms with his sexuality. If he was attracted to a woman or a girl, and the situation was such that an affair were possible, then there should be no limitations, regardless of age.

But now he wondered, and he wondered about other things as well. He'd thought he'd also overcome fear and yet he had recently been afraid. He'd thought he knew what to expect from life and yet suddenly his expectations were falling apart. He had thought he knew himself as well as any man knew himself, yet he had suddenly experienced feelings and thoughts totally alien to what he considered his nature.

"Isn't Isidra eating with us?" he asked.

"You are rested now," said his grandmother. "I wish to talk with you alone. Isidra knows this. She will eat when we have finished talking."

McGregor followed his grandmother into the kitchen, where she'd placed his breakfast of muffins and eggs on the dining table. "What is it you wish to talk about?" he asked, sitting down.

"I will talk as you eat. Then if you would talk, you may."

McGregor nodded, feeling strangely apprehensive, an emotion that also made him feel slightly ridiculous.

"Louis said I could expect you," began Mrs. Beleforte, staring at her grandson across the table. "At first I was happy and I listened to the birds in my heart sing as I remembered their doing when you lived here. But then I remembered how it was when you left. I had hoped that you would learn, and when I saw you last night I knew that you had, but not what was necessary. You had good teachers for what you learned. You are a man, a strong man, a beautiful-looking man, and you have power, but you are not who you should be. . . ."

The fork in McGregor's hand stopped in mid-swing. A rush filled his ears and a buzzing rang in his head as he remembered Riley Dancing Waters' words: "The chiefs say you are of the greatest, McGregor, but you are not yourself. How can they trust someone who is not himself?" *What is happening to me?* he thought.

"You were hurt," continued Mrs. Beleforte, apparently unaware of the effect of her words on her grandson, her voice calm and deliberate. "I am sorry for that, but I can give you no love. You came home after many years expecting love, but what you found, what you will always find, is a mirror to yourself. You will never find love until you are able to give love, and that is something that takes more courage than all your manliness can muster.

"You see Isidra, who has not been hurt, and you lust for her, for what she represents, and you would make her like your mother, who hurt us all, you would make her like yourself, unable to love or trust anymore. And you would do this with no understanding of what you did.

"I will not be hurt again by your carelessness and I will not have Isidra hurt. You are wrong for this place, Richard. Tonight you will talk to Louis, but tomorrow you must leave."

Mrs. Beleforte stopped, and her face was firm and uncompromising. McGregor had trouble finding words. Something in him had shattered and he was frantically trying to salvage the pieces. "I . . . I didn't come here . . . for that. . . ." he stammered. "I came . . ."

"Why did you come, Richard?"

"I have a job to do. . . ." began McGregor, knowing even then that what he had been about to say was a lie. He stopped. Mrs. Beleforte nodded.

"Finish your breakfast," she said. "You will get thin," and she stood up and left the room.

It was a while before McGregor tried to eat again. When he finally took a bit of egg he felt physically sick to his stomach, shoving the plate aside.

He left the house unmindful either of his grandmother, who was watching from the porch or the girl Isidra, who was toweling off after her shower. He walked for fifteen minutes before he was aware of his surroundings. Either intentionally or by accident he found himself standing under an old oak in which he had once built a tree house when he was a child. The tree house had been his refuge from the world, a place where he felt safe from the pain he felt whenever the jokes about his mother got too bad to bear. Now he clenched his teeth, mentally cursing himself for giving in to the childish feelings that washed over him.

I must be going crazy, he thought, and then remembered something Bastanchury had once said:

"Craziness is just another state of consciousness. Nothing to worry about."

But Bastanchury was gone now, and this pain was still with him.

Chapter Forty-Five

WHEN McGregor finally returned to his grandmother's house it was afternoon. The girl, Isidra, had gone but would return later that evening. McGregor's grandmother was canning fruits in the kitchen, and McGregor thanked her for her words. As he spoke, her stern face began to soften.

"They were hard for me," she said. "They were against my nature."

"I understand."

Mrs. Beleforte smiled sadly. "No. Not yet, but perhaps someday."

McGregor picked up his bags to leave, but his grandmother stopped him. "You must see Louis tonight," she said. She appeared almost anxious.

McGregor had forgotten about the old man, but now the questions from the night before had returned. He questioned his grandmother about Louis, but she refused to answer, saying only that it would do him good to talk to Louis.

"Then I guess I'll have to see him," said McGregor finally. Mrs. Beleforte nodded and returned to her canning.

McGregor spent the rest of the day wandering about Dominique, sightseeing and remembering. He was almost surprised at himself when he realized how many happy memories he actually had about the place. Dominique had scarcely grown in twenty-five years, and little had changed. Friendly, laughing locals, children running naked around the old central fountain, the smell of Jamaica heavy in the trade wind, old men singing and playing homemade instruments on doorsteps as they watched the last of their lives pace slowly by—it was as he remembered.

Isidra was back when he returned to the house. He still wanted her but now he looked at her in a different light. There was an innocence about her, something very delicate. He had noticed it earlier and been sexually attracted to it, but now . . .

"Grandmother told me you once lived in my room," said Isidra while McGregor watched a horsecart go past carrying bananas. He had been sitting on the front porch, as he had sat for two hours in his old tree house, thinking, but now his thoughts were not so painful. "That must have been some time ago."

While the girl spoke, she looked directly into McGregor's eyes. He was aware of little else but her presence.

"A long time ago," he answered.

"You must love her as much as I do, then," continued the girl.

McGregor didn't speak for a moment. "Perhaps," he said finally.

"You must," said the girl with assurance.

"Do you have many friends?" asked McGregor.

"I stay by myself a lot, but I have some friends. I like staying by myself."

"Do you have any boyfriends?"

The girl laughed impishly and shook her head. "No," she answered. "But I know who I am going to marry."

"How do you know that?" asked McGregor.

"Louis told me."

"Louis? How could Louis know that? Is he obeah?"

Isidra looked shocked and shook her head vehemently. "Oh, no. Louis has nothing to do with voodoo. Louis . . ." She paused, searching for words.

"Louis is just . . . Louis. He sees."

"And can he make cars disappear from dark roads at night?"

Isidra shrugged. "Louis doesn't do things like that, but sometimes he makes other people see also."

"See? See what? See reality?"

Again the girl shrugged. "I don't know about that," she said. "Just see things you want to know. Sometimes things you need to know. He said what I want and what I need are the same, but what most people want and what they need are two different things."

"You wanted to see who you would marry?"

Isidra smiled again. "Oh, I knew who I would marry. I just wanted to see if he knew also."

"And who are you going to marry?"

Isidra stood up from the seat she had taken next to McGregor. "I can't tell," she said solemnly. "Then it wouldn't happen." And she turned and left.

Evening came quickly and Mrs. Beleforte began lighting the oil lamps. As the last of the sun's light finally gave way to darkness McGregor heard the rasping sound of an old flathead V-8 engine and he looked out the window to see the old black Ford pickup stopping in front of the house. Seconds later there was a soft knock on the door and Mrs. Beleforte let in the aging black man, Louis.

"Good evening, Renée," said the old man, his sharp eyes seeming aware of everyone in the room at the same time. McGregor was watching him closely, with the intent gaze of a trained observer, for any signs of something unusual but he could find none. Perhaps that in itself was a sign, he thought.

The old man was dressed in a threadbare but clean off-white suit whose color matched his surprisingly long hair. He had a certain ease of movement that was unusual in a man who must have been over seventy.

"Mr. McGregor, so nice to see you again," said Louis.

"Then you were there," said McGregor, taking the offered hand and finding it, as he expected, firm and steady. "I'd begun to have a feeling that I dreamed you, the way you took off out of there."

Louis laughed. "I do like to drive fast," he said.

"My grandmother told me you knew I was coming three days ago," said McGregor.

"Felt it was time," said Louis. "But you never really know."

McGregor felt put off, and he was just about to question Louis further when Mrs. Beleforte interrupted. "Dinner's ready," she said. "You can talk afterward."

Louis laughed again. "Women have a much better sense of timing than men," he said. "You know, there really is a time for everything. That's one of man's biggest problems, knowing when a thing's time is up, or when another thing's time has come. Take love for instance, feels so good when it's happening, man he wants to hold it, but it's like everything else, got its time and place and when it goes nothing goin' to stop it. On the other hand you got to be ready when its time is come, which takes a lot of courage, more 'n most ready to shove out."

Louis irritated McGregor though McGregor couldn't have said why. He was interested in him, like he was interested in the Taos Indians, because there was obviously something to learn there, but the old man's attitude was strangely offensive to him, as if he were trying to teach McGregor a lesson McGregor didn't think he needed.

"Love's a pretty broad subject," said McGregor. "Lots of different types."

Louis shook his head and laughed sadly. "No," he said. "Only one Love. Man, he splits up everything and thinks he knows it, but there's only one Love and you know it when you're there. Most people hurt so much not being there, they're afraid. Make up all sorts of substitutes that they talk about and write songs and poetry about and get married because of, but it isn't the real thing. Only a man who's been there know what I talk about."

The old man's eyes shone with the reflection of the oil lamps.

"Bad word, love," continued Louis. "Irritates men to talk about it. We all been there one time or another, usually when we're children, but something happens later." Louis sighed and repeated himself. "Something happens and then the rest of our lives are spent trying to forget because it hurts too much to remember, and trying to remember because it hurts too much to forget."

"You can finish your talk after dinner," said Mrs. Beleforte again. "The fish will get cold."

McGregor was thankful for the interruption. Sometimes these old men knew some good tricks, some good techniques, like predictions. McGregor did want to talk to Louis about how he knew he was coming to visit his grandmother three days before he'd even known himself, and he was still curious about the night he'd met the old man, but if he had to put up with more rubbish about love . . .

Dinner was rice, squash, fruit salad, fish, and white wine. Isidra ate quietly while Mrs. Beleforte and Louis made small talk about local happenings. When it was over, Louis stood up and gave a slight bow to Mrs. Beleforte.

"Thank you again for dinner, Renée."

"You're leaving, Louis?" Mrs. Beleforte didn't sound surprised.

"I've things to do and places to be. Goodbye, Isidra."

"Goodbye, Louis." Isidra didn't sound surprised either.

Louis turned to McGregor, who was still seated, feeling confused.

"It was nice meeting you, Mr. McGregor," said Louis, holding out his hand.

"Likewise, Louis, but do you have to leave? I did want to talk to you about some things. . . ."

Louis laughed and his bright eyes twinkled in amusement. "Those things are unimportant and always have been," he said.

"Those things you wanted to talk about?"

"Yes . . . ?"

"Sometimes they can make a person see that something else is going on other than what he thinks," continued Louis. "But they aren't what you need."

"Need?"

"You aren't Richard Francis Burton, Mr. McGregor. You are someone else. Mr. Burton had his time and his place and his task, you have yours. The enemy is the same, but everything else changes. When I was a boy Mr. Burton was needed. Had to show some things. Those things been shown." Louis bowed again to Mrs. Beleforte.

"Good night," he said, and left McGregor staring at his grandmother and Isidra in silence.

"Strange man," said McGregor finally. "I thought he wanted to talk to me."

"No," said his grandmother. "You needed to talk with him."

"Then why wouldn't he talk?"

"He said everything which was necessary to say."

"That's ridiculous," said McGregor. "He didn't say anything. Some crap about love and then that Burton thing. What in hell did Burton have to do with love? Burton was a man, he lived a man's life. Why—?"

"And a man can't love?" asked Mrs. Beleforte quietly.

"No, I didn't mean that. . . ." McGregor wanted to explain himself, to tell his grandmother how a strange major in the Green Berets had told him about Richard Francis Burton, explorer, writer, orientalist, athlete, unafraid, his own person. How McGregor had grabbed on to the image and how it had helped him understand and forgive his mother, how he'd tried to follow his namesake's example, how his life had been based on that example. . . .

But then he remembered his own doubts that he could ever follow Burton's example. How many lands were there still unexplored? How many mountains left unclimbed? How many specialists were there in this world that made everything Burton did seem amateurish in comparison? What was the challenge in the world of today, what would Burton have been like if he'd lived in the twentieth century, in a land of atomic weapons and mega-corporations, of specialists and mass media, of computers and preplanned, antiseptic scientific expeditions, where the men involved were no more than the pieces of machinery they carried or flew to the moon in?

The doubts had always been with McGregor, even when Bastanchury had advised him to *do*—not to rationalize, not to think, just to decide and then to do. McGregor had learned to do, but now the structure that had informed his decisions was crumbling.

"Sometimes it takes time for a person to understand Louis," said Isidra gently. "Sometimes it takes time to understand yourself."

"Tomorrow you must leave," said Mrs. Beleforte. "You may return someday, if you feel right about doing so."

That night McGregor dreamed his nightmare again. This time the Gypsy was his grandmother and the man who pointed was the old man, Louis.

Chapter Forty-Six

IT was the shoes that gave the man away. McGregor couldn't be sure at first sight of him, but the shoes clinched it. All the way back to Kingston from Dominique his mind had been working, chewing over old memories and new ones, old thoughts and new ones, his attention wandering from his surroundings until he was barely aware of them. It was a dangerous state for McGregor to be in and he knew it, but the thoughts kept coming until he finally gave in to them.

The sight of the shoes brought him back. They were expensive shoes, polished leather, hand stitched. Out of place—like the man who wore them—in the hall that led to McGregor's room in the ancient Port Royal Hotel. The Port Royal was off the main tourist beat and was frequented mainly by down-and-outers or students traveling on a low budget. McGregor stayed there because he liked the place, its old wood siding, shuttered windows, and Victorian architecture.

The man wearing the shoes was seated in an antique captain's chair in the hall, reading that morning's copy of the Kingston *Pilot*, his face hidden. McGregor noticed his manicured white hands and the stylish cut of his tropical suit. McGregor also wondered why the man didn't bother to glance out from behind the newspaper. He was positive the man was aware of him.

"Excuse me, do you have the time?"

The man lowered the paper. He was youngish, clean-cut but fairly rugged-looking, like an Ivy League football player. His eyes narrowed and he tried to appear nonchalant as he consulted his watch.

"It's twelve-fifteen."

McGregor nodded, thinking that he must be carrying his gun on his belt in the rear, like an FBI man. An unhandy place when sitting in a chair.

"Thank you," said McGregor, and he walked down toward his room carrying his two bags. He put the bags down by his door. Then, as if he'd forgotten something, he went back down the hall and entered a communal bathroom. Removing one shoe, he took off a sock, which he filled with sand from an ashtray next to the sink before wetting it. He tied a single knot in the sock stem, both to hold the sand in and to give him a better grip. He didn't have much grasp in his injured right hand. Then he put his shoe back on and left the bathroom.

The man in the chair didn't have time to lower the newspaper again before McGregor hit him. The wet sand slammed into his temple with a dull sound and the man slumped back in the chair. McGregor searched him, taking out a wallet, a passport, and a Walther PPK pistol from a holster on the man's belt in the rear. The passport and ID were issued to someone named John Kastler, Langley, Virginia. There was no ID connecting him to the Agency, but McGregor knew that many junior field agents carried Walthers, a sign of status in some circles as a certain brand of ski would be in others, or the type of car you drove.

McGregor replaced the wallet and passport but kept the Walther. He laid the newspaper across the man's face to make it appear that he was sleeping, hitched the sand-filled sock to his belt, and walked back down toward the door to his room.

"Room service," he called, knocking twice loudly. There was no answer. He knocked again and then put his key in the lock, making sure to rattle it noisily.

"Come back tomorrow," came a sudden voice. "I'm trying to get some sleep."

"Ah'm jus' goin' change the linen," called back McGregor, and then he threw the door open.

"Freeze, you sons of bitches, or you're dead!" The voice he used was something he'd learned long ago; the louder you were, the ruder your words, the less chance the people you were covering would think to react.

There were two men in the room: a youngish, grim-faced, ascetic-looking man in a conservative gray suit, and a black man, as tall as McGregor but weighing more, dressed in a three-piece brown suit that looked as if it had just been taken from the rack at Brooks Brothers. Neither man moved, though both controlled their surprise well, a fact McGregor gave them credit for.

"Get down on the floor. Put your hands over your head, fingers together, legs apart."

The ascetic-looking man tried to protest. "Really, McGregor, all this isn't necessary. I—"

"Get down before I blow your heads off!"

Both men moved. McGregor searched them, his borrowed Walther held first to the black's head and then the other's as he took out their wallets and passports. Neither carried a gun, but McGregor found a wicked-looking folding stiletto in the black man's coat pocket. McGregor moved back to the door.

"Nat Bishop?" he asked, reading one of the passports.

The ascetic-looking man started to move. "I tried to tell you, McGregor—"

"Shut up and keep your hands where they are. I didn't say you could talk."

"McGregor, I'm your employer. I have a right—"

"You lost your rights when you entered my room without my permission and left that college boy out in the hall with a gun."

"McGregor—"

"I said shut up." McGregor looked at the other passport. The name was unfamiliar to him; Adrian Idris; aged 42. Nationality: American.

"Idris," said McGregor thoughtfully. "Unusual name. You an agent? I thought I knew most of the good ones. I didn't think a man in Bishop's position would travel with anyone less than the best, but I have my doubts after seeing that boy outside."

"I'm not employed directly by the Agency," said the black calmly. "If that's what you mean." He spoke with the trace of an accent McGregor couldn't place. Soft *r's* and a roll that could have been Caribbean, but McGregor doubted it. Spanish Caribbean, possibly.

"I'll ask you directly, then, Idris. Who are you?"

The black was silent. "I'm sorry," he said finally. "But I'm not at liberty to tell you that."

"I could find out another way."

"Perhaps."

McGregor was thoughtful for a moment, then tossed the wallets and passports back to the two on the floor.

"You can get up, but I'm still keeping the gun out. Tell me what this is all about."

"What did you do to Kastler?" asked Bishop as he stood up.

"The man outside? He'll be unconscious for a few more minutes. Have a headache when he wakes up. Nothing more. If you wanted to talk to me, there were certainly other options not so dangerous for you or your men. What's this all about?"

The black man sat down in a chair and crossed his legs. His eyes watched McGregor carefully and there was a slight smile on his lips. Bishop remained standing.

"You're off the mission, McGregor," said Bishop. "We just came to tell you."

"May I ask why?"

"After that debacle in Vegas, you have to ask?"

"I've seen agents do worse. What's the real reason?"

"You're unstable, McGregor. The mission is too important to leave in the hands of a . . ."

"Madman," finished McGregor. "Strong words, considering I still have a gun on you." He turned to the black. "Mr. Idris," he said. "You wouldn't happen to know a certain Mr. Meade, would you?"

Idris widened his smile. "I might," he said.

"I thought you might. Sloppy job, that search back in Laguna."

"There was a reason."

"I figured that there was, but not what it was."

"We thought it best you knew you weren't alone."

"All this is wasting time, McGregor," broke in Bishop. "You have no right to question us. I told you you're off the case and that's it. You can keep the advance money. Other than that there's nothing more to be said."

"Oh, but you're wrong, Mr. Bishop. There's a lot more to be said, and do I have to keep reminding you that I do have a gun, and as you said yourself, I am rather unstable."

"You're about as unstable as the rock of Gibralter," said Idris. "I think you just have to be understood. And I have some questions, too: Why did you beat up those men in Las Vegas, and what gave you the clue that Rumison had gone back to Nicaragua?"

"He did go back, then?"

Idris nodded. "We couldn't decide any other reason why you would have gone back to Jamaica, so we began checking: boats, airlines, every means possible Rumison may have used to get over there. Found a charter skipper here named Luís Echeverría, a Cuban refugee, who remembered a man resembling Rumison's description paying him ten thousand dollars American to let him off in or near Bluefields in Nicaragua, not more than a month ago. But what gave you the clue?"

"Feelings," said McGregor simply.

"And the men in Las Vegas?"

McGregor shrugged. "Just something I had to do."

"I had a feeling it was something like that," said Idris.

"This is getting us nowhere," said Bishop. "McGregor, you're off the mission and that's that. We don't need you anymore. You're a liability now." Bishop started to move toward the door, but McGregor stopped him.

"Not so fast. We've still got a lot to talk about. I'm not even sure you are who you say you are. I've never seen Nathaniel Bishop, for one thing. Why isn't Norris here? He ought to be the man to call me off."

"Norris is off the mission also," said Bishop stiffly.

"Is he? And do you have proof of all this?"

"McGregor, I warn you—"

"By the way, Idris, or Meade, or whoever," continued McGregor, turning to the black, "that was quite a job you did on the Van Mannon family, but was all that really necessary? I mean, it did leave a lot of loose ends lying about."

Idris frowned. "That wasn't us, McGregor," he said quietly. "We didn't even know about the girl until you called in."

"Then somebody else is interested in Rumison."

"Lots of people," said Idris. "More than you could possibly know."

There was a sound out in the hall, and McGregor stiffened. Idris and Bishop were silent. A smell of the sea and poincianas came in from the room's open window. Outside McGregor could hear the sound of light traffic and the singsong pidgin language of the West Indies as pedestrians talked in the streets. Off in the distance, barely audible, came the klaxon horns of emergency vehicles. There was another sound in the hall.

"Tell him to come in," whispered McGregor.

Bishop hesitated.

"Tell him!"

"It's all right, Carter. Come on in."

"You'd better come out, Mr. Bishop," said a voice from the hall apologetically. "I don't know who is in there with you."

McGregor reached behind him with his bad hand and slowly opened the door. Another college type was standing in the hall with a drawn pistol, a Walther.

"Damn it, it's all right, Carter," said Bishop irritably. "Mr. McGregor just feels nervous with you out there."

"If you say so, Mr. Bishop, but I found Jack unconscious out in the hall and—" Carter lowered his gun.

"And you're going to be unconscious also, if you don't put that gun away," said McGregor, motioning the agent in with his gun and wondering where the Agency was getting its people from these days. A Boy Scout wouldn't have made the mistakes Carter had. Idris smiled again as he watched McGregor, and Bishop looked disgusted. Outside, the blare of the klaxons grew louder.

"Did you call the police?" asked McGregor.

Carter shook his head slowly.

"We don't want them involved any more than you do, McGregor," said Bishop.

The klaxons turned onto the street the hotel was on, and McGregor didn't wait. "Somebody called them," he said. "Down on the floor. All of you. Hurry, same position, hands on head, fingers linked. Down, damn it!"

McGregor didn't wait for the men to reach the floor. The sock whirled, and Carter fell to the floor, then Bishop. McGregor could hear the police cars pulling up outside the hotel, and he looked at Idris. There was no sign of fear in the black's eyes.

"I'm glad I finally met you in person, McGregor," said Idris. "But I'm a little disappointed. I thought I had understood you, but this move throws me off again. You are in for a lot of trouble, you know. You don't know how much."

McGregor nodded. "It doesn't matter," he said. "I do what I have to do."

Idris smiled in understanding and the sock fell one more time.

Chapter Forty-Seven

McGregor closed and locked the door to the room, grabbed his bags, and ran toward the door leading to the fire exit. Behind him he could hear the footsteps of police as they swarmed up the stairs to the second floor, and their voices as they discovered the unconscious Kastler. He hoped it would take them a little longer to find the room the other three men were in. He didn't know what story Bishop would tell, but whatever happened there were going to be people after him. In a way this knowledge was a relief. Now he didn't have time to think, to let his mind wander. Now all he had time for was to react.

Throwing the bags over a low brick wall at the rear of the hotel, McGregor glanced around to see if anyone was behind him. Seeing no one, he quickly climbed over, and pushed the bags near the wall. Then he walked around to the front in order to get his car. There were two police cars in front with a driver standing by each. They didn't notice the man across the street with only one sock on who calmly climbed into a little M.G. and drove off. Their attention was on the hotel. McGregor breathed in relief after he retrieved his luggage, turned off onto another street, and finally lost the hotel from view.

It was a hot, humid day in Kingston. King Street was crowded with hawkers, traffic, and tourists. The sound of steel bands and calypso music gave a distinctly Caribbean beat to the noise of the traffic.

McGregor ignored the spectacle and cursed the traffic for slowing him down. He parked the M.G. near the charter slips down by the bay, took his bags out, and began walking. Hundreds of small boats, both motor and sail, were lined up in their slips, waiting for charter. McGregor hailed the first man he saw on board a thirty-foot power cruiser.

"Nicaragua?" said the man, a black sporting a weathered yachting cap and a white beard. "You might try the Professor. Has a forty-eight-foot ketch down the way a bit called *Zygote.*"

"Zygote?"

The man shrugged. "I didn't name her."

McGregor thanked him and continued walking. He found the *Zygote,* a sturdy-looking teak-hulled ketch, and climbed the ramp to board.

"Hello."

There was a sound from the cabin and a man appeared, bare to the waist, tanned and fit-looking but obviously middle-aged. "Did you call?" he asked, staring at McGregor with undisguised curiosity.

"I need to get to Bluefields. Man down the way recommended you."

"Bluefields? You can drive over there. Why hire a boat?"

"Nicaragua, not Jamaica."

The man smiled. "That's different," he said. "Five hundred dollars in advance."

McGregor frowned. Something suddenly didn't seem right. He hadn't thought about it before, but now it seemed very important.

"Too much?" asked the man who McGregor assumed to be the Professor. McGregor shook his head.

"Too little," he said.

"Too little?"

"Who would pay ten thousand dollars to be taken to Nicaragua?"

The Professor looked puzzled. "I don't understand. Nobody. Nobody in their right mind. It's an easy crossing."

"An American?"

The man shook his head. "It's risky sometimes with Americans," he said. "But not that risky. You can hire twenty boats around here would do it for less than a thousand. Why, you an American?"

McGregor nodded. "You know a skipper named Luís Echeverría?"

"Sure. Everyone in Kingston knows him. Nasty sort. Has a sloop called *El Conquistador* not far from here, slip 37. I just saw him not more than an hour ago. Cuban. Anything-for-a-buck sort, but a capable seaman. What's this all about, anyway?"

"Can you be ready to go in half an hour?"

The Professor looked dubious. "I don't know. I have to get my crew together. The *Zygote*'s ready, but . . ."

"I'll give you an extra two hundred."

"I'll be ready."

"I'll be back. I have to see a man about an overly large fare he collected."

"If you're talking about Luís," said the Professor, "I wish you luck."

McGregor smiled grimly. "I'll be back in half an hour," he said. "Just be sure your boat's ready to sail."

"I'll be ready and so will the *Zygote.*"

McGregor left his bags on the *Zygote* and ran back to his car. The exertion was making his ribs ache. He hoped Luís Echeverría was at his slip.

McGregor stopped a young deckhand walking down the boardwalk. "Hey, you want to make a quick twenty?"

"Sure, mon. I'm always up for a quick money. What you got me to catch?"

"Take my car up to Fort Charles and leave it with the keys in it. Take a taxi back."

"Sure, mon. That all?"

"That's all. Here's twenty and a couple for cab fare."

That done, McGregor began looking for the finger dock that held slip 37, finding it only six down from the one the *Zygote* was docked at. Echeverría's sloop, *El Conquistador,* was older by two decades than the *Zygote* but well maintained, recently painted and trimmed with gleaming brasswork, and had unstained sails furled neatly. McGregor could see no one on deck, so he climbed aboard and knocked on the cabin door. The door opened and a seaman stood there.

"Are you Luís Echeverría?" asked McGregor.

The man shook his head and motioned McGregor to follow him. He led McGregor to the stern cabin and knocked once on the door. A gruff voice answered.

"Qué pasa, Ramón?"

"Un hombre aquí, Señor Echeverría."

"Entre."

The seaman, a burly, dark man with a seamed and scarred face and black, unkempt hair, opened the cabin door and waved McGregor in. McGregor had hoped the man would join them in the cabin; he didn't want someone around whom he couldn't observe firsthand, but the door closed and the seaman remained outside.

"What can I do for you?"

McGregor appraised Luís Echeverría before answering. The captain of *El Conquistador* sat behind a carved mahogany ship's desk and stared back. His eyes were the first to break contact and McGregor noted this. Echeverría was dark and swarthy, like the deckhand, but smaller. He had the air of a degenerate about him, self-indulgent but probably clever and good at what he did. McGregor looked at his watch. Twenty two minutes before he was due back at the *Zygote.*

"I'm interested in a passenger you took to Nicaragua last month," said McGregor quietly.

Echeverría immediately stood. "I have already talked to the authorities about this man," he said too loudly. "I have nothing more to say."

"You haven't talked to me," said McGregor.

Echeverría's answer was halted in midsentence as he suddenly noticed the gun in McGregor's hand.

"What is it you wish, *señor?*" he asked.

"Tell me everything."

The sailor shrugged. "There is little to tell," he said. "Last month, a man—"

"What did he call himself?"

"Señor White. He called himself Señor White. He wished to go to Nicaragua. He was an American. I said the risks were great, that my sloop ran the risk of being impounded by the Nicaraguan navy. He said he didn't care how much it cost, so I took him to Nicaragua. I left him off four miles south of Bluefields, on the beach. That is all. There is no more."

"There is more," said McGregor.

Echeverría shook his head, but his eyes were narrowed and McGregor knew he wasn't telling something.

"There is more," said McGregor. "And you are going to

tell me what it is or you will never tell anything to anyone again." He knew how to be threatening when he wanted to be. All you had to do was be sincere. Echeverría felt this and McGregor could see fear growing in the Cuban.

"What more?"

"The trip to Nicaragua is easy. I've been told," said McGregor, "that a man, even an American, can be taken there by any charter for less than a thousand. That what little navy Nicaragua has is mostly on the west coast and that the Nicaraguan government doesn't mind American tourists. That it's the United States that doesn't want Americans to go to Nicaragua. Why would a man pay as this man paid you just to take him to Bluefields?"

"You—you know how much he paid me?"

McGregor nodded. "Ten thousand dollars."

"He was scared," said Echeverría. "He had something to hide. He didn't want anyone to know about the journey—"

McGregor shook his head. "He wasn't scared," he said. "He knew what he was doing. Why are you lying, Luís?"

"*Señor,* please . . ." The captain's eyes shifted at the last moment, and McGregor was ready when Echeverría shoved the desk at him and leaped for his gun. McGregor's bad hand brought the sock over in an arch, striking Echeverría's jaw and knocking the Cuban to the floor. McGregor had aimed the sock carefully. He hadn't wanted to knock the man unconscious.

"My jaw," cried Echeverría. His words were slurred and he held his chin.

"You can still talk. You're lucky. I'm going to hurt you more, much, much more, if you don't tell me the truth."

There was a slight noise behind McGregor and he turned to see the cabin door open. The seaman who had taken McGregor to the cabin entered carrying a gun. McGregor hit his arm with the sock and the gun dropped to the floor. Echeverría tried to jump him but McGregor kicked him in the knee. The seaman grabbed McGregor's bad hand and the pain was intense but McGregor forced the Walther into the man's chest and pulled the trigger. The man fell to the floor. McGregor didn't think he was dead yet—he'd tried to miss the heart—but he didn't have time to find out. He took the groaning Echeverría by the arm and swung him across the desk.

"I have no time, Echeverría. You either tell me the truth or I will hurt you bad and then kill you. Do you understand? Do you understand me?" The Cuban nodded dumbly.

"What luggage did White have? Did he have a small black suitcase?"

"No, no, *señor*. He carried only a large pack. It was blue."

"You took the money from him, didn't you."

The Cuban didn't answer, and McGregor hit him across the face with the pistol. Then he took out the stiletto he had taken from Idris and opened it.

"If you don't tell me what I need to know I will cut your fingers off and then your ears and then your nose."

"*Señor*, please . . ."

"And then if you still haven't told me . . ." To make his point, McGregor hit Echeverría in his groin and all the man's defenses suddenly crumbled.

"He offered me a thousand," he sobbed. "I agreed, but Ramón saw more money in his case."

"So you robbed him."

Echeverría nodded.

"And you got ten thousand?"

"*Sí*. And Ramón got five thousand."

"That was all? Only fifteen thousand?" The knife pressed down on one of Echeverría's fingers and the Cuban screamed.

"*Sí*, I swear by the Holy Mother. That was all."

"And you killed him then?"

"No, *señor*. In truth, I am not a murderer. We gave him up to the port authorities in Nicaragua."

"And what story did you give them?"

"Only the truth. That he was from the United States, that he was trying to sneak into their country."

"And they believed you?"

"They kept him."

McGregor felt that the Cuban was telling the truth. He eased the pressure on the knife. Echeverría sighed.

"You are the lowest form of scum, Echeverría," said McGregor. "I only wish I had time to teach you a lesson." The sock rose again and the Cuban captain fell unconscious on the desk. McGregor wiped his fingerprints from the Walther and forced it into Echeverría's right hand. He picked up the pistol the seaman had dropped, a Smith and Wesson .38, and put it in his belt. The seaman was still breathing, but McGregor now saw he would die shortly, even with medical help. The bullet had missed the heart but must have touched an artery. A bright red rhythmic surge of blood soaked out of the wound.

I've burned all the bridges, thought McGregor. *All the bridges there are.* He remembered Bastanchury once talking about dangerous actions.

"Once you make a move, you have to learn to be totally committed to it. Otherwise you leave room for personal error. The move may be totally insane, but if you are not committed to it you multiply its insanity."

McGregor was committed. To what he wasn't yet sure, but he knew it was more than a black attaché case and a runaway Air Force sergeant.

Chapter Forty-Eight

CHESTER MELLON PIROSH, better known around Kingston as the Professor, regarded his passenger with a thoughtful look on his weathered patrician face. They were seated on cots in the stern of the *Zygote*, several hours out from Jamaica. One of the hands, a young boy named Constantine, was at the wheel; the other hand, Constantine's older brother, was cooking an early supper in the galley below.

"A zygote is the cell produced by the union of two gametes," said the Professor, answering the question all his passengers asked. "Or the individual produced from that union. I consider the *Zygote* to be the result of several creative forces at work in my life."

"I take it you weren't always a charter skipper," McGregor said.

The Professor smiled and lit the pipe he had been toying with. "No," he answered. "I really was a professor once. Vermont College. I taught English."

The trade wind was blowing lightly, moving the *Zygote* along at eight knots, quartering across her as the rigging slapped and pots banged in the galley. McGregor hadn't wanted to leave his small cabin. He hadn't wanted to talk to anyone until they reached Nicaragua, but the pitch of the boat had upset his stomach in close quarters and he'd been forced on deck. The Professor had tactfully refrained from mentioning either McGregor's visit to Echeverría or his reason for wanting to go to Nicaragua and McGregor was thankful for this.

It didn't seem to bother the Professor that McGregor was

a total stranger. "Long ago I wanted to find out who I was," he mused after a long draw on the pipe. "I studied and went to war and got my doctorate and studied and read and finally realized that I would probably never find out who I was because there was no one I trusted enough to tell me. Since I would never know myself, I thought, then why not the next best thing, decide who I wanted to be and become that. Lately I realized that who I am and who I want to be are one and the same."

"And you wanted to be a charter skipper?" asked McGregor, finding himself listening in spite of himself. The Professor's story echoed many of his own recent thoughts.

The Professor nodded. "Among other things," he said. "A great writer, for instance. I write a lot nowadays when I take the time. I visited Jamaica many years ago when my wife was alive—she died in an automobile accident ten years ago—and fell in love with it. At the time I was still too tied to my old self to follow the call of my heart."

"How long you been doing this?"

"Three years. I was having an affair with a coed, a beautiful girl who was taking my Comparative Literature class, and got caught having intercourse with her on the mock stage in the Drama Department by the chairman of the department. . . .

"Beautiful girl but not too bright. A Cadillac body and a mo-ped mind, but very sweet nonetheless."

"You were fired?"

"I resigned. It was a fairly liberal college and I wasn't alone in my extracurricular interests. It would have been shoved under the rug with everything else, but I had decided that I'd had enough. It was time to leave school behind and put the knowledge I had gained to work trying to realize my dreams."

Both men were quiet, listening to the sounds of the *Zygote* and the rhythm of the ocean.

"It's a good dream," said McGregor quietly.

The Professor nodded. "I think so," he agreed and then he laughed. "You know," he said, "one of my biggest worries was that there wouldn't be any more coeds. That now that I wasn't a professor, that I didn't have the gimmick of grades and all that pompous prestige, that I wouldn't have any more—but you know . . . I don't know what it is, but I find that women are dangerously attracted to older sea captains."

"Have you ever been in love?" asked McGregor.

"All the time now," answered the Professor. "In love with the *Zygote* and the sea, with the Caribbean, with life."

"I mean with a woman?"

"Yes," said the Professor shortly.

McGregor didn't press. "There was a man I once wanted to be," he said. "I was named after him. I tried to be him, but a man like he was couldn't exist in today's world."

"Don't be too sure," said the Professor. "A man worth wanting to be can exist in any time. The enemies change but courage remains. The mountains are climbed but there are always more, even if we no longer call them mountains but something else."

"You're quite a romantic, Professor."

"There's an old saying, Mr. McGregor. A Persian said it a long time ago. It began, 'Life is a caravan of dreams, a dream of caravans.' Why not dream a romantic, worthwhile life for yourself rather than some nightmare?"

"I wish it were that easy."

"It wouldn't be worthwhile then, Mr. McGregor."

"Soup's on," called Constantine's brother from the galley.

The Professor stood up. "Will you join me, Mr. McGregor?"

"I'm not really hungry. I think I'll stay up here a bit."

"I understand. It took me a while to get my sea legs."

McGregor watched as the Professor went below decks, and then he returned to his thoughts. He couldn't seem to focus on any particular problem. They all seemed fused inexorably together. Where was Rumison now? In jail? Did the Sandinistas know who he was, or did they just think he was a misguided American tourist? The restriction on U.S. tourism to Nicaragua was fairly recent, just the last two months. Maybe they let him loose. But why had Rumison wanted to return to Nicaragua in the first place? Was Bastanchury still alive? And what had Rumison done with the black case that seemed so important? Why had Norris been taken off the mission and why had Bishop tried to take McGregor himself off it and what was in that damn case that had gotten Norris and Bishop personally involved? Who was Adrian Idris, and who had killed the Van Mannons if he hadn't?

And who was Richard Francis Burton McGregor?

The questions flooded his mind, breaking over the dams erected by long years of practice. *If only I'd had more time to question Bishop and Idris. If only I'd had more time with Echeverría. If only . . .* McGregor cursed himself for doing the very things he'd trained himself not to do—fantasize, daydream, fill his mind with useless conjectures and might-have-beens. There were always might-have-beens.

"What is, is," Bastanchury had said once. "It's funny, but you'd be surprised how hard that is to accept for some people."

What is happening to me? thought McGregor in anguish. He hardly noticed the quiet approach of the Professor.

"You look troubled, Mr. McGregor."

McGregor didn't answer.

The Professor sat down next to him. "I don't mean to intrude on your private affairs, Mr. McGregor," he said, "but I have to admit I am terribly curious about some things."

"Oh?"

"A man comes along wearing one sock and wants a charter to Nicaragua. The man is large and has obviously just recently been injured; bruised face, broken hand, moves carefully as if his ribs hurt. . . ."

The Professor was a clever and observant man, McGregor decided. Somehow, however, he didn't feel threatened.

"He wants to leave quickly," continued the Professor. "But first he visits a rather disreputable charter skipper named Luís Echeverría who I later hear on the radio has been arrested for murdering his number-one hand—"

McGregor started at this, and his eyes narrowed in on the man sitting next to him.

"Easy, Mr. McGregor. I'm just curious is all. I personally detested Luís, as did most who knew him."

"Luís turned a man in to the Nicaraguan police after robbing him of fifteen thousand dollars," said McGregor. "I suspected that and confronted him with it." He shrugged.

The Professor nodded and took out his pipe. He filled the bowl with new tobacco and lit it.

"You killed Ramón?" he asked.

"Would I tell you if I had?"

The Professor was quiet, as if thinking. "Was this man a friend of yours?" he asked. "The one Echeverría robbed?"

"No. I never met him."

"Then why . . . ?"

"I don't know. I've been hired to find him, but somewhere along the line our fates got mixed up and now it's more a matter of finding myself." McGregor was surprised at himself. He hadn't let himself open up like that since his time with Bastanchury in Viet Nam. What was happening to him? He looked out at the sea trying to calm his thoughts, the thoughts that he so desperately wanted to spill out to this white-haired man next to him who reminded him of the father he'd never known.

"I thought it was something like that," said the Professor calmly. "I recognize the symptoms, having gone through them myself."

"Symptoms?"

The Professor nodded. "When a man looks too hard at a thing, sometimes that thing disappears. This happens if a man looks too hard at himself. When that thing disappears . . . well, then what replaces it?" He took a draw on the pipe and followed McGregor's gaze out to sea.

"It gives a man a certain look," he continued. "A tortured look quite unlike the grimaces of discomfort that go with ordinary pain."

"What does replace it, Professor?"

"Only two things can replace it, if a man keeps looking and doesn't run from the fear of what he might find."

"What are those?"

"Death and wholeness, Mr. McGregor. Death for the unwary. Wholeness for those that make it."

"I understand death."

"I'm sure you do, but do you understand wholeness?"

McGregor shook his head.

"Perhaps you will understand it when you find this man you are looking for, Mr. McGregor. Perhaps then."

The Professor stood up to watch as Constantine's brother came out of the cabin and threw the day's garbage into the sea. A small flock of seagulls that had been following the *Zygote* swooped down with cries of bird greed and began picking the pieces out of the water. McGregor watched also, and it wasn't until the last scrap of garbage had been retrieved by the gulls that he realized he'd stopped thinking for a moment. The chain of internal dialogue that had begun building ever since that day in Taos when Norris had told him about Bastanchury had come to an end at last.

"It's going to be a beautiful sunset," said the Professor to no one in particular. "A beautiful sunset."

"Hurricane sunset," said Constantine's brother.

"Hurricane sunset?"

The Professor nodded. "Clouds like those form a day or so before a hurricane."

"Are we expecting a hurricane?"

"Tropical storm is all. Small one. We'll be east of it and in harbor if it shifts. Probably get some rain squalls. Marine radio weather doesn't expect anything nasty."

The Professor sighed and stared out at the horizon, at the golden-yellow-orange lights on the clouds, the grays and blacks and light against the incredible blue backdrop of the early-evening sky.

"A beautiful sunset," he said again.

Chapter Forty-Nine

THE *Zygote* was within fifteen miles of land before Constantine called "Land ho!" The main center of the storm had hit farther east, crossing over Puerto Rico, Cuba, and Jamaica, but the sky had been overcast for a day and the swells had increased ten feet.

McGregor hadn't talked any more to the Professor about his mission. The Professor sensed his reluctance and spoke of other matters. McGregor enjoyed the two days of conversation and almost felt inclined to confide in the older man, but Constantine's cry brought him back to his problems and his immediate danger.

"How far from Bluefields?" he asked.

"Seventeen miles, more or less."

McGregor was thoughtful. Undoubtedly Bishop would have traced him onto the *Zygote,* probably aware of its destination. He'd certainly left enough signs. How far the Agency would go to stop him was another matter, or whether they'd even try. And there were still those other nameless parties Idris had hinted at. The ones who had killed the Van Mannons.

"Professor, do you think you could let me off along the coast farther to the north?"

"Sure. How far?"

"Couple of miles."

"Expecting trouble?"

McGregor shrugged. "Maybe, maybe not."

The Professor nodded and gave the new course to Constantine, who dutifully swung the wheel another quarter-peg to starboard. It was nearing twilight, but there was no sunset because of the overcast. McGregor had gotten used to the pitch of the boat but he still preferred being above deck. When the *Zygote* was two miles out he went below and began packing, putting the few items he thought essential in a canvas duffle bag the Professor had given him, the items that might be harmed by ocean water, his gun, ID, and money, in a sealed plastic container. The rest he put back in his suitcases and shoved under the bed. When he'd finished, the bag weighed less than twenty pounds.

"McGregor. A boat's coming. Looks like a small government gunboat."

"How far off, Professor?"

"Miles. Coming directly at us."

"How far out are we?"

"Mile, mile and a half. We can't outrun them."

"I know that. I'm going over the side. Will you cover for me? I'm leaving you an extra thousand. Say a boat picked me up or you lost me overboard."

The Professor laughed. "You're that sure they're after you?" he asked.

McGregor nodded. "Will you do it for me?"

"Sure. Why not? I don't envy you the swim to shore, however. Not with these swells, sharks, your hurt body. Don't envy you at all."

The Professor smiled again, wistfully.

"Maybe I do envy you after all," he said. "Among other things, I've always wanted to be an adventurer. Life's pretty placid in Jamaica. Good luck, McGregor."

McGregor followed the Professor out of the hatch with his duffle bag. Off the port side of the *Zygote* he could make out the fast-approaching profile of a power boat, its running lights winking green and red. West lay the dark and ominous Mosquito Coast rain forest of Nicaragua. McGregor knew he was taking a chance, at night, alone, but he had little choice if he wanted to find Rumison. The swim to shore was the least of his worries, even with his sore ribs and injured hand. He knew most sharks feed at night and he also knew the area was rampant with them, but the danger of sharks was overrated and he'd dealt with them before, at other times. Sharks were a known quantity, though he knew he would feel different once he was in the water alone, a mile from shore with the last light of day slipping quickly away.

"I'll fill the boys in," said the Professor. "They won't talk. Good boys, both. That's one thing I've learned in my life, McGregor. It's people. I've never been let down." He looked at McGregor for a long moment.

"I suppose there will always be a first time, however," he answered.

McGregor took his shoes and most of his clothes off and put them in his bag, then climbed over the gunwale.

"Thanks, Professor. Maybe we'll meet again."

"There's a bay about ten miles to the south of Bluefields, McGregor, called Cuastacomote. I'm sailing down there in a few days. Probably stay a week. Beautiful place. If you need a ride . . ."

"Thanks. I may take you up on that."

"And there's a man in Bluefields," continued the Professor. "A good friend. Used to be a teacher also. Named Ho Feng Hua. Lives at 112 Brandy Street. He may help you. He was one of the good ones. Very few left—teachers, that is. The ones that are good aren't teaching. He is a merchant now. Import and export in lumber and machines."

The water was warm as McGregor lowered himself into it. The sealed container in the duffle bag acted as a float for the bag and McGregor felt the water tug at him as the current threatened to pull him away from the *Zygote.*

"Why are you helping me, Professor?" he asked, staring up from the water as he held tightly on to the ladder.

The Professor shook his head. "Who knows," he said. "I left introspection back in Vermont. Just say it seems like the thing to do." He waved a short salute.

"Good luck, McGregor. I hope you find what you are looking for."

McGregor let go of the ladder and immediately was swept away from the boat. It was a lonely feeling. Chester Pirosh had been the first person he'd felt at home with in a long time. He watched for a moment as the *Zygote* swung to the south. Then he started a one-armed crawl toward the shore, his other arm around the duffle bag. It was nearly dark and the clouds hid the light of the stars, but off in the distance he could see the motorboat as it swung in next to the *Zygote.* For some reason, McGregor knew the captain of the *Zygote* would keep his word.

Chapter Fifty

WITH only one arm to swim with, a water-soaked duffle bag to pull, and a weak breaststroke kick, it took McGregor over an hour to reach the shore. The swells were large and the water was filled with phosphorescent plankton that left tracks of glowing light whenever his arm broke the water. It grew dark, and at one point McGregor lost all sense of direction. That terrible feeling of panic that he had experienced in Las Vegas when Kirkpatrick's people had kicked him returned momentarily, but he suppressed it and continued doggedly onward until a swell lifted him up and he could see the even darker outline of the Mosquito Rain Forest, broken here and there by the occasional light of a house. To his south was a soft glow from the lights of Bluefields, and he used these as a homing beacon.

The beach was long and must have been white during the daylight. McGregor pulled himself out of the surf and fell exhausted onto the sand, exhausted not so much from the swim as from the fear that he had battled ever since leaving the *Zygote*. The fear disturbed him, because he knew it was growing and would continue to grow until he found some answers for himself. He lay on the sand, drained, as he tried to stop the trembling of his body. After several minutes he collected some dry driftwood and lit a fire with one of the matches he had put in the watertight container. He'd never been to Nicaragua and he knew little about its topography. He built the fire up near the forest, out of view of passing boats or anyone walking along the beach. It took a long time for his soaked clothes to dry. Two hours later he put them back on and began walking toward the Nicaraguan port of Bluefields, using the beach as his highway.

He'd dressed as a sailor, bell-bottom denim trousers, canvas deck shoes, and a blue turtleneck T-shirt. With the duffle bag thrown across his back he hoped this was what people would mistake him for. He left his gun in the bag, because with the tight-fitting clothes there was no place to conceal it. By the time he reached what he took to be a main road his clothes were wet again, this time from sweat. It was hot and muggy, even at night and even with the winds of the storm still blowing. He saw a car approaching and he held out his thumb. The car, an old and battered Oldsmobile, slowed down and then drew to a stop. McGregor could feel the driver sizing him up.

"I'm not going to kill you," said McGregor, using the Jamaican accent he'd had as a kid but had lost somewhere in his adolescence. "Mon, I jus' need a ride to a hotel somewhere."

The driver laughed. "Get in, sailor," he said. "Can't tell these days anymore, not that you ever could. Get in, I'll take you to a hotel."

"Where you comin' from?" asked the driver, a large, aging black with gray hair and gold teeth. McGregor climbed into the seat next to him, laying his duffle by his feet.

"Up the beach a ways," he answered.

"You no local. Where you be from?"

"Kingston, mon. Private yacht till I had me a run-in with de skipper's woman."

The driver looked sympathetic. "Tough luck, mon."

"Don't s'pose many cars come by dis way," said McGregor.

"No, mon, an' you was lucky it was me. I'm comin' in from Tadobrady fishing camp. I be de cook dere till all the tourists leave when de revolution fuck things up. Come into town, now and again. Most folk don't give no stranger de time of day no more. Me? I'm big 'nough to take care of meself. Got Gretel here."

McGregor looked down to see the driver holding a wicked-looking meat cleaver in his lap.

"I'm jus' lookin' for a place to sleep, mon," said McGregor quickly.

The driver laughed. "Don't you worry. Gretel only for bad men. You may look hard, mon, but not bad." He laid the cleaver on the seat and, chuckling to himself, returned his concentration to the road.

The road was dirt and still muddy in places from recent rains, but the old Oldsmobile cruised along as though it had four-wheel drive. As they neared the lights of Bluefields, what McGregor saw reminded him of Jamaica; rundown shacks with palm-frond roofs, the larger buildings in no better repair, with rusty tin roofs, few people on the narrow streets who looked as though they had somewhere to go, women in doorways or looking out dirty windows as the old Oldsmobile drove past. The population seemed mostly black, with a few orientals and fewer Anglos.

"Used to be a wild place," said the driver of the Oldsmobile as he looked out at a small group of men in Cuban army uniforms who were buying tickets to a ramshackle cinema. The marquee read: "All Night Kung Fu Entertainment."

There was a trace of sadness in the driver's voice. "Damn Cubans coming in now. All too damn serious."

"Is there a Brandy Street around here, mon?" McGregor asked suddenly.

The driver nodded. "Sure, but ain't no hotel on it."

"There's a mon I heard live dere. Ho Feng Hua . . ."

"Ho?" asked the driver, startled. "You know old Ho?"

"Mutual friends," said McGregor. "A mon told me to look him up. Maybe I'll go dere 'stead of de hotel."

"Ho a good mon. One of de few making it, dese days. I'll be glad to take you to Ho's."

A mile farther on the driver turned the Oldsmobile onto a cobblestoned side street lined with ancient and weathered Victorian townhouses and dying pepper trees. Farther on the houses looked in better condition and the car pulled to a stop in front of a large house with a well-kept front yard surrounded by a wrought-iron fence.

"Dis de house," said the driver. "Good luck. If Old Ho ain't home, mon, the Port O' Spain Hotel ain't far."

McGregor thanked him and got out. The driver waved as he drove off and McGregor opened the iron gate and approached the large front door. He used the brass door knocker and waited. Before long he heard footsteps. The door was answered by an oriental houseboy in a white coat.

"Yessah? May I help you?"

McGregor didn't answer. He was staring past the houseboy through a short entrance hall into the interior of the house where he could see two men seated in a well-furnished living room. One of the men's faces was hidden by a lamp, but the other McGregor recognized immediately.

"Professor!"

"Glad to see you made it," said the Professor, appearing calm and not at all surprised to see McGregor. He was dressed in clean slacks and a knit shirt and was holding a glass of red wine in one hand.

"I've been telling my friend Ho about you."

"Take the man's bag, William," said the man who McGregor took to be Ho Feng Hua. He looked to be about the Professor's age and was dressed in a red velvet housecoat. He was short, but appeared to be in good shape. He held out his hand in greeting as McGregor entered the room. His grip was assured and his manner pleasant, but his brown eyes were alert and appraising.

"Chester has told me about you," he said, offering McGregor a seat. "Would you care for a glass of wine? Or perhaps some food. I understand you've had quite a swim."

McGregor declined the food but accepted a glass of Cabernet from a crystal decanter on the table, still trying to sort out the surprise he had felt at seeing the Professor again. The reunion had come as a definite surprise. He wondered at the feeling of warmth that had accompanied his surprise.

"You're probably wondering what happened after we left you," said the Professor. "You were right about that patrol boat. They were after you, but luckily they weren't sure you were on the *Zygote*. It was no difficulty convincing them I had never seen nor heard of you."

"You've been kind, Professor," murmured McGregor.

"The Sandinista government is paying people to keep a watch out for you, apparently. The patrol boat's boarding the *Zygote* was a routine check. They searched around a bit, spotted your suitcase, the stuff you left, but luckily your name wasn't with it. I said it was mine and they believed me. Might have helped that I knew the skipper. He said they'd been on alert for you for four days."

McGregor looked up from his wine. Something was wrong. "Four days?" he asked.

Ho Feng Hua was watching him closely. "That seems to upset you, Mr. McGregor," he said quietly.

"Did they have my name?" McGregor asked.

The Professor nodded. "Knew your name and had a picture."

"A picture? Could you describe it?"

"Certainly. A very clear photo of you getting out of a Volkswagen. You were wearing a suit."

McGregor's mind was racing. Four days? A recent photo. How . . . ?

"Perhaps you would like to tell us what this is all about?" said Ho Feng Hua.

McGregor sipped at his wine without tasting it. Somebody, some people were closing in on him. Bishop? Adrian Idris Meade? The person or persons who had killed the Van Mannons, tortured the girl?

He settled back in his chair, tired from the evening's exertions, warmed by the wine and perhaps, though he had yet to admit it, by the presence of the Professor and his friend. After a moment, surprising himself, he said, "All right. I don't suppose there is any reason not to," and he told his story, leaving out little. Somehow the fact that he was breaking one of Bastanchury's, and by definition one of his own, cardinal rules no longer seemed to matter. When he'd finished there was quiet in the room. Somewhere in the room a clock ticked.

Finally Ho leaned forward in his chair. "When you were ordered off the mission," he said, "why did you not comply?"

"Isn't it obvious, Ho?" interrupted the Professor before McGregor could reply. "What other choice had he? When a man's god dies, he must find out why."

"God?" McGregor asked.

"With a little *g*. Anything becomes a god when we center our thoughts around it."

Irritated, McGregor shook his head. "I've hardly seen Bastanchury in ten years."

"Perhaps," said Ho, "you made the mistake of identifying this Mr. Bastanchury's teachings with Mr. Bastanchury."

"And when he died," picked up the Professor, "your world began to crumble."

"What is this?" McGregor asked, attempting a smile to cover up his growing irritation. "Two professors get together to analyze the new kid on the block? I'm not even sure Bastanchury is dead. There's a good chance he isn't."

"But not one you believe in."

McGregor's anger broke out. "Look, Mr. Ho . . ." he began, but Ho quickly interrupted.

"Please, Mr. McGregor. Neither of us is trying to be rude. How many languages do you speak?"

The unexpected question caught McGregor off guard. Remembering Bastanchury, he felt a moment's *déjà vu.* He took a deep breath. "Ten," he said, trying again to sort out his emotions. His anger was unreasonable.

Ho smiled thoughtfully. "Ah. So many. Then you must be aware of the problem of trying to find a way to say something in one language that has no words for what you are trying to say, but another language you know can express it very clearly."

McGregor nodded.

"Then you see our problem."

"Both you and the Professor speak excellent English, Mr. Ho."

"I am not speaking of English, Mr. McGregor. I am speaking of the language of the heart. It is a language the mind does sometimes not want to hear. If my friend Chester and I are clumsy in trying to express our feelings, then forgive us."

McGregor remained quiet, not knowing what to say.

"Why did you seem so disturbed that it has been four days the Sandinistas have been looking for you?" asked the Professor. The apparent change of subject was a relief for McGregor.

"Because," he answered, "it means Bishop probably wasn't the one who put the word out. Someone has anticipated my actions. There's a good chance they already have Rumison, if Echeverría wasn't lying about having him arrested here."

"You are tired, Mr. McGregor," said Ho suddenly. "Tonight it is useless to dwell on these matters. In the morning we will find out the truth of some of these matters."

"Oh?"

"I have many connections in Nicaragua. We will find out what has become of Mr. Rumison."

McGregor nodded, suddenly too tired to object. Briefly he wondered if the wine had been drugged. It didn't seem to matter.

Chapter Fifty-One

McGregor was having more and more trouble sleeping at night. That night at Ho Feng Hua's house was a bad one. In spite of his exhaustion he didn't fall asleep until well after four in the morning, and then he entered a fitful sleep full of dream images and phantoms whose identities he could never pin down.

Madness was something McGregor had never thought about, never worried about, never considered, but now he was apparently breaking down in the face of a host of doubts and fears and nameless anxieties that he thought he'd long ago conquered.

When he awoke it was late morning, and he felt anything but rested. Sunlight was pouring in through the large window next to his bed, and he knew the storm clouds had passed. Out the window he could see Brandy Street and its rows of ancient English-style houses, the cobblestoned street, and the sun, which looked too big in the sky. McGregor knew it must be hot outside, but Ho's electric air conditioners kept the house temperature near seventy-five degrees. He went into the bathroom adjacent to the guest bedroom, where he showered and shaved off a three days' growth of beard before dressing. Then he went downstairs. The houseboy, William, was waiting for him with a breakfast of eggs and ham.

"Mr. Ho and Mr. Pirosh went out early," said William. "Said be back before noon. Suggested you wait." William spoke with a strange mixture of street jargon and the cultured phrasing and tones Ho used.

"Did they say where they were going?"

William shook his head.

"Does Ho live here alone?" asked McGregor, as he sat down at the dining table.

"Yes. But he has many friends always."

"Your Mr. Ho seems like quite a gentleman."

"The best, sir."

McGregor nodded thoughtfully and finished the meal. Just as he finished he heard the front door open. He got up from the table to find Ho Feng Hua regarding him, a phlegmatic expression on his round face. Ho was wearing white slacks and shoes and an embroidered short-sleeved shirt. For some reason he reminded McGregor of a statue of Buddha he had once seen.

"News, McGregor," said Ho.

"About Rumison?"

"It seems Echeverría was telling the truth. Rumison was taken off his boat for entering the country without a visa and fined. Since he had no money to pay a fine and refused to supply references, he was given thirty days in jail. He was using the name White then. But last week, four days ago to be exact, a man named Colonel Preitas showed up with several soldiers and took Rumison as their own."

"Preitas!" said McGregor. "Shit!"

"I see you have heard of Preitas also. Not a man I would willingly invite to dinner," said Ho. "But it is not so bad as it sounds. Preitas and his men questioned Rumison for two days, but got nothing. The Chief of Police, Caswar Kelly, a friend of mine and a good man, objected so strongly to Preitas' methods, Preitas decided to fly Rumison back to Managua. Caswar feels bad about the whole matter and was happy to tell me what he knew."

"You said it was not so bad as it sounds," said McGregor. "It sounds worse."

"It would have been much worse if Caswar were not there. But let me continue. Near Lake La Perla Preitas' helicopter developed engine trouble. Rumison escaped."

McGregor sighed. Ho's sudden smile threatened to split the taut skin over his cheekbones. "He jumped, McGregor. Jumped out eighty feet above the water into the lake. He was heavily guarded on the ground when they transferred him to another helicopter but the minute his guards relaxed, he broke free and jumped through the open door."

Ho Feng Hua shook his head in disbelief. "Who would have thought a man with his hands and feet bound would willfully jump from a helicopter eighty feet into a lake? Caswar knows all this because he insisted on sending three of his men along as witnesses in case Preitas resumed his interrogation before the authorities in Managua could have a chance to view Rumison."

"He must be dead," said McGregor thoughtfully.

Ho shook his head. He brimmed with delight. "They are searching the lake now, but Preitas has brought in jungle trackers in the event that Rumison managed to survive. Personally I believe Rumison is alive. Such a magnificent act has its own rewards. I do not believe, as does Caswar, that it was the act of a desperate man, a suicide in effect. I believe, after talking to Caswar, that it was the act of a man who knew exactly what he was doing. A well thought out act that took courage and a strong purpose."

"It's possible," said McGregor, still thinking. "Rumison was a competitive swimmer in college. It depends on his condition after two days with Preitas, on whether he could swim with his hands and feet bound, on whether he could survive in the jungle."

"He lived," said Ho with conviction. "He lived and is even now making his way to his destination."

"You seem to have some definite ideas about him," said McGregor, "for a man who had never heard of Michael Rumison until last night. Perhaps you know where he is headed?"

Ho shook his head. "No, but wherever or whatever it is, it must have the same sort of power that a lover has over her beloved."

"A god with a little *g?*"

"Perhaps a God with a big *G,*" said Ho.

"Please, Mr. Ho. Let's not get mystical. I've enough trouble dealing with the rest of what you've said."

Ho didn't look sympathetic. He wiped perspiration off his forehead with a white handkerchief as he asked William, the houseboy, to pour him a glass of iced tea. He took a seat and regarded McGregor across the kitchen table.

"If we can see what drives your Mr. Rumison," he said,

"we will be closer to seeing where it drives him. Perhaps we can reach there before Rafael Preitas."

"We?" McGregor asked, amused.

"Chester and I have decided to help you in this matter."

McGregor's reply was ironic. "That's thoughtful of you. Where is the Professor anyway?"

"He went to check on the *Zygote*. He never . . ."

Ho was interrupted by the cry of skidding tires and locked brakes from outside the window. McGregor had picked up a kitchen knife and was waiting by the kitchen door when the Professor burst in, out of breath and perspiring heavily.

"Somehow they found out you were on my boat, McGregor," he blurted out. "Word must have come from Kingston. Caswar, the police chief warned me. I've got to get back, get the *Zygote* out to sea before the Federals arrive. They know I've stayed with you, Ho. They'll be here before long. Checking."

Ho looked unperturbed. "Easy, Chester. Nothing is gained by being frantic."

"I have to go," said the Professor, peering out through the curtains on the kitchen window. "I can't chance having the *Zygote* impounded. I think it was only luck that Caswar allowed me to leave."

"Go to your boat, Chester," said Ho. "McGregor and I will look after ourselves. I'm sorry you will miss out on the adventure of locating Rumison."

"I'm still planning on being at Cuastacomote," said the Professor, breathing easier now that he'd brought his news. "I'll take the *Zygote* out to sea and head down in two days. If you need a ride, McGregor, I'd love to hear the end of this thing."

"You'll be risking your boat," said McGregor, alarmed at how quickly things had gotten away from him. Not since he'd been in Viet Nam with Bastanchury had he trusted his life to others. Now, it seemed, he had no choice but to trust two aging romantic ex-schoolteachers. He searched for a way out but could see no immediate answer. Why were they helping?

"Cuastacomote is isolated. No one goes there. I'll be there in two days, McGregor. Goodbye."

Chester Mellon Pirosh turned and ran from the house.

Outside they could hear his rented car as he roared off down the street. McGregor immediately went to the guest room where he had slept the night. He put on a loose sports shirt that would conceal the Smith and Wesson in his belt and hurried back downstairs. Ho was waiting for him.

"William is bringing up my Land Rover," said Ho, who had replaced his own shirt with a khaki jungle outfit. "It's gassed and I think it will make the journey with little trouble."

"Journey? Just where are we going, Mr. Ho?"

Ho was taking an expensive-looking Browning hunting rifle out of a cabinet. He checked the bolt and then put two boxes of ammunition in his pockets. "Only one place to go," he said. "O'Brien's plantation. The last place you said Rumison was seen before disappearing from Nicaragua. It is the logical place to begin our search, since it seems Rumison is so desperately trying to reach somewhere in this country.

"Unless," he added, regarding McGregor with a quizzical eye, "you would rather go to Lago La Perla and join Colonel Preitas' men in their search?"

McGregor saw no need to answer. He stood facing the older man. "I can't take you, Ho," he said. "You must know that."

"You would kill me?" asked Ho quietly.

"I could stop you without killing you."

"Perhaps."

In that moment as he made his decision, McGregor realized two things; that it indeed would be very difficult to stop Ho Feng Hua from joining him, and secondly, that he did not really want to. "All right," he said. "But I warn you . . ."

Ho smiled. "I understand, Mr. McGregor. I told William to park the Land Rover away from the house. There is a side door that we can leave through. Shall we go?"

McGregor nodded shortly.

Chapter Fifty-Two

ONCE the Land Rover left the settled area and reached the rutted and almost overgrown road that Ho insisted was the only way to get to the O'Brien plantation by land, McGregor began to relax and organize his thoughts. He drove while Ho sat next to him, his rifle at his feet. By the map it was less than fifty miles to the plantation, but with the poor condition of the road, the Land Rover could average less than ten miles an hour. Several times Ho and McGregor had to get out and remove fallen logs from the road or cut through thick vines with the machetes Ho had in the truck.

"It used to be a good road, at least for these parts," said Ho. "Before the revolution. When the embargo hit, most of the plantations went out of business. Those that didn't, save a few owned by local citizenry, were nationalized."

"The man I caught a ride to your house with said Bluefields was dying because of the revolution."

Ho nodded. "The east coast was never for the revolution," he said. "Especially Bluefields. Their ties are with the Caribbean, England, the U.S. Few are happy about the state of affairs, which is why Caswar and most of the other officials are rather less than willing to help the Marxists."

"Is that why you are helping me?" asked McGregor.

"Good Lord, no," said Ho. "My business depends on the embargo."

"Just what is your business, Mr. Ho?"

"I am a smuggler."

McGregor almost stopped the truck.

"Don't be so surprised, Mr. McGregor. The officials

know my occupation, and the Marxists themselves look on with friendly eyes. I deal with machine parts. American. The east coast couldn't keep its machinery in repair if it wasn't for my operation. It will be a long while before all of Nicaragua's machinery is replaced with parts from Russia or some other industrial country that hasn't ceased trade with us. In the meantime U.S. machine parts are in constant demand and bring a high price. It is really quite simple."

"I'm sure it is. Is the Professor in this with you?"

"Chester? Oh, no. He knows, of course, and manages to bring me brandy and other luxury items that I find difficulty getting, but he is in his own world, just like I am in mine. We were both college professors once, you know. He taught in Vermont, I in New York."

"Why are you risking your business to help me?" McGregor asked.

Ho didn't answer immediately. A log was blocking the narrow road and McGregor had to stop the truck and move it. A brightly colored bird flew out of a tree blooming with yellow flowers and insects buzzed around his head. Back in the truck, Ho was still seated quietly. McGregor put the Land Rover in gear and they started off again.

"When I was a young man, I fought the Japanese in China," said Ho. "I knew both Mao and Chiang. My life was very intense. When the war was over and the country fell to the Communists, I moved to America. I respected Americans, liked their youth and energy. I did not like Communism nor did I like Chiang Kaishek. I went to school in New York. I spoke poor English and it was difficult, but I was like Aladdin with three wishes; a new land, with so many opportunities. My life was very intense there also."

Ho sighed, remembering. "I became a teacher of Chinese culture. It was many years before I realized my life was no longer meaningful, no longer intense.

"And then," he continued, "in the sixties, I became involved in the antiwar movement and later the resultant search for consciousness. My life took on intensity again, purpose. But after the war all the fine people I had met, with few exceptions, returned to being just what they had been, inside, all along: teachers, lawyers, doctors, dishwashers and housewives."

Ho's eyes seemed far away, lost in memory. McGregor didn't interrupt.

"By this time, though my popularity with the students was high, my academic reputation had suffered considerably. I had no more interest in bored students and self-righteous instructors who knew less about life than many sixteen-year-old Chinese soldiers I had fought with as a youth. I never married. I am not celibate, mind you. I had several long-term mistresses, but I had few attachments. Taking what money I had managed to save, I traveled. Seeking. For what, I was not sure of. I happened to be in Bluefields when the revolution broke out. During the anti-war days I had made many connections, so . . ."

Ho shrugged and spread his hands. "So this is just another adventure for you?" McGregor asked. "To make your life intense?"

"You don't understand," said Ho, looking at McGregor. "I joined those causes not just for adventure. I believed in them. They were my gods, but as I grew older and more experienced, I saw them for what they were: mere historical phenomena. Any higher significance they may have had rested in another area entirely. My business arrangements in Nicaragua, well, it is something to do and it pays quite well, but it is not enough."

"I'm still not sure what you are saying," said McGregor.

"You don't?" Ho asked. "You do not feel it? In the language of the heart?"

McGregor didn't answer.

"We are the same, you and I," said Ho. We are both looking for God. We follow this man Rumison because somewhere we both sense that part of the puzzle will be answered when we find him."

It was nearing dark when they finally arrived at the O'Brien lumber plantation. The last three miles had been particularly difficult. The Land Rover had gotten stuck twice and McGregor had to free it using the winch on the front and a cable looped around a tree. After Bluefields the road had turned inland for about ten miles, but it had curved back toward the coast until they could hear the sound of surf lapping on the sand-covered beach.

"What do you know about this guy O'Brien, Ho?"

McGregor hadn't yet turned the Land Rover's headlamps on and had pulled to a stop just after the road had broken out of the jungle. A large plantation house, surrounded by a large field of uncut grass, stood before them. Off to the right were more buildings, probably the mills and workers' quarters. A dock jutted out into sea on the far side of the field. A light shone through one window of the house but the other buildings were dark. McGregor thought it was a depressing and gloomy sight.

"Not very much," said Ho, answering his question about O'Brien. "He had a large and apparently profitable operation. He minded his own business. Rarely came into Bluefields. I never met him."

"Something's cut into his profits," said McGregor, staring out at the darkened compound, trying to see some sign of life other than the light in the window.

"It was rumored O'Brien left Nicaragua last month," said Ho. "A vacation. There were other rumors."

McGregor didn't ask what they were. He turned on the Land Rover's headlamps and slowly let out the clutch. "Someone's here. Maybe they have some answers."

McGregor had a strange sense of foreboding about the plantation. He took out his pistol and placed it on the seat. Ho checked his rifle and brought it to his lap. The evening was absolutely still. If it had not been for the light in the window, McGregor would have thought the plantation abandoned. The little four-cylinder engine of the Land Rover seemed overly loud. They came to a stop in front of the front terrace to the house and McGregor turned off the motor. There was no other sound other than the distant swell of the sea.

McGregor got out. "There may be trouble," he said. Ho nodded, waiting with his rifle on the far side of the Land Rover. McGregor approached the front door and listened. When he still heard nothing, he knocked. The sound seemed to echo inside. There was a long moment of waiting and then the sound of movement from within. The thick mahogany door opened several inches against a locking chain. McGregor couldn't see who had opened it, but the voice that came from inside was a woman's voice.

"Yes?" it asked. It was a strange voice. The sound of it made an immediate impression on McGregor. He didn't know how, but he felt with certainty that whoever had spoken was not far away from total despair.

"I'm looking for Mr. O'Brien," said McGregor gently. "We've come from Bluefields."

"He's gone," came the reply, and again McGregor sensed deep sadness. "I'm sorry. But he went back to Ireland. It's been several weeks."

"Ma'am, I don't mean to disturb you, but I was looking for someone who may have been around this plantation last May."

There was a hesitation. McGregor could feel it. Then he heard the sound of the chain being slipped off its catch and the door opened. A girl stood in front of McGregor, or a woman. McGregor couldn't be sure of her age. She was blond and tall and had an odd kind of dignity which shone through the aura of despair surrounding the girl and overshadowing everything else about her. Her green eyes looked lost, almost uncaring, but no one who didn't care would have felt the pain McGregor knew she was hiding. It was so overpowering that he could feel the pain almost as if it were his own. Her presence so hypnotized him that it was several seconds before he realized she had spoken.

"I was here then," she said. "I am Whitney O'Brien, Mr. O'Brien's daughter."

McGregor had almost forgotten why he had come to the plantation. He forgot nearly everything but the pain he saw in the girl's eyes. It was as if the young girl, Isidra, had grown up without losing her innocence, her openness, but because of this had no defenses with which to battle the world.

"Is something wrong, miss?" The words sounded thin and inadequate, even to McGregor, but he didn't know what else to say. The girl looked at him but didn't answer. He heard a movement and looked beyond her into a large front room to see another woman standing there, watching. The woman was black, with a beautiful gleaming body dressed in a provocative print dress. Her face was tilted at an off angle, as if there were a malformation in the neck, but aside from this she was breathtakingly beautiful.

"The Chinaman die today," said the black girl, her dark eyes looking with unhidden disdain at the blond girl. "Finally. I wait a long time for it."

"Hermilia, you don't—" began Whitney O'Brien, but then a sob choked her words and she collapsed on the floor.

"Ho!" cried McGregor. "Get in here!" He didn't wait for an answer but picked up the girl and carried her to a large couch in the front room where he laid her down. Ho came running in moments later, carrying the Browning. When he saw what was happening he put the rifle by the door and ran over to McGregor. The black girl watched without comment.

"What happened, McGregor?"

McGregor looked over at the black girl. "Maybe you could answer that question," he said.

The girl laughed, a strange laugh, half flirtation, half cackle. "Certainly," she said. "Jus' Whitney there is weak, jus' like her father. Her old Chinaman died. He was old, should have died long ago." She moved closer to McGregor, moving with an exaggerated sexiness that was only a little diminished by the deformity in her neck.

"I don' have much more reason to stay roun' here," she said. "One more thing is all."

"Miss, I would appreciate it if you would leave this room." McGregor looked up in surprise to see Ho glaring at the black girl, his hands clenched. He looked as if he were facing a hated enemy and McGregor wondered what had set him off.

"Another Chinaman," spat the girl. "You got no right telling me where I can be. Not in this house."

"Leave, Hermilia!" The person who spoke was Whitney O'Brien, and the words held an authority that wasn't lost in the sobs.

Hermilia's eyes burned with sudden hate as they looked at the girl on the couch. Then she shrugged.

"I be aroun'," she said. She gave McGregor a quick smile that lingered for just a moment, and then left the room. Ho Feng Hua's hands and teeth were still clenched for several minutes after her departure.

Whitney O'Brien was sitting up on the couch, trying

hard to hold back her tears. Without thinking, McGregor put his arm around her and drew her to him. She lost the battle with her tears and began to cry again, burying her face in McGregor's chest. He stood without speaking, but McGregor could tell by his expression that he too felt the girl's pain.

Finally the crying subsided and Whitney O'Brien raised her head. "Please excuse me," she said.

"There's no need."

"I should have an explanation," said the girl, rubbing tears from her eyes.

"A friend has died. We understand."

Whitney shook her head and looked as if the crying were about to start again. "No. You couldn't possibly understand."

"Try us."

Ho looked very serious. "There is more than a friend dying here," he said. "Much more."

Whitney looked up at Ho Feng Hua as if seeing him for the first time. "I . . ." she began, but the effort was too much and the tears returned in wracking sobs.

"We should leave her alone," said Ho. "Let her sleep the night."

McGregor nodded agreement. He looked at Ho, who watched Whitney with an odd, withdrawn look on his face.

"Will you watch her?" said McGregor. "I want to go talk with the black girl."

Ho nodded. "Of course," he said. "But watch her, McGregor. Watch her closely."

McGregor wanted to ask Ho why he had reacted so strongly to Hermilia's presence, but Ho no longer seemed interested in anything but the girl on the couch. McGregor stood up and went in the direction Hermilia had taken from the room.

Chapter Fifty-Three

THE large plantation house seemed well kept, but everywhere there were bare spots as if things were missing—hooks on walls where pictures should have hung and odd bare spaces where furniture should have stood. Other than the two women, McGregor hadn't seen anybody else around, and he felt sure there was nobody else.

He found Hermilia in a room that must have been the library, though now the floor-to-ceiling shelves were empty of books. She stood looking out a window that gave onto the long rolling front lawn. McGregor had the distinct and uncomfortable feeling that she had been waiting for him. Now that the girl named Whitney was no longer present, the lines of hate had almost left Hermilia's face and McGregor saw how beautiful she would be if not for her deformed neck. When she smiled, when she moved closer to him, he almost forgot that deformity.

"I would like to talk with you," said McGregor.

The girl nodded. "Of course," she said, looking up at him with her cocked head. From that angle her neck didn't seem malformed at all. McGregor found himself reluctantly attracted.

"That girl, Miss O'Brien," said McGregor, trying to keep his mind from Hermilia's melonlike breasts as they rose and fell with her breathing. "She said O'Brien went back to Ireland. Perhaps you could tell me what I need to know."

"What's that?" Hermilia moved closer to McGregor, and her voice was husky. He tried to remember her face of only a few minutes before, twisted and ugly, but he couldn't.

"Everything, beginning in May when three men apparently visited this plantation. They were called Michael Rumison, Robert Rosso, and Michael Black."

For a brief, unguarded moment Hermilia's eyes flared with hatred before she succeeded in masking the emotion in them, and again they were staring back into McGregor's, deep and promising. "Why do you need to know this?" she asked. "The police already know everything."

"We are not the police. We are after Michael Rumison. This is the last place he was known to have been in Nicaragua."

"Why are you after him?"

"He may have information we need."

"You are from the United States, then?"

There was something in the girl's voice that made McGregor hesitate before answering, something that wasn't quite right.

"Miss, you seem to be asking all the questions. I think that perhaps it might be to your advantage to start answering a few." McGregor put just enough menace in his voice to get his point across, but the girl drew back in anger. McGregor couldn't tell if it were feigned or real.

"You think you can scare me, Mr. who ev' you be. I don' scare no more, not since this." The girl jerked her head sideways and pointed to her neck. "You either tell me who you are and what you want or I'm not gon' tell you nothing."

"We can always ask that girl in the other room, when she's ready to talk."

The black girl spat. "She's gon' die just like her ol' Chinaman," she said, but then she smiled and moved closer to McGregor again, her hand reaching out tentatively, touching the middle button on his shirt.

"But there's no need for us to fight. Maybe we both got something to give each other."

McGregor smiled back at her. "Maybe," he said. Her hand played with his button for a few moments and then she pulled it back.

"They come one day trying to get a way out of the country," she said. "My husband—"

"Your husband?"

"Sean O'Brien was my husband. He owns this plantation."

"You mean you are Mrs. O'Brien! That girl's mother?"

"Not her mother. Never that bitch's mother. She wen' crazy and kill herself. I marry Sean later."

McGregor could see there was much that remained to be known, but he didn't want Hermilia to get sidetracked, so he kept his questions to himself for the time being, nodding at her to continue the story.

"Sean, he don' want to mess with the government—he was lucky to keep the plantation when they went around taking them away from all the foreigners. When the Americans come, Isaiah and me, we don' like them, but Whitney, that bitch, she have this crazy idea, talk Sean into helping, take us a while to talk him out of it."

Hermilia's hand moved back to McGregor's shirt and she began playing with the button again. "Maybe you tell me some things now," she said.

"Finish your story first," said McGregor.

Hermilia's hand brushed down McGregor's front and she looked petulant. "You not gon' tell me what you here for?"

He reached out his own hand and began stroking her neck lightly, then her ear.

"Finish your story," he said.

"I haven't had a man in a long time," said Hermilia, her voice low, her hand moving. She felt his hardness and pressed.

"You sure you not gon' tell me what you here for?" she asked, her hand moving, slowly, lightly.

"McGregor!"

McGregor hadn't heard Ho enter the room but Ho's angry voice jerked him back to awareness. Ho's face was livid as he watched from across the room, and McGregor felt a strange mixture of embarrassment and rage in the presence of the older man. The black girl looked up, her face filled with the same hate McGregor had seen on it earlier.

"Get out of here, you shithead Chinaman," she screamed. "Go back out with that white cunt!"

Hermilia's hatred was so intense McGregor shuddered involuntarily. Suddenly she turned on him and her eyes were vicious.

"You go to hell too, you bastard. Next time I rip your damn cock off."

McGregor slapped her. He slapped her so hard she fell to the floor, where she lay writhing, looking up at him through eyes lit with hatred.

"You will die," she said, her voice as intense as anything McGregor had ever heard. "You will die within the week." Her eyes locked with his and McGregor felt the battle of their wills. Then the thing on the floor became what it had been, a young black girl once beautiful, whose face was now so distorted by hate that he could see no beauty in it. McGregor wondered what had gotten into him, and then he turned and walked away.

"You will die within the week!" screamed Hermilia. McGregor shuddered again but didn't look back. Ho closed the door behind them as they left the room.

"I'm sorry," said McGregor.

Ho's face looked more concerned than angry now. "I told you to be careful, McGregor. I thought you would sense it."

"Sense what? I wanted to ask her some questions. And I got carried away."

"Don't you sense the blackness?"

"Blackness?"

"Blackness. She's *black obeah!*"

McGregor's mind stopped, its logic halted by a flood of images from his childhood in Cockpit Country where voodoo was a dreaded word. Much of McGregor's later interest in Indian rituals, shamanism, occultism and hypnotism stemmed from his early childhood experiences. Hermilia's last words to him floated hauntingly in the air. Then he shook his head.

"That's silly," he said, but Ho's face looked more concerned than before. He took hold of McGregor's arm tightly. "Easy, McGregor," he said. "Don't dismiss this. You're a strong man but you've lost your center. You know how these things work?"

McGregor shook his head, feeling childish for even listening to the older man whose sanity he now questioned.

"Doubt, ambiguity. Obeah creeps in the cracks and plants what it wants to plant. You have to keep constantly on your toes to weed those plants out if they start to grow."

"I know about those things," said McGregor. "Suggestion and all that. I'll watch it."

"More than suggestion, Mr. McGregor."

McGregor shrugged. "When I was a child, I saw some things, but . . ."

"We've all seen some things," said Ho, interrupting. "They mean little. See them clearly, not through the memories of a child. That black girl, she has a power, but she is sick and the power is no good if you know that."

"You're sounding like an old gentleman I met in Jamaica the other day," said McGregor."

"I'm sorry," said Ho. "I don't mean to be mysterious. It's just that . . ." He paused and looked sharply at McGregor.

"What, Mr. Ho?"

"I'm sorry, McGregor. It's just that I don't think anything I could say right now would mean much to you. But I do feel that from this point onward both of us are going to have to stay completely alert."

"No need to tell me that," said McGregor. "I've felt that for some time."

"Have you? Have you really?"

"Of course."

"Follow me, Mr. McGregor. We have work to do."

"Work?"

"I'll show you."

Chapter Fifty-Four

Ho Feng Hua led McGregor through the front room where Whitney now slept on the couch. The smuggler had found a pillow and placed it under her head, and McGregor thought how much like a little girl she looked.

"How did you get her to sleep?"

"It wasn't hard," said Ho. "She was near the end of her energy anyway. A suggestion, given rightly . . ."

"Perhaps you have a little obeah in you," said McGregor. He meant it as a joke but Ho nodded.

"Perhaps," he said.

In a bedroom down the hall from the room where Whitney slept lay an old Oriental man in a four-poster bed, looking small and frail in his silk nightgown. Rigor mortis had set in, but he couldn't have been dead for long. His face looked peaceful, as if he had died an easy death.

"We have to bury him," said Ho. "It is best that the girl not wake up to find him still unburied."

"You're pretty concerned for a girl you don't know."

Ho Feng Hua looked back at McGregor with unfathomable eyes and didn't respond.

"I'll go find a shovel. You haven't seen sign of anyone else around, have you?"

He shook his head.

"I haven't either. I wonder what two young girls are doing out here alone, especially since they don't appear to like each other much?"

Again Ho didn't answer. His reticence irritated McGregor, who managed, with effort, to catch his anger before it reached a critical point.

"I'll be right back."

Outside it was warm and quiet, with a light onshore breeze cooling the humid air and carrying the sound of the light surf out into the jungle to mingle with the whispers of the trees and the occasional cry of an animal. It was dark in spite of bright stars, and McGregor took a flashlight from the Land Rover before going over to a large barn near the house to look for a shovel. A side door was locked, but the lock was a simple tumbler type and McGregor had no trouble picking it with a sharp wire he had also gotten from the car. Once inside he found a light switch and turned it on. Apparently the building was a garage. Inside were two beat-up pickup trucks and a newer tractor, along with maintenance equipment and some tools.

A large rat, disturbed in its foraging by the light, startled McGregor by scurrying under the nearest truck. When he saw what it was, McGregor put his gun back in his belt.

He found a pick and shovel against the wood siding and returned to the house. Ho was waiting for him.

"I'll dig the grave, Mr. McGregor. It would be difficult for you, with your bad hand."

"My hand is all right."

"I insist."

McGregor shrugged. "Where?" he asked.

"I noticed a knoll with a fountain on it across the grass there. I thought that would be a nice place."

McGregor watched as Ho left the house with the shovel. "I'll spell you if you get tired," he said.

"I will not get tired." Ho spoke with a determination that increased McGregor's wonder at what had come over the urbane, phlegmatic man he had ridden out to the plantation with.

Ho Feng Hua returned to the house an hour later, his shirtsleeves rolled up and his clothes damp with sweat. McGregor had wrapped the body of the dead Chinese man in a sheet for burial, and with Ho carrying the flashlight and leading the way, McGregor carried him out to the freshly dug grave and laid him down in it. Then he watched as Ho shoveled the dirt over the body. When it was over, Ho stood back from the grave and said a few words in Chinese that McGregor translated to himself.

"Old one, revered old one," Ho whispered in Mandarin. "Why do you die so far from home?" McGregor recognized the line from an old Chinese epic poem, but he couldn't remember the rest save that it ended, "And in the graves, the people are smiling, and in the swaddle the babies are crying." The words sent a chill down McGregor's spine. Ho turned and began walking back toward the house without waiting to see if McGregor was following. Off in the distance came the cry of a large cat and then there was silence again. When the two men were back inside the house, McGregor confronted Ho.

"What's this all about?"

"About?"

"Don't give me that blank stare, damn it. You know what I mean. Ever since we got to this plantation you've been acting strange, like you're a different person. And don't give me any crap about voodoo or that mystical bullshit you're so fond of putting out."

"I'm sorry, McGregor," said Ho. "Perhaps I've been inconsiderate, but I do not think there is time to explain."

"Explain what?"

"Tonight it is best we get some sleep. We will need to be rested in the morning," continued Ho, ignoring McGregor.

"In the morning I'm going to find out from that girl what this is all about, and then I'm leaving after Rumison."

He shook his head. "That will not be necessary," he said. "Mr. Rumison will be coming here."

"What makes you think that?"

"I know," said Ho simply. "And we will need our rest, because I assume that whoever else is following Rumison will not be far behind."

"God damn it, Ho, what in hell are you talking about?"

Ho Feng Hua sighed, and the lines on his rounded face grew softer. "Before the girl went to sleep," he said, "she told me that the old man, the man who we buried tonight, had told her to wait. Her words were, 'Sun told me to wait, but now he is dead and I can't wait any longer.' "

"So?"

"Don't you see, McGregor? Rumison is coming back for the girl."

The silence that followed Ho's statement was broken by

McGregor's laugh. "I think you've gone a bit mad, Ho," he said. "According to what we know, Rumison, Bastanchury, and Rosso couldn't have been at this plantation for more than a few days, hardly long enough for Rumison to fall in love to the extent he'd do what he's done for her."

"Don't be too sure of that, Mr. McGregor, but in any case I did not say Rumison was in love with the girl."

"Then why?"

"I don't know why. It's something. Don't you feel it, McGregor?"

McGregor didn't answer because he too felt something, a pattern that was somehow coming together but that he was reluctant to acknowledge to the other man. For some reason the idea threatened him.

"I think you're crazy, Ho, but assuming you're right, at least about Rumison's intentions, then we shouldn't have long to wait, if Rumison survived the jump and then after. If Preitas doesn't find him first. If, in fact, he is headed here."

"Do we have a choice but to wait?"

"I don't know. We'll see in the morning after I talk with the girl."

"In the morning then, Mr. McGregor."

"In the morning."

The man known as Adrian Idris among other names sat calmly in a leather easy chair in front of Nathaniel Bishop's bare formica desk. From outside the rented office came the street noise on a busy afternoon in Kingston, muted by the double-paned windows. The windows were designed to keep the air-conditioned atmosphere inside the building and the sound out. Like most things in Kingston, the soundproofing didn't quite work.

"Well?" Idris asked. He felt no need for formalities. He didn't like Bishop, but then he didn't like most of the people he was forced to work with. Idris' likes and dislikes were lost on Bishop, who ignored them not so much from tact as indifference.

"Our information about the boat McGregor chartered was apparently correct," said Bishop, glancing irritably up at the other man. He had been working on a report for the director's eyes only. He had called Idris to the office but it bothered him that Idris had entered and taken a seat without knocking.

"Seems Preitas also got the word McGregor was in the Bluefields area somehow," he added. "There's apparently a search going on for him, but the locals haven't come up with anything."

"Not surprising," said Idris. His words were made almost unnoticeably softer by the accent that he hadn't altogether lost, even after twenty years of dealing with English-speaking peoples. "It's known the authorities in that area aren't sympathetic to Preitas or the Sandinistas."

"They also let that charter boat sail off."

Idris shrugged.

"I am worried about the accuracy of their information," said Bishop. "They must have an agent in Kingston."

"We've assumed leaks since that Van Mannon thing," said Idris, unconcerned.

"Why do I think McGregor is behind much of it?"

Idris laughed. "Extremely unlikely. Probably just some very good agent somewhere; Russian, possibly Cuban. Or perhaps one of our other competitors."

"Preitas is still looking for Rumison," said Bishop. "McGregor has probably left Bluefields and probably with a man named Ho Feng Hua, an expatriate Chinese-American who runs a minor smuggling operation in machine parts out of Nicaragua."

Idris' interest perked. "Ho Feng Hua. An agent?"

"Probably," said Bishop shortly. "He has to have some vested interest in helping McGregor."

Idris was thoughtful. "I think it's time I visited Nicaragua," he said.

Bishop nodded. "That's why I asked you here. A seaplane has been arranged. You'll leave this afternoon."

Idris took a cigarette from a gold case and lit it. After a moment he said, "You know, Bishop, that was a stupid move, trying to call McGregor off. You warned him."

For the first time since Idris had met him, Nathaniel Bishop looked actually angry. "He was and is a menace to the operation, Idris," said Bishop. "We'd already learned the whereabouts of Rumison and we don't need that sort of unstable personality, McGregor, mucking things up."

"I've heard Norris is flying in here in the morning," said Idris, exhaling a long puff of smoke.

"I've heard."

"He doesn't agree with you about McGregor."

"Don't you have a plane to catch?" said Bishop.

Idris smiled. "I guess I do."

Chapter Fifty-Five

McGregor awoke with the sunrise. Both he and Ho had elected to sleep outside in light sleeping bags on the grass next to the Land Rover. The sky overhead was clear of clouds. The heat was already in the nineties. Heat waves rose off the dirt of the road as McGregor gazed back at the jungle. He got out of his bag slowly, stretching sore muscles. The night had been another bad one. Ho was still asleep. McGregor ignored the cloud of insects around his head and began walking, his pistol in his belt, wanting to see the surrounding territory in the daylight. When he returned to the Land Rover an hour later, Ho was gone. McGregor put the sleeping bags back in the Land Rover and then drove it a quarter of a mile up the road before parking it under a tree in the jungle, out of sight from either the road or the house. This done, he returned to the plantation house.

"In here, McGregor. Miss O'Brien has fixed breakfast for us." Ho's voice called from the dining room. McGregor entered to find Ho, Whitney O'Brien, and Hermilia seated at the table with a breakfast of eggs, rolls, and fried Spam in front of them. Ho was eating his meal with relish, apparently undaunted by Hermilia's presence.

McGregor was relieved to see that Whitney had regained her self-possession, though she looked pale and drawn.

"I suppose Ho's told you who we are," said McGregor. Whitney nodded and Hermilia smiled at him provocatively, but McGregor felt nothing for the black girl now. It was the blonde who interested him. Her resemblance to

Isidra was remarkable, not in physical appearance but in the aura about her, an aura of . . . not naïveté but . . . openness, trustfulness, receptiveness. Again McGregor found himself drawn to her as he had been drawn to Isidra, though his grandmother's words sat uncomfortably in his mind, warning him.

"I want to thank you and Mr. Ho for . . ." Whitney seemed at a loss for words as she sat staring at McGregor with wide-open eyes incapable of hiding her feelings.

"We did nothing. We're sorry about the old man."

"Thank you for burying him."

Hermilia had been silent, but now she spoke. "And why have you come here, Mr. McGregor?" she asked pointedly. "You were about to tell me last night, when this new Chinaman interrupted."

"Do you mind if I sit down?" he asked, choosing to ignore her, and wondering how he could have been attracted to her the night before. "Ho and I did miss dinner last night."

"Of course, Mr. McGregor," answered Whitney. "I'm sorry all we have to offer is canned Spam and some eggs, but . . . lately . . . I . . ." She looked almost as if she might cry again, but then she lifted her head with determination and continued.

"Lately we've been living off the stores."

"The help left when the government closed the plantation down," said Hermilia unconcernedly. "Last month, jus' before Sean left."

"And why are you two still here?" asked McGregor, after he had taken several bites from his plate.

Whitney O'Brien looked strangely embarrassed, but there was a wicked gleam in Hermilia's dark eyes. "Should I tell them, or will you, Whitney, dear?"

Whitney was silent, her face turned downward. Hermilia laughed. "She don' believe it herself anymore," she said. Whitney shuddered. McGregor had an urge to slap the black girl, but sat immobilized in his rage. Ho, who was seated next to Whitney, took her arm gently.

"It's all right," he said. "Perhaps we might really understand."

"Why are you here?" said Whitney quietly, looking at Ho's face as she had looked at McGregor's.

It was McGregor who answered. "We're looking for a man named Michael Rumison. We have heard he was here with two others last May—" He stopped when he saw what color Whitney O'Brien still had drain from her face at the mention of Rumison's name.

"Do you remember him?" he asked, knowing the certain answer.

Whitney nodded jerkily. Hermilia laughed, a short, unpleasant laugh.

"Why are you . . . looking for him?" asked Whitney warily.

"He was on a mission," McGregor said. "For the U.S. Air Force. We're trying to find out what happened to him after he left your plantation and why he came back to Nicaragua without reporting to his unit."

Whitney's face went into total shock. "Back?" she managed to whisper. "He's come back?"

God, thought McGregor. *Ho was right!* The thought upset him in an almost physical manner. He could feel the muscles in his stomach and solar plexus tighten. Hermilia's face had turned dark and unreadable.

"Yes, he's come back. We thought maybe we could learn why here."

Whitney O'Brien underwent a startling metamorphosis, the despair in her face replaced suddenly by a tentative, almost exploratory joy. McGregor could sense her trying to fight off the new feelings, as if they were something to fear. Ho was smiling widely at McGregor as if to say, "See, McGregor, I told you so," but Hermilia's face grew darker. McGregor wondered what had gone on between Rumison and this girl to have caused such a reaction, and the answers he could guess at only increased the tightness in his midsection. Was he feeling jealous of Rumison? *What is going on here?* he wanted to shout.

"I knew it," burst out Ho like a little boy who had suddenly learned a great secret that he had guessed at all along. Ho almost chortled.

"McGregor, I knew it. I could feel it. Don't you feel it? Don't you see what's going on here?"

"Damn it, Ho, don't start on that," said McGregor sharply, but Ho ignored him.

"It's what I felt all along. I knew there had to be something like this."

McGregor felt like a blind man in a land of crazy people who could see. "Miss O'Brien," he said, trying to regain some of his initiative. "Maybe you could tell me what happened here last May."

"Of course. I'm sorry, it's just that . . ." Whitney's face was beaming now and just as her pain had spilled over, before, almost hypnotizing McGregor, so now did her happiness. At that moment he knew with certainty why Rumison had returned to Nicaragua, but the feeling was fleeting and somehow threatening and McGregor shoved it from his consciousness.

"Your friends came here in May," said Hermilia, her voice hard. "Isaiah say they were bad. I don't know at first, but I know he was right. Have to be, they killed him. . . ."

"He turned them in!" cried Whitney.

"You weren't so damn forgivin' after they shot Sean."

"Ladies, please," said McGregor. Whitney stopped, but McGregor could see the anger still smoldering in her eyes, and he thought how much healthier that anger was than what he had seen in them earlier.

"Continue, please."

Hermilia snorted but continued her story. "Isaiah tell me and I tell Sean, but Whitney there . . ." Hermilia's eyes burned with the hate McGregor had seen the night before. "She believe some bullshit my mother tol' her when she was a kid, 'bout how a prince—"

"Hermilia, shut up."

"I'll tell my own story," shouted Hermilia.

Ho put his arm around Whitney to comfort her. "It's all right," he said.

" 'Bout how a prince gon' come down here and run away with her. She thinks that man her lover, but I talk Sean into locking 'em up until the police arrive. There was a reward—"

"I heard," said McGregor. "About ten thousand dollars, wasn't it?"

Hermilia spat. "They say. They say they pay me, but all I ever get is doctor bills and Isaiah dead. They never pay."

"They had them in the storage room," said Whitney, quietly now. "My father, Isaiah, and Hermilia had Michael and Mr. Black in the storage room. Something happened and Isaiah and my father were shot. Hermilia's neck was broken."

McGregor thought of Bastanchury being kept in a storage room by three amateurs, and he could guess at what had happened. Bastanchury was . . . had been . . . the best. For nonprofessionals to threaten him or put a gun on him was suicide.

"There was a report they escaped in a small airplane."

Whitney nodded, calmer now, the color returning to her face as her strength grew. McGregor suddenly realized how beautiful she was. He had made love to many women who had been prettier, but Whitney's beauty was . . . total. His stomach muscles tightened again and McGregor cursed himself for his irrational feelings.

"After the shootings a helicopter arrived with soldiers on it. Michael, Mr. Black, and the other one, Rosso, who had been left at the plane to guard it, took off—it was my father's plane he used for tree spotting—but Rosso was killed."

"What happened to the helicopter?"

"It was pretty well shot up."

"And afterwards? After Bast—Black and Rumison escaped?"

Whitney faltered. "I . . . I'm not . . ."

"She didn't know," interrupted Hermilia. "She don't remember, but I know, even though my neck was broke. Isaiah was dead, once 'tween the eyes, but the man who shot him, he don't live no more either, both probably resting next to each other in hell. . . ."

"How do you know that? That the man is dead? Was it Black?"

"It was Black. He dead. I just know. Sean was shot also, by Miss Princess' prince there. He didn't die, but might as well have. Wasn't a man no more. The soldiers, they flew Sean and me to Bluefields to the hospital."

Hermilia's face was contorted with the strength of her hate and things were becoming clear for McGregor.

"I was in a daze," said Whitney quietly. "I really don't remember much . . . trying to stop my father's bleeding, the soldiers, one man in particular, asking questions, refusing to help until I answered, my father's pain, carrying

Isaiah away. They brought in Bob Rosso and I began to cry, but this man, this little man, kept asking these questions. . . ."

"Take it easy, Miss O'Brien."

"I'm all right now. It's good for me to talk about it, but at the time . . . But now my father has recovered, in spite of what Hermilia said. She's mad because he saw what he had been doing and he felt guilty, and I knew this but couldn't help him. He left for Ireland."

"He wasn't a man no more," insisted Hermilia.

"That's not true. He just saw you for what you were."

"And you stayed here?" asked McGregor, not wanting another fight to start.

Whitney nodded.

"Even after the government closed the place?"

"I had to take care of Sun."

"The old man?"

Again Whitney nodded. "He wouldn't leave."

"Why don't you tell him the truth," cried Hermilia. "You stayed because you still believed your lover, the man who shot your father, who did this to me, who killed Isaiah, would come back for you."

Ho, who had been silent for much of the conversation now looked at Hermilia. "And why did *you* stay?" he asked quietly. Hermilia's eyes narrowed as she turned her fury on the Chinese man.

"You will die also," she said. "Just like this other man here. Just like Whitney and her lover, if he returns," and she stood up from the table and left.

"I felt sorry for her," said Whitney, apologetically.

"You shouldn't have," said Ho. "People like her, they use sympathy like a weapon. She is an evil person."

"She wasn't always so. We were friends when we were little girls. Her father returned one day and then she was different. She turned to him more than her mother. And suddenly she was with my father."

"You don't have to be telling us these things, Miss O'Brien," said McGregor, feeling uneasy with the girl's sudden openness.

"Oh, it's all right, Mr. McGregor. Everything is all right."

"Was Hermilia right? Did you wait here because you

had fallen in love with Michael Rumison and felt he would return?"

Whitney looked down at her plate and didn't answer. Ho nodded thoughtfully. "He is returning, you know," he said.

Whitney looked up and there was a bright, joyous smile on her face. "I know," she said. "I know."

The muscles in McGregor's stomach clenched until they almost hurt. "Come on, Ho," he said. "There's a lot to do before Rumison gets here, if indeed he does get here."

"What do you intend to do, McGregor?" Ho asked.

"I'm still a professional. As a professional I expect I'll try and finish the mission, even though I'm no longer on it, according to a man I don't trust. To me, now, that means getting Rumison out of Nicaragua."

"And Miss O'Brien?"

"Her too, if it comes to it."

"I think it has come to it, Mr. McGregor."

Chapter Fifty-Six

"How far are you into this thing, Ho?" asked McGregor, after he and the older man had left the house.

"Far?"

"Yeah, how much are you willing to do? This morning I got up and walked around. There's no way to defend this place, even if we wanted to. I knew when you said that this was the logical place to begin looking for Rumison that we could possibly expect others to reach the same conclusion. Now that I think this is Rumison's destination, that possibility raises to a probability of extremely high odds. All this Preitas has to do is chart Rumison's direction of flight and he'll likely send at least a few men here ahead of Rumison."

"I came to the same conclusion quite some time ago, McGregor. But I thought you understood me. I am in all the way, to the end."

"Ho, I don't think—"

Ho held up his hand and gave McGregor a searching look before speaking. "McGregor," he said finally. "Have you any idea as to why you have done what you have done so far in regards to this 'mission' you're on?"

McGregor was quiet. "Of course," he answered after several minutes seemed to have passed.

"And you know what's involved?"

"There is a lot involved."

"Exactly," said Ho. "Not just a lot, there is everything involved, isn't there?"

McGregor didn't answer.

"Well, you see, McGregor," said Ho. "It is the same with me."

"How could it be the same, Ho? You didn't know Bastanchury, you have no connection with this whole affair other than some romantic notion I don't understand at all."

Ho smiled. "There are connections all right. If I told you what they were you still wouldn't understand. Perhaps someday you will."

Ho's manner irritated McGregor. "All right," he said abruptly. "Then this is where we stand. We can't defend this place, so we will have to run. It won't do any good to run with Preitas right behind us, so any plan we have will have to include getting away secretly or keeping trackers from following."

Ho listened attentively. McGregor noted this, and his anger with the older man lessened.

"I've parked the Land Rover in the bushes off the road. Maybe Rumison likes running through jungles, but I think that's suicide. We can assume Preitas will either come in force or send a few men to check out the plantation first. In any event they will have to have transportation; helicopter or small aircraft, boat, or truck. I think truck or helicopter would be the most likely."

"I'm listening, Mr. McGregor."

"The three ways they can arrive are by this road, by air, or by water. This morning I found a shed over by the compound marked with 'Danger' signs. I got inside and found cases of explosives, melignite, used by foresters. It's my intention to mine any possible helicopter landing areas—the road and the front yard of the house."

"Pretty drastic, isn't it?"

McGregor shrugged. "Hopefully we won't have to use it. Hopefully Rumison will arrive and we can be out of here before anybody else knows."

"And what if Mr. Rumison himself isn't willing to listen to us? After all—"

"I'm aware of that possibility," snapped McGregor. "I don't know what in hell he's got going with that O'Brien girl, but—"

"Don't you, Mr. McGregor?"

"No, damn it, I don't, but I'm going to talk to her and explain the situation. Then she can talk to him. There are a lot of ifs, Ho, but the whole thing from start to finish is insane anyway."

"How are you planning on getting to Cuastacomote from the road?"

"It's eight miles. We'll have to walk. Do you have any other suggestions?"

"I'm a smuggler, Mr. McGregor. I have lots of suggestions, but they all entail returning to Bluefields."

"I'd rather not. I'd rather count on the Professor."

"I think he'd like that," said Ho. "But let me talk to the girl, McGregor. I think I understand her."

McGregor started to object, but his reasons for objecting were vague and he pushed them from his mind. "All right," he said.

"One more thing, McGregor."

"What's that?"

"Hermilia."

"Hermilia?"

"Why do you think she is staying at this godforsaken place, McGregor?"

"You tell me."

"She's waiting also," said Ho quietly. "For Rumison."

"You think she blames him?"

"Among other things."

"But how could she possibly know he was coming back? Don't tell me they both believed that story about princes and whatever. . . . Damn it, Ho, what is going on around here?"

"As to Hermilia, McGregor, she is obeah, with strong juju, power, bad, negative, however you want to call it. Unhealthy at best. People like that know things, however they use that knowledge. As to what is going on . . ." Ho smiled. "Well, I think we will all find out soon enough."

Using the pick and shovel Ho had used to bury the old Chinese man, McGregor began to cut shallow trenches in the ground around the plantation house and the road where it emerged from the jungle. The work was difficult with his taped fingers, and the temperature was over a hundred degrees in the direct sun. Ho didn't return from the house for several hours. When he did he seemed happy to take over from McGregor, who sat down under the shade of a large banana tree. As he sat and watched Ho work, wondering at the stamina of a man who must have been twenty years older than he, Whitney O'Brien came out of the house carrying a pitcher of cold water and a glass. McGregor accepted thankfully, and when Whitney turned to go he held her hand and asked her to talk. There were things he wanted to find out, but that wasn't the reason he stopped her. It was a reflex action, an action of the heart, and as she stood next to him, her face serious, her eyes wide, the aura of pain that had surrounded her the night and morning before gone, McGregor felt suddenly at a loss.

"Did . . . did Ho tell you what we plan?" he asked.

Whitney nodded.

"And you're willing to go along with it? It'll mean very probably not being able to return to this place again."

"I hate this place, Mr. McGregor. I've hated it ever since . . ." Whitney faltered but then continued. "Ever since Hermilia seduced my father, and my mother found out. I won't be sorry to leave."

"You know Rumison may very well never show up."

"He'll come."

"You're so sure."

Whitney lowered her eyes. "After that day in May," she began slowly, "I didn't know what to think. It was all so . . . so . . . wrong, but Sun kept telling me to believe, to wait, and then my father got better and moved to Ireland, and I stayed on and thought it would happen any day, but when he died . . ."

"When the old man died?"

"Yes, when Sun died, there seemed to be nothing." Whitney looked up at McGregor and she smiled, and her smile hurt McGregor in a way he couldn't describe.

"But then you arrived," she said. "And you told me Michael had come back."

For some reason the question McGregor wanted to ask wouldn't leave his lips. Why was Whitney O'Brien waiting for Rumison? Why did she think Rumison was coming back for her? Had they fallen that deeply in love in the few short hours they had known each other? Instead he said, "Things don't always work out like they do in fairy tales, Miss O'Brien."

The smile increased. "They do if you believe they will, Mr. McGregor," she said.

"But how can you believe so strongly?" This was as close as McGregor would allow himself to get toward asking what he really wanted to know.

"I just do," answered the girl and, still smiling, she turned and left McGregor standing under the banana tree, wondering how a man might have the courage to do the things that he had done and still be afraid to ask a rather romantic young girl a simple question.

Late afternoon the sky began to cloud up. Both Ho and McGregor were exhausted from their efforts and returned to the house after planting charges in seven different places. A wind had begun to blow and the clouds began to form in a pattern of high cumulus that McGregor now found familiar.

"Hurricane sunset," he said.

"Fitting weather," said Ho.

"For what?"

"For what's coming."

"And what's that, Ho?"

Ho shrugged. "I don't know, McGregor, but I'm a warrior, as you are. I've only been in petty squabbles for some years now, but I still remember the feeling I would get before a battle. It's what I am feeling now."

McGregor didn't answer because he was beginning to feel it too—an increased heart rate, a nervous expectancy and yet the strange calmness that comes of knowing how to wait, committed to whatever you are waiting for. Whatever McGregor felt had little to do with the darkening clouds and the coming storm. He didn't understand it yet and couldn't help feeling a little foolish for putting faith in an old man's curious behavior and a young girl's romantic folly, but he too knew against all reason that Rumison would return to the O'Brien plantation.

"I'd better close the storm shutters," said Whitney, looking out the front window at the clouds and the growing wind that was even now sweeping sand off the narrow beach and sending it gusting northward.

"Where's Hermilia?" asked Ho casually.

"In her room. She spends a lot of time in her room."

"I think I'll have a talk with her."

McGregor looked at Ho, but his expression was unreadable. "I'll help you with the shutters," McGregor said to Whitney. They went outside.

The plantation house was large and strongly built of mahogany and other hardwoods. The shutters were two inches thick and they locked with wrought-iron clasps from outside.

"This is a large place," said McGregor as he finished latching the last shutter. "Desolate area too. I'm surprised you two women alone didn't have trouble."

"We were never alone, Mr. McGregor. The last of the field hands didn't leave until last week, and Sun was here."

"But wasn't he sick?"

"Oh, no. He was quite healthy until he died. That was one reason it was such a shock for me."

"Do you have any idea what he died of?"

The wind had increased to above fifty knots, and McGregor had trouble hearing Whitney's answer, it was so softly spoken. "I think now I do," she said.

It hadn't started raining yet, but McGregor knew it wouldn't be long. Out where the sky met the Caribbean the slate-gray streaks of rain could be seen and the wind was blowing them toward shore.

The piercing sound of a woman's scream carried out from the house above the wind, interrupting McGregor's next question. The scream was one of anger or humiliation, not pain, and McGregor was more curious than alarmed as he ran around to the front of the house followed by Whitney. Inside he found Ho just coming out of the hall that led to Hermilia's room. His face was scratched and bleeding, and in his hands he carried five roughly carved wax dolls.

McGregor had seen voodoo dolls before, but always as curiosities, in picture books or museums. The sight of these, so grotesquely lifelike, sent shivers up his spine. Whitney stood back in shock.

"I found them in her room," said Ho, a half-smile on his face. He put the dolls down on a coffee table and motioned McGregor over.

"Look here," he said.

"Two aren't finished," said McGregor, examining the statues.

"She was working on this one when I entered her room." Ho held up a doll for McGregor to examine. "Look familiar?"

The doll was only partially carved and reminded McGregor of one of Michelangelo's *Captives* as its form struggled to escape from the wax bar holding it, but it was clearly intended to portray Ho.

"Perhaps this one is easier to recognize." Ho handed him the other unfinished doll. It was larger than the first doll, with sharp, clearly defined features. Its right hand had a small, cleverly tied bandage on it.

"Who are the others?" asked McGregor.

Whitney came forward and took three of the finished dolls from Ho's hand. They were complete with human hair and sewn pieces of cloth for clothes. "They are my father, myself, and Michael," she said quietly.

"There are holes in those three, pinholes, and some of the cloth looks scorched, as if they were held to a candle."

"You don't think this stuff works, do you?" said McGregor.

Ho shrugged. "What I think or don't think hardly matters in this case. It's what Hermilia thinks and what she intended the dolls for. But bad will never helps anyone. And a bad will trained and directed will do worse. One could certainly say that the persons whom the three finished dolls represent have had a bad time of it."

"You're avoiding a direct answer to my question, Ho."

"Of course they work, McGregor," Ho finally snapped. "How? You tell me. But you must know as well as I do that it works, being from Jamaica, being who you are."

McGregor was quiet. Outside, the force of the wind was increasing, its sound whistling heavily through the shuttered windows.

"I'll cleanse the dolls," said Whitney. Ho nodded and handed her the one he still carried. Strangely reluctant, McGregor hesitated before giving her his. After she had left, Ho reached into a pocket and took out yet another doll. It was dressed in black cloth and broken in two pieces. The hair on its head was steel gray and the features of the face were sharp enough to be nearly recognizable.

"I didn't want the girl to see this," explained Ho. "The doll is dead, and whoever it was intended for is also either dead or free from it."

McGregor took the pieces from Ho, who must have seen something in his eyes, because he asked, "Do you know who it was for?"

McGregor nodded. "Bastanchury," he said. "But I can't believe this thing had an effect on him. I once saw him slap a Montagnard magician for preaching doom before a battle. The villagers believed in the magician and didn't want to fight. Even I was getting worried. I'd seen the guy do some strange things, but Bastanchury walked up and slapped him in front of the whole village. We won the battle, and a week later the magician died of *mahri* fever. Bastanchury used to say magic was all belief."

"He was right in theory, I suspect, but not many people have strong enough beliefs to fight things such as this. I would like to have met Bastanchury."

McGregor stared at the broken doll for several moments before handing the pieces back to Ho. "What did you do to Hermilia?" he asked.

He chuckled. "Nothing to her," he said. "Though she did manage to get off a few good ones at me. I took the dolls and broke up some apparatus she had in her room. She's still dangerous, even more so perhaps, but in a different way. I wouldn't be surprised if she tries to slit my throat, but I suspect she'll wait."

"For Rumison?"

"Aye, for Rumison."

Like the sound of a river, the rain began, and lightning flashed through the cracks in the shutters.

"Are we all crazy?" asked McGregor after a bit.

Ho smiled gently. "I think we must be," he answered.

Chapter Fifty-Seven

HERMILIA didn't leave her room that night, not even for dinner. Outside, the storm grew in intensity. It seemed violent enough for a full-fledged hurricane, but Whitney insisted the house had withstood worse and McGregor had no reason to doubt her, though he did wonder about Rumison and the chances of his surviving such a storm.

"Relax, Mr. McGregor," said Ho. "If he has lived though what he has lived through and made it through the jungle, then this storm won't stop him." Oddly, Whitney O'Brien seemed the least troubled.

"What about the Professor?"

"That is a question, but Cuastacomote is the best place a boat such as his could be in this storm. A small, perfectly formed bay. There are low cliffs at the south end that will protect the *Zygote* as much as anything will."

McGregor's uneasiness grew but he tried to keep it to himself, not wanting to alarm Whitney. He was growing increasingly more conscious of his desire to protect her. She was showing herself to be strong in ways that constantly surprised him, but her sense of trust, her receptiveness, her incredible emotional openness made him fearful for her.

He balked when she insisted on standing a watch along with Ho and himself that night, an idea he had raised with Ho in case Rumison—or his pursuers—should come that night. He also had in mind watching out for Hermilia, but this he didn't say out loud. Whitney hadn't spoken about the black girl since she'd taken the dolls. McGregor wondered if she was really aware of the danger Hermilia represented. But Whitney was adamant, and it was agreed Ho should stand first watch, McGregor mid and the girl morning watch.

Half an hour after dinner, while the three were in the living room, the electric lights went out, leaving the house in total darkness. Whitney lit some storm lamps.

"The generator's in a shed in the compound. It may be out of fuel. I haven't checked it since . . . since Sun died."

"I'll look after it in the morning," said McGregor. "I'm exhausted anyway."

"And the watch?" asked Ho.

"The lamps will last the night. Miss O'Brien—Whitney—do you have any weapons in the house?"

Whitney nodded. "In the library. They're locked in a case."

"Could you show me?"

"Certainly."

Whitney carried a lamp and McGregor followed her into a room adjoining the living room. The room was paneled in mahogany and shelved from floor to ceiling, but most of the books that had lined the shelves were now packed in cardboard boxes that lay haphazardly on the floor. Whitney removed a small key from a desk drawer and opened the glass panel on a beautifully carved rosewood gun cabinet. There were two Weatherby hunting rifles of safari grade, two .22 rifles, an M-1 army rifle, and several shotguns as well as ammunition and several pistols. McGregor took out a twelve-gauge automatic shotgun, a Weatherby, two Colt .45 Army pistols, and several boxes of ammunition for each weapon, before he had Whitney lock the panel again. The case was constructed in such a way that even if someone had broken the glass, a stout hardwood bar would keep him from the rifles unless he had a key or a saw. If someone really wanted the weapons he'd have to make a lot of noise getting them.

"You'd better keep the key," said McGregor.

"You think Hermilia . . . ?"

McGregor shrugged with his load. "Better to be safe."

"You look like you're planning to fight a war," said Ho as they returned to the front room.

"We have to make contingency plans because of the

storm. I know we can't defend this place, but we need some cover fire if it comes to that." He put the weapons down and began loading the shotgun. It was unfamiliar to him, a Japanese imitation of the Browning automatic called a Suisan, and carried twelve shells to the Browning's six. Whitney saw him fumbling with the catch on the shell housing and took the gun from him.

"It's a lock you twist like this," she said, and dropped the housing expertly down from the barrel. She took twelve shells of double-O buckshot and loaded them into the housing, then locked the housing back to the barrel.

"Can you shoot that thing?" asked McGregor.

"I am a very good shot with all my father's weapons. Why do you seem so surprised?"

"I just thought . . ."

"You just thought that I was a rather naïve young girl with some rather overly romantic childhood notions about life? Maybe you are right, Mr. McGregor, and maybe not, but I assure you I have seen more in my life than most my age, and that I can use these weapons."

Ho burst out laughing. "Well said, Whitney O'Brien. Well said."

McGregor was embarrassed. She had described his thoughts exactly and now he didn't know what to make of her. She had cried at an old man's death and nearly killed herself with pain when she thought a childhood fantasy might not come true, yet here she was calmly loading shells into a twelve-gauge shotgun with two men she hardly knew, while they waited for who knew what to happen.

"I think the living room is the best place to sleep and keep watch," he said to hide his embarrassment.

Whitney put the shotgun down on a table. "I'll get some bedding," she said.

The wind was getting worse and the house groaned like a ship in a heavy sea, but McGregor fell asleep instantly. He awoke with a start when Ho tapped him on the shoulder and told him it was time for his watch. An oil lamp burned low at the far end of the room, leaving the area where the watch sat and the other two slept fairly dark, but casting shadows that were distracting to the point of hypnosis if watched too closely. McGregor was fairly alert for the first hour of his watch until he began to brood over his thoughts, and to drift with the shifting shadows. He jerked himself erect when he discovered his mental wanderings and, standing up to rouse himself, walked to the far end of the room to get away from the light. But the shadows were still visible there and he found his attention constantly drawn by them.

One shadow seemed to have more form than the others, to be darker and to move in a rhythm unlike the movement of the lamplight that created it. McGregor was instantly alert, but then the shadow merged with the others again. He listened for many minutes, but there was nothing to indicate that anyone was moving about in the house—only the wind and the hammering rain, the rattle of the shutters, the pieces of forest being blown against the house, and the groans of the house itself.

McGregor had served many watches in his life, with Bastanchury in the jungles of Viet Nam and on his own in his later years as an agent. He had taken the mid watch for himself because he knew it to be the hardest, but as his eyes shifted with the light and fell into the rhythm of the shadows he did what he had never before done in his life. He fell asleep.

The dream began, but it didn't seem to be a dream this time. He knew it was a dream and yet he was awake, or was he? The storm raged outside and he knew any minute the walls were going to collapse and the piece of broken window was going to shatter his right eye. The pressure increased and there was an explosion, the sound of glass shattering, and McGregor screamed.

"Wake up! Wake up, McGregor."

It was the old Gypsy. She must have already removed the glass from his eye because it no longer hurt.

"Mr. McGregor, wake up. You're having a nightmare."

He opened his eyes. Whitney knelt over him, her eyes filled with concern.

"You scared the daylights out of me, McGregor," said Ho, who was standing behind Whitney. His head was partially covered in shadow making it appear as though he wore a flat-brimmed hat low over the eyes. "I thought the devil had arrived, the way you screamed." The Chinese man's words were light, but McGregor could feel his concern. He looked back up into Whitney's eyes and their warmth nearly overwhelmed him. Surrounded by such caring, he felt like a child again and boyhood memories flashed through his mind, one in particular of his grandmother holding him while he cried after a bad nightmare.

But he couldn't cry now! It was absurd. He was McGregor, Richard Francis Burton McGregor. One of the best agents in the game. He'd been through a war, murders, assassinations. . . .

There was such caring in those green eyes. Honest caring without thought of self. Warmth. Hide it, a voice screamed. Force it down, don't let them see you cry, see who you really are. Who I am?

"Who am I?" A fourteen-year-old boy sent away from his home by a mother who no longer loved him? A green Army lieutenant, scared, defensive, vain about questionable achievements? A seven-year-old slapped by the same mother because he happened to walk in at the wrong time and caught her in the act of making love to a strange white man who smelled of brandy and expensive cigars?

Hide it! Control it! But something in McGregor could no longer hold back and he began crying. The harder he fought for control, the deeper came the sobs. So deep that his whole body, his whole being seemed involved in them.

"It's all right, Mr. McGregor," said Whitney, taking his head in her arms. "It's all right."

The wracking sobs continued. For an hour, it seemed to McGregor, but in reality only a few minutes had passed before his tears began to lessen.

"I . . . I'm sorry. . . ."

"It's all right. We understand. It happens to many. It's a good thing, a strong thing to be able to let it out."

Ho was still standing behind Whitney, but McGregor was aware only of the girl, soothing him, her hand stroking his forehead. Finally the control began to return. It balanced for a second and then slipped onto the other side. McGregor felt happy, relieved, and he almost giggled, but he caught that also and then he remembered who he was and the hurt returned and then the balance and finally he sat up. Whitney sensed that he'd returned from the edge, and pulled herself back from him.

"I don't know what happened," said McGregor. "I'm sorry. It was a bad dream."

"I said there was no need to be sorry."

"Can you sleep again?" asked Ho quietly. "It's time for Whitney's watch."

McGregor nodded. It would be best to go back to sleep, he thought, and wake up in the morning believing everything had been just a bad dream. "I thought I heard a crash," he said.

"A tree fell against a shutter, knocking it inward enough to break the glass. It still holds," answered Ho. "Get some sleep, McGregor. Sleep is the best antidote for all our hurts."

McGregor nodded again and lay back down on his bedding. He slept well until morning.

Chapter Fifty-Eight

NEITHER Whitney nor Ho mentioned McGregor's emotional breakdown during breakfast, but Hermilia, who had apparently decided to rejoin them, had a strange look in her eyes whenever McGregor caught her glancing toward him. No one mentioned Hermilia's voodoo dolls either, and the black girl seemed to have accepted their loss, though she was unusually subdued. The storm had abated somewhat, so McGregor decided to look around the plantation again, perhaps see if he could repair the generator.

Outside, the house looked like a trash heap, with rubbish and pieces of the jungle lying everywhere. Save for the fallen tree which had stove in the shutter, the house itself was undamaged, as were the barns and sheds of the compound yard. The trouble with the generator had come when a fuel line from the storage tank outside the shed had ruptured, probably broken by flying wood. Luckily the tank was half empty, and the pressure had kept fuel oil from leaking out onto the ground. McGregor found some new piping in the shed and repaired the broken line. On his way back to the house McGregor heard Ho shouting for him. Running around to the front he saw the Ho kneeling down by something near the road. McGregor had noticed it earlier, but there was so much debris on the ground he had thought it just another fallen log. Ho had been examining the explosive charges for damage and had gone up for a closer look.

"He's still alive," said Ho. "Help me get him inside."

A strange mixture of emotions ran through McGregor: a

kind of wonderment combined with relief, and resentment too, the resentment of a runner-up athlete toward the eventual winner of the gold medal. He knew it was Rumison. He had no doubt, though the man's face was cut and swollen beyond recognition, his clothes torn nearly to shreds.

"God, he made it," said Ho, who also apparently had no doubts about who the figure was. "You know, McGregor, you have these feelings about things . . . but I guess you never really believe until . . . Lift him up. There, that's it."

Rumison was light. McGregor remembered that the dossier said he weighed a hundred and eighty pounds, but he must have lost thirty or more.

"Doesn't look like he'll make it, Ho."

"He'll live, McGregor. He'll live."

Between them they carried the unconscious man to the house, where both Whitney and Hermilia were waiting. Whitney seemed neither surprised nor upset that Rumison had returned and had returned in such bad shape, but McGregor saw her eyes glaze over with tears as she looked into the man's mottled face, and when the mist cleared after a moment he could see the same open, unselfish concern that had looked down on him the night before. His stomach muscles began to tighten as he saw another emotion in the girl, an emotion quite unlike any she had shown him.

"He don't look so good," said Hermilia, her voice wintry. She hadn't seemed surprised either when Ho and McGregor had brought the man into the house.

"Shut up, Hermilia," said Whitney. "And keep your obeah away from him, I'm warning you."

"You warning me, you . . ." Hermilia stopped as she noticed Ho moving closer to her, his face set firmly. "Well, anyhow, don't look like I need juju anyway."

"I think you'd better return to your room," said Ho quietly. The black girl's eyes narrowed, and for a moment McGregor thought she actually seemed afraid of Ho.

She laughed. "No matter," she said. "You all goin' to die anyway," and she left the room without looking back.

"The first time I saw him he was like this," said Whitney without taking her eyes from Rumison, her fingers stroking his face. "Not so bad, but bad enough. I knew he was who he was, though everyone else laughed, or wanted to."

"There's a medical kit in the truck."

"No need, Mr. Ho. We have supplies here."

Whitney stood up and left the room, to return a minute later with a canvas medic's kit, which she set on a table next to the couch Rumison was on.

"I'm not a doctor," she said. "Perhaps one of you . . . ?"

McGregor didn't wait. He began checking the bag's contents and came up with a hypodermic, a bottle of buffered penicillin, and a bottle of epinephrine, a heart stimulant, which he set aside. Then he ripped off what remained of Rumison's clothes and checked him over for obvious major injuries, finding none. Ho had found a large pan. He poured hot water in it; found soap and towels, which Whitney took from him. While she bathed Rumison McGregor gave him a full dose of penicillin, inserting the needle in the upper inner part of the buttock in order to miss the sciatic nerve.

"I'd say that aside from infection he's just suffering from fatigue and malnutrition," said McGregor. He put the hypodermic away in its plastic case and then took out a stethoscope.

"Heart rate forty-eight."

"Is that good or bad?" asked Whitney.

McGregor shrugged. "Could be either. Normal is in the sixties or seventies, but Rumison was a champion swimmer, so his is bound to be lower. I'm not a doctor either, just had some medic training in the service. His pulse is fairly strong."

"Do you think he is in good enough shape to move him?" asked Ho.

"No way of knowing. He may have a reaction to the penicillin. I wouldn't worry about it for a while. Not till this storm eases. I think we're in the eye. We won't have to worry about Preitas until then. I certainly wouldn't want to risk being out in it."

"Look at his arm."

McGregor nodded as he saw the long series of needle marks covering the veins on both of Rumison's arms. Many of the dots were red and infected-looking, as were many of the cuts on his body.

Whitney looked concerned and a little bit frightened.

"Interrogation technique," said McGregor. "Truth serum. He couldn't have told them much, though."

"Why is that?"

"They'd be here by now if he had. A lot of people are drug-conscious these days, something a Nicaraguan interrogator might not be aware of. Then again, they might not have believed him . . . I know I sure as hell would have a hard time." McGregor paused. "Maybe I still do," he added.

"But they'll probably be here?"

"We'll just have to wait for the storm to pass."

McGregor spent the rest of the day in nervous activity. The storm had picked up again, and with Ho and Whitney caring for Rumison, he had little to do but pace the floor, check and recheck the guns and detonators for the explosives, and peer out the peepholes in the shuttered windows hoping that no tracker in his right mind would be out in that storm.

Toward evening Rumison's breathing seemed to grow stronger. Whitney refused to leave his side even for dinner, so Ho and McGregor ate alone, with Hermilia coming down for a bowl of stew, which she took to her room after casting a contemptuous look at Whitney and her patient.

"We'll have to watch her closely," said Ho. "Very closely from now on."

McGregor didn't answer. He hadn't felt like talking for some time, as his sense of expectancy grew with every passing hour. At nine that evening by McGregor's watch, Rumison regained consciousness. Ho and McGregor were out of the room, and when they returned they saw Rumison and Whitney O'Brien gazing into each other's eyes, their right hands clasped tightly together. Neither had spoken. He grabbed McGregor's arm and shook his head.

"Give them this moment," he said quietly. McGregor felt the pain in his stomach return, but he obeyed. As he watched the scene unfolding before them he remembered his own scene with Whitney the previous night, and for a horrified second he thought he might be going to cry again.

Finally Rumison spoke. "I knew you'd be here," he croaked, his voice dry and brittle and weak.

"I knew you'd come."

"Your father . . . ?"

"He's all right. He's in Ireland."

Rumison relaxed with a deep sigh. "I'm sorry—" he began, but Whitney interrupted.

"It's all right."

Only then did Rumison's eyes shift from Whitney's face to the two men standing behind her in the darkening room. They were calm eyes, thought McGregor, yet aware and rather hard.

"They're friends," said Whitney.

Rumison seemed to take in Ho with one glance, but his gaze stayed on McGregor for a long time. For the first time since Bastanchury, McGregor felt himself intimidated by another's stare.

"Friends?" said Rumison.

"I was hired by the U.S. government to find out what happened to the mission you were on, and why, when you returned to the U.S., you didn't report in," said McGregor, more harshly than he meant.

Perhaps recognizing something of McGregor's feelings, Ho spoke. "Mr. McGregor was a friend of one of the men on that mission," he said.

"Who?"

"Bastanchury."

"Bastan—?"

"You knew him as Michael Black."

Rumison's eyes didn't waver. "You remind me of him in a way, Mr.—ah . . . ?"

"McGregor."

"Yes, McGregor."

"Is he dead, Rumison?"

Rumison nodded, the effort causing him pain as he grimaced. Whitney immediately began stroking his head again and Rumison smiled.

"How did he die?" It was the question McGregor had begun the mission with but now it seemed less important than the questions he still didn't know how to ask. Rumison acknowledged the question with his eyes but didn't speak. Finally he said, "I'm tired, Mr. McGregor. Your question deserves a good answer. I can't give it to you now."

"Of course," said Ho, stepping between McGregor and Rumison. "Perhaps tomorrow when you've had some sleep. Right now I believe you could use something to eat. I don't imagine you had much out in the jungle."

Whitney spoon-fed Rumison a small amount of stew. When he'd eaten enough he shook his head.

"Sleep now," said Whitney.

McGregor could not sleep at all that night. He knew the symptoms: his body was preparing for action. When he checked his heart rate, he found it to be over eighty per minute when normal for him was in the low fifties. Wanting to make up for his performance of the night before, he offered to stand the night's watch alone, but Ho objected and McGregor reluctantly acceded.

"You fell asleep last night, McGregor," said Ho. "I think that might be more dangerous tonight."

McGregor was honest enough to know Ho was right. His falling asleep was just another symptom of what he considered his general mental deterioration. Maybe Bishop had been right to want him off the case, he thought. He no longer trusted himself; his once finely tuned and hardened body and mind now seemed to be playing tricks on him.

He stood the first watch with Ho. With the generator working again they didn't need the lamp, and the light they had left on didn't create the same type of moving shadows.

"It's beautiful, isn't it," said Ho as they sat, backs against a wall, the lightning flashing intermittently through the shutter cracks and the cry of the storm drowning the sound of his words.

"Beautiful? What?"

Ho's round face, crisscrossed with the lines of age and stress, looked relaxed and somehow at peace. "What is happening," he answered.

"I'd hardly call it beautiful, Ho."

Ho looked over at McGregor and smiled. "Perhaps you don't yet see what is happening, McGregor," he said.

"Maybe I don't, Ho. Why don't you tell me."

"Don't be angry, Mr. McGregor. I think you know more than you're willing to admit. I can see it in your eyes when you look at the girl."

"What?"

"Calm down, I don't mean to be rude."

"What do you see?"

Ho shrugged. "I see that you sense what she is, and wish that you instead of our Mr. Rumison was the center of her life."

The stomach muscles tightened and McGregor shuddered. Ho was getting too close. "What—exactly—is she?" asked McGregor, forcing the words out.

"I'll tell you a story from my birthplace," said Ho. "About a Shoulin monk who was exiled from the monastery for failing to attend to his proper duties. This monk decided on a plan of revenge, a plan to discredit the other monks, so he put a sign up at a nearby lake that said: 'On February 2, this year, a dragon will arise from this lake and fly off toward the moon,' and he signed it, 'The Shoulin Monks.' It was his hope that when the dragon failed to materialize, the monks would be discredited. Well, the word spread throughout the countryside, and on the morning of February second the shores of the lake were crowded with villagers waiting to see a dragon rise out of the lake."

Ho paused for dramatic effect. McGregor waited.

"Well," Ho said finally. "As the hour approached when the dragon was supposed to rise, a great sense of expectancy overwhelmed the crowd, and at the appointed time . . ." Another pause. "At the appointed time a dragon was seen rising out of the water, flapping its scaly wings and flying off toward the moon. The poor monk, overwhelmed with guilt, returned to the monastery to confess the whole story, but naturally the other monks would not believe that he was the one who had put up the sign and predicted the rise of the dragon."

"Well?" asked McGregor, after a number of seconds had passed and Ho didn't explain how the story related to anything. The wind howled outside and Ho Feng Hua sighed.

"I thought you would see it, McGregor," he said.

"I don't see anything, Ho. What are you trying to say?"

"I said I was a warrior, McGregor. As a warrior one is only satisfied if one has an enemy, but as one grows older one sees that the enemy is not necessarily what one imagined it to be. Sometimes one becomes so forgiving, so broad-minded, that as someone once said, one's brains slip out one's ears. In the war we had an enemy, the Japanese, but now the Japanese are our friends. Later the enemy was myself, my mind, my thoughts, my cultural habits, and then the enemy became the American establishment."

"You create your own enemies," said McGregor. "Bastanchury said that you decide what to do and then you do it, and your enemies are whoever or whatever gets in the way of your doing it. But I still don't see how this all relates."

"I am sure your Bastanchury knew many things," said Ho, "and was a very strong warrior, but I am afraid he left out an important aspect of enemies."

"What's that?"

"They must be real. You must believe totally in the rightness of your cause, and it must *be* right. It cannot be some fabricated action that you arbitrarily decide on, thereby creating your enemies and your friends out of your own ego."

"It's all fabricated," said McGregor. "Everything. It's all our own creating. It's just who we are programmed to like and hate."

Ho shook his head. "No," he said. "Who we think we are is not real, and therefore our enemies are not real, nor our friends. The real enemy uses this fact."

"Who am I, Ho, if I am not who I think?"

"We each must learn that for ourselves, but I will tell you this. There is a real enemy. It takes many shapes, sometimes as the invading Japanese, sometimes as the people who have been invaded, sometimes as the rude waiter at a restaurant, sometimes as a bigoted narcotics agent, and sometimes as the drug dealer the agent is trying to arrest. Sometimes it is a combination of factors that are all trying to keep destiny from operating."

"Destiny? Ho, really . . ."

"You feel it, McGregor. You might not be aware of what it is you feel, but you feel it."

"The girl and Rumison?"

Ho nodded.

"And you think the enemy is everything that is trying to stop this?"

"I know that is the enemy."

McGregor couldn't accept Ho's words. They went against too much that he believed in. There was no destiny. There is only yourself, alone, and what you see as the world. *What you see!* The words set something off in his mind.

"How does the dragon story fit in?"

"If you can't sense it, then I doubt my words will help."

"Try me."

"There are feelings we have about things, McGregor. About who our real enemies and friends are. Most of the time we ignore them, sometimes to the extent of marrying an enemy or working for one, or hurting a friend. We do things we feel are wrong because we think they are right. Our expectations, our thoughts do create our world, just like the thoughts of the villagers created the dragon, but if our creations don't coincide with those inner feelings of right and wrong, then we are in for a bad time, because this gives our real enemies an advantage.

"When I first met you, McGregor, I felt that you were engaged in a positive activity. Kingsley mentioned it also. He said he believed you were looking for your soul. When you told me the story of Rumison I had such a feeling about him, too, and so I decided to come along. When I met the girl, Whitney, I knew immediately what it was that Rumison was coming back to. It was not necessarily love, though I am sure that is a part of it. It was a simple feeling of rightness, of destiny, if you will. A destiny that the girl may have created out of her faith, but more real than most of what I have encountered before. Who knows where the dragon came from, whether it was real or not? This young girl's destiny feels right. There is nothing else I can say, McGregor."

Ho waited until two o'clock before leaving McGregor to stand the mid-watch by himself. The thoughts and shadows began to plague McGregor as soon as Ho was gone. He'd told himself he was going to let Whitney sleep the night, but she woke by herself and he was almost glad. He talked little with her, not wanting to disturb either Ho or Rumison, but he was happy for her company. By four McGregor's eyes were blinking shut and he lay down, hoping to get some sleep, but the thoughts wouldn't leave him, and the best he could accomplish was an hour of twilight rest, half sleeping, half awake. In the morning he was jerked to awareness by the realization that the storm had passed and bright sunlight was coming in through the cracks in the shutters.

Whitney was already in the kitchen making breakfast. McGregor jumped to his feet and tapped Ho awake with his foot.

"Ho, wake up. We've got to get going."

Ho was instantly awake, his eyes taking in the sunlight as it traced its patterns on the carpeted floor of the living room. McGregor bent over the still-sleeping Rumison and put his hand to his forehead.

"Fever's down," he said quietly.

"Can he make the trip to Cuastacomote?"

"We may have to carry him, but we can't stay here."

Ho looked at McGregor with a wry smile on his face. "You sound as if you are beginning to believe in destiny," he said.

"I'll get the Land Rover," said McGregor shortly.

After the storm the heat returned, drying out the puddles of water and the mud. Despite the lack of sleep, McGregor felt alert as he walked toward the Land Rover. He carried the automatic shotgun and two boxes of extra shells with him. The road was littered with debris, but nothing the vehicle couldn't handle. Birds cried overhead and seagulls dove into the litter, searching for scraps the storm might have turned up. McGregor waited while a huge snake, the kind the natives called matabuey or oxen killer, crossed the road looking for shade. Then he heard the dogs.

The sound was hardly noticeable at first, among the whine of insects and the cries of the birds, but it was insistent and growing louder. A pack, on a scent and moving fast down the road. McGregor began running back toward the house.

McGregor had been hunted by dogs before, during a training course the CIA had required certain of its trainees to attend. He'd learned about hound dogs, the kind that just followed scents, other dogs, trained to hold the prey, and vicious attack dogs, trained to kill. He'd learned how to throw them off a trail and how to deal with them once they caught up to their prey. An attack dog went for the throat and if it got an arm instead it would hang on until the other dogs could finish the kill. But if you were fast enough you could split its skull with a rock or board. These thoughts crowded McGregor's mind while he ran, trying to remember everything that course had taught him about dogs. But the dogs weren't after him. They were after Rumison. And they were gaining.

If the road had been straighter McGregor could have seen them. Their speed indicated they were loose with their handlers trailing behind. It also indicated that the handlers knew the quarry was close by. McGregor reached the house before the dogs burst into sight, six of them, four large German shepherds and two that looked like Airdales, coming down the road at a full run. They weren't hound dogs, but McGregor didn't think they were the attack kind either. He was sure that whoever was after Rumison wanted him alive.

"Ho!" he cried. "We've got to get out of here. Dogs."

Ho and Whitney had already heard. Rumison was awake now and sitting up.

"I thought I'd lost them," he said.

"What do we do?" asked Whitney. Her voice showed no trace of fear. *But then, why should she?* McGregor asked himself angrily. *She believes in her damn fairy tale so much. Why should she be afraid?*

"How you feeling, Rumison?" he asked.

"Better."

The dogs were at the door now, barking wildly. The jungle had been McGregor's plan. The only sane one left. Trying to defend the house against the Nicaraguan army . . . ? But then, the army hadn't arrived yet. Maybe if they could hold out just long enough to . . . to what?

McGregor looked at the faces before him: Ho, his expression as inscrutable as only the Chinese were supposed to be; Whitney, looking calm and ready; Rumison, also calm.

"Rumison, you said you'd thought you'd lost the dogs. Did you know how many handlers they had? How many people were after you?"

"I never saw them."

"If there are a lot of them we don't have much of a chance."

Rumison shrugged. "You can leave," he said.

"Ho?" asked McGregor.

The Chinese smiled. "I'm here, McGregor. I'm staying."

The barking of the dogs was growing more frantic and McGregor ran to the slot in the shuttered window and looked out. Four men carrying rifles were trotting down the road toward the house.

"Four," said McGregor. "Grab some weapons. Ho, get in the kitchen. Rumison, stay down behind the couch. Whitney, you'd better go in another room."

"I'm staying," said Whitney.

McGregor started to object, but Rumison handed a pistol to the girl, and McGregor sighed in defeat.

"What about the dogs?" asked Rumison.

"Don't worry about them. Just stay still if they get in. They won't attack if you stay put. It's their handlers we're after."

A pounding at the door and a voice with a Spanish accent called, "Open up! We are the police!"

Whitney was standing off to one side of the door. "Tell them the door is open, to come inside but leave the dogs," whispered McGregor.

Whitney nodded and obeyed. There was a commotion outside as the handlers leashed the dogs and then cautiously opened the front door. Whitney was the only one in view of the three men who entered slowly, alert, M-16 rifles at ready.

"What do you want?" asked Whitney. McGregor thought how strong she looked, standing there, facing the enemy. Quite a change from the nearly broken girl of two days before.

It was obvious the trackers felt something was wrong. Their leader was a young man, a Latin with sharp eyes and a thin mustache. He didn't answer immediately. He peered around the room, which was still partially darkened by the shuttered windows.

"A man," said the soldier. "We are looking for a man." He said it coldly, without emotion or apology in his voice, and then his eyes seemed to see something and the barrel of the M-16 swung in McGregor's direction. McGregor didn't wait. Two blasts from his shotgun cut down the leader and the man behind him before they had a chance to fire. The third man died from shots fired nearly simultaneously by Ho from the kitchen doorway and by Whitney and Rumison.

The dogs rushed through the door, released by the man who had remained outside, and McGregor's shotgun worked frantically. He was vaguely aware that the others in the room were also firing. In ten seconds nearly all the dogs were dead. One German shepherd lay wounded on the floor, whimpering. McGregor took out his Smith and Wesson and shot it through the head.

The room was not a pretty sight as McGregor reloaded the shotgun. He'd seen worse and he imagined Ho had also, but the girl was a mystery. She had taken the clip out of the Colt and was looking around for another, apparently unmindful of the death all around her. Rumison got weakly off the couch and handed her another clip from the small pile where McGregor had left them.

"There's one left," said McGregor, not knowing exactly what else to say. Ho came up next to him and put a hand on his shoulder.

"She is a very strong person," said Ho quietly. "Perhaps, in her own way, stronger than you or I."

McGregor wondered how Ho had read his mind. "I have to get that last man," he said aloud.

McGregor couldn't see anything out the window, so he took a step out the door. A burst of automatic rifle fire coming from the jungle slammed into the house, splintering the hard wood of the door and creasing McGregor's right leg. He fell back into the living room, his hand covering the wound.

"McGregor! How bad?"

"Scratch, Ho. Hardly bleeding. You see where the fire came from?"

"Near that tall tree, but I can't see a thing now, not even through the scope." Ho was looking through the sight on his Browning, scanning the jungle.

"I'd better get him. We can't stay here."

"I'll go," said Ho.

"No, I'm a better runner."

"Your leg?"

"Nothing. I'll go out the back, so keep up a good diversionary fire."

McGregor left the shotgun in the house, carrying only a pistol and the knife he'd gotten from the black man in Kingston. There was an open area behind the house and he sprinted across it, circling the plantation yard into the jungle while Ho, Whitney, and Rumison kept firing at the jungle in front of the house.

He came to the road and waited, trying to pick up the soldier's position, but the soldier wasn't returning the fire and McGregor had to wait. Ho must have known what was happening, because after several minutes he stuck his head out the door. Immediately another burst of M-16 bullets chattered from the jungle and Ho ducked quickly back inside.

It was too late for the soldier, however. McGregor had seen his position and began closing in.

The soldier was young, possibly not out of his teens. He was hidden in the undergrowth next to a tall pine, lying down and impossible to hit or even be seen from the house. A low sound far off down the road startled the man and he turned only to see McGregor behind him. McGregor ignored his youth, the look of unbelieving surprise on his face, then the horror as McGregor slit his neck with the knife. He bent down and quickly stripped the soldier of his weapon and extra ammunition before lying down in approximately the same position as the dead man. The noise that had disturbed the man had been the mechanical grumble of a truck's engine. McGregor waited. While he waited he put a broad-leafed branch over the open eyes of the corpse next to him.

Two vehicles came slowly down the road, picking their way over the debris scattered by the storm—a canvas-backed truck and a civilian C-J5 Jeep. Three men were in the jeep, a uniformed one driving while two others sat in back. One was dressed in a neatly pressed white suit, small and middle-aged with thinning light-colored hair, a man McGregor would have discounted had it not been for his eyes, which were cold and hard behind aluminum-framed glasses. It wasn't this man who interested him, however. McGregor had last seen the other man in a small hotel room in Kingston. Adrian Idris looked as much at home seated next to the man in the white suit in the company of Nicaraguan Army soldiers as he had with Nathaniel Bishop back in Jamaica.

The truck pulled up in front of the house while soldiers disembarked from the rear. The men in the jeep, perhaps sensing something wrong, waited away from the house. There were shouts and orders in Spanish, and then the truck blew up. Ho had detonated the explosives he and McGregor had buried.

Men were screaming, some from pain, some from shock. The soldiers stood, unable to believe what they saw; a few tried to run for the safety of the jungle but were cut down by fire from the house. McGregor looked through the smoke, trying to find the occupants of the jeep, but it was empty and Idris and the man in the white suit nowhere to be seen.

The battle was over in minutes. Bodies lay across the front yard; McGregor counted at least seven. It had been like target practice on an easy range. When the smoke cleared and there was no more movement outside the house, McGregor circled around through the jungle and entered the house. Among all the dead he didn't see either Idris or the white suit, and that worried him.

"Easy," he said as a gun was jabbed into his ribs. Rumison was standing behind leaning against the wall. He lowered his pistol when he saw who it was.

"There are still some alive," said McGregor. "A man I know and another in a white suit."

"That was Preitas," said Rumison grimly. "He and the other got into the jumgle. So did their driver."

"I'll have to go back out there," said McGregor, looking out the window. "Get our Land Rover. That jeep looks done in. Flat tires. I—" He stopped as he turned around and saw the black girl Hermilia. She was standing purposefully, quietly, a shotgun cradled in her slender arms.

Ho cried out just as the girl pulled the trigger. The first blast caught Ho Feng Hua in the stomach, doubling him over and throwing him against the door. McGregor had his pistol out but he was too late. Another blast hit him, spinning him, and he fired as he turned. He didn't know if he hit anything. He didn't know anything but blackness for some time.

Chapter Fifty-Nine

FOR the second time in a week McGregor awoke to pain. It was general at first, but as the blackness that clouded his senses lessened, it became more localized. The worst was the head, near the right temple, but there was also pain in his shoulder. He concentrated on the pain, a trick he'd learned from Bastanchury. Pain was good, you had to face it, live it, feel it. It was a warning, a reminder, a guard. It told you you were alive. If you couldn't feel pain you were dead. If you tried to hide from it you were as good as dead.

The pain eased and McGregor opened his eyes.

"Well, McGregor," said Adrian Idris, the first person he saw. "You are indeed very lucky. Welcome back to the living."

McGregor's vision began to clear. Behind Idris stood the little man in the white suit; Rumison had identified him as Colonel Rafael Preitas. He looked on with cold fish eyes. In a corner, guarded by a uniformed soldier, sat Whitney and Rumison, both alive, both watching him. Whitney smiled tentatively when he looked at her. Rumison nodded. Another soldier stood by the front door. All the dead had been removed from the room, but there were still large bloodstains on the floor. The blood was still red, not very old, which told McGregor he hadn't been unconscious very long.

"Ho?" asked McGregor.

"Dead, I'm afraid," said Idris. "The girl with the shotgun also. Your last shot evidentally killed her. Hit her right between the eyes. She got you in the shoulder. One slug grazed your temple. You won't be using your right arm for a long while. Nasty wounds."

McGregor caught an odd stress in Idris' words. The man was trying to tell him something. His head hurt like hell, but he could feel that his shoulder wasn't as bad as Idris had indicated. The bandages someone had put on looked massive and bloody, but McGregor could flex his muscles, feel them respond in his arm. Aside from the pain in his head he didn't feel weak, as he would have, had the wounds been worse.

"You two know each other?" asked Preitas.

"Jamaica, wasn't it?" said Idris. "McGregor was working for the British, and I, naturally, for the Cubans."

McGregor nodded. Whatever game Idris was playing, he had no choice for the moment but to follow the other's lead.

"My agents have been aware of you for some time," said Preitas quietly. "We know why you are here, so there is no use lying or playing uninformed."

"No use at all," said Idris.

"But perhaps we could arrange a deal," continued Preitas, his eyes quiet, unemotional, waiting. They were the eyes, thought McGregor, of someone who was dead inside.

"Deal?"

"You are a free agent. As such you have worked for many different employers. Even the Chinese, I understand."

"The CIA was always aware of my activities," said McGregor. "I couldn't act without their approval."

Preitas shrugged. "The question is, would you if you could . . . for a large enough fee, of course . . . ?"

"I'm listening," said McGregor.

Preitas tilted his head and began rocking back on his heels in a way McGregor found irritating. "We must have that case," he said finally.

"A lot of people want that case," said McGregor. "I don't know where it is."

"No. I know that. Rumison is the only one who knows that. We will deal with that matter shortly."

"There is no need," said Rumison. "I'm perfectly willing to give the case up. I always was. I never wanted the damn thing in the first place."

"Then why did you return to Nicaragua?" asked Preitas harshly, turning toward Rumison.

McGregor could visibly see Idris tense as Rumison answered Preitas' question with a shake of his head.

"I'm sorry," said Rumison, "I can't answer that, but I can tell you what I've told you all along. It had nothing to do with that damn case or the mission. It was a personal matter."

"He came back for the girl," said McGregor.

"You don't expect me to believe that!" snarled Preitas. For some reason, the little man who had appeared so calm before was now getting very emotional about something. Idris smiled.

"It would answer a lot of questions, Colonel," he said.

"It would bring up many more than it would answer, Idris," said Preitas sharply.

"It's easy enough to prove," said Idris. "Just have Rumison tell us where the case is, and then see if he's telling the truth."

"There must be more to this than that case," said Preitas. "Where did that other agent, Black, disappear to, and why did Rumison return? The story of the girl is patently ridiculous. No man would do what Rumison has done for a . . ." Preitas looked scornfully over at Whitney, who was listening quietly. "No," he continued. "It was something else, and I suspect this plantation is the key. After all, this is the last place we saw Black. If Rumison is willing to let us have the case, then the case must not be what it is we are searching for."

"What are you searching for?" asked McGregor.

"If you do not know that already," said Preitas, "then I am sorry for you, because I will have no use for you and you will die in a very painful manner while I try and decide whether or not you are telling the truth."

"Where is the case, Rumison?" asked Idris.

"A deal," said Rumison. "Our lives for the case."

"No!" said Preitas. "I am getting tired of these games. The questioning will begin, and this time there will be no idiot of a police chief to interfere. Hernán, *traiga la mujer aquí!*"

The soldier Preitas had called Hernán slung his M-16 over his back and jerked Whitney to her feet, using her hair and the bindings on her hands as levers. Then he dragged her over to the colonel and threw her down. Rumison lay still, but his body was as tense as a guitar string. Idris' expression was unreadable.

"We will work with the girl first," said Preitas. "I doubt she knows anything, but perhaps her pain and ultimate death will remind one of the truth."

With Hernán's help Preitas took some manila cord and tied Whitney's legs apart, lashing each to a leg of the couch on which McGregor lay. Whitney struggled wildly at first, but Preitas slapped her repeatedly until she subsided into silence. She didn't cry, and McGregor wondered at this as he felt his own body tighten in anger, his jaw clench and his knuckles turn white as they ground into fists.

Preitas took a small penknife from a pocket on his white suit and cut Whitney's blouse off, exposing her breasts. Then he began cutting her denim pants, unmindful that the tip of the knife left a thin bloody line on her flesh where he pressed too hard.

Rumison screamed. "Stop it!"

The colonel ignored him, the knife working. Hernán stood by watching in interest as Whitney's pants were stripped away, his rifle still over his shoulder. The other soldier was by the door, his neck craned to see the girl on the floor. Idris was a problem. Where did he stand? What would he do if McGregor attacked?

Preitas stood up, put his knife away and called to the soldier at the door. *"Traígame el equipaje."*

It was the opening McGregor had hoped for. He waited, flexing his muscles, especially those of his wounded shoulder, assessing his strengths and weaknesses. The soldier left the house to get the interrogation equipment Preitas wanted—McGregor counted off twenty seconds before he struck. His left leg kicked out, catching Hernán in the small of the back and knocking him to the floor. While the soldier struggled to get the weapon off his shoulder, McGregor was off the couch. Preitas' eyes flickered toward Idris in puzzlement as the big agent just stood without moving. Then the colonel's hand went for a gun hidden in a shoulder holster, but McGregor grabbed it before he could fire, his thumb lying across the hammer while his free arm struck at Preitas' throat.

"Ramón!" cried Preitas, and then he fell to the floor, his thin neck broken by McGregor's blow.

McGregor looked toward Hernán but Hernán was also dead, a stiletto sticking out of his chest. Idris had finally committed himself. McGregor grabbed Hernán's M-16 and ran to the door just in time to meet the other soldier, who had heard Preitas' shout and come running. McGregor didn't bother shooting him, instead using the rifle like a club over the soldier's head. A dizziness settled over him as he looked down at the dead soldier, and he dropped the rifle. Strong arms held him up and pulled him back over the couch.

"Easy, McGregor," said Idris. "You've done enough for one day."

McGregor watched in a daze while Idris cut Whitney's bonds and then Rumison's.

"Get some clothes on, girl," said Idris.

"A boat should be waiting at Cuastacomote."

"Pirosh's?"

McGregor nodded. "How did you get in with Preitas?" he asked.

Idris smiled. "Cuban intelligence supplied the papers," he said. "Preitas was a tough cookie. I fed him just enough."

It sounded reasonable enough, but for some reason McGregor didn't quite believe Idris. "There are some trucks in the garage, but our best bet would be the Land Rover. I stashed it in the jungle a quarter mile up the road on the right."

"I'll get it. You and the others get ready to leave. There'll be others following. Preitas was a methodical man."

Whitney returned a few minutes after Idris had left for the Land Rover, dressed in jeans and a man's shirt. Rumison approached McGregor.

"I want to thank you," he said.

McGregor felt awkward. "I knew Idris was with us," he lied.

"Is he with us?" Rumison asked.

"He helped, didn't he? I met him with my boss—ex-boss—in Kingston not more than a few days ago. He said he got in with Preitas pretending to be a Cuban. I suppose . . ." Rumison's question brought McGregor's own doubts to the surface. After all, he still didn't know who the black really worked for, only that Bishop had accepted him. But what was Bishop's game?

"I don't trust him," said Rumison.

It's funny, thought McGregor, but neither do I, never did. Aloud he asked, "You trust me?"

Rumison nodded. "I trusted Ho," he said. "Ho must have trusted you."

The mention of Ho Feng Hua had an instantly sobering effect on McGregor. Seeing Whitney and Rumison together, holding hands, also made him sad. To hide his feelings, he asked Rumison about Bastanchury—Mr. Black, as Rumison called him.

"He killed himself," said Rumison. "A bird startled him when he was making a difficult move up a waterfall. He fell and broke his back. I wanted to get help, but he said no and later shot himself."

McGregor was quiet. It didn't seem to matter much now.

"I learned a lot from him," continued Rumison, "but in the end I think he'd failed himself."

"I learned a lot also. He was my friend . . . my teacher really . . . for two years."

Rumison nodded. "I see a lot of him in you."

"Why do you say he failed himself? He chose his death, didn't he?"

"Maybe, maybe not. Maybe the bird chose it for him. Who knows. I do know that he didn't die for something he really believed in. He was afraid to fight for what he really believed in."

"He used to say you choose what to believe, that nothing was more important than anything else, that the act of choosing was what was important, and keeping to this," said McGregor.

"I think he was half right," said Rumison.

McGregor wanted to ask what Rumison meant, but his question was interrupted by the horn of the Land Rover outside. Whitney and Rumison had gathered up several guns and a small pack of supplies and taken them outside. When McGregor followed he saw the bodies of the dead, lined up in front of the veranda where Preitas' remaining two soldiers had dragged them during the time McGregor was unconscious. Eleven of them, lying in a row, the flies and mosquitos gathered in hordes large enough to form small clouds above them. Several yards away from the dead soldiers lay the bodies of Ho Feng Hua and Hermilia. McGregor put his shotgun and an M-16 in the Land Rover.

"I'm going to bury Ho," he said.

Rumison and Whitney nodded, but Idris looked peeved. "We have little enough time as it is, McGregor," he said. "The guy's dead, makes no difference if he's buried."

"Yes it does," said McGregor and he turned to the others. "I'll need help."

"Of course."

Idris looked exasperated but, turning off the key to the truck, finally gave in. "Shit, the condition you guys are in you'd take a year to get him under. I'll dig the hole."

"I want him by the fountain," said McGregor.

"By the . . . what in hell . . ."

"By the fountain," insisted McGregor.

When it was done, McGregor repeated as much of the Mandarin poem that Ho had recited over the grave of Sun as he could remember. Idris brought the truck up and they got in. McGregor didn't speak for some time afterward.

Chapter Sixty

THE Professor had kept his word despite patrols and hurricanes, and the *Zygote* was waiting at Cuastacomote Bay as he had said it would be. The trek from the road to the bay had been hard, but Whitney, Rumison, Idris, and McGregor made it before sunset, to find the *Zygote* silhouetted against the evening sky, waiting for its passengers. For Rumison and McGregor the short hike from the road through the jungle to the coast was particularly hard, Rumison because of his general debilitation and McGregor because of his wounds, which, though not serious in themselves, had thrown his body into minor shock after his exertions. He had to be carried across the sand beach to the water's edge and lifted onto the little Boston Whaler that served as the *Zygote*'s dinghy, but he remained conscious enough to tell the Professor about Ho's death. The Professor didn't seem surprised.

"He was a good friend," he said sadly, "but I always knew he wouldn't die in bed."

McGregor remembered little about the next two days; the bed in his cabin was too soft, his rest needed too much by both his mind and body. The Professor looked in on him occasionally, and he seemed to remember Whitney bringing him soup and talking to him, but this could have been a dream. He dreamed a lot during this time, though not his nightmare. It had gone and he knew it wouldn't return. With it had gone something else—what, he couldn't have said—but he wasn't sorry it had gone. All he knew was how good it was to sleep.

On the morning of the third day McGregor felt well

enough to dress and walk up on deck. The rest of the crew and passengers were already there: Rumison looking stronger and pounds heavier; Whitney starting an even tan that was turning her into quite a woman; Idris, quiet, by himself; the Professor; Constantine at the helm and his brother fishing off the transom with a shark bucket and light chain. Everyone smiled as he appeared.

"Morning, McGregor," said the Professor. "Good to see you up. You're looking better."

The bright sun hurt McGregor's eyes, and he had to squint until they adjusted. It was a clear day, and off in the distance perhaps forty miles McGregor could make out a land mass.

"Jamaica. We'll be in Kingston before tonight."

McGregor nodded without talking. Somehow talk didn't seem important. He took off his shirt and did some mild stretching exercises, grimacing with the pain and effort it cost his body. When he'd finished he left his shirt off and lay out in the sun. The Professor sat down next to him.

"It must have been rough," said the Professor, pipe in mouth, wearing a stained T-shirt and torn shorts. "Was it worth it?"

"What's that?" asked McGregor.

"Whatever."

"I don't know yet."

The Professor took this with a nod. "It was the girl," he asked after a bit. "Whitney. She was the one he went back for, wasn't she?"

"That's what Ho thought."

"You can see it. It's something special. Makes me feel left out, like I'm missing something. It's not their words, their actions, the way they look at each other or anything. It's something else, like a heavy connection . . . a rightness. . . ." The Professor was quiet for a moment.

"Makes me wonder if I've been missing something all my life. I wonder if that's love."

"Ho said it wasn't. Said it was destiny."

Pirosh shrugged. "It's something," he said.

The sun was hot, and after a while McGregor went below decks. He found Rumison seated alone in the small salon, apparently thinking. When he saw McGregor he looked up.

"What's going to happen?" Rumison asked.

"Happen? You mean when we get you back?"

"Yeah."

"I don't really know."

"You know," said Rumison, "when I returned to the States I figured I was a dead man if I reported in. After everybody buying it the way they did and then calling the unit and finding out that Major Hawkes was dead also . . ."

"That was you? An NCOIC out there told me about the call."

Rumison nodded. "I figured that whatever was in the case was so important that somebody wanted everybody connected with it dead. I didn't really care too much at the time. The state I was in, that didn't seem too important. Now it does."

"So you're wondering . . ."

Again Rumison nodded. "I think I might trust you a little, McGregor, at least enough to talk about it."

"I don't know much, Rumison. I don't even know what's in that case."

"That's what Black said. He said it didn't matter."

"I'd like to help you, but I've got my own problems when we get back. All I'd say is, you've got the damn case. Use it as a bargaining tool and don't let them deal you out of it. Be tough."

"I'd already come to that conclusion. I was wondering about not reporting in at all. About disappearing again."

"They'd find you."

"Maybe not."

There was a silence. For an inexplicable reason it embarrassed McGregor. He sat down next to the younger man and looked out the porthole.

"Why did you go back to Nicaragua?" he asked finally.

Rumison smiled. "Preitas asked that question and didn't believe my answer. That was the only reason I didn't break in Bluefields. He wouldn't go on until I answered what he thought was the truth. He stayed with that question and kept asking and asking. . . . And then the police chief finally stopped it."

"Why?"

"Well, it's hard to say. I went through a lot in that jungle . . . the first time. Involuntary. Not my choice. Pretty bad time. The only thing out of the whole experience that seemed positive was Whitney, and I'd run out on her after shooting her father. I couldn't forget the look on her face. . . ." Pain darkened Rumison's features and he shuddered.

"Anyway, when I'd gotten home nothing was the same. Nothing mattered. And then I remembered Black saying that that's the way it was, that nothing mattered but what you wanted to make matter and I realized that the one strong feeling I had was the look on Whitney's face, and I felt I ought to do something about it. It seemed right that I do something about it. It still seems right."

The trades were blowing strongly in the wake of the hurricane, and the *Zygote,* in spite of some minor damage to her rigging caused by the storm, was responding well. She'd weathered the storm in the lee of a low cliff at the south end of the bay and the Professor and his two hands had jerry-rigged repairs before McGregor and the others were spotted on the beach. The lights of Kingston Harbor were spotted at dusk and the *Zygote* was safely moored in her slip before midnight. Everyone spent the night on board, and in the morning Idris called a cab and he, Whitney, Rumison, and McGregor left for Bishop's rented office downtown.

"We'll see you later, Professor," said McGregor. "Have dinner together."

"You'd better. I want to see how this all turns out."

Idris gave the driver directions and the taxi took off, leaving the Professor and his two hands back on the boat, getting ready to finish damage repairs and wash it down.

The taxi stopped in front of a three-story glass-and-metal office building on Palace Street several miles from the port. The building looked innocuous enough, secretaries and businessmen, black and Anglo alike, coming in and out of the thick glass doors. A sign read *Palace Professional Building.*

The group was met by two men near the door—Kastler and Carter. McGregor nodded in a friendly fashion, but his smile was met with scarcely concealed hostility.

"You're all wanted inside," said Kastler, glaring at McGregor.

"As if we didn't know that."

"Watch it, McGregor. I owe you."

"Anytime."

They were led to a suite of offices titled "American Cultural Institute." There were four other men inside: two McGregor had never seen before, middle-aged and professional-looking, like doctors, and two he had met before—General Gwilyn Norris and Nathaniel Bishop.

"McGregor," greeted Norris, still boyish, still exuding goodwill and all-American charm, though McGregor thought he detected a note of strain in his act. "Glad to see you made it. I told Bishop you'd do it, that he shouldn't have tried to take you off the case."

Introductions were made and seats were offered. McGregor noticed that all the men in the room with the exception of Idris and Bishop were taking particular interest in Whitney, who stood quietly next to Rumison, dressed in faded denim pants and a blue T-shirt.

"Now then," began Norris. McGregor noted that he seemed to be in charge, rather than Bishop, and wondered what kind of infighting had been going on. "Adrian gave us as much of the story as he could. Some of it I find hard to believe. . . ." He smiled. "But I suppose stranger things have been done in the name of love."

Rumison grimaced openly but Whitney took his hand and held it. Norris continued.

"We've learned from this end that Preitas had agents working in the States. With Preitas dead and certain other loose ends gathered in, we only have one more problem—the attaché case that was taken off the jet last May. Sergeant Rumison, I presume that you can answer this last question for us?"

"I'm not a sergeant," said Rumison. "Not anymore. You guys saw to that. But yes, I know where it is."

"Good. Then perhaps you could tell . . ."

Rumison shook his head. "I want some guarantees first."

Good man, thought McGregor. He'd been afraid Norris's act might have deceived Rumison.

"Guarantees?" asked Norris, a mild questioning look on his face.

"Look," said Rumison, angrier. "I've gone through a lot

the last few months. I still don't know what in hell this whole thing is about and don't want to know. But I do know—that the chances that all those people that were involved in it died by accident or happenstance is against all the laws of probability, and I don't want to be hit by a car like Major Hawkes because someone thinks I know too much."

Bishop's mouth twitched, but he still didn't speak. Norris looked slightly offended. "Come now, Serg—I mean, Mr. Rumison. You don't really believe . . ."

"I've told you what I want."

"If it's guarantees you want, you've got them."

"I don't believe you. Words won't do."

Bishop's face had been growing darker. "Damn it, Norris," he said finally. "I told you Rumison had sold out to someone. Who was it to, Sergeant?"

A tension that had been present from the beginning in the room began to erupt. Rumison stared straight back at Bishop. "No one. I've told you the truth."

"Come now," said Norris. "There's no need for this. If Rumison has told us the truth, then there's an easy way to prove it. With the case."

They're trying to box him in, thought McGregor. The old Mutt-and-Jeff approach. But apparently Rumison wasn't buying it.

"Sorry," he said. "Not until I get those guarantees."

"There are ways . . ." began Bishop, but Norris stopped him with a wave of his hand.

"What kind of guarantees, Mr. Rumison?"

"A week's head start. That's all. I'll mail you a letter saying where the case is in one week. And there will be a document placed somewhere to the effect that if something suddenly happens to myself or Whitney, the news services will find out everything that has happened."

There was quiet in the room. McGregor sensed something wrong but couldn't place his finger on it. Maybe it was the two faceless individuals behind Norris and Bishop who had been watching the scene with clinical detachment. Maybe it was the game Norris and Bishop were playing on Rumison.

Norris looked suddenly sad and he shook his head. "I'm

sorry," he murmured. "But we can't allow that. If you were killed accidentally, for example . . ."

Norris hesitated after glancing at Bishop. The implications of his next words sent a chill down McGregor's spine. "Perhaps if we explained the whole matter."

Rumison shrugged. "You can try."

McGregor wanted to shout, "No! Don't listen, Rumison! If they tell you any more than you already know, your life isn't worth shit, no matter what happens. If they're willing to tell you what's in that case, that means he doesn't care if you know because it doesn't matter. You're dead. And Whitney also."

McGregor shifted his weight onto his left leg, trying to move as inconspicuously away from Idris as he could while Norris removed a slender red file from a briefcase on the desk. He loosened the zipper on his windbreaker to allow easier access to the pistol he had stuck under his belt.

"Some five years ago," Norris began, but then, as though he had read McGregor's mind, Rumison suddenly raised his hand.

"I'm sorry," he said. "I don't want to hear it. I've realized nothing can change my mind."

Norris let out a deep sigh. "I'm sorry," he said apologetically, as though he really were. "Maybe Nat is right. I'm sorry it had to come to this. You must realize we don't enjoy these things."

Bishop nodded, waving toward Kastler and Carter who grabbed Rumison's arms, fastening handcuffs on him. Whitney cried out and McGregor had a momentary urge to help, but Idris was watching him with a thoughtful expression on his dark features and he restrained himself. Rumison hadn't resisted until one of the agents slapped Whitney to the floor, and then he charged head-first into Kastler.

It was short and brutal. Seconds later, half-conscious, Whitney and Rumison were cuffed together and dragged from the room. They were followed by the two nondescript men McGregor now realized to be professional interrogators. McGregor looked at Norris, who wouldn't meet his eyes. Bishop, on the other hand, almost smiled. Idris waited for a moment, gauging McGregor's reaction, then followed the others into the interrogation room.

"Don't worry about it, McGregor," said Norris sympathetically. "You're clear. Nat here argued like hell, but I know you can be trusted. You're a good agent, if a little unconventional. We wouldn't want to lose you."

Norris reached down into his briefcase and came up with a fat manila envelope, which he handed to McGregor. "There's fifty thousand dollars here. Perhaps not as much as we originally discussed, but considering the problems you've caused, not bad."

Slowly McGregor reached out and took the envelope.

"You can tape your report tomorrow. You'd better get some more rest today."

McGregor turned to leave, but then looked back toward Norris.

"What about Rumison and the girl?"

Norris had the grace to lower his eyes, but Bishop smiled coldly. "Terminal, McGregor."

McGregor had known it. It had been a weakness to ask. He nodded shortly and started to leave again. We all die someday, he thought to himself. What did it matter, two people he hardly knew. His work was finished. He had found out how Bastanchury had died. Norris and Bishop would find the case.

He had found out what he'd wanted to know, hadn't he?

The question bothered him and he found he couldn't leave the room, couldn't open that door that led outside to the real world in the hall outside, of scurrying secretaries and harried Jamaican businessmen. And if he couldn't leave?

There was only one other alternative. Almost without thought, McGregor drew his pistol out from under the light jacket and turned. He shot Bishop first. The bullet hit Bishop just above the left eye, distorting his features with the impact. Norris' eyes widened, but he didn't cry out. There was no boyish candor in them now, only an aging and unhappy man who realized in that brief moment that it was all finally over. And maybe, McGregor thought, was almost grateful for it. McGregor took better aim with Norris because he found his arm was shaking. As he fired, the door to the other room flew open and Carter and Kastler charged in, guns drawn, apparently heedless of their own safety.

They weren't very good, McGregor thought as he pulled the trigger two more times. Vaguely he wondered again why they had been chosen for such a supposedly top-level operation. Perhaps, in the end, they would have been expendable also.

When McGregor was certain that he had made good hits on the two agents, he moved closer to the door that led to the other room. He took a deep breath, trying to steady the shaking that had started in his arm but was now threatening to spread to his entire body.

"McGregor?" Idris called from the other room.

McGregor didn't answer. Taking one last breath, he dove into the room, his body crying out in agony as he rolled across his wounded shoulder into firing position. Idris stood without moving, his hands up and palms out in surrender. McGregor knew he should have killed him then anyway, but somehow the sight of Whitney, handcuffed to a chair next to Rumison stopped him.

"Let them loose," he said, ordering the two frightened interrogators who stood dumbly by their prisoners. McGregor didn't take his eyes off Idris.

The two interrogators quickly obeyed.

"You're a fool, McGregor," Idris said calmly. "We'll get them sooner or later."

Again McGregor didn't answer. Instead he reached in his pocket for the money Norris had given him and threw it in the direction of Rumison.

"Take that money. I'll meet you back at the *Zygote.* If I'm not there five minutes after you, have the Professor take you someplace. Someplace far away."

Whitney hesitated. "Mr. McGregor . . ."

"Don't talk! Just do as I say!"

Rumison had more sense. He took Whitney by the arm and pulled her from the room.

"Why, McGregor?" Idris asked.

"You wouldn't understand."

"I've studied your career, McGregor. I've studied you like I studied Le Clerc, Karamasov, Bastanchury."

"Shut up, Idris."

"The psyche reports called you unstable, given to moodiness and flights of romanticism that made you unsuitable for certain missions. You could have been the best."

Idris' eyes slipped momentarily in the direction of the two interrogators. McGregor turned just in time to see one reaching for a scalpel on a small surgical table near the chairs. McGregor shot him and then the other, who fell heavily across the portable polygraph machine and the drug tray. A sharp pain caught McGregor in the chest. He looked down to see the obsidian hilt of a stiletto protruding from his left pectoral, not far from his heart. He tried to bring the pistol back to bear on Idris, but his reactions were strangely slow. Idris grabbed his jacket and then the hilt of the knife. McGregor could feel the blade twisting, searching for vital arteries or the greatest prize, the heart.

McGregor's strength was ebbing fast. Blood poured from his chest. He could taste its copper sweetness in his mouth as he tried, ineffectually, to hold Idris' arm. He screamed.

For a moment, as the pain cleared his senses, McGregor stared into Idris' eyes. They were bright and full of certain victory. With one last agonized effort, McGregor jerked his right arm free. With complete concentration of purpose, he jammed his straightened thumb into one of those triumphant eyes.

This time it was Idris who screamed; a high-pitched, pain-racked sound as he let go of the knife and tried to free himself. But McGregor had found a hold on the inside of the eye socket bone and wouldn't let him. Idris grabbed his wrist. McGregor's left hand, suddenly free, jerked the knife out of his chest and shoved it up under Idris' sternum, cutting through the solar plexus ganglion and into the aorta. Idris ceased his struggles and McGregor shoved him away.

McGregor's world was gray and turning black but he forced himself back to the outer office. On a shelf he had seen a large oil lamp, some decorator's apology to the world for the plastic sterility of the rest of the office. Somehow McGregor managed to unscrew the cap. He sloshed oil over the desk and floors and into the room where Idris lay, and then he lit a match.

He was thankful for the heavy soundproofing of the rooms. It would give him time. Already the linoleum floor and polyester carpets had caught and the flames were growing.

Oil had spilled on his hands, but he didn't feel where the

flames were charring his flesh. He didn't notice the heat or the smoke or the insistent wail of the automatic fire alarm. He was somewhere else, thinking about a lake in the mountains near Taos, about a small house in Jamaica, about Isidra and Whitney, about Ho Feng Hua and Riley Dancing Waters. He remembered his grandmother and he knew now that he could return home.

Epilogue

I DON'T know why I woke, I just did. Before morning, while still dark out the porthole. Whitney lay next to me, sleeping soundly. I had to go to the head, so I got up. Afterward, not feeling like returning to bed, I went on deck. Constantine's brother was at the helm. We said a few words, but he wasn't much for talk and I didn't feel like it, so I went forward and sat with my back against the foremast and watched the stars twinkling overhead.

I suppose I should have felt bad, considering all the people who had died, many of them friends: Rosso and Barney, Cordobes and Hawkes and Ponce's father and Ho and all the others; and considering that I could never again be who I had been, never be Michael Paul Rumison again, never return home for fear the Agency or whoever all those assholes had been would be waiting.

But I didn't feel sad. All that was gone, past, and whatever had happened, I was here and Whitney was with me and somehow I didn't really feel as if I could never go home because that home was gone and now I carried it around with me.

My body still hurts and I suppose there are mental scars in there somewhere, but in spite of this I felt whole and well for the first time in a long while. I would have liked to have known McGregor better. He never made it to the boat, though we waited. I don't know what finally happened to him, but I have the distinct feeling he made it in the end, somehow. That damned black case is sitting at Mr. Black's feet in a cave somewhere in the mountains of Nicaragua. The money I'd made from the sale of my house, most of it anyway, was still in the safe-deposit vault in a bank in Miami. It would be some time before I went back to get that. The first priority was to get totally, completely lost, and then we'd see.

I heard a sound and looked up to see Whitney standing above me. "I woke and found you gone," she said and sat down, resting her head on my shoulder. "Sometimes it's not good to be alone."

The stars were fading and the sky lightened in the east. The air was fresh with salty spray and the bow broke through the ocean's wavelets with an even rhythm. Whitney was smiling and I knew she didn't feel sad either.

It would be a good sunrise.